By Heidi Cullinan

With Marie Sexton: Family Man

COPPER POINT MEDICAL
The Doctor's Secret

TUCKER SPRINGS
With Marie Sexton: Second Hand
Dirty Laundry

Published by Dreamspinner Press
www.dreamspinnerpress.com

THE DOCTOR'S SECRET

HEIDI CULLINAN

DREAMSPINNER
PRESS

Published by
DREAMSPINNER PRESS

5032 Capital Circle SW, Suite 2, PMB# 279,
Tallahassee, FL 32305-7886 USA
www.dreamspinnerpress.com

This is a work of fiction. Names, characters, places, and incidents either are the product of author imagination or are used fictitiously, and any resemblance to actual persons, living or dead, business establishments, events, or locales is entirely coincidental.

The Doctor's Secret
© 2019 Heidi Cullinan.

Cover Art
© 2019 Kanaxa.
Cover content is for illustrative purposes only and any person depicted on the cover is a model.

Mass Market Paperback ISBN: 978-1-64108-100-9
Trade Paperback ISBN: 978-1-64080-855-3
Digital ISBN: 978-1-64080-854-6
Library of Congress Control Number: 2018943361
Mass Market Paperback published April 2019
v. 1.0
Printed in the United States of America

This paper meets the requirements of
ANSI/NISO Z39.48-1992 (Permanence of Paper).

For Kwanna Jackson

ACKNOWLEDGMENTS

THANKS FIRST and foremost to Dan Cullinan, who put up with ten million medical questions and was the only reason I was able to say, "Yes, I can do a medical trilogy."

Thank you to Tracy Cheuk and to the commenters on the Formosa forums, who kindly helped me make Hong-Wei more accurate and gave me insight into his life.

Thank you to Anna Cullinan and her mad mapmaking skills, which not only made Copper Point feel more real, but kept me from sending people in ten different directions.

Thank you to Elizabeth North for helping me dream up Copper Point and giving it a home at Dreamspinner Press.

Thank you to my patrons who kept me company as I drafted this work, who peeked at early drafts, and as always gave me the life and love I needed to keep going. Thank you especially to Rosie M, Pamela Bartual, Marie, and Sarah Plunkett.

Thank you to my readers, whether you have just found me or have been along for the ride for all ten years. Let's make stories for thirty more.

CHAPTER ONE

DR. HONG-WEI Wu cracked as he boarded the plane to Duluth.

He'd distracted himself on the first leg of the flight from Houston with a few drinks and the medical journal he'd brought in his bag. He nibbled at the in-flight meal, raising his eyebrow at their "Asian noodles" beneath a microwaved chicken breast.

He realized how long it would be until he ate his sister's or his grandmother's cooking again, and his chest tightened, but he pushed his feelings aside and focused on the article about the effects of perioperative gabapentin use on postsurgical pain in patients undergoing head and neck surgery.

When he disembarked at Minneapolis to transfer to his final destination, the reality of what Hong-Wei was about to do bloomed before him, but he faced it with a whiskey neat in an airport bar. Unquestionably he'd require some adjustments, but he'd make it work. If he could succeed at Baylor, he could succeed at a tiny hospital in a remote town in northern Wisconsin.

Except you didn't succeed. You panicked, you let your family down, and you ran away.

The last of the whiskey chased that nagging bit of truth out of his thoughts, and when he stood in line for priority boarding for his last flight, he was sure he had himself properly fortified once again.

Then he stepped onto the plane.

It had fewer than twenty rows, and either he was imagining things, or those were propellers on the wings. Was that legal? It had to be a mistake. This couldn't be a commercial plane. Yet no, there was a flight attendant with the airline's logo on his lapel, and the people behind Hong-Wei held tickets, acting as if this was all entirely normal.

He peered around an elderly couple to speak to the flight attendant. "Sir? Excuse me? Where is first class?"

The attendant gave Hong-Wei an apologetic look that meant nothing but bad news. "They downgraded the plane at the last minute due to low passenger load, so there isn't technically a first-class section. You should have received a refund on your ticket. If you didn't, contact customer service right away when we land."

Hong-Wei hadn't received a refund, as he hadn't been the one to buy the ticket. The hospital had. He fought to keep his jaw from tightening. "So these are the seats?" They were the most uncomfortable-looking things he'd ever seen, and he could tell already his knees were going to be squeezed against the back of the person ahead of him. "Can I at least upgrade to an exit row?"

The attendant gave him an even more apologetic look. "I'm so sorry, those seats are sold out. But I can offer you complimentary drinks and an extra bag of peanuts."

An extra bag of peanuts.

As Hong-Wei stared at his narrow seat on the plane that would take him to the waiting arms of his escorts from St. Ann's Medical Center, the walls of doubt and insecurity he'd held back crushed down upon him.

You shouldn't have left Houston. What were you thinking? It's bad enough you ran, throwing away everything your family sacrificed for. Why did you take this job? Why not any of the other prestigious institutions that offered for you? Why didn't you at least remain close to home?

You're a failure. You're a disgrace to your family. How will you ever face them again?

"Excuse me, but do you mind if I slip past?"

Hong-Wei looked down. A tiny elderly white woman smiled up at him, her crinkled blue eyes clouded by cataracts. She wore a bright yellow pant-suit, clutching a handbag of the same color.

Breaking free of his terror-stricken reverie, Hong-Wei stepped aside. "Pardon me. I was startled, was all. I wasn't expecting such a small plane."

The woman waved a hand airily as she shuffled into her seat. "Oh, they always stuff us into one of these puddle jumpers on the way to Duluth. This is big compared to the last one I was on."

They made commercial planes *smaller* than this? Hong-Wei suppressed a shudder.

With an exhale of release, the woman eased into the window seat in her row.

More people were piling into the plane now, and Hong-Wei had become an obstacle by standing in the aisle. Consigning himself to his fate, he stowed his carry-on and settled into the seat, wincing as he arranged his knees. When he finished, his seatmate was smiling expectantly at him, holding out her hand.

"Grace Albertson. Pleasure to meet you."

The last thing he wanted was conversation, but he didn't want to be rude, especially to someone her age. Forcing himself not to grimace, he accepted her hand. "Jack Wu. A pleasure to meet you as well."

Ms. Albertson's handshake was strong despite some obvious arthritis. "So where are you from, Jack?"

Hong-Wei matched Ms. Albertson's smile. "Houston. And yourself?"

"Oh, I grew up outside of St. Peter, but now I live in Eden Prairie. I fly up to Duluth regular, though, to see my great-granddaughter." She threaded her fingers over her midsection. "Houston, you say. So you were born here? In the United States, I mean."

"I was born in Taiwan. My family moved here when I was ten."

"Is that so? That would make you… well, do they call you first- or second-generation? Bah, I don't know about that stuff." She laughed and dusted wrinkled hands in the air. "My grandmother came here when she was eighteen, a new bride. Didn't speak a word of English. She learned, but if she got cross with you, she started speaking Norwegian. We always wondered if she was swearing at us." Ms. Albertson lifted her eyebrows at Hong-Wei. "You speak English quite nicely. But then I suppose you learned it growing up?"

"I studied in elementary school and with private tutors, but I struggled a bit when I first arrived."

What an understatement that was. It was good Hong-Su wasn't here. Even Ms. Albertson's status as an elder wouldn't have protected her from his sister's lecture on why it wasn't okay to ask Asian Americans where they were from. Though simply thinking of Hong-Su reminded him he wouldn't be going home to her tonight to complain about another white person asking him where he was from.

Have I made a terrible mistake?

Ms. Albertson nodded sagely. "Well, it's a credit to you. I never learned any language but English, though my mother told me I should learn Norwegian and talk to my grandmother properly. I took a year of it in high school, but I'm ashamed to tell you I barely passed the course and can't remember but three or four words of the language now. You must have worked hard to speak as well as you do. I wouldn't know but that you were born here, from the way you talk."

Before Hong-Wei could come up with a polite reply, a bag hit him in the side of his head. A steadier stream of passengers had begun to board the plane, and a middle-aged, overweight businessman's shoulder bag thudded against every seat as the man shuffled an awkward sideways dance down the narrow aisles. Either he didn't realize he'd hit Hong-Wei or didn't care, because he continued single-mindedly on… to the exit row.

Well, for that alone, Hong-Wei resented him.

His seatmate clucked her tongue. "Some people have no manners. Is your head all right? Poor dear. Let me have a look at it."

Definitely a grandmother. Hong-Wei bit back a smile and held up his hands. "I'm fine, but thank you. It's close quarters in here. I think a few bumps are bound to happen." Hong-Wei was glad, however, he was in the aisle and not the frail Ms. Albertson.

"Well, scooch in closer, then, so you don't get hit anymore." She patted his leg. "I'll show you pictures of the grandchildren and great-grandchildren I'm flying north to see."

Not knowing what else to do, Hong-Wei leaned closer and made what he hoped were appropriate noises as Grace Albertson fumbled through her phone's photo album.

He was rescued when the flight attendant announced they were closing the flight door, and a series of loudspeaker announcements meant for the next several minutes conversation was impossible, so outside of Hong-Wei's polite decline of Ms. Albertson's offer of a hard candy, he settled into silence.

The engines were loud as they taxied on the runway, so loud he couldn't have listened to music even if he had headphones. He wished he'd bought some in the Minneapolis airport, or better yet had made sure to pack some in his carry-on. He supposed he could ask for a headset from the flight attendant, but they were always such poor quality, he'd rather do without.

Headphones were just one thing he should have prepared for. He'd rushed into this without thinking, full of the fury and headstrong nonsense Hong-Su always chided him for. It had felt so important to break away when he'd been in Houston, pressed down by everything. Here, now, with the roar of takeoff in his ears, with nothing but this last flight between him and his destiny, he didn't feel that sense of rightness at all. He had none of the confidence that had burned so strongly in him, fueling his wild reach into the beyond.

I can be a doctor anywhere, he'd told himself defiantly as he made the decision to take this job. *I can do surgery in Houston, Texas, Cleveland, Ohio, or Copper Point, Wisconsin. The farther away I am from the mess I made, the better.*

Trapped, helpless in this plane, his defiance was gone, as was his confidence.

What have I done?

He was so consumed by dissolving into dread he forgot about his seatmate until they were in the air, the engines settling down, the plane leveling out slightly as Ms. Albertson pressed something that crinkled into his palm. He glanced down at the candy, then over at her.

She winked. "It's peppermint. It'll calm you. Or, it'll at least give you something to suck on besides your tongue."

Feeling sheepish, this time Hong-Wei accepted the candy. "Thank you."

She patted his leg. "I don't know what's waiting for you in Duluth that has you in such knots, but take it from someone whose life has knotted and unknotted itself more than a few times: it won't be as bad as you think it is, most likely. It'll either be perfectly fine, or so much worse, and in any event, there's not much you can do at this point, is there, except your best."

The peppermint oil burst against his tongue, seeping into his sinuses. He took deep breaths, rubbing the plastic of the wrapper between his fingers. Any other time he would say nothing. Here on the plane, though, he couldn't walk away, and he had no other means to escape the pressure of the panic inside him.

Talking about it a little couldn't hurt.

"I worry perhaps I didn't make the right choice in coming here."

He braced for her questions, for her to ask what he meant by that, to ask for more details about his situation or who the people saying such things were, but she said only, "When you made the choice, weren't you sure you were right?"

Hong-Wei sucked on the peppermint as he considered how to reply. "I didn't exactly make a reasoned choice about my place of employment. I all but threw a dart at a map."

Ms. Albertson laughed. "Well, that explains why you're so uneasy now. But you still had a reason for doing what you did. Why did you throw a dart at a map instead of making a reasoned decision?"

His panic crested, then to his surprise rolled away under the force of the question, and Hong-Wei chased the last vestiges to the corners of his mind as he rolled the candy around with his tongue. "Because it didn't matter where I went. Everything was going to be the same. Except I thought… I hoped… if I went somewhere far enough away, somewhere as unlike the place where I'd been as I could possibly get, maybe it would be different."

"Ah." She smiled. "You're one of *those*. An idealist. Just like my late husband. But you're proud too, so you don't want anyone to know."

Hong-Wei rubbed at his cheek. "That's what my sister says. That I'm *too* proud, and my idealism holds me down."

"Nothing to be ashamed of. We need idealists in the world. No doubt wherever you're going needs them too. Good for you for taking a leap. Don't worry too much about it. Even if it's a disaster, you'll figure it out, and you'll make it work."

"Except I don't want it to be a disaster. I want to make it right, somehow." He thought of his family, who had regarded him with such concern when he'd said he was leaving. *I want to become someone they can be proud of, instead of the failure I am now.*

"Of course you don't. No one wants trouble. Sometimes a little bit of it isn't as bad as we think." Covering her mouth to stifle a yawn, she settled into her seat. "You have to take risks. You'll never win anything big if you don't."

As his seatmate began to doze, Hong-Wei stared at the seat ahead of him, her advice swimming in his head. *Take a risk.* Without meaning to, he'd subliminally internalized this philosophy by accepting this job and moving here. The trouble came with his logical brain trying to catch up.

His whole life, all Hong-Wei had done was study and work. He'd been at the top of his class in high school, as an undergraduate, and through medical school. He'd been praised throughout his residency and fellowship and courted for enviable positions by hospitals from well beyond Baylor's scope before any of his peers had begun to apply. A clear, practical map for his future had presented itself to him.

He still couldn't articulate, even to himself, why he'd leapt from that gilded path into this wild brush, navigable only by dubious commercial jet.

Coming to Copper Point—the town seeking a surgeon the farthest north on the map, a town nowhere near any other hospitals or cities of any kind—felt like an escape that settled his soul. He knew nothing about Wisconsin. Something about cheese, he thought he'd heard. What it *felt* like to Hong-Wei was a clean slate.

Would it truly be different, though? Certainly it wouldn't be Baylor, but would it be different in the right way?

Grace Albertson had called him an idealist with a smile. Hong-Su had always chided him for it. What he needed from Copper Point was some kind of signal that they valued him, idealism and all. That they appreciated the fact that he could have gone anywhere in the country but he'd chosen them. An indication that here might be the place he could find himself, make something of himself. One small sign to show they understood him. It didn't seem too much to ask.

Ms. Albertson woke as the plane landed, and Hong-Wei helped her gather her things, then escorted her down the long walkway to the terminal and out through security.

"You seem to have found some of your confidence while I napped," she observed.

He wasn't sure about that. "I've decided to accept my fate, let's say."

She nodded in approval. "Remember, mistakes are the spice of life. If you arrive and it's a disaster, embrace it. I promise you, whatever you find when you land, if you're lucky enough to get to my age, when you look back at it from your twilight years, you'll think of it fondly, so long as you approach it with the right spirit."

They had come to the end of the walkway leading into the waiting area. Hong-Wei turned and made a polite bow to his companion. "Thank you, Ms. Albertson, for your advice and for your company. I'll do my best to remember what you've said."

She took his hand and held it tight in her grip, smiling. "Best of luck to you, young man."

Hong-Wei watched her go to her family, watched them fold her into their embraces with no small bit of longing in his heart. Turning to the rest of the crowd, he looked for the welcoming party from Copper Point, ready to see what happened next on his adventure.

No one appeared to be waiting for him.

Hong-Wei paused, confused and concerned. There should be a large group, composed chiefly of the hospital board, poised with smiles and coming forward to greet him. They'd mentioned how eager they were to see him and assured him they'd have a delegation sent to collect him in Duluth. It wouldn't be difficult for them to identify Hong-Wei—they'd seen his photo, and there were at best four Asians in the entire airport. The waiting area was small as well. The entire airport was small. What was going on?

All his apprehension came rushing back, swamping the peace Grace Albertson had given him.

This is going to be a failure before I even begin.

Then he saw it—just as he'd asked for, there was a sign. A literal sign, small and white, and it had his name on it, sort of. It read DOCTOR WU in block letters, but underneath it was the Mandarin word for doctor in hànzi followed by Wu, also written in Chinese character. Except it wasn't quite the right word for doctor, and the character for Wu wasn't the one Hong-Wei's family used. The order was also incorrect, with the character for doctor written before Wu—in Mandarin, the proper address would be *Wu Dr.* instead of *Dr. Wu.*

Still, Hong-Wei *had* asked for a sign, and here it was.

The man who held the sign appeared to be alone. He was young, about Hong-Wei's age, perhaps a bit younger. He looked nervous and haggard. He was also, Hong-Wei couldn't help noticing, attractive. *Cute* was definitely a word that described this individual. Light brown hair, bright hazel eyes, a thin strip of beard on his chin, the suggestion of muscles beneath a tight shirt….

The man's eyes met Hong-Wei's, and something crackled in the air.

Hong-Wei threw up walls as quickly as he could. *No.* Good grief, no. He'd said he would consider opening up, but he wasn't interested in romance, or even simple sex, and absolutely not with someone associated with the hospital.

But those eyes. And he'd made a sign. An incorrect, awkward sign. Hong-Wei could tell by the way the man smiled at Hong-Wei—uncertainly, hopefully—that the Chinese had been his idea.

Gripping the strap of his bag tightly, Hong-Wei stepped forward and did his best to meet his disaster head-on.

No ONE had told Simon the new doctor was beautiful.

He hadn't wanted to drive the hour and a half from Copper Point to Duluth and back again to pick up the new surgeon, especially when he'd been asked at the last minute during an extended shift. He'd worked odd hours seven days in a row, and then they'd wanted him to fetch the doctor everyone had been raving about as if he were some kind of second coming for St. Ann's? It wasn't as if Simon could refuse, though. Erin Andreas, the new human resources director and son of the hospital board president, had asked him personally.

"It's fitting for the surgical nurse to pick up the new surgeon, don't you think?" Andreas had punctuated this remark with a thin, apologetic smile. "I'd originally planned to go myself with a team of physicians, but everyone was summoned for call, and I have an internal crisis I need to deal with. So, if you would do this for us, please."

He hadn't waited for Simon to agree, only given him directions on when and how to meet Dr. Wu. He'd also sent along another copy of what Owen called That Damned Memo, the one reminding everyone of the strict new penalties for dating between staff members. Simon had no idea if Andreas meant it for him or for the new doctor.

As he clutched his hastily cobbled welcome sign, his pulse quickening with each step the surgeon took closer, Simon decided he'd definitely been the memo's intended target. Dr. Wu could have starred in an Asian drama, he was so beautiful. In fact, he looked a lot like Aaron Yan, one of Simon's top five favorite DramaFever stars. He was also *tall*. Simon wasn't particularly short, but he was compared to Dr. Wu.

Tall. Handsome. Chiseled. Short black hair, not dyed, artfully styled into messy peaks. Dark eyes that scanned the airport terminal with sharp focus, then zeroed in on Simon. A long, defined jaw lightly dotted with travel stubble below the most articulate set of cheekbones Simon had ever seen.

I'm going to work beside this man every single day. Hand him instruments. Follow his every instruction. Except if he smells even a fraction as good as he looks, I'm going to pass out in the OR before the patient arrives.

Mentally slapping sense into himself, Simon straightened and smiled, holding his sign higher as the man approached. "Dr. Wu? Hello, and welcome. I'm Simon Lane, the surgical nurse at St. Ann's Medical Center. It's a pleasure to meet you."

Dr. Wu accepted Simon's hand, but he also looked around, searching for something. When Simon realized what it probably was, he lowered his gaze, his cheeks heating.

"I... apologize that it's only me here to greet you. We're a small hospital, as you know, and the team members who planned to greet you were all called away on emergencies. I hope you're not offended."

Wu cleared his throat, not meeting Simon's gaze. "Of course not."

Simon was sure Wu was at least a *little* offended, which made Simon feel bad, but it wasn't as if the man didn't have a right to be upset. It was also pretty much on par for the administration to shove a nurse into the middle of its mess to take the heat for a mistake he had nothing to do with.

This wasn't the time to feel sorry for himself or sigh over the man. Dr. Wu had traveled a long way and deserved some professionalism. Forcing a smile, Simon gestured to the hallway. "Shall we collect your luggage?"

Wu adjusted his shoulder bag and nodded, setting his jaw. "Please."

They walked in silence to the baggage claim area, where the rest of the flight from Minneapolis was already gathered, for the most part. An elderly woman in yellow, surrounded by children and adults, waved at Dr. Wu as he passed, and he waved back. Simon almost asked if it was someone the surgeon knew, decided that was a stupid question, and kept his focus on the matter at hand. *Professional. Be professional.*

"It says your bags will appear at the second claim."

Dr. Wu glanced from side to side, then raised his eyebrows in a look of quiet disdain. "Well, if not, there are only the two."

Simon followed his glance. "I guess there are. I never thought about it. I haven't been to any other airport baggage areas. I haven't so much as been on a plane, myself." Realizing he should probably not have said that, he rubbed his cheek. "Sorry, I didn't mean to give away that they'd sent the B-team to escort you. I may not know anything about the rest of the world, but I'm an expert on Copper Point."

For crying out loud, Lane, the man is going to think they sent the village idiot to fetch him. Except even as he thought this, Simon noticed Dr. Wu was smiling a real smile.

It was gorgeous. If the man sent too many of those Simon's way, he was going to need a cardiologist, not a surgeon.

The baggage carousel hadn't started to move yet, so Simon filled the gap with conversation he thought might interest Dr. Wu. "The administrators told me to take you out to eat before we headed to Copper Point, but if you're too tired, we can skip that. I think someone stocked your condo with some starter groceries, but we could also stop somewhere on the way to get anything you might need." He paused, biting his lip and glancing sideways at Dr. Wu. "I should warn you. Our grocery options are seriously limited in Copper Point. I mean, we have food, obviously, but because the population is small and homogenous, anyone who wants to cook beyond the church cookbook greatest hits has to drive to Duluth or order online. A good friend of mine is a bit of a gourmand, and he's always complaining about it. So if you want, we can stop at a store too. But it can also wait."

Crap, now he was babbling. The carousel wasn't moving, though, and the surgeon wasn't talking. A stolen glance revealed he was still smiling, however. *Wider* now, in fact.

Simon swallowed a whimper and clenched his hands at his sides. When he spoke next, his voice cracked. "It's nice to have someone new come to town, and we do need a surgeon at the hospital. An official surgeon on staff, I mean." He could tell his cheeks were blotchy, the stain of his blush leaching onto his neck. "Sorry. I talk too much when I'm nervous."

Wu's voice was like warm velvet falling over him. "I'm sorry I make you nervous."

He *did* make Simon nervous, but Simon didn't want his new superior to know that, and he *especially* didn't want him to know why. "I... you... you don't make me nervous. I mean… I feel bad that you had to be met by me, is all. You deserve a better reception. I'm sure the hospital will make up for it once we arrive in town."

"Your reception is more than adequate. Thank you for coming."

Dr. Wu sounded almost gentle, and Simon couldn't breathe. Also, he was pretty sure his entire face and neck were as red as a strawberry.

The baggage carousel began to move, collecting suitcases spit from the chute, and Dr. Wu stepped away from Simon to retrieve his bags. "Where was it you thought of stopping for dinner?"

Simon fumbled for his phone and called up the list of food options Andreas had given him. "There's an Italian restaurant with good reviews. Oh, but it's in the other direction." Most of the places were, though. He resigned himself to returning home after midnight. Trying not to let his frustration show, he rattled off the other choices on the list. "There's a place called Restaurant 301. 'American classics with a local bent.' I'm not sure what that means, but I could look at the menu. There's another Italian restaurant. Wow. There are, like, five." He scrolled some more. "Tavern on the Hill has Greek wood-fired pizza." He frowned. "What makes pizza Greek? Is that really a thing, or do you think this is a gimmick to punk tourists?"

Dr. Wu had ducked his head, and when he lifted it, he looked as if he were trying not to laugh. Before Simon could apologize for whatever foolish thing he'd said, the surgeon spoke. "I'd prefer a burger and a beer somewhere low-key, to be honest."

Simon was sure *low-key* was nowhere on Andreas's carefully curated list. He opened Yelp, typed in *burger*, and scanned the results. The first hit immediately jogged his memory, and he knew where he wanted to take Dr. Wu. "What about Clyde Iron Works? It's a lot more casual, but the food is good, and they have an extensive list of microbrews. I won't drink, obviously, since I'm driving."

"Sounds perfect."

Once Wu had collected his suitcases from the belt, Simon claimed the handle of the larger one. "Let me take this. You have your carry-on and the other."

Dr. Wu hesitated, then inclined his head. "Thank you."

As Simon had feared, the surgeon's suitcases completely filled his trunk and much of the back seat. "Sorry we're so cramped." Simon's cheeks were hot with shame as he paid the ticket and drove them away from the airport. "I was going to borrow my friend's car, which is bigger, but it ended up in the shop."

"It's not a problem."

At this point Simon couldn't tell if Wu was simply being nice, or if he didn't mind. Uncertainty made him babble again. "You'll meet Owen soon enough. He's one of my best friends from middle school and the anesthesiologist at St. Ann's. He was on the original team that was coming to meet you. Kathryn, another friend of mine and our resident OB-GYN, was going to come too, but too many of her patients had babies."

Wu gazed through the window, taking in the scenery as they passed. "You mentioned you knew Copper Point well. Have you lived there long?"

Simon laughed. "My whole life, and possibly my previous one. I'm one of those people who can trace a great-great-grandparent to the town. When I was four, the town had its one hundred fiftieth anniversary, and they put me on a float in some kind of settler getup with the other kids who were descendants of the founding families." Come to think of it, that meant he'd stood next to Erin Andreas, who would have been just a few years older.

"Tell me about the town. I saw a little online, but of course it's not the same thing as firsthand experience."

"Well, it's on the bay feeding into Lake Superior, and it's one of the first settlement areas in what was the Northwest Territories. Lots of fur trading here before that. The European settlers came for the mining, I think." Simon bit his lip. "Okay, so I don't know the *history* of Copper Point so well. But I can tell you that we have a sandstone mine—I think it was copper the first time, but it's sandstone now—and a college. It's called Bayview University, but it's a small liberal arts college. We have a campus town, which has more places to eat than our downtown and some fun shops. Because we're so far away from everything, our Main Street does okay, even with the big box stores. It's a midsized town, but it's small enough everyone knows everyone. Sometimes more than you want.

"You're moving here from Houston, right? I looked it up while I was waiting. Wow, it's really big. Did you come there from somewhere else in Texas before you went to school? They didn't tell me much about you. I know you were born in Taiwan and did your residency at Baylor, but that's about it." Simon's hand brushed the sign between them, and he decided this was a good time to get his apology over with. "Sorry if the sign was over-the-top. I misunderstood and thought you were more recently from Taiwan than you are."

Dr. Wu glanced at the sign with an affectionate smile. "No, I liked the sign. Thank you. I moved to Houston from Taipei with my family when I was ten. It worked out that the university I wanted to attend was in the same city, and I was fortunate enough to be matched with Baylor for my residency."

"Wow. I would think you'd have more of an accent, if you moved here that late."

"My sister has one, sometimes, but the two of us worked hard to practice our American accents as well as our English. It was important to us both to blend in." He shook his head, rueful. "We watched *so many* movies. She would find the scripts, and we'd read along with them."

Simon hadn't meant to confess, but the road ahead of him was hypnotic, as was Dr. Wu's low, smooth voice, and it tumbled out of him. "I wish I could do that to learn Korean or Chinese. I watch so many Asian shows on DramaFever, but I've only learned how to say *I'm sorry* and *thank you* and *I love you*, and I'm not entirely sure about the last one."

There was a moment's awkward pause where Simon cringed inwardly and Dr. Wu said nothing.

"You... watch Asian television?" Wu said at last.

Simon nodded, refusing to be uncomfortable about his confession. "The romances. They're my favorite. I stumbled on one on Netflix one day and loved it, and of course Netflix kept recommending more, and I was down the rabbit hole. I found out there was an entire network devoted to them, and it was all over. Now I watch the new ones as they're released, but I've also gone back and watched a lot of older ones as well." He resisted the urge to apologize for himself and forged on. "I think it's better than most of the stuff on American television. It makes me wish I could travel."

"Is there some reason you can't?"

Simon shrugged. "I haven't had the opportunity, I guess." Deciding to be honest, he added, "Also, I'm a little scared. I used to want to go everywhere, but the older I get, the more impossible it seems. I still want to do it, but I don't want to go by myself, and…." He forced a smile. "Anyway. You're certainly not scared. I look forward to working with you, Dr. Wu."

Wu made no reply to this, only stared out the window, an unreadable expression on his face. Simon was working up to apologize for whatever it was he'd said wrong when he noticed the surgeon had closed his hand over the edge of Simon's cardboard sign, holding on to it like an anchor.

Maybe he'd messed some things up, but he'd done the sign right. At least he had that going for him.

THE RESTAURANT Hong-Wei's escort took them to had a funky urban-industrial theme, and the menu was more than promising, full of burgers, pasta, and as Lane had said, a vast selection of local beer. Hong-Wei ordered two different types and a large bacon cheeseburger, as well as a side of onion rings.

Lane, who had a smoked salmon salad, blinked as he watched Hong-Wei dig into the beer-battered rings. "So… you're not a health-conscious doctor, then?"

Hong-Wei shrugged as he wiped his mouth with a napkin and dusted crumbs from his fingers. "My mother and grandmother always nag me to eat properly, so whenever I escape their influence, I tend to go wild." He pushed the basket of rings toward Lane. "Try one. They're excellent."

Lane held up a hand and shook his head, eyeing Hong-Wei curiously. Hong-Wei retreated into his food and drink, reeling a bit from Lane's declaration that Hong-Wei wasn't scared. Now he felt as if the pressure was on, which was difficult since the closer he got to his new reality, the more terrified he became. Junk food and alcohol seemed the best refuge.

He liked hearing Lane talk, so he searched for a prompt. "You told me about the town. What about the hospital? My schedule didn't allow me to come to Wisconsin for a proper visit."

As Hong-Wei had hoped, Lane relaxed and launched eagerly into speaking about the hospital. "St. Ann's is a small critical access hospital, which I suppose you already knew. I guess the thing I can tell you that's most important since it sounds like you've always dealt with large hospitals is small hospitals have a different feel. I worked at a larger hospital after finishing my degree, and the atmosphere at a place like St. Ann's is very different. Unlike large hospitals where there are multiple floors and departments separated from each other, we're all in each other's laps at St. Ann's. There's only one nurses' station. One doctors' lounge. One bank of elevators, though we do have a service elevator in the laundry area. Technically we have one hundred beds, but because of the way the critical access rules read, we only ever use seventy-five. Also, though everyone has their specific role, we fill in everywhere. I'm supposed to be the surgical nurse, but I do whatever shift needs doing. The doctors are in the same predicament."

None of this had come up when the administration had interviewed him, Hong-Wei thought as he sipped his beer, but he wasn't surprised. He wondered how much else he could get Lane to confess. "What's the work environment like? Do people get along? Are they competitive with one another?"

Lane seemed confused. "Competitive? I'm not sure what you mean. As far as getting along… well, it depends on who it is. Owen—he's Dr. Gagnon—is known for being difficult, but I think that's overblown, personally. The nurses gossip a lot, which I don't care for, but it's not like anybody can stop that either." He sighed. "The hospital board is a little… scary. They're all old, which would be fine, but they're a total good-old-boys club. The hospital CEO is a solid guy, I always thought. He was friends with one of my friends in high school. The HR director, though, is the son of the hospital board president, and he makes me nervous. You know Roz, that woman from *9 to 5*?"

9 to 5 was one of the movies he and Hong-Su had used to improve their English. "I'm familiar with her, yes."

"He reminds me of her, sometimes. I feel like everything I say goes directly to the board."

Lane toyed with his straw, first with his fingers, then with his lips as he stared off to the side, ostensibly considering something deeply. Hong-Wei paused with an onion ring halfway off his plate, arrested by the sight of Lane's full lips teasing the straw.

Stop it, he chided himself. *He's a nurse. Your nurse.*

The spell was broken when Lane sat back, a determined look on his face. "I'm going to tell you this because you're going to hear about it eventually anyway.

We've had our share of scandals recently at St. Ann's. The CEO before Nick Beckert was fired due to embezzlement, and before the air was clear, a married clinic doctor was caught sleeping with his nurse. It was like watching a soap opera live at work, except it got ugly and made the papers and the TV news. I don't think the board was paying as close attention then as they are now, though they've been worried about money since forever. Anyway, we got a new CEO, and the new HR person. The latter is really bringing down the hammer." Lane aimed his fork at Hong-Wei. "Don't be fooled by how Erin Andreas appears either. He seems small and sweet, but he smiles while he bites you. He's already fired four people since he arrived last month."

Interesting information. Hong-Wei digested it as he drank more beer. "Has he fired any doctors?"

Lane laughed, the sound startling for its bitterness. "Are you kidding? Not a chance. The doctors are never wrong." Apparently remembering he was in the presence of a doctor, Lane averted his gaze and cleared his throat. "I mean, the hospital gives doctors the benefit of the doubt, always."

"That will be an interesting change, then." Hong-Wei picked up his burger and took a bite, thinking as he chewed. "I've been a surgical resident up until now. Things were my fault even if I was at home sleeping when they happened."

"Nothing will be your fault. I thought things would get better once we switched to the electronic record-keeping system, because finally the doctors couldn't blame us when we couldn't figure out what their insane handwriting meant or when they wrote the order wrong and the pharmacist yelled at us. Now they still ask for the wrong dose of medicine, and when the pharmacist says an order would kill the patient and calls to tell them so, we get yelled at for letting them interrupt the doctor."

The beer was unloosening things in Hong-Wei, making it easier to laugh. It also silenced the voice warning him not to notice how the lighting in the restaurant was making soft halos dance on top of Lane's light brown hair, casting pleasant shadows across his broad shoulders. "This sort of thing happened to me in my residency as well. I hadn't planned on passing on the experience to my nurses, though. I thought I'd prefer to be a competent surgeon instead."

Oh, but Lane had a nice smile. "About that. I don't know the full story, but I heard the other doctors and some administrators talking. I hear you're an exceptionally good surgeon, or that you have some kind of special skill? I didn't understand all of what they were talking about, but what I gathered is we're very fortunate to have you at St. Ann's."

Hong-Wei held his glass to his lips longer than necessary as he tried to decide how to reply. He hadn't given the full truth to St. Ann's in his interview. Had they uncovered it on their own? It didn't matter, he supposed, but it made him uneasy. The whole point in coming here had been to step back and be a simple general surgeon.

He cleared his throat and set down his glass. "I had many places to choose from for my postresidency employment, yes. I decided to come to St. Ann's, however, because I wanted a more intimate, uncomplicated hospital experience."

"Well, I don't know about uncomplicated, but you'll probably get more up close and personal with people than you care to." Lane's smile was crooked, apologetic, and impossibly endearing. "That includes me, I'm afraid. We have a few other backup nurses trained, but in the same way you're the only surgeon at St. Ann's, I'm the only surgical nurse. So we'll be seeing a lot of each other, Dr. Wu."

"Call me Jack."

Lane's eyebrows lifted. "Oh, that's your first name? Huh, not what I expected. Do most people in Taiwan have Western names these days?"

The beer had relaxed Hong-Wei's tongue to the point of no return. Or perhaps it was Lane's smile and gentle eyes. "No. Jack is the name I use with people outside my family, since Americans don't have an easy time with Asian names."

"Would you mind telling me your given name? I'll use Jack if you prefer, but I'm curious about who you really are."

Who you really are. He was both Jack and Hong-Wei equally at this point, but Lane was so clumsily charming, Hong-Wei couldn't resist him. He shifted on his chair. "Wu Hong-Wei." Why did he give it in Taiwanese order instead of Western order, with his surname first? Now he was just being silly.

You're an idealist. Grace Albertson's voice came back to him. Hong-Wei had to agree. Though now he wondered if he didn't have to admit to being a romantic as well.

"Wu Hong-Wei."

Hong-Wei shivered and went still.

Lane's pronunciation came out as clumsy as any American's attempt, maybe worse because he was clearly trying to mimic Hong-Wei.

Ever since the airport, the yearning to connect had been apparent in Simon Lane's gaze, but now Hong-Wei saw the truth behind the nurse's longing for what it was, a truth his escort probably didn't want him to see. He'd come all this way to pick up the new surgeon because he'd been asked, because he was a nice guy… and because he was lonely.

Without a moment to prepare for the attack, Hong-Wei's walls crumbled into dust.

He finished off the first beer and picked up the second, indulging in a long draught. "You may call me Hong-Wei if you like, Simon."

Simon smiled so wide it lifted his ears and made his hazel eyes twinkle.

Losing himself in that smile, Hong-Wei couldn't remember why, exactly, he shouldn't pursue a flirtation with his nurse. Something told him the harder he tried to resist Simon Lane, the more he'd be sucked in.

A relationship wasn't the adventure he'd come to Copper Point to pursue, and yet every instinct Hong-Wei had told him Simon would be the adventure he ended up taking.

CHAPTER TWO

WU HONG-WEI.

The surgeon's name rang in Simon's head as he drove home after dropping Hong-Wei off at his condo. *Wu Hong-Wei.* All night Hong-Wei had spoken perfect English, but when he said his Taiwanese name in Mandarin, Simon felt a ridiculous thrill.

Which Simon reminded himself he shouldn't have. Setting aside the fact that Dr. Wu—Hong-Wei—*the new surgeon*—was practically his boss, there was the new policy to bear in mind. Even so, Simon still floated as he parked the car and drifted up the path into the house. He shouldn't think about the man that way, but for tonight at least, he would allow himself to dream.

Of course, he needed to be careful how he fantasized. Simon had two roommates, Owen Gagnon and Jared Kumpel, his friends from childhood who were doctors at the hospital. They were also two of the biggest gossips in Copper Point.

Owen and Jared were home, Jared in the kitchen washing dishes, Owen sprawled in the overstuffed chair with one foot on the ottoman and one on the floor as he surfed his laptop. Owen glanced up over the top of his glasses as Simon came in.

"The prodigal returns." Owen removed his glasses and shut his computer. "So, what's the verdict on the new surgeon?"

Jared wiped his hands on a towel and waved Simon over. "Come get your dinner first. I held it in the oven for you."

"Oh, sorry, I already ate." Simon toed off his shoes and hung up his jacket, determined not to show any signs of embarrassment. If they saw weakness, they would have no mercy. "I took Dr. Wu somewhere because he was hungry."

Owen rubbed his hands together. "Excellent. This means you got *more* dish on him. Come on. Spill. Is he an arrogant asshole? I mean, to a degree it's a given. He's a surgeon."

Jared pulled Simon's plate out of the oven and put the food into a storage container. "I've met decent surgeons."

"Your definition of decent doesn't count. *You* are an arrogant asshole." Owen gestured impatiently at Simon. "Out with it. What's he like?"

Simon sat in the corner of the couch and drew his favorite afghan over his legs. How could he describe Hong-Wei without sounding ridiculous? "He's a little reserved, though he warmed up after I talked to him for a bit." He was also slightly aloof in a way Simon hadn't expected to be so tantalizing. "He didn't want to go to a fancy restaurant. He wanted to go to a pub-style place." Simon searched his brain for more information. "He has a sister. He just finished his residency."

He told me his real name.

Jared glanced at Simon, glass and towel in his hand. "I still don't know why someone would come to Copper Point from Baylor St. Luke's. Either he's terrible, or he's crazy."

"Not a chance he's terrible." Owen rested his elbow on the armrest and leaned on his hand. "Beckert has been running around bragging about his catch ever since the hire was official."

Jared snorted. "He might have seen *Baylor* on the app and lost his common sense."

Simon thought of Hong-Wei, of the cool, confident way he'd handled himself at the airport, how graceful his hands were when doing something as simple as navigating a fork. "I don't think Dr. Wu is incompetent."

"He's crazy, then." Jared turned back to the sink. "I guess I don't care, as long as he gets his work done."

"You haven't told us much about what you thought of him, Simon." Owen pushed his glasses higher and raised his eyebrows at Simon. "You're being quite cagey, in fact."

Simon deliberately didn't meet Owen's gaze. "I think he's nice. I mean, obviously I don't know him well. All I did was have dinner with him and drive him home. He was quiet in the car. He was on his phone for a while, and he slept a little."

He'd seemed to flirt a few times, but Simon had probably imagined things. At any rate, he wasn't sharing *that*.

Owen looked ready to press for more, so Simon told him the rest. "There's nothing at his place but the gift baskets everyone dropped off, mostly food and towels and toiletries. I tried to take him to Walmart to get some pillows and a blanket at least, but he didn't want to go out again, so the building supervisor lent him some."

Simon had given Hong-Wei his phone number in case he wanted to go shopping, and Hong-Wei had said he'd definitely be texting him. Simon didn't share this detail either.

"The guy does his residency at one of the most prestigious med schools in the country, takes a job at a tiny hospital in a tiny city as far north as you can go without hitting Canada, and shows up without so much as a pillow. Jared's right. Guy's nuts." Sighing in satisfaction, Owen threaded his fingers over his chest, shifting his body so his laptop nearly tipped into the recesses of the chair. "So, that's settled. Next question. Did we get new hospital eye candy or not?" When Simon hid his face inside the blanket, Owen laughed. "*And* the answer is yes. *Delicious*. Are you calling dibs, Si?"

Popping out of the blanket again, Simon glared at Owen. "Of course I'm not. Andreas is running around waving the no-dating-between-staff-members policy in everyone's face and making threats."

Owen rolled his eyes. "Andreas is full of shit. Nobody's going to obey his damn edict. It's an idiotic order, especially in a town this size. The hospital is the number two employer. The odds alone mean people are going to meet their significant others there."

"That's fine for you to say, Owen. There's no way they'll fire their only anesthesiologist."

Owen opened his laptop. "All I'm saying is you're a fool if you turn down action with a hot surgeon because Andreas has a bee up his pert little butt."

"Maybe you should put something else up Andreas's butt," Jared called from the kitchen.

Owen chucked a throw pillow at Jared, who dodged it neatly.

Simon's daydreams about Hong-Wei began as soon as he went to bed. He wondered if Hong-Wei would call him. He imagined a shopping date where Simon helped Hong-Wei pick out furniture, decorations, and other apartment necessities. He got a thrill thinking maybe Hong-Wei would rely on him for all his errand needs, and he pressed his hands to his cheeks, visualizing himself rushing off to help. Hong-Wei would be waiting on the steps of his condo, looking off into the distance with his aloof expression, wind in his hair, wearing highly fashionable clothes. Then he'd see Simon, and his expression would ease.

Simon Lane, you're completely, utterly ridiculous.

It was true, he was, but he fell asleep thinking romantic thoughts all the same, and he woke to his alarm, feeling a bit breathless. He hummed in the shower, and he smiled to himself as he got his lunch ready. Unfortunately he forgot to wipe the expression away before Owen came into the kitchen, and his friend nudged him in the small of his back.

"You're *giddy*. He must have flirted with you."

Simon nearly dropped the sandwich he was making. "I— He didn't."

"You stick your tongue out and touch your top lip when you're lying. He flirted." Owen popped Simon's sandwich in its container and touched Simon's nose with it. "The question is, why are you trying to hide it?"

Simon brushed Owen's hand away and reached for the bag of carrots. "I don't know if he actually did, but yes, I'm attracted to him. Are you happy? Now leave me alone. I need to get ready to go to work."

Owen stole one of the carrots Simon put into his vegetable container. "I want to meet him. Do you think he'll come in to the hospital today?"

"I wouldn't know. He didn't tell me."

"He doesn't have a car. How's he getting around?"

"I don't know." Though Simon had wondered the same thing, which was why he'd given Hong-Wei his number. *One* of the reasons he'd shared his number.

"I suppose his condo is only a few blocks from the hospital. It's not far from us. On the days you walk to work, you'd pass him. Are you by chance walking to work?"

Simon glared at Owen. "Why are you so obsessed with this?"

Owen's smile made Simon shiver. "Because it's so *interesting*. You're always polite about everything, and the few times you've dated, you were so luke-warm you practically yawned. Judging by your re-action to one evening with him, this guy must be so charming he breaks hearts just by walking by."

Simon caved. He was going crazy without some-one to tell, and it wasn't as if he could confide in the nurses. "He reminds me of Aaron Yan."

Owen frowned. "I don't know who that is. One of your Asian drama guys, I take it?"

Putting down the carrots, Simon pulled out his smartphone. When he had a photo—a still from *Refresh Man* promos—he showed Owen.

Owen whistled low. "Hot *damn*. If you don't call, Si, I'm going in."

Heart skipping a beat, Simon clutched his phone to his chest. "You don't know he's gay."

"I'll know pretty damn quick." Owen raised an eyebrow. "Not going to tell me I can't try?"

Simon wanted to tell Owen absolutely not, no way. Even if he wasn't naturally shy, though, all he could think of was Andreas and his memo. He twisted the carrot bag shut and sealed it with a clip. "I told you. I'm not getting caught up in the no-dating policy."

Owen sighed and pushed off the counter. "Whatever. I'm going over in a few minutes. You want a ride?"

Simon shook his head. "I need to do some shopping after work, so I'm going to drive myself."

When Simon arrived at work, every secretary, janitor, home health worker, and nurse wanted to know about the new surgeon.

"What's Dr. Wu like?"

"Did he have a good flight?"

"Did you take him to dinner? Where did you go? What did he order?"

"Is he handsome?"

"Is he married?"

"Is he young?"

"Is he nice?"

"What did you think of him?"

Simon answered them politely, giving them as few details as possible, especially as they got personal. "Dr.

Wu is polite and professional. I believe he'll be good member of the staff, though I suspect he'll be exacting and strict." When they pressed him on the issue, he added, "Yes, he's handsome. I think he's in his late twenties, maybe early thirties at the latest. I have no idea if he's married or not. I don't think it would be right to ask him."

"*Pish*." Christie, the charge nurse, waved this objection away. "We need to know if we should take over something for his wife as well when we bring him welcome baskets."

The poor man's condo was full of welcome baskets and nothing else. "A partner didn't come with him." *Why are you assuming a wife? It could be a husband.*

"She might be arriving later." Dante, one of the nursing techs, leaned on the top of the nurses' station. "He mention anything?"

"No." Simon shuffled the files in front of him, not liking the thought of a wife, husband, or any significant anyone joining Hong-Wei. "I need to check my patients."

His patients, however, were as nosy as the staff, and they all asked the same questions. Everyone wanted information about Dr. Wu. Most of all, they wanted to know when he was going to come in to the hospital.

"He didn't tell me," Simon kept saying, "but I highly doubt it will be today. He must be tired, and he has so much to do, getting his place set up." Everyone agreed Simon was probably right.

Despite this, just after lunch, while Simon was helping Mrs. Mueller into her shower, he heard a great commotion in the hallway.

Mrs. Mueller, who had severe dementia, tried to get off her chair and go see what was going on. "Is that Bobby?"

Simon shifted the spray nozzle to his other hand
and eased her onto the shower stool. "Bobby's coming
for dinner, Mrs. Mueller. We need to get you showered
and into a nice dress before he gets here. Will you let
me help you, please?"

"Oh, yes." Her expression was soft and absent-
minded as she settled down. "Bobby will take me
somewhere nice to eat. There's a festival this weekend, you know."

Bobby Mueller was Carole Mueller's husband, a
swindling cheat who had run out on her years ago. Simon had discovered, though, that Mrs. Mueller would
happily dream of him, waiting forever for the day he
would arrive.

"Let's wash your hair, then, and make sure you're
pretty for the festival." Simon slipped the hair guard in
place and lathered the elderly woman's hair with the
shampoo he brought in special for her. He kept talking
soothingly to her, but the noises in the hall continued,
and they distracted her.

"Are hoodlums breaking in?" She fidgeted and
attempted to rise.

"No one can break in. I promise we're safe, but
if you keep trying to stand up in the slippery shower,
you might get hurt."

She patted his arm. "You take such good care of
me. Almost as good of care as Bobby."

He managed to finish the shower, at which point
he toweled her off, got her into her Depends and a
lovely nightgown one of the techs had bought for her
at Goodwill. She touched her cheeks, trying to twirl as
she felt the fabric swish around her ankles.

"Bobby will love this dress." She clutched Simon's hand and kissed his cheek. "Thank you so much."

Simon smiled. "It was nothing at all. Now let's get you in bed so you can rest for your big day."

She would forget, within hours, about the festival, about Simon, and possibly even Bobby—definitely she wouldn't understand where she was and why she was there. Simon didn't know if it was better or worse that they couldn't tell her what was wrong. No one could figure out what was going on with the strange mass in her abdomen, wedged in a place that left her reluctant to eat. The fill-in surgeon was unwilling to touch it because of its placement, so she was stuck in limbo, hopped up on painkillers until the tumor grew so large she died.

Simon took time with her, more time than he was supposed to, coaxing her into eating some of her lunch despite the pain, doing the jobs a tech was meant to do because he knew no one would care for her the way he would, and by the time he left her room, she was asleep.

He barely made it into the hall before Dante cornered him.

"Simon—your guy was here!" Dante gestured excitedly in the direction of the nurses' station. "You'd think a rock star arrived from the way everybody behaved. All the women were starry-eyed and giggling like schoolgirls, and when he left, all they could talk about was how hot he was. I mean, even I had to admit he was gorgeous. If I were gay, he's who I'd go for."

Simon's heart was beating in his ears, and he smoothed his hands over his hair and scrubs. "He's here?"

Dante gave Simon a once-over. "What happened to you? You're wet, and you have food smeared all over you. Is that... oatmeal in your hair?"

Gasping, Simon winced as his fingers found the nest of oatmeal. "I gave Mrs. Mueller her shower, then got her to eat before her nap. It was a bit of a struggle."

"Dude. I keep telling you, that's not an RN's job." Dante shook his head. "I'll cover for you while you shower. You got spare scrubs in your locker, yeah?"

"I do. Thanks, Dante, I owe you one." Simon hurried down the hall.

"You can introduce me to the cute new night nurse," Dante called as Simon disappeared around the corner. "Obviously don't tell Andreas."

Simon wasn't sure why he was so nervous, or why he thought he needed to shower in case he ran into Hong-Wei. Probably he'd already left or was in a meeting, and if he wasn't, he'd be out of the main area of the hospital by the time Simon was showered. Still, Simon couldn't help rushing to the locker room, telling himself if he was fast, he might have a chance—

When he opened the door to the locker room, he ran straight into Hong-Wei.

Literally, he ran into the man, right into his chest. Hong-Wei's scent hit him, some kind of subtle cologne mixed with aftershave and a peppery essence of male that curled into Simon's belly and made his knees waver.

Hong-Wei caught Simon as he wobbled, then wrapped an arm around the small of his back, holding him in a sturdy grip. "Are you all right?"

No, Simon was going to die of embarrassment. He was a mess, and he'd nearly run Hong-Wei over. "I'm fine. Thank you." Simon righted himself as best he could and tried to hide his dirty tunic with crossed arms. Of course Hong-Wei appeared incredible, wearing a tasteful gray mock turtleneck and black trousers that rippled every time he shifted his body. He had on a long, slim-fit white lab coat, unbuttoned, flowing around him.

No oatmeal in sight.

Simon scraped together what dignity he could manage. "It's good to see you, Dr. Wu. I didn't expect you to come to the hospital so soon."

Hong-Wei seemed as if he wanted to say something, but he was also frowning, studying the mess in Simon's hair. Before Simon could say anything to explain, another voice from behind Hong-Wei piped up.

"Simon, let Wu through so I can get out already."

Owen. Blushing, Simon shuffled down the side of the wall and remained there, flat as he could, as Hong-Wei moved aside so Owen—and God help him, Mr. Beckert and Mr. Andreas—could come through. To Simon's surprise, Hong-Wei remained beside him, meaning once all the men had exited the locker room, they ended up in a circle at the edge of the hallway.

Beckert, ever the politician, took it in stride. "Thank you again for picking up Dr. Wu last night. I apologized to him that none of us were able to come with you, but he says you were more than an adequate host."

Simon resisted the urge to hide the oatmeal in his hair. "I'm always happy to help."

Hong-Wei was still fixated on Simon's disarray. "Did something happen to you?"

Simon gave in and tugged at the oatmeal, which was firmly glued to his head. "I was trying to get Mrs. Mueller to eat."

Andreas narrowed his gaze at Simon. "Feeding patients is a nursing assistant's job, Mr. Lane."

Owen smiled one of his brittle smiles. "Simon takes special care with his patients. You won't find a more conscientious nurse at St. Ann's. He can assist with all surgeries, but he doesn't mind lending a hand when we're short-staffed in any department. I've seen him taking out trash on occasion as well." Owen rubbed his chin. "Mueller. That's the benign stomach tumor case. You might find it interesting, Jack."

Jack? Simon blinked, surprised Owen and Hong-Wei were already on a first-name basis.

Hong-Wei perked up. "I would?" He turned to Beckert. "May I see the patient's file?"

"With pleasure." Beckert looked like a cat with cream. "We're off to get you into the system now so you can see the electronic files. We'll find you someone to take you on errands as well, while we're at it."

"I already have that arranged." Hong-Wei's hand fell on Simon's shoulder, and he glanced sideways at him. "Unless Simon has changed his mind?"

Simon was sure his face had to be in flames. "I— Of course not. I'll take you wherever you need to go. Just give me a call."

"I'll do that."

Hong-Wei lifted his hand and strode away from Simon, lab coat rippling in an invisible breeze as if he were in some sort of ad for sexy hospitals. As the group disappeared around the corner, Owen gave Simon a heavy wink.

Andreas gave him a long, narrow look.

Simon hurried into the locker room, stripped out of his clothes, and ran into his shower, setting the stream on full blast.

IT HADN'T been Hong-Wei's plan to go to the hospital, but with nothing in his apartment and no means to rectify the problem but his tablet and a credit card, he eventually grew bored of online shopping and decided to check out his new place of employment. He'd deliberately chosen a condominium near the hospital so he could walk to work, so when the empty rooms had become too much for him, he gathered his things and went to see what would happen when he arrived unannounced.

It was frightening to imagine what they would have done if they'd known he was coming. St. Ann's treated him like visiting royalty, or perhaps a god. The way the CEO joked about red carpet made Hong-Wei think they had some stashed somewhere and had been trying to figure out how to lay it out for him. Oh, there had been some racism, most of it clumsy stuff rather than aggressive. Largely, though, as he toured the hospital, everyone from janitor to CEO gave him the princely reception he'd assumed he'd receive at the airport.

The day ended with dinner at a local steakhouse, members of the board and a few other doctors in attendance. The board was exactly as Hong-Wei had anticipated them to be: rich, white, and dripping with good-old-boy smiles. The hospital CEO he'd already known to be black from his Skype interview, but he was surprised to discover the OB-GYN, Dr. Kathryn Lambert-Diaz, was also black, and her partner was Dominican. He'd noticed two Hispanic nursing staff members during his tour as well. No other Asians, but that Hong-Wei wasn't the only person of color in the hospital was something of a relief. In fact, glancing around the steakhouse, he saw that though most people were white, there was the occasional burst of melanin. Several individuals appeared as if they might be from India or Pakistan. Hong-Wei wondered if they were associated with the college Lane had told him about.

Dr. Kumpel, the pediatrician, and Dr. Gagnon, the anesthesiologist who had toured with Hong-Wei, were also present at the dinner. Hong-Wei liked Kumpel and Gagnon, who were apparently friends outside of work. They behaved more casually with Hong-Wei than most of the other doctors, insisting he needed to come over to their house sometime for dinner.

Hong-Wei digested this information, sitting up straighter as he examined the closeness between Gagnon and Kumpel with new eyes. "You live together?"

Kumpel nodded. "Roommates since medical school, friends since we were old enough to get in trouble. Simon lives with us too—the surgical nurse who picked you up from the airport."

Simon. Hong-Wei remembered the way the man had blushed when he'd run into him, how charming he'd looked even with oatmeal stuck in his hair. So he lived with Kumpel and Gagnon, did he? Hmm. "I'd love to come over for dinner sometime."

They made a promise to set a date soon, and then the daughter of the one of the members of the hospital board gave Hong-Wei a ride home. She was a kind middle-aged woman, a professor who worked with a number of nurses at the college.

"We're so glad you're here," she told him as she dropped him off.

Then Hong-Wei was alone in his condo again, with nothing but his makeshift bed, the contents of his suitcase, and a mountain of welcome baskets. He wasn't bored any longer, but he didn't feel any better about staying in the space.

This was probably why, when his sister called, he answered. "Hey."

Hong-Su's snort had an edge of dubiousness that could have cut glass. "Finally, you answer. All right. Go ahead. Tell me all about the mess you've gotten yourself into. Because I can tell by your *hey* it's a mess."

Hong-Wei sat cross-legged on the pile of blankets. "It's not a mess. It's just… strange."

"Of course it's strange." In the background he heard the telltale sounds of a busy hospital. "I have a twenty-minute break before I make my next rounds. You can be stubborn and hem and haw about how you don't have anything to say, or you can use this time wisely and talk it out."

Hong-Wei had only one reservation. "Mom and Dad aren't around, are they?"

"You're really paranoid, aren't you? Why don't you want them knowing I'm talking to you?"

Because they'd want to talk to him too, and Hong-Wei wasn't remotely ready for that. "Are they around, or not?"

"First of all, this is a huge hospital, and the odds of them being in this exact section of it at the same time I'm talking to you and walking by me are incredibly low. But since I know that won't be good enough for you, no. They're not in the building."

"You're sure?"

"Positive. They're off at a fundraiser."

Hong-Wei lay on his back and stared at the ceiling. "I don't know where to start."

"Is it terrible? Are you sorry?"

He was a little sorry, but not enough to run home. He let his vision relax as he unpacked his thoughts. "I guess I assumed it would be bad in a sitcom kind of way. It's less slapstick and more bleak. I thought I was one of two surgeons, but I'm the *only* full-time surgeon. The other surgeon is someone they hire on rotation from a service. Their anesthesiologist situation is the same. They have one full-time and one who is hired to cover his vacations and the off times. They don't have enough nurses or nursing techs. When I arrived for a tour today, my surgical nurse was feeding oatmeal to a patient. He's the only surgical nurse, by the way, though a few others are trained as backup."

Thinking of Simon relaxed him. He smiled.

Hong-Su made a grim sound, half grunt, half sigh. "I'm not surprised to hear it's bleak. You picked an incredibly remote location. Few health care professionals want to take employment there. Few locals would want to stay. A degree is a ticket out. Have you not listened to our parents' sermons?"

Hong-Wei wasn't in the mood to have *them* brought up right now. "It's not what I expected, is what I'm saying." Steeling himself against self-pity, he tried to rally. "I'll figure it out. I'll be fine."

"I have no doubt you will." In the background, a machine beeped quietly. "I have some time tomorrow, so I'll send those boxes you set aside. Is there anything else you want me to ship while I'm at it?" Before he had a chance to think, she continued. "Did you pack any dishes? Noodle bowls, spoons, chopsticks?"

"No, I didn't." No way in hell they'd have any of that here. "I guess I'll have to order some." Except he already regretted not taking his favorites along. Why hadn't he taken that into consideration?

"I figured you'd forgotten. You were so bent on proving to the family you could stalk off on your own, I'm surprised you had underwear. I'll send some dishes along, as well as some of the instant noodle packets you like. You can order a lot of them on Amazon, you know. I'll send you links. Not the same as when I make it, but it's not as if I ever had the time to do it anyway. Maybe you'll meet a nice boy in Wisconsin who wants to cook for you, and I'll teach him."

Hong-Wei flinched, which was stupid. He knew Hong-Su was on his side, but hearing her talk so casually about getting him a *nice boy* made him want to roll inside this makeshift bed. "Your twenty minutes have to be up by now."

It had been maybe five, ten tops, but she didn't point this out. "Don't make me call every time, okay?"

She's not the enemy. "I won't. Promise."

"And if you didn't bring along a Bluetooth speaker for your phone, go get one. You need your music almost more than you need furniture."

"I have headphones." He'd found those, at least, packed inside his suitcase.

"Not the same thing. They have to have big box stores there. Get on a bus or take a walk or phone one of these grateful hospital people and get to somewhere that sells one. As soon as possible."

"Yes, ma'am." Hong-Wei smiled despite himself. "Thanks, Hong-Su."

"Anytime."

He stayed where he was for several minutes after he hung up, considering everything she'd said. Then he checked the time and did a search for stores that might sell a speaker. He found several that would be open for a few hours, but none were close to his apartment, and Copper Point didn't have a bus system.

Hong-Wei thought of enduring the heavy silence of his condo for another evening, and he twitched.

Holding his mobile above his head while he lay on his back, he pulled up the entry for Simon Lane and opened up a text message bubble.

Is your offer to help me get things for my apartment still good?

He felt a thrill when the reply to his text came in under twenty seconds.

Absolutely. Were you wanting to go now?

Yes, Hong-Wei wanted to go instantly. *If it isn't too much trouble.*

No problem. Let me get my coat and shoes, and I'll be over in ten minutes.

He didn't meet Simon on the front steps, because that seemed desperate, but he did answer the bell quicker than Simon had answered the text message.

Simon was as cute as Hong-Wei remembered, possibly cuter. He wore jeans and a plain T-shirt, and a thin blue coat that brought out the color of his eyes.

"Ready to go?" Simon gestured to the street, where an SUV sat idling. "I brought Owen's car because it has more cargo room, in case you wanted to get a lot of things."

"Ready. Thanks again for giving me a ride."

"It's no trouble, really. Though eventually you'll want to get a car. The walk to the hospital will be no joke in the winter."

The stroll he'd taken to the hospital had been enough to get his attention, and it was April. "How cold does it get here, exactly?"

"This is northern Wisconsin on a bay off Lake Superior. It gets cold. And snowy. You paid for a garage with your condo, didn't you?"

"I did. It's beneath my first floor—if you drive to the rear of the building, the ground is a story lower. A car was next on my list, but my sister reminded me tonight I go a bit batty if I don't have music playing, so Bluetooth comes first. At some point I'll get a proper stereo system, but this will do in the meantime."

They were almost to Simon's car, but at this comment Simon stopped and gave Hong-Wei a reproachful look. "You didn't let me play anything for you on the drive back from the airport. I asked what Spotify station you wanted, and you told me it didn't matter."

He could hardly say it was because he'd had too much fun watching Simon be adorable, that for Hong-Wei, doing so had taken the edge off the terror of what he'd just done. He settled for an abridged version of the truth. "The company was too good to spoil."

If it was possible to get Simon to be flustered like this but still handle instruments properly in surgery, St. Ann's might not be so bad after all.

Of course, unless the man was out and open to being flirted with at work, Hong-Wei wouldn't do much more than make flattering comments. The last thing Hong-Wei would do was be *that* doctor.

"Did you know where you wanted to go?" Simon asked as he climbed into the car. "We could hit Electronics Barn before they close, or you could see what they have at Target."

"Electronics Barn, definitely."

Simon nodded, but he had a pensive expression as he drew the seat belt over himself. "What about furniture?"

Hong-Wei did want furniture, but he wasn't getting it at Target. "I'll take care of that tomorrow."

"I wish I could help you run errands tomorrow, but I have a double shift. Surgery, then filling in on the floor in the evening. But I'm happy to leave you my car and get a ride with Owen so you can get around."

Neither Simon nor Gagnon had said anything to make Hong-Wei think the two of them were anything but roommates, and yet Hong-Wei couldn't help a ridiculous flare of jealousy at the idea of Simon riding with Gagnon. "If I were going to borrow your car, I'd give you a ride. I couldn't put you out, though."

"Oh, I wouldn't mind. It's not as if I'd be using it while I'm at work. Besides, you rode in my car already. You might be the one put out." Simon gestured at the road ahead. "What kind of car were you thinking of getting? I could take you past the dealerships too, unless you wanted to go to Duluth for something nicer."

Hong-Wei shrugged. "Probably a Honda or Toyota, a few years old. Nothing fancy. Though I suppose I should consider four-wheel drive with the snow."

"You only need four-wheel drive if you're going off-road or in the country, and I doubt you are. A good set of snow tires will do you fine on whatever vehicle you want otherwise once winter hits. However, if you want a foreign car, you'll need to go to Duluth. We only have Chevy, Ford, and Dodge dealerships in town."

Hong-Wei laughed, but when Simon didn't, he immediately sobered. "You're serious?"

Simon nodded, clearly embarrassed. "Sorry. We're lucky to have those. The auto crisis about did us in. Without the bailout, we'd have lost those too." He smoothed the side of his hair in an awkward fidget. "I have Saturday off. I could run you to Duluth then. Jared will want to come along too. He loves cars. Owen would enjoy coming as well, but he's on call."

Hong-Wei was still reeling from the idea that Cooper Point only dealt in domestic vehicles. Vaguely he'd known places like this existed, but he hadn't been prepared for the reality. It seemed so odd. He wanted to point out that most Hondas and Toyotas were built in the United States and plenty of US-owned companies were sending factories and parts to Mexico, but he didn't. That was the kind of antagonism that got him in trouble.

He didn't want trouble with Simon. Not like that, anyway. He wasn't sure what he wanted with Simon yet, but it wasn't to make him upset.

"I'd be grateful if you took me on Saturday, thank you."

"Sure. No problem." Simon gestured to a small strip mall on the left. "We have a bakery, and a repair shop, and a home and garden center. Several restaurants are on the next block, and a few bars, but between you and me, I wouldn't go in there. The ones on Main Street are nicer and friendlier. The restaurants here are okay. Family Table is a home-cooking kind of place, but they focus on fried food. The burger place next door is one of my favorites. The Mexican place is good as well, and China Garden—" He cut himself off, blushing. "Well. I mean, it's fine for me, but maybe you have other ideas."

A Chinese restaurant, eh? He supposed it could be an outlier, but since most restaurants in the Midwest featured American Chinese cuisine, he doubted it served the sorts of dishes he craved. Still…. "Are the workers native Chinese?"

"Oh, yeah. A few speak decent English, but for the most part just enough to say *hello* and *thank you* and *excuse me*."

"Do you know what region in China they're from, especially the cook?"

Simon blinked. "I—I don't know. I'm sorry."

"It's all right." Hong-Wei sighed. "I wonder if they know how to make proper beef noodle soup. I'll have to ask."

A lull in their conversation caused him to worry that he'd made Simon uncomfortable, but when he glanced Simon's way to check, Simon only looked deep in thought. When he spoke at last, Simon said, "Can I ask you a question?"

Shifting in his seat, Hong-Wei studied Simon's profile in the semidarkness of the car. "Of course."

"Why did you move to the United States?"

"My father had been studying abroad in medical school and was accepted into a surgical residency at McGovern. My family moved to Houston to join him."

"And you really learned English from movies?" He frowned at Hong-Wei. "Because now I'm feeling guilty for not learning anything from Asian dramas."

"I learned from movies *and* studies, first in Taiwan and then here, at school and with tutors. Also, you're watching foreign films with zero pressure to learn the language. I'd come home to the next DVD of *Friends* knowing it might keep me from being beat up."

Simon winced. "Fair point."

"Our private school had a strong support system for international residents, and they helped us find affordable tutors. My mother helped us study as well, when she wasn't working, and my grandparents took care of the house so my parents could focus on work and parenting. Once my father got through his residency and became a practicing surgeon, we had more money, and my mother was able to finish her hospital administration degree. Now we're all grown, my grandparents live like royalty in my parents' suburban home, and my family raised two doctors, just like they wanted."

He hadn't meant that to come out as acerbic as it did, but thankfully Simon didn't pick up on it. "So your sister is a doctor too? What's her specialty?"

"Surgical oncologist."

"You're all surgeons? What's your father's specialty?"

"Orthopedics. He's a hand surgeon."

"Wow. So specific. And then you're a general surgeon. How lucky for us. Oh, here's the electronics store. Will this do?"

Hong-Wei studied the red and yellow sign. *General surgeon.* He had to practically bite his tongue to correct Simon, to explain that no, he wasn't *just* a general surgeon. Which was ridiculous. That had been his entire point in coming to Copper Point, to be *just* a general surgeon.

*You came out tonight to get a Bluetooth speaker,
not dump your dirty laundry on your new friend.* "Yes,
let's stop."

The store was about a quarter the size or perhaps
smaller than the one by the same company near the
condo Hong-Wei had shared with his sister in Houston, and the poor selection of Bluetooth speakers and
stereo equipment had him feeling anxious. Lucki-
ly, the store clerk not only helped him find a decent
speaker to take with him, they also placed a special
order for the stereo system and speakers he'd been
eyeing in Texas but couldn't get because Hong-Su had
threatened him with her scalpel if he did. Hong-Wei
left the store buzzing with anticipation.

"I've wanted this model for so long. It's *exactly*
what I want."

"So what is it you're going to listen to on your
incredible system? What's your audio poison?"

Hong-Wei was so high on his euphoric bubble
he almost answered. He didn't feel like sharing that
part of himself, not yet. *Be a normal general surgeon.*
"This and that. What about you?"

"Oh, a little of everything." Simon cleared his
throat and ran a hand through his hair. "So, you talked
about furniture shopping tomorrow, but if it's not too
late, I know a place you could go tonight. Good quality and variety, and if there's something you wanted
to order, you could. If you'd rather wait, though, no
pressure."

Frowning, Hong-Wei checked his watch. "Sure,
but I can't imagine anywhere is open at this hour."

"Trust me, I can get you in. Is there anywhere else
you want to hit first?"

Hong-Wei wanted nothing more than a real bed and somewhere to sit. "No, by all means, let's go."

Simon drove them into the downtown area of Copper Point, to a building off the cross street opposite City Park and Main Street. Hong-Wei saw the sign first, an old but well-maintained double-faced sign reading *Petersen Home Furnishings* displayed over a metal awning above a long spread of glass windows, well-lit despite the fact that the store was clearly closed for the day. Yet as soon as Simon parked the car and got out, an affable-looking man with a thick mustache wearing a driving cap and tan jacket came out to meet them, beaming.

"Hello, Simon. So good to see you."

Simon waved at him. "Hello, Uncle Jimmy. This is Dr. Wu, the new surgeon I told you about on the phone. Dr. Wu, this is my uncle, James Petersen, the owner of Petersen Home Furnishings."

Petersen held out his hand, eyes twinkling, mustache lifting as he grinned. "A pleasure to be at your service, Doctor. We're so glad to have you here in Copper Point."

Hong-Wei accepted the handshake. "Call me Jack, please. Especially if you're going through the trouble of opening your store at this hour just for me."

"Nonsense. I escaped hauling junk out of the basement and clearing out drains to come here. Besides, the way Simon put it, you're in the mood to furnish an entire apartment, and I'm always happy to help a man part with his money." He laughed at his own joke but quickly sobered, placing a hand on Hong-Wei's arm as he led him inside. "That said, Jack, you take your time checking everything over, and if you need to place any special orders, I have plenty of catalogs. Plus, we work with Amish craftsmen direct from Cashton, and if you see anything close but not quite right in any of our fine wood furnishings, we can get something custom designed exactly the way you want it. Above all, I want you to let me know precisely what you need. Furnishing your home is the most important thing you'll do. It's your refuge at the end of the day."

Hong-Wei had to hand it to Petersen. The man knew his business. He was a born salesman, using just enough grease to ease Hong-Wei into more purchases than he planned to make and at higher prices than he'd originally intended. Petersen had him book an appointment with a local interior designer to help him set up his condo as well. Normally Hong-Wei would have balked at the idea, assuming anyone from a place this small wouldn't share his design taste, but once Petersen showed him the sample design options in the designer's portfolio, he had an appointment for a free initial consultation with her the following afternoon. When he finally left the store two hours after he entered it, he was over seven thousand dollars lighter, and he had a good chunk of his condo coming the next day with several items on order.

"Your uncle is exceptionally good at his job," Hong-Wei said as they got into the car.

"I hope he didn't talk you into spending too much." Simon frowned as they drove away. "It was my only reservation in calling him."

"Oh, no. It saved me a lot of headache, because I didn't know where else I was going to get most of these things. I don't care for ordering furniture online because you can't tell the quality until you touch it. I like having a nice atmosphere, but I don't care to put in the work of setting it up. I let my sister design our condo in Houston. I asked her to come here and help me get organized, but she laughed."

"Well, I'm glad it worked out, then."

"It did. Thank you very much. It was kind of you to take me."

"Are you kidding? Uncle Jimmy pulled me aside three times and thanked me and told me to pick out whatever recliner I wanted, and once you special ordered the bookshelf and stereo cabinet, he told me I could make it a leather one. There's a rival furniture store on the other end of town. He's going to get all the bragging rights that the new doctor bought *all* his things from Petersen's."

Hong-Wei attempted to wipe away his smile, but it didn't work. "I'm grateful all the same. Not the least of which because tomorrow night I get to sleep in a real bed."

"You're welcome. Is there anywhere else you want to go?"

Back to his place to hook up his new Bluetooth speaker. "I'm good. If you're still offering to let me borrow your car during the day tomorrow, I won't say no."

"Oh, sure. Did you want me to leave it with you now?"

Taking the car now was a sure bet Lane would get a ride with Gagnon in the morning. "No, go ahead and pick me up on your way. Then when I'm done, I'll park it, bring you the keys, and walk back to my condo."

He was ready for Lane to make noise about putting Hong-Wei out, but he didn't. "If it turns out you need to keep it, don't worry. I can always get a ride home."

Mmm-hmm. Hong-Wei let him pretend this was an option, since it made him feel better. "Sounds like a plan."

He waved at Lane as he drove off, then hurried inside, where the emptiness of his condo still nagged at him, but now that he knew exactly how temporary it was, it didn't bother him quite as much.

Also, Hong-Su was right, as usual. He wasn't sure what he was doing with his surgical nurse or why he cared who gave him a ride to work, but once he had the speaker hooked up and a violin concerto echoing through the room, the world felt a lot better.

CHAPTER THREE

SIMON TRIED to make it out of the house without Owen or Jared cornering him, but he couldn't escape the kitchen before the pair of them confronted him while he packed his lunch.

"So." Owen took up Simon's right flank, leaning against the cupboard. "Someone came home awfully late last night and snuck into his room before he could be properly interrogated."

Jared blocked the other side. "I heard a rumor a certain surgeon spent a handsome chunk of change at Petersen Home Furnishings. You wouldn't know anything about that, would you?"

This revelation alarmed Simon. "What, did Uncle Jimmy post it on Facebook?"

Owen laughed. "No. Your aunt told my mother, who texted me wanting more details. Which sadly I don't have, because I wasn't given any."

Simon did everything he could to avoid their gazes, but since they were practically boxing him in, he had to stare at the floor. "Dr. Wu needed to do some shopping, so I helped him out. And yes, I called my uncle so Dr. Wu could get some furniture. There's nothing else to tell."

Jared rested his elbows on the countertop and withdrew a tomato from the bowl by the sink, examining it casually. "What do you think, Owen? Is Si blushing *this* red, or is he more the color of a strawberry?"

"I think he's the color of someone smitten by a handsome surgeon who, out of the thirty-some people who offered to shuttle him on his errands yesterday, chose our boy to be his escort instead."

Simon pressed his hands to his cheeks and shut his eyes. "*Stop*. Both of you."

Jared popped Simon lightly on the ass. "I'm about to head in, and since the golden surgeon hasn't started yet, I'm the lucky draw for the empty ER shift tonight. Do you want a ride, since we're both wallowing in St. Ann's shorthanded misery today?"

Simon felt his blush spread across his body as he realized they were about to get worse. "I… I can't. I told Dr. Wu I'd pick him up so he could borrow my car for the day."

They were merciless, lighting into him to the point he was still rattled when he got to Hong-Wei's condo, and Hong-Wei commented on it, frowning at Simon as he climbed into the car. "Are you all right? You look flushed. Are you coming down with something?"

Simon touched his cheeks. "No. My housemates were teasing me this morning, is all."

He meant the remark to dismiss the matter, but when he glanced at the passenger seat, he was surprised to see Hong-Wei was angry. "Were they bullying you?"

It shouldn't make Simon dizzy, having him rise to his defense, but it did. "No—thank you, but no. Like I said, they were only teasing. We're old friends, the three of us. It's just the way they are." When Hong-Wei didn't look convinced, Simon kept babbling as he pulled onto the street. "Owen, Jared, and I went through a lot in middle school, survived a sometimes small-minded town by turning ourselves into the Three Musketeers. We went to University of Wisconsin at Madison and roomed together, then decided to come back to Copper Point. Even when they drive me nuts, I still love them both to death."

Somehow this wasn't mollifying Hong-Wei much. "Hmm. So none of you dated or married?"

"There have been dates, but not much for me since college. No one ever serious. Work doesn't leave a lot of room for a social life, and we don't exactly have much of a nightlife here. Not a lot of guys I'm interested in."

His stomach danced with butterflies as he glanced at Hong-Wei to check his reaction at that subtle come-out, but Hong-Wei didn't seem fazed by Simon's revelation. Probably it wasn't much of one. "So you haven't dated Gagnon or Kumpel?"

Simon blinked in surprise. "We all dated each other at one point, but it was a disaster, so we agreed to stay friends." When Hong-Wei remained weirdly quiet, Simon flipped the tables. "How about you? Have you dated much?" *Would you like to confirm your orientation while you're at it?*

He regretted the question immediately when he saw the way it shut Hong-Wei down. "No."

Well. Damn.

Simon would have redirected the conversation, but they were at the hospital now, meaning he had to leave on an awkward note. He forced a smile, trying to make the best of the situation. "So, here we are. You can leave the keys with the front desk if you want to return the car when you're done, or I can stop by to get them later and find a ride home. Jared said he has to work late—"

"I'll bring them by."

How *that* upset Hong-Wei, Simon had no idea. "Okay. I'll look forward to it, then. Have a good day."

"You too."

Simon was still flustered when he went inside, and dealing with Dr. Orth all day long wasn't going to help his case. Since Dr. Stevens's retirement four months ago, St. Ann's had relied on a rotating roster from local hospitals to fill in their general surgery slate, and while none of them were exactly stellar, Dr. Orth was absolutely the worst. He was young, full of himself, and he hated Simon as much as Simon hated him, which made working together oh so pleasant. By the time his surgery shift was done and he was showering for a quick changeover before he ate dinner and took his turn in the ER, Simon was grinding his teeth and muttering curses under his breath.

When he came into the locker room, scowling, Owen met him. "Hey there. I see Orth has you in a fine mood as always."

"Please tell me he's the one we're letting go as soon as Dr. Wu starts." Simon shut his locker and frowned at Owen, who wore his scrubs. "You got called in?"

"Probable cesarean. Kathryn says there might be two, but it's only the one for now. You going to send me some fun and games from the ER while you're on shift?"

"Bite your tongue." Simon pulled his ER scrubs on. "So Jared and I are in ER, and you're here for OB."

"Fair warning, Jared has a peds patient he's going to want a performance for before the weekend's over." Owen grinned, a twinkle in his eye. "First, though, you need to go to the nurses' station. You have a delivery."

That must be where Hong-Wei had left his keys. Simon thought about collecting them later, then considered how many places they could get moved in a shift and decided it would be best to retrieve them now. "Thanks. Good luck with the cesareans."

"Not me having them. I'm just keeping the ladies comfortable." He winked at Simon. "Go to the nurses' station."

After he clipped his badge to his lapel and exited the locker room, Simon hurried down the hall, trying to shake off the afternoon with Orth. He hoped they didn't have any emergency surgeries for the next few hours, since Orth was on call until seven. After that they'd have no surgeon until Orth returned on Monday. Simon wondered when Hong-Wei would start. He'd asked Andreas multiple times, but the only answer he ever got was basically "whenever Dr. Wu wants to," which wasn't much help. Surely the man had a start date.

As long as they stopped hiring Orth to fill in, Simon didn't care what else happened.

At the nurses' station, an unusually large cluster of hospital staff as well as several patients had gathered at the far edge of the long counter. Probably someone had baby pictures, and since Simon didn't much feel in the mood to see them, he ignored the throng, heading for the desk. "Hey, did any of you guys see where Dr. Wu left my keys?"

When his question was met with only giggles, whispers, and a round of *shhh*s, Simon glanced up and saw Hong-Wei himself, looking sexy as hell in a dark gray thermal and black jeans as he leaned over the nurses' station, smiling as he dangled Simon's keys and held up a delicious-smelling bag of takeout.

"Do you have time left before your shift to let me thank you with dinner?"

More giggles, more whispers, and oh, but the tips of Simon's ears were on *fire*. Here he'd thought he'd somehow said something to upset Hong-Wei earlier because he'd been so quiet, and now the man was openly flirting at the nurses' station. *Flirting*. There was no mistaking the expression on his face. Simon wanted to drown in it—if it wasn't a look that could get him fired.

Pointedly turning his back on the clutch of gawkers updating Facebook and sending texts to the entire city, Simon focused on Hong-Wei. "I start in the ER in a few minutes, unfortunately. But thank you so much."

"Hopefully you have time to eat later, then. I'll walk you." Hong-Wei cupped Simon's elbow, and Simon swore he heard the sound of fifteen status updates in their wake.

Simon caught a better whiff of the bag Hong-Wei held as they went around the corner. "That smells amazing. What is it?"

"Me showing off. Do you remember when I said I was going to go to the Chinese restaurant and put in a request? I did."

Now Simon was incredibly curious. "What did you ask them to make?" He inhaled again, trying to guess. He couldn't. "Is it spicy? Because I'm not going to pretend to be brave. I can't eat spicy foods."

"I had them make *tsao mi fun*, which is stir-fried rice noodles. With pork, in case you didn't like shrimp. Not spicy. Most Taiwanese food isn't spicy, in fact. I wanted beef noodle soup, but that's a bit much for me to ask for on the spur of the moment."

"It smells incredible." Simon glanced over his shoulder, bit his lip, and gave in. "I might have a *few* minutes before my shift starts."

Hong-Wei grinned. "I thought you might."

The longer Simon smelled the food, the hungrier he got. "So you simply went to the restaurant and custom-ordered this?"

"It was slightly more complicated than that, but basically, yes." They were near the entrance to the elevator, and Hong-Wei paused in front of it, glancing around. "Where would be a good place to eat?"

Simon ran a hand over his hair. "Well, probably the cafeteria."

Hong-Wei gestured at the door to the doctors' lounge. "What about here?"

Simon wasn't supposed to go in there, and he *definitely* wasn't supposed to eat there. That said, Owen and Jared had dragged him in plenty of times, and it was after five now, on a Friday to boot. Everyone who might get him into trouble had almost certainly gone home.

"Sure, just this once." When Hong-Wei regarded him oddly, Simon pointed at the sign. "Nurses aren't allowed."

Hong-Wei flattened his lips. "Oh. I'd hoped these ridiculous rules weren't observed at smaller hospitals."

"I think it depends on the hospital." Simon put his hand on the door, pushing it open. "It's all weird now, because as I said, we had the administration shakeup, and—"

He stopped talking as he stepped inside the lounge and saw the administration shakeup in question talking heatedly to Owen at the table near the pop machine.

Andreas looked as if he wanted to reprimand Simon, but as soon as he saw his new surgeon, he was all smiles and politeness. "Dr. Wu, back again I see. I'm glad you feel at home at St. Ann's. Is there something I can do for you?"

Hong-Wei waved the bag of takeout. "I came to thank Mr. Lane for showing me around yesterday and loaning me his car today. Brought some special noodles to give him before his next shift."

Owen raised his eyebrows and drifted over, peering intently at Hong-Wei's bag. "Oh? What did you bring? Enough to share?"

Simon so longed to strangle Owen.

Hong-Wei blinked, momentarily stunned by Owen's forwardness. Simon wanted to get rid of his friend, but before he could do that, Andreas stepped in, literally, drawing Owen away. "I believe *you* are needed in OB."

Owen glared at the top of Andreas's head. "I haven't heard any pages for me." When Andreas only smiled back at him, Owen pursed his lips and rolled his eyes. "Fine. I'll go to OB."

"I'll go with you." Andreas nodded at Simon and Hong-Wei. "Dr. Wu. Mr. Lane. Enjoy your meal."

Simon watched them go, thinking that, for the first time, he was grateful to Andreas for something. Unfortunately, one of his roommates remained.

Jared crossed lazily toward them, laughing. "God, I love watching Owen and Andreas fight." He sat at a table near them and plunked his feet on a chair. "You better eat fast, though, Si. Andreas is sticking around tonight to do one of his assessments."

Simon sighed as he sat opposite Jared. "You're kidding. It's Friday night. Doesn't he have a life?"

Jared snorted. "Andreas? Absolutely not."

Hong-Wei frowned as he opened the bag and withdrew two Styrofoam containers. "I thought Erin Andreas was the human resources director. Is this some sort of employee performance thing?"

"It's an Andreas thing." Jared toyed absently with the straw in his cafeteria cup. "He's the HR director, yes, but his father is also the president of the hospital board and owner of half the county. Their family is so old money some say you can trace them to the French traders who settled Copper Point before the miners."

Simon was feeling sour, still thinking about the hell Andreas could wreak during his shift—his double shift—when Hong-Wei opened the container in front of him. The smell hit him full force this time, as well as the sight of the glimmering, wonderful noodles. "Oh my *God*."

"Eat them while they're hot." Hong-Wei passed him a packet of takeout chopsticks, then hesitated. "Or do you need a fork?"

Simon regarded the chopsticks longingly. "I always wanted to learn how. I've tried, but I'm a disaster."

Hong-Wei smiled. "I'll teach you, but not while your noodles are already half cold." He glanced around the lounge. "Are there forks in here?"

"I'll get him one." Jared got up and fetched a disposable utensil from the drawer by the microwave. When he returned to the table and handed it to Simon, he studied the two of them with interest. "You two seem to be getting along well."

Simon wanted to kick Jared, but at that moment Hong-Wei had caught a long section of noodles between his chopsticks and sucked them into his mouth. God, the man was even beautiful when he ate. Simon forced himself to focus on his own noodles and spun some around his fork, then took a bite. And groaned. "*These are amazing.*"

Hong-Wei wiped his mouth with a napkin after finishing his second bite. "They're not bad. A little different than I'm used to, but they're good. I'm glad you like them too." He shifted his gaze to Jared. "I thought it would be wise to get to know my nurse, since we'll be working closely together."

"Mmm-hmm." Jared sipped his drink through the straw. "You still need to come over and have dinner. What about tomorrow? Simon and I aren't working, and Owen's on call. A rare Saturday off."

Simon sat up straight, remembering. "Oh. I told Dr. Wu I'd take him to Duluth to buy a car tomorrow."

Jared brightened. "Oh yeah? I'll come along."

Hong-Wei's smile was smooth. "You don't need to trouble yourself."

"Who's troubling? I'm looking for some excitement in my life. Plus it'll bug Owen, which is a bonus." He set his cup down and grinned. "What are you thinking of getting?"

They talked cars for a few minutes, so Simon focused on eating his noodles. He told himself not to resent Jared for stealing his time with Hong-Wei, that even if Hong-Wei was interested, which he wasn't, Simon couldn't go there.

Still, it would've been nice to eat his thank-you noodles *alone* with Hong-Wei.

He was finishing up when Jared rose, stretching as he pushed back his chair. "Well, I'm going to go check the lay of the land. Hopefully we have a nice, boring night." He patted Simon on the shoulder. "I'll cover for you if Andreas shows up, but don't take too long. I only have so much charm. And the price is a performance for my peds patient when she's discharged Sunday."

Hong-Wei raised an eyebrow at Simon once Jared was gone. "Performance?"

Simon really was going to kill Jared. "When he has a pediatric patient in the hospital, he likes to give them a treat when they go home, and he's become famous for putting on something of a show. He drags Owen and me into it as much as he can."

"This place is so quirky. I like it."

"Well, it gets quirkier, so I hope you can hold on to your attitude."

Hong-Wei picked up their garbage as he stood. "I'm thinking I'll start on Monday."

On *Monday*? "Does Andreas know you plan to begin so soon?"

"He told me to come whenever I was ready. We didn't plan to have me begin actual surgeries until the end of the month, or at least for another two weeks. I'm talking more about coming in and establishing procedure, getting to know you and the rest of the nursing staff, things like that. It sounds like the hospital is always shorthanded, so I'll help out when needed, and I thought maybe if you have any free time and are willing, we could go over the way I prefer the OR set up. Andreas said he'd find me coverage for you when I was ready to begin the transition."

Simon's heart skipped a beat. The idea of working with Hong-Wei instead of Orth was almost too much to hope for. "I'll help any time I'm free, and I'm eager to work with you."

"I feel the same way." Hong-Wei sorted the remainders of their meal into the recycling, compost, and garbage bins, then tapped his finger thoughtfully on the counter. "Would you mind, actually, if I hung around the ED tonight to begin going over some things now? Or will I get you in trouble with Andreas?"

"If you clear it with him first, I think you can have anything you ask for. St. Ann's is so happy to have you here, they'd give you the moon if you put up an order for it."

"I don't think my condo has enough space. But I'll go find Andreas and ask him. Thanks. I hope to see you soon."

Simon practically floated all the way to the ER. The ED, as Hong-Wei had called it. Technically all ERs were Emergency Departments now, and when he'd worked in the larger hospitals in Madison they'd called them that, but here at St. Ann's the throwback name stuck. He liked that Hong-Wei called it an ED, though. It suited him, made him seem special and fancy and… well, more *Hong-Wei*.

He tried to wipe the stupid grin off his face as he arrived, but it didn't work. When Jared saw him, he gave him a thumbs-up. "Way to score, Si. Bringing you dinner? He's *totally* into you."

Simon shushed him and glanced around fervently, but fortunately the other nurse was gossiping with the tech and the receptionist as the workers from the other shift prepared to leave. "Can you not? God, what if Andreas were here?"

"He's harassing Owen in OB. I know because Owen's texting me every thirty seconds complaining. Sometimes he sends me Snaps too." Jared held up his phone, which was indeed blowing up with text and Snapchat notifications. "I'm serious, Simon. Wu is into you."

Simon busied himself filling a cart with supplies it didn't need, then taking them off again. "He needs a friend in a new place, and I'm friendly. I'm sure it's nothing more."

"If Owen or I joke-flirt with you, which we keep doing just to see him react, he all but growls at us and barks *mine*."

Simon pressed his hands to his cheeks. He did? The idea made his heart leap, but…. "I can't do anything about it, though, if he's interested."

Jared rolled his eyes. "*Si.* Yes you can. You have to be smart and careful, is all."

"In this town? With the surgeon everyone was so sure we'd never get, from a prestigious hospital? I couldn't cross the street with him without seeing the news as a banner headline on the *Copper Point Gazette* the next day." He shook his head. "Besides, I think you're misreading it."

"I'm not. He's into you. Even if you don't date him, you should at least take him to bed."

The very idea made Simon's nerve endings short-circuit. "I can't. The policy."

Jared leaned in close. "You want to pursue this, I can see it in your eyes. But you're scared. You're using the policy as a shield. What are you actually afraid of, though?"

Simon abandoned his fussing with the cart. "I'm not risking my career to get laid."

"You *are* dodging the question."

He was, and he'd continue to do so. "Do you have any rounds to make?"

"Nope. Did them all."

"Well, I'm going to go take report from the nurse leaving shift and do my job instead of listening to you gossip."

He left Jared at the cart, picking up a clipboard as he passed and clutching it tight to his chest in an attempt to still his rapidly beating heart.

What are you actually afraid of?

For a moment, Hong-Wei's slow, lopsided smile drifted into his mind. Then Simon pushed the image out as quickly as possible, lest it stir up answers he didn't want to hear.

HONG-WEI FOUND Andreas in the OB ward, arguing with Gagnon. When Andreas saw Hong-Wei, he held up a hand in front of the anesthesiologist's face and smiled at Hong-Wei. "Dr. Wu. Is there something I can do for you?"

He stifled a laugh as Gagnon mimicked Andreas, exaggerating Andreas's posture and mouthing *Is there something I can do for you?* before curling his lip and turning away from the director to read something on a monitor.

Hong-Wei cleared his throat. "I think I'd like to come in on Monday, unless you have any objections."

Andreas's expression took on a mercenary quality. "I'm absolutely pleased to hear you're ready to work right away. We have a fill-in surgeon scheduled for another seven days on contract, but I'm still negotiating the week after that, so if you decide you'd like to take on the surgical schedule for that week, say the word. Basically, tell me what you'd like to do, what you need to get set up, and I'll make it happen."

Simon was right. This man did indeed seem to run much more than HR. "For now, I want to spend some time with Simon and any other surgical staff I'll be working with so they understand my expectations. That's my first priority."

Andreas nodded. "I'll send out a memo letting people know the surgical team members might be called away to work with you while on shift. As you've noticed, we all fill in wherever we can here, so your staff might be doing things in odd places. I'll send you a roster. But as you noted, Simon will be who you work with the most. We have fewer surgeries right now since we're working with a skeletal staff. I'm eager to have our sub staff work the weekends you're unwilling to take call instead of the weekdays. I'm going to have marketing let people know we'll have surgical staff on the weekend again soon."

Hong-Wei blinked. "You—you don't have surgical staff on the weekends right now? At all?"

"Unfortunately, no. We're lucky to have a resident OB-GYN. Dr. Lambert-Diaz generally keeps track of when her mothers are due and doesn't go far out of town unless she can help it, because when she does, if her mothers go into delivery, they have to go out of state. Ironwood, Michigan, has the closest hospital, and it's not in much better shape than we are. We have to call ahead and make sure *they* have surgical staff if we send someone there. Otherwise it's a hot ambulance ride to Duluth or Eau Claire. Duluth is closer, but depending on what insurance or Medicaid people are on, we have to keep them in the state if we can. Dr. Lambert-Diaz is going to be thrilled you can cover for her if she needs to take a weekend off."

Hong-Wei couldn't believe this. "So if someone comes in tonight with acute appendicitis, you have to send them away?"

Andreas looked Hong-Wei dead in the eye. "If someone comes in tonight with emergency surgery needs, I'm getting on my knees in front of you, Dr. Wu."

The revelation there was no surgical coverage if he left town shook Hong-Wei to the point that he

closed himself in the office Andreas had told him was
his in the clinic area and called his sister. He literally sagged with relief when she answered, though he
didn't let her get more than two words into her ribbing
before he cut her off.

"They have no surgical coverage on the weekend.
None at all."

She whistled low. "Grim. Makes sense, though.
Only emergencies on the weekend."

"Yes, but they have to ship them hours away. I was
going to leave town to buy a car tomorrow. There's no
way, now. The whole time all I'll think about is who's
dying because I wanted to—" He cut himself off before he could say *flirt with my nurse*. He decidedly
wasn't telling Hong-Su about Simon.

"Hon, you can't start with that attitude. This job
will bury you. You have to be able to leave town."

"They're going to switch the sub coverage to
weekends I don't want to take call, apparently. The
bottom line is, I don't think I get a car this week."

"Why do you have to leave town to get a car?"

"They only sell domestic in town."

"Wow. Okay. Well, you know, you could probably tell one of the local dealers what you want used,
even in an import. Or you could build a new car online, send it to a dealer, and have them tell you when
it's ready. You have plenty of money hoarded to make
a down payment. If not, I'll spot you."

He'd spent a lot of his money on the furniture,
but he'd kept enough aside for a decent used car. He
hadn't considered buying new. He'd gotten a signing
bonus, and he could likely get more if he told Andreas
he'd work call for the first month. But that would

make it tricky to pick up his car. "Do you think they'd deliver my car to me?"

"Depends on how much money you spend. Think one of your new fans would go get it for you?"

He could see Gagnon rubbing his hands together at the prospect. It wasn't as if Hong-Wei actually *wanted* to go to Duluth anyway. Maybe he could send Gagnon and Kumpel and, while they were gone, spend the day with Simon. "I think that could be arranged."

"See? It'll work out. Remember, too, these people have gone a long time without a regular surgeon. Just because you're there doesn't mean you have to save the world. You ran away to the boonies to *stop* everyone from pressuring you. Don't you be the first in line to start it up again."

She was right. She was always right. "Okay. I'll remember. Thanks."

"This place sounds like something else. You're starting to make me curious. Maybe I'll come visit you."

His entire body went tense. Much as he wanted to see her, he couldn't handle his family seeing him here, not yet. "Absolutely not."

"Okay, go be a hero. Gently and at a sedate pace."

Hong-Wei did his best. Over the next hour, he sent emails to the staff Andreas listed, introducing himself and letting them know he'd be pulling them aside to go over procedures for how he wanted to run the OR. He went down to the ED and talked to Simon, but he was less able to keep his cool there, too distracted by each patient coming in, even though not a single one of them went to surgery.

"You okay?" Kumpel asked after Hong-Wei hovered during the dressing of a young boy's broken arm in the ED. "You seem out of it. I can't tell if you're bored or worked up or both."

Probably it would be best to confess, since being at the hospital was settling his anxieties. "Andreas told me we have no surgical staff on the weekends."

"Yeah, it's not ideal, but we've figured out our workarounds." Kumpel gave Hong-Wei a long look. "Is that why you're hanging out? At first I thought it was because of Simon, but now I'm starting to wonder."

Hong-Wei startled at the casual way Kumpel called out his interest in Simon. He decided to ignore it. "I stayed initially to talk to Simon about surgical procedures, but... yes. I think I'm on trauma watch. Tonight and for the whole weekend. There's no way I can leave town knowing someone might need a surgeon while I'm gone. I couldn't focus on anything."

"You're worrying a tad bit much, but I can't say I mind. Usually our fill-ins can't run out the door fast enough on Friday night. I like what this says about you, that you haven't finished orientation and you've put yourself on call." Kumpel leaned on the counter of the exam room and tapped his fingers against the side. "You certainly don't need to hang out here for that, though. Don't you have a condo full of new furniture to try out?"

It would take some getting used to, everyone knowing everything about his life. "I do, but I don't mind being here."

Kumpel snorted. "Nobody wants to be here. You must be restless. Well, I have the cure for that, shy of the person you want to cure your restlessness with." He picked up his phone and punched out a text.

Rising, he put an arm around Hong-Wei's shoulders. "Come on, Jack. Let's go find you some scrubs and a patient to play with."

Hong-Wei meant to object, but he didn't, and he ended up seeing several patients and doing rounds with Kumpel in the general wing. Nothing serious came through the ED, mostly the usual Friday-night drunks and weirdness, and a few sick babies that were firmly Kumpel's territory. He kept dragging Hong-Wei along anyway, though, introducing him to patients and parents as if he were visiting royalty. "This is our new surgeon, Dr. Jack Wu. He's helping us out in the ER and getting to know the staff. We're incredibly lucky to have him here."

Kumpel was amazing with kids. Not only did he clearly know his discipline, he put his patients at ease and made them laugh more often than not. He also played well off Simon, who was a competent ED nurse.

"Have you worked with kids much?" Kumpel asked during a lull in the shift. Simon was with them this time, updating a patient's chart.

Hong-Wei shrugged, trying not to feel edgy at the question. Kumpel was simply getting to know him. "I did some moonlighting in pediatric surgery. Among other places."

"I still can't get over someone from Baylor coming here. I won't ask you too many questions in case I break the spell and send you away, but I'd love to know more about your background. All Andreas told us was you were a general surgeon."

General surgeon. Simon had said the same thing. Well, he was one now, he supposed. He set down his cup and cleared his throat. "It's complicated."

"That's what I figured you'd say." Yawning, Kumpel stretched in his chair. "Oh, hey—Simon, I forgot to tell you. Mrs. Mueller got discharged to the nursing home today."

Simon sighed, not looking up from the monitor. "She'll be back here within a week."

"It's the truth." Kumpel turned to Hong-Wei. "She has the inoperable stomach tumor I showed you the other day."

Hong-Wei remembered. The scans were poorly done. He wanted to see new ones, but apparently he'd have to fight Medicaid. "You'll let me know when she's a patient again?"

"Absolutely."

They had no operations that night, and before Hong-Wei could try to get a ride with Simon, Kumpel captured him. As he dropped him off at his condo, the doctor leaned over the center console to speak to Hong-Wei.

"I'll swing by tomorrow morning around nine and pick you up. Owen makes a great Saturday brunch—if he's on call, I'll cook and send Simon for you. Speaking of Simon, you don't have any worries, he's totally into you."

Hong-Wei stilled and carefully stared straight ahead out the windshield.

Kumpel continued on, calmly. "I've seen you eyeing him all night. For the record, Owen and I are also queer, and the three of us are out. You don't have to be, though. That actually might work well, because Andreas's no-dating policy between staff is trash, and Simon's freaked about getting fired. The point is, I'm saying I've got your back, and Owen does too. We love Simon and want to see him happy. If *you* make him happy, so much the better."

This town was so strange. "It would be my pleasure to come over for breakfast tomorrow." Sweat dripped down his brow.

What was his problem, anyway? Hadn't he left Houston so he could do things exactly like this: make friends, fall in love, enjoy his life?

I don't know, honestly. I don't know what I went away for.

"Great. I'll get your number from Si, and I'll be in touch. Sleep well. And don't worry about emergencies. If they happen, we'll figure them out. That's the St. Ann's way."

Nodding, Hong-Wei slipped out of the car and drifted up the walk to his condo. After letting himself inside, he flopped on his new couch—so wonderful to have furniture—turned on the Bluetooth stereo with the remote, and played Chopin until he felt calm.

CHAPTER FOUR

Nothing about the weekend went the way Simon expected it to, but that turned out to be fine.

He hadn't expected Jared to go out for milk and come back with Hong-Wei, to start, or for Hong-Wei to be against going to Duluth to shop for a car. Jared seemed unsurprised by this too. When Hong-Wei mentioned he wanted to look into shopping online for a new car, Owen pounced, leading him into the den with his laptop, and an hour later Hong-Wei emerged with a 2018 Toyota Avalon on order. Until then, Owen promised he could borrow his car whenever he needed one.

As a thank-you, Hong-Wei took them all to dinner at the Chinese restaurant because Owen had heard about the magic of personalized ordering and wanted to see it for himself. Simon worried this was going to end in disaster, but Jared winked at him.

"Don't fuss. Everything's going to be fine. If Owen gets too crazy, I'll reel him in."

To Simon's surprise, Owen behaved, too enraptured with watching Hong-Wei address the waitstaff in Mandarin. The spell was broken, however, when two nursing techs came in, saw Owen, whispered in panic to one another, and left.

Hong-Wei glanced at Owen, then at the door. "What did you do to them?"

Owen shrugged, indifferent.

Simon answered for him. "Owen is only friendly with the two of us. And now you, I guess. Everyone else calls him Owen the Ogre."

"I'm not an ogre." Owen ran his finger around the Chinese zodiac on his place mat. "I don't care for other people, is all. They always want me to do things for them, and I hate that."

Hong-Wei laughed. "I guess I'm glad I passed the test?"

"Sure. You like Simon, and he likes you, so it's automatic." Owen squinted at his place mat, oblivious to the way Hong-Wei had gone rigid and Simon went as red as the decor around them. "I hate being an ox. I want to be a snake."

Hong-Wei shook himself out of his paralysis and focused on his own place mat. "So you were born in 1985? So was I. You're not just an ox. You're a wood ox. You're decisive, straightforward, and always ready to help the weak and the helpless." When Owen beamed, he added, "You're also restless."

Jared laughed. "That's him to a T. Okay, so I'm 1984. A rat."

"Also a wood rat." Hong-Wei got out his phone. "Enterprising, and you go straight to the core of the matter."

Now it was Simon and Owen's turn to laugh. Owen waved at Simon. "You're a little younger. What are you?"

Simon checked the place mat. "1986. Tiger."

Hong-Wei winked. "*Fire* tiger."

Owen threw up his hands.

Hong-Wei ignored him as he consulted his phone. "Tolerant, talented, and have strong will. Faithful and popular, but easily taken advantage of."

Jared and Owen pointed at him at the same time, their eyes wide. "*You*. It's *you*. *Fire tiger*."

The meal was excellent—Simon wasn't sure what they ate, except it wasn't anything similar to what he usually had at Chinese restaurants. Also the entire staff of the place seemed to wander past their table to talk to Hong-Wei, who was patient with them. Owen was fixated on the food, but Jared, like Simon, was fascinated by Hong-Wei's admirers.

"I can't think they're coming by here because you speak the language," Jared said at last.

Hong-Wei shook his head. "It's the doctor thing. I let it slip when I was placing the noodle order."

Jared and Owen raised their eyebrows and exchanged knowing glances. "Ah," Jared said. "You ended up giving free medical advice?"

"Yes, except they were confused I didn't know Eastern medicine too. I explained I've lived most of my life here, but they want to know why my grandmother didn't teach me medicine."

Simon frowned. "But by that logic, *their* grandmothers could have taught them medicine."

Hong-Wei smiled. "I think they're teasing me at this point, which is kind of nice, as if I've been adopted. It's nice to use my Mandarin, in any event. The owner is a good person who treats his staff well. Some of these places can be brutal."

Simon put down his fork. "What do you mean?"

Hong-Wei raised an eyebrow. "How much do you know about the history of Chinese restaurants in the United States?" When they all looked at him blankly, he continued. "In the late 1800s, the US cut off all immigration from China, but in 1915 a court case made an exception for restaurant owners. This began a machine which expanded across the country and fueled a network of immigration that still exists today, some through legal immigration, some illegal. In a lot of the restaurants, the workers stay for six months at a time or less, moving on with little or no notice via buses that exist only to take them to the next restaurant. They sleep together, live together, work together. As a rule, they get every other Sunday off. They're often paying off a mammoth debt they incurred to arrive in the States, or they're sending money home to family in a small village. But Mr. Zhang appears to be running a respectable establishment, and he's a kind man who treats his workers well."

Simon, Jared, and Owen all stared at Hong-Wei, dumbfounded. "I never considered the lives of the people who work here," Jared said, recovering first. "I don't know what I assumed. I guess I thought they seemed so professional—God, the more I talk, the more idiotic I feel."

Hong-Wei glanced around the restaurant. "This place is good. It would be important for Mr. Zhang, though, because working here means complete isolation. There isn't even another Chinese restaurant nearby."

Simon considered. "We have a Chinese bar at the grocery store now."

Hong-Wei rubbed his lips to hide a smile. "I know. They laugh about it. It's not part of their restaurant network, and it's apparently not very good."

Simon had to agree, it was pretty bad. He still reeled from the idea that the workers here had been so cut off from the Copper Point community all this time. Had they wanted it that way? Or had Copper Point been that unwelcoming?

He thought a lot about the restaurant on Sunday when he got asked to cover a shift on the main floor for a nurse who called in sick. He thought about Hong-Wei in general, the way his voice sounded when he told stories, when he laughed. Much as Simon longed to see him again, he was glad Hong-Wei wasn't at the hospital when Jared dragged him over to the cafeteria for a farewell performance for one of his peds patients. That was laughter Simon didn't need to hear.

Still, Simon kept thinking about Hong-Wei as the day wore on, remembering the casual way Owen and Jared kept tossing him together with Hong-Wei during dinner, and how Hong-Wei didn't seem to mind.

Did Simon mind, though? He wasn't sure. He couldn't shake the vague sense of panic he had over the surgeon's potential attention. Jared was right, his nerves weren't entirely about the policy. Simon didn't exactly want to be the next doctor's secret liaison exposed, no, but his unease was more complicated than that.

What was he scared of? Why did Hong-Wei inspire this reaction in him?

At this point, he wasn't sure if he was eager to see Hong-Wei on Monday or not, lest his feelings—or fears—get more complicated, but it turned out his relationship with the new surgeon was the least of his workplace worries that day. The real fireworks ended up being between Hong-Wei and Dr. Orth.

Before Dr. Stevens had retired, Simon regularly came in for work Monday through Friday at five thirty in the morning, prepared the operating room, and then assisted throughout the day until it was time to go home. Now his schedule was erratic, depending upon when and if surgeries were scheduled at all. St. Ann's had lost quite a bit of business since Dr. Stevens's retirement, though they'd seen fewer and fewer scheduled surgeries for some time before that. Initially, Dr. Stevens had helped fill in some of their gaps, but then he had moved to Florida.

This particular Monday, Simon came to work at six in the morning, and after he prepped the OR, he helped on the main floor since no surgery was scheduled until eleven. To his surprise, he had barely finished his first hourly rounding when Hong-Wei approached him, wearing scrubs and his lab coat.

"Dr. Wu." Simon threw his gloves into the biohazard bin, using the moment to will his heartbeat to calm down. It would never do to get a thrill simply from making eye contact with the man. "Good morning. How can I help you?"

Hong-Wei passed over a clipboard. "Andreas gave me free rein to commandeer you in order to go over how I want to run things. It's important to me you and I work well as a surgical team."

"What happens with the surgeries scheduled today? Who will assist for those?"

"Andreas met with the charge nurse, who arranged for your backup nurse to take your place for the week."

The backup nurse was Rita Taylor, who Orth openly despised, more than he did Simon. Simon worked to keep his face blank. "Have you informed Dr. Orth of these changes?"

Hong-Wei seemed annoyed. "Not yet. He's late arriving, so much so that he's put the surgical schedule in jeopardy. I've informed the administration we'll take on his surgery if he doesn't appear by ten. It's a standard gall bladder via scope, so I don't anticipate trouble taking it on."

No way would Orth make it by ten. He was routinely late on Mondays, to the point the scheduling staff often told patients later arrival times to compensate. Orth would likely be furious at being end-run.

Though Simon wondered if he should mention this to Hong-Wei, he didn't have much of a chance as Hong-Wei whisked Simon away to his office—Dr. Stevens's old office. It was clean and organized, emptied of the trash the visiting surgeons had littered the place with. Now it was tidy, and the shelves were dusted and lined with a few books and binders Stevens had left behind, and some new ones Simon didn't recognize.

"Some of my things arrived late Friday. I had them shipped directly to the hospital," Hong-Wei explained. "More are on their way." He withdrew a binder from the shelf and passed it to Simon. "You can go through a lot of my overall procedures and preferences on your own, but I'd like to go with you personally as we set up this first time, because I'm quite exact about how I want my instruments arranged, and my trays, and I have strong opinions about the lighting of the room. Also, you should know I find I'm most productive if music is playing while I work, especially during longer or difficult surgeries. I ask a tech to change the songs if it comes to that, but I'll want you to get the music ready. Is this something you feel you can do?"

Music. During surgery. It wasn't something Simon had ever had a doctor request, and certainly never with this kind of exactness. "I'll do my best to make things right for you, and if I fail, I'll work hard to make sure things go smoother the next time."

"Excellent. I want to start implementing as many of them as possible right away."

Simon held up his hands, every warning bell going off inside him at once. "Wait—you want to do this *now*, while the other surgeons are still working?"

The cool mask Hong-Wei had worn when they'd first met at the airport slid into place. "Yes. I can't imagine it's a secret to my subordinate surgeons that I've arrived. They must be expecting some changes. Nevertheless, how they react to my policies isn't something you need to concern yourself with. I'll speak to them in due time, and of course when they're in surgery, they'll be able to direct matters to a certain degree, but this is my department now, and they answer to me."

If Hong-Wei spoke to Orth this way, the odds were good Orth wouldn't come back to St. Ann's at all. *Does Andreas know about this? Beckert?* Owen would tell Simon this was above his pay grade, and Owen was right. Still, it wouldn't hurt to be around to assist in case things got hairy.

The fantasy of rescuing Hong-Wei from anything quickly fell away as Simon scrambled to keep up with his new surgeon. The hospital did have two operating rooms, one dedicated for OB, one for general surgery and any specialty clinic surgeries, which were set up in the afternoons on Wednesdays and Fridays. Hong-Wei didn't like the idea that he had to share his surgery area with visiting surgeons, so Simon's first task was figuring out how to keep things for visiting surgeons as separate as possible, and to create a manual for all fill-in nurses so they knew how to put the room back.

Simon didn't mind slipping into a follower role. It was a relief, frankly, after having to deal with Dr. Stevens's absentmindedness and inconsistency for so long, to serve under a surgeon who knew exactly what he wanted and what Simon was supposed to do. Before he knew it, he stopped worrying about what the other surgeons would think and what trouble might be coming, and he did as he was told.

This changed when ten o'clock arrived and Dr. Orth hadn't. Simon broke out of his bubble of calm and tensed, bracing for trouble, but Hong-Wei only calmly ended his orientation and led Simon to the room where the scheduled surgery patient waited.

"You will follow my lead." Hong-Wei opened the door and entered the room, smiling and extending his hand.

His bedside manner was incredible, especially for a surgeon. Granted, Simon hadn't encountered a terribly large number—most of them had been at UW-Madison while Jared and Owen finished medical school and their residencies. He'd worked with enough to know they didn't always have the warmest personalities. Their job was to cut you open and remove or fix the problem, not chat you up. Hong-Wei doled out the charm, distracting the woman from her fears about postoperative pain, promising her the discomfort she'd been feeling because of her gallbladder would be gone and she'd be home with her baby that night. He explained the drugs she'd be given pre- and postoperation, confirmed what Kathryn had already told her about when it would be safe to nurse her baby, and in general was incredibly patient, as if he had all the time in the world for her. When she seemed relaxed, he left her in Simon's care to get ready for surgery.

"Get her started, then have a tech take over so you can double-check the OR for us, please," he said as they stepped out in the hall together.

"Yes, Dr. Wu."

With Hong-Wei in charge, Simon forgot about the impending confrontation and took care of his patient. Even when Hong-Wei left and Simon was in the OR alone doing a last-minute check, Simon was more concerned with making sure he met Hong-Wei's expectations than he was with whether or not Orth would appear and be upset. When Hong-Wei was in charge, things felt easy and right.

This was only day one of working with him too. Simon felt like he'd won the nursing lottery.

On his way back from the OR, he heard Orth's angry shouts in the hallway outside of the patient's room.

Orth stood arguing with the patient tech and Rita, who'd been called down in the confusion and showed up to assist with surgery. "What's the meaning of this? This is my patient—why is she prepped for surgery when I'm nowhere near ready for her?"

The tech pressed her hands tight against her stomach. "I'm sorry, Dr. Orth, but Dr. Wu said—"

Orth sneered and cut the tech off. "*Dr. Wu.* He isn't supposed to start yet, and he's in here disrupting my OR? I'll be giving this new guy a piece of my mind. Where is he?"

Before Simon had a chance to move, Orth spotted him and marched over, glaring at him over the tip of his pointed nose. "*You.* You're supposed to be the surgical nurse today, but *this one*"—he pointed to Rita—"tells me she's been assigned to me instead. Yet here you are. What's going on?"

Simon braced himself for impact. "I'm assisting Dr. Wu today."

Orth's skinny nostrils flared as he aimed a bony finger at the center of Simon's chest. "Listen here. I don't care what this wise guy told you. I'm still the surgeon this week, and I'm running this place the way I see fit. This is my patient, my OR, and you're *my* nurse. Understand?"

What was Simon supposed to say to Orth? *I'm only following Dr. Wu's instructions* would fuel the fire, and abandoning Hong-Wei's directive would be insulting to the man he *did* want to obey.

"Is there a problem?"

Simon couldn't help letting out a small breath of relief. *Hong-Wei.* He felt the surgeon's body heat as he walked up behind him, standing so close he almost touched Simon's body.

Orth curled his lip, running his gaze up and down Hong-Wei. "So you're the hotshot from Baylor who thinks he can come in here and do whatever he wants in my OR? You've got a lot of nerve."

Hong-Wei tucked his hands behind his back with an icy smile. "You must be Dr. Orth. Hello. Allow me to introduce myself. I'm Jack Wu, the new head of surgery at St. Ann's. I've had your schedule rearranged so the two of us can meet later today, but for now you can review some policy changes I have waiting for you in the small conference room upstairs. Since you were delayed, I'm taking over the scheduled surgery this morning. I didn't want the patient to be inconvenienced."

Orth turned red and began to sputter. "Listen here, you can't—"

Hong-Wei glanced at the wall clock and frowned as he put a hand on Simon's shoulder. "We're about to run late. Please make sure the patient is still on schedule and move us to the OR."

Nodding, Simon stepped forward, ready to get the hell out of the confrontation, but Orth immediately blocked him. Simon stiffened as Orth gripped his wrist.

Orth brandished Simon's arm like a prize. "This is *my* patient and *my* nurse."

Simon held his breath.

Hong-Wei's gaze narrowed, but otherwise he didn't react. The more Orth ramped up, the calmer Hong-Wei became. "It's not a problem if you don't wish to work under the new rules. I can adjust my schedule to absorb your surgeries and begin this week."

"You *son of a bitch*. You think you can waltz in here and run this place? Do you have any idea what a cesspit you've signed on for? Now you want to cut off support of the only surgical relief you have? I have to haul ass all the way from Eau Claire to get here. You can't get surgeons from Ironwood or Duluth because they're out of state. We're it. And if I tell them what an ass the new surgeon is, you're cut off."

Orth's grip was now so tight Simon couldn't help but wince.

Hong-Wei's stare was flinty, but he spoke quietly. "Please release my nurse so he can do his job."

Orth jerked Simon closer to him, and Simon lost his ability to keep up a mask and shot Hong-Wei a desperate plea over his shoulder.

Hong-Wei grabbed Orth's arm, touched something at his elbow, and the next thing Simon knew Orth was backing away, clutching his biceps and glaring.

Simon was, briefly, flush against Hong-Wei's body, half in an accidental embrace as he stumbled backward into him. For a moment he lingered there, stunned. Blushing, he drew away.

More footsteps sounded behind them—Andreas and Beckert had arrived. Andreas surveyed the scene, regarding Orth coolly. "Dr. Orth. I believe I had Sally call to tell you that since you were running late, we'd rearranged the surgery schedule and you weren't needed here today."

Mr. Beckert tugged on the cuffs of his shirt and nodded gruffly at Hong-Wei. "Dr. Wu. My apologies this has kept you from your patient. Please, you and

Simon go ahead and continue with the surgery, and we'll settle things with Dr. Orth."

Hong-Wei shielded Simon's body and led him past the sputtering Orth and around the corner, away from the scene. Instead of taking Simon to the patient's room, he led him into a supply room near the OR. As soon as they were inside the small space, he gently pressed Simon to the wall and locked the door.

"Are you all right?"

Breathless, dizzy, Simon glanced up at Hong-Wei. Oh, he was so close. So handsome. Simon could still feel the ghost of the heat of Hong-Wei's chest against his back, that temporary feeling of being cradled. Now Hong-Wei stood in front of him, one arm braced against the brick as he leaned in close, his face full of concern.

Simon ached for him. He knew he shouldn't, knew he *couldn't*, but in that narrow space, with the object of his affection a literal breath away, there was no way to stop himself.

Especially when Hong-Wei lifted his hand to stroke Simon's face. Nothing more than a brief, lingering brush, but Simon shuddered all the same, his lips parting on a gasp as he stared, caught in Hong-Wei's gaze.

"I'm sorry I got you involved." Hong-Wei rested his hand on Simon's elbow. "Are you hurt?"

Unable to make a sound, Simon shook his head. He couldn't move, couldn't look away.

Simon chided himself for letting his fantasies run amok. Hong-Wei was simply checking on him after an intense encounter. Any second now he'd smile, release Simon, and they'd go to the OR for surgery.

Except Hong-Wei didn't smile, and he didn't let him go. If anything, he moved closer. His smell engulfed Simon: spice, crisp linen, and Hong-Wei. Simon's hands itched to fall to Hong-Wei's hips, and he had to ball his fists, resting them on his thighs so he didn't reach out. Hong-Wei leaned closer, his lab coat draping around them as his arm bent against the wall. His gaze never left Simon's.

Wu is into you.

Simon couldn't exactly argue with Jared's assessment any longer. The question was, what did he want to do about it?

Never mind, that wasn't a question. Simon *wanted* him like he'd wanted nothing in his life. But he didn't know if he *should* have him. Not the doctor he worked with. Not with Andreas's policy hanging over his head.

What he *should* do was an easy answer. Funny how knowing that didn't motivate him to move at all.

Hong-Wei touched Simon's cheek again, stroking with more purpose this time, his thumb scraping Simon's chin, lingering on his neck. "Should I stop?"

Such a terrible thing to do, to make him choose. And yet how like Hong-Wei. *Should* and *want* became tangled in Simon's heart, a snarl turning over and over. *Should* they stop? Yes, probably. Did Simon want to? No. He wanted this so much. He wanted this strange, wonderful moment where, after charging in like a surgical white knight, the new doctor whisked Simon away into a closet and kissed him.

The want swelled until it lifted Simon's hands, settling them on Hong-Wei's shoulders. "I don't… we shouldn't, but… I want…."

Hong-Wei's knees brushed against Simon's, his hand that wasn't cradling Simon's face drawing Simon's body closer. "I want *you*, Simon."

Simon clung tight to Hong-Wei, compensating for his legs, which had abruptly turned to jelly. "I don't want to lose my job. I don't want to make things awkward in the OR." He shifted his hands so they skimmed the lapels of Hong-Wei's coat. "But I want this." His pulse pounded in his ears as he said the words, and he scarcely recognized himself. He tamped down the fear that threatened to rise and make him doubt himself, and pressed forward. "I don't know if it's a good idea. Probably it's not. But right now, just this once, I want to do what I'm not supposed to do."

The look on Hong-Wei's face wasn't quite surprise. It was as if something in the last part of Simon's confession had caught the edge of his heart. Hong-Wei cupped Simon's face gently with his hands.

"I'll protect you, always. As a doctor, as a friend, as…."

As a lover hung unspoken in the air between them.

Simon shut his eyes, waiting.

The kiss was soft at first, a tease at his bottom lip, until Simon opened and let him in. Then it quickened, tongues tangling deeper as hands drew bodies closer. When Simon gasped as fingers curled into the sensitive hairline at the back of his neck, his cry was swallowed, absorbed into the kiss. Simon mapped the hard sides of Hong-Wei's body as Hong-Wei ran a hand beneath the hem of his scrubs, seeking skin.

Hong-Wei broke the kiss enough to speak against Simon's mouth. "We need to get to the OR."

Simon nodded in agreement, gasping as Hong-Wei's hand dipped inside his waistband to tease the flesh of his hip.

Panting as he sought his breath, Hong-Wei pressed his forehead to Simon's. Simon shut his eyes, willing the moment to last a little longer. Every part of him felt alive. He wanted more. He *needed* more.

Why in the world had he said *just this once*?

Hong-Wei drew back, nuzzling Simon's nose. With a sigh, he shifted from amorous to professional mode, smoothing first Simon's and then his own clothes. "Our patient is waiting."

Simon was so dizzy he didn't think he could stand. "Hong-Wei." His voice came out a whispered plea. Except he had no idea how he should beg for what he wanted.

Hong-Wei adjusted Simon's badge. "I'll go ahead to the OR and tell them you'll be along shortly. Take your time."

Unlocking the door, he slipped out of the room.

For several seconds, Simon stared at the place where Hong-Wei had disappeared. Then he slid to the floor.

HONG-WEI HADN'T meant to kiss Simon yet.

He'd had a plan for how to woo Simon. It involved long, drawn-out courting, some slow-build flirting, and then, when the timing was right, he'd invite Simon into a discreet relationship that wouldn't upset the hospital policy. Instead, here he was, making out with Simon in a closet when he should have been scrubbing in for surgery.

Had he completely lost his mind?

Apparently.

He wanted to blame it on Orth, but he had to take a great deal of the responsibility on himself. He'd lost control when he'd seen Orth holding on to Simon's arm, and he'd handled the situation poorly. It could have gone south in so many ways. If Orth had fought back, one or both of them could have injured their hands.

The kiss, though. Hong-Wei had imagined kissing Simon a few times, but nothing had prepared him for the reality. It had been like stealing a fingerful of a luscious dessert. Now it was all he could think about, knowing there was so much more to savor.

If only he hadn't done the sampling in the supply closet.

If only Simon hadn't said *just this once*.

He shoved thoughts of kissing Simon aside and focused on the surgery instead, going over the notes one last time before entering the OR. The patient was already there, sedated, and Gagnon checked her as Hong-Wei scrubbed in.

Simon was present also.

He inspected instruments and told the techs where they should be, reminding them of the new procedures. Gagnon watched all this with mild interest, heedless of the fact that his presence seemed to unnerve every nurse and tech in the room but Simon.

Simon was only unnerved by Hong-Wei.

Gagnon waved at Hong-Wei. "Everything's fine on my end. Though I heard you had some excitement getting in here. Sorry, Orth's an ass. Glad you socked it to him."

Hong-Wei felt as if he were both watching Simon and avoiding him at once. "My priority is the patient."

The circulating tech inclined her head at Hong-Wei after an awkward glance at Gagnon. "I have the room ready per your requests, Dr. Wu. Let me know when you'd like the music to start."

Hong-Wei nodded at her as Gagnon raised his eyebrows. "Music?"

"Yes, I find it helps me clear my mind as I operate." Hong-Wei surveyed the patient, the instrument tables, the staff, everything but Simon's face. "Are we in order for surgery, first assistant?"

"Yes, Dr. Wu," Simon answered.

Did he sound subdued? Uneasy? Oh, Hong-Wei wished he'd stuck to his plan. Except he honestly couldn't bring himself to regret the kiss.

Gagnon chuckled. "First assistant? You keep a formal room. I'd better get in line."

Thank God for Owen Gagnon. "Something tells me there's no power on earth that could keep you in line." Hong-Wei rode the moment of levity and rolled his shoulders. "All right. Let's begin."

The surgery went smoothly, far better than Hong-Wei could have hoped for his first time with a new team in a new place, considering the rough start they'd had thanks to Orth. He and Simon made a good team, even with the elephant of the kiss between them. Simon had clearly taken his instructions about the OR to heart and set everything up better than Hong-Wei had dreamed.

Of course, there was the small problem of *afterward*.

He wanted to talk to Simon about the kiss, but he didn't know how, and he wasn't sure he should. Simon was always a bit demure, but he seemed especially so that afternoon. Hong-Wei debated asking Simon to go to lunch with him, and normally he would have, but Simon looked nervous, and Hong-Wei worried he might make him uncomfortable.

In the end he wasn't free for lunch anyway. Andreas and Beckert commandeered him and apologized for Orth, then smoothly delivered the bomb he'd been expecting: because Hong-Wei had insisted on taking over the surgery, Orth wouldn't be back, and now they had no other coverage.

Hong-Wei shrugged as he cut into his food. "We don't have many surgeries this week, and they're all fairly routine. I'll have Simon call the patients and let them know I'll be their surgeon. Do you anticipate any difficulties?"

Beckert exchanged an enigmatic glance with Andreas, who shook his head as he dabbed his mouth daintily with a napkin before replying to Hong-Wei. "I don't foresee any particular problems, but sometimes people in Copper Point can be fussy about change. I'll have letters sent out before the end of the day to everyone scheduled for surgery in the next few weeks, letting them know how excited St. Ann's is to have you on board and how confident we are in your abilities. As for the patients themselves, I'm sure you've dealt with nervous grandmothers and grumpy old men before."

"I possess a nervous grandmother and grumpy grandfather, so yes, I'm familiar with the drill. I'm sure there will be a few bumps as we transition, but I've been winning people over my whole life. I don't anticipate I've lost my touch now."

"Excellent. This is what I expected you'd say." Andreas leaned back in his chair. "So, that's settled—now it's only a matter of adapting you to our quirky St. Ann's schedule. I'm hoping with a surgeon on staff again we'll get a regular schedule for you, but at the moment, as you've seen, the surgery load is light to say the least."

Hong-Wei waved a hand. "This isn't a problem. It will make the transition easier."

Andreas raised an eyebrow. "Would you be open to taking some rotations in the ER in the meantime? I'll try to keep your turns to day shifts as much as possible, but we may ask you to fill in evenings and weekends and occasionally overnights. I'll give you plenty of advance notice for those except in emergencies. I only ask because we usually had the fill-ins take some of these positions as well. Excepting the weekends, of course."

Hong-Wei indulged a glance at Beckert, but the man didn't seem to mind his human resources director was completely running this meeting. Interesting. "I have no objections to any of this. I don't mind work, and I'm not proud. I've moonlighted almost anywhere I can. I also understand I'm essentially on permanent call until you can restore backup coverage. I hope you're looking to have weekend surgeons at some point? For the record, I want to be called in if there's a weekend surgical emergency. I don't want my patients sent on a three-hour ambulance ride for something I can come in to do."

Beckert finally woke up at this. "Yes, we're working on that, but it's going to take some time. Thank you for being willing to step up in the meantime."

"The other detail worth bringing up to you from a staffing standpoint," Andreas continued, "is that especially given the erratic surgery schedule, your nursing team is currently a bit in flux. Technically Simon Lane is our dedicated surgical nurse, with Rita Taylor as our backup first assistant during surgery, and we're looking for another so we have more than two trained nurses on staff because of vacations, maternity leaves, and so on. Our usual protocol would be to have Mr. Lane's schedule mirror yours as much as possible, using him as a float nurse when you're filling in elsewhere or having him fill in the same shifts in the ER, though that doesn't always work with the nursing schedule. I assume this would be amenable to you?"

Of course Hong-Wei wouldn't mind spending as much time with Simon as possible, thereby giving him even more opportunity to flirt. If only this no-dating policy weren't in the way. "It seems the smoothest arrangement, and I have no argument with it. Simon Lane is a highly capable nurse, and I enjoy working with him."

"Excellent. Granted, as you add surgeries, this problem will sort itself out, and Mr. Lane will largely be working as your first assistant and consulting with your patients pre- and postoperation. Sadly, I think it will take you half a year minimum to get there. Our patients have become accustomed to driving to Duluth or Ironwood or even Eau Claire for their care, and despite the hassle, some of them will continue to do so because, as I mentioned, Copper Point resists change."

Everyone everywhere resists change, Erin Andreas. Hong-Wei suppressed a sigh. "As I said, I'm not afraid of work."

Beckert leaned forward, bright with his eagerness. "We're here to help you, Jack, so say the word if you need anything to make your work easier. We're glad you chose St. Ann's."

Andreas gave Beckert a more overt glare that practically screamed *down, boy*, and Hong-Wei took a drink to hide his smile.

He left lunch feeling more positive not only about his direction at St. Ann's but his prospects with Simon. He decided he'd let things simmer between them and do exactly what he'd promised: focus on building trust. How better than to work beside Simon, deepening their personal and working relationships? A few shifts where things returned to normal would make it easy to ask the man to dinner—a harmless, professional dinner. He'd woo Simon over the same way he'd woo the rest of Copper Point: with determination and constant attention.

It was a good plan, and he was ready to put all his energy into it. However, on his way back to the clinic after rounds, he discovered Dr. Gagnon and Dr. Kumpel lingering outside his office.

"There you are. We've been looking for you, *Jack*."

Gagnon turned to Hong-Wei with a terrible smile, and too late, Hong-Wei understood why the nursing staff feared him so much.

CHAPTER FIVE

AFTER USHERING them into the office and closing the door, Gagnon threaded his fingers over his abdomen and fixed Hong-Wei with his gimlet stare as Hong-Wei took refuge behind his desk. "I couldn't help noticing some interesting friction between you and Simon during this morning's surgery. After Jared went to our housemate for some recon, he came back with some *very* interesting reports."

Jared's smile was less jagged, but by no means nonthreatening. "Si seems to think you might not be out, and we're not here to cast stones on that subject. However, he *is* nervous about getting caught up in Andreas's stupid new dating policy, and there is the not insignificant matter of you being, essentially, his boss."

Owen leaned closer. "As the two guys who've protected him since middle school, we're taking it upon ourselves to give you a Simon Lane orientation whether you're interested or not. Also, if you plan on hurting him, remember I'm not a surgeon, and I don't give a shit how much I damage my hands when I punch a guy out."

Hong-Wei studied the pair of them for a moment, completely at a loss as to how to respond. "I take it Simon has no idea you're here?"

Kumpel laughed. "Oh, he'd kill us. We don't advise telling him about this visit, though."

Gagnon added teeth to his smile.

Hong-Wei held up his hands. "I was mostly trying to make sure I understood the situation. Does he—?" He cut himself off and changed direction. "Do you do this because Simon is so… openhearted?"

Gagnon snorted. "Such a diplomatic way to put it. Yes. We do it because Simon has a history of getting stepped on, in and out of love. He's an easy man to crush, and it happens whether or not we're around, so we try to be around when we can."

The corner of Kumpel's mouth lifted. "We vowed whoever attempted to win his heart had to be worthy."

Good Lord. "I assume no one has ever passed your test?"

Kumpel waved a dismissive hand. "Oh, don't be silly. Several guys have been fine, but… well. Simon is gun-shy. We don't know what he's afraid of, but we know we're here to make sure whatever it is doesn't hurt him."

Gun-shy? Hong-Wei thought back to the supply closet, his pulse quickening. *Gun-shy* wasn't a word he'd use.

Gagnon checked his watch and frowned. "I have a lot more I want to interrogate you about, but I have to check in with OB. You better not have dinner plans, because you're on my menu."

The terrifying thing was Hong-Wei couldn't decide how much of the statement was metaphorical. "What is it you want to know?"

"Everything." Kumpel crossed his arms over his chest. "How serious are you? Are you taking Simon's concerns about this no-dating policy to heart, or are you assuming they don't apply to you? Do you have any comprehension of what it's going to mean for the two of you to attempt to see each other, in public or in secret, in a town like Copper Point?"

"Also, what the hell is with the way you tense up every time we've teased you about being hot for Simon?" Gagnon narrowed his eyes at Hong-Wei. "Si thinks it's because you're not out, but I don't buy it. I think it's you being an arrogant control freak, and let me tell you, buddy, that role is *taken*."

Hong-Wei had a sudden, sharp longing for Hong-Su to be there. He wanted to go home tonight, drop his bag, and tell her everything about this odd duo and their insane demands, about Gagnon and his terrifying smiles and the pissing contest over which one of them got to be the asshole. He even wanted to tell her about Simon.

Which was all both wonderful and stunning, because the complaint everyone made about Hong-Wei, especially Hong-Su, was he never told anyone anything.

He cleared his throat, brushing his hand over his lips to remove his smile before he replied. "I'm interested in dating Simon, and I want to be careful both for the sake of the dating rule and because I'm new to

St. Ann's and Copper Point. I don't want to make him uncomfortable, and I don't want to draw inappropriate attention to us. I've already regretted my hasty action today. I'd planned to move more deliberately."

Gagnon's gaze sharpened. "*What* hasty action would that be?"

Ah, so Simon hadn't told them. "I don't believe that's your business." Hong-Wei sat back in his chair. "As for my being out, it's mostly that I haven't ever advertised. Largely I've been married to my career and haven't had time for relationships. However, one of the perks of moving to a quieter setting was having more time for such things." Hong-Wei lifted an eyebrow at Gagnon. "I don't concede the title of arrogant control freak to anyone. It can't be claimed, only earned. It absolutely can be stolen, however."

Gagnon's grin became positively evil, but with a lilt at the edges it hadn't had before. "*You* are coming to dinner, Wu."

Hong-Wei opened a folder on his desk and pretended to read through it absently. "Fine, but I'm cooking."

AFTER THE way Owen had eyeballed Simon postsurgery and the questions Jared had asked in the locker room, Simon had anticipated some kind of confrontation when he got home, and he'd rehearsed how he'd dismiss his housemates all afternoon. His speeches had gone out the window, however, when he'd come in the back door and found Owen and Jared hovering, arms folded, as they watched Hong-Wei chopping vegetables on the island.

"What—?" Simon couldn't get anything else out and remained frozen in the doorway.

Brightening, Jared waved him over. "Si, welcome home. We're watching Jack hack peppers into bits. Come join us."

Hong-Wei nodded a greeting at Simon, gave a small, slight smile, then continued dicing his vegetables. Simon saw no evidence of hacking, and in fact, he'd never seen peppers cut finer.

Owen had his gaze fixed on Hong-Wei's knife. "Dinner's going to be late. Not only did I have to haul this guy to the store and watch him fuss over every vegetable in stock, but he insulted our knives and sharpened the three he planned to use before he'd even start preparing anything. He complained about our sharpener too. Made me order a new one online."

Hong-Wei didn't look up. "I'm not working with dull knives, and any chef worth their salt has a whetstone, not an electric sharpener."

Simon didn't care about dinner. He wanted to know why Hong-Wei was here at all. "I can wait to eat. Does anything else need to be done? I can—"

"*No*," Jared and Owen said in unison, glaring at Hong-Wei as if they expected a challenge.

Simon gave up. "Am I supposed to stay in here and watch you stare down Hong-Wei, or can I go get changed?"

Too late he realized how he'd addressed their guest. Naturally it was Owen who picked up on his slip first. "Hong-what? What did you call him?"

"My name." Hong-Wei still didn't look away from his work. "My birth name is Hong-Wei Wu. Wu Hong-Wei if you use Taiwanese order, not Western. I've gone by Jack since I moved to the States to everyone but my family."

Simon kept his gaze on the floor as Jared spoke. "And yet Simon uses it. Interesting."

Hong-Wei said nothing, simply continued to slice. Simon became incredibly interested in the peeling Formica against the cabinet near Hong-Wei's feet.

"So do *we* get to call you Hong-Wei?" Owen asked.

"*You* call me Jack."

Clearing his throat, Simon started for the stairs. "I'm going to get changed and maybe lie down. Call me when dinner's ready."

Unfortunately Simon discovered being trapped alone in his room was a torture worse than watching the three of them bicker. Sleeping was out of the question, and lying on his bed meant he had nothing else to do but imagine what Owen and Jared were telling Hong-Wei about him. In the end he went downstairs well before anyone called him, and he arrived just in time. Owen was on the computer pulling up Simon's Spotify playlists.

"*What* are you doing?" When Owen moved the mouse toward the Play button, Simon yelped and slammed the laptop shut, nearly hitting Owen's fingertips.

"*Hey*," Owen complained, but Simon ignored him, aiming an angry finger at his face.

"I didn't give you permission for that."

Owen blinked innocently. "But I thought you'd like it if we played some of your music—"

I will kill you, Simon telegraphed. "I would *not* like it if you played some of my music."

The damage, of course, had been done. In the kitchen, Hong-Wei looked up from a fragrant skillet. "Why not? I'm curious to hear what you listen to."

Simon lifted a threatening fist briefly at Owen, then forced a smile. "A lot of things," he replied to Hong-Wei.

"Excellent. Put one of those things on."

Shoving Owen out of the desk chair, Simon opened the laptop and hastily cobbled together a sanitized playlist. While focusing on Owen, however, he'd forgotten about Jared.

"You've heard about our performances, haven't you?" Jared sat on one of the barstools at the island as he watched Hong-Wei at the stove. "When I have a peds patient in the hospital and they're scheduled for release, or sometimes simply if things are getting grim and they need a pick-me-up, on request Simon, Owen, and I do lip-synched dance numbers."

"Yes, I've heard of that."

"It's because of Simon's music, actually, and because he was always running around the house dancing to—"

"*Jared, I'm going to murder you in your sleep.*"

Jared pressed a hand to his chest. "What? What did I do?"

Simon started the playlist and stalked toward Owen and Jared in the kitchen. "You can both stop. Immediately."

Hong-Wei's shoulders shook, and when he spoke, his voice had a hint of laughter. "You guys are making me miss my sister."

"You do lip-synch dance numbers with her too?"

"*Owen!*"

Laughing out loud, Hong-Wei set down the spatula and wiped his eyes.

Simon was now close enough to the stove to get full appreciation for the pasta dish Hong-Wei was making, and when he opened the oven and saw fresh bread, Simon couldn't focus on anything else but the impending food. When they finally were ready to eat, the taste was as good as the anticipation, and he forgot his nervousness over being kissed and his fury over Owen and Jared's meddling and simply settled in to enjoy.

"This is amazing." Simon sopped up sauce with his bread, took a decadent bite, and melted. "Hong-Wei, you're an incredible cook."

"Yes, *Jack*, I have to admit, you're not bad." Owen speared a tube of pasta with a look of regret. "I'll study up and best you next time, dull knives and all."

"Here I am feeling like an idiot assuming you'd cook something Asian," Jared said. When Simon glared at him, he held up a hand. "Hey, he's the one who brought the fancy Taiwanese dish to the hospital. It was a fair leap."

"I'm afraid I don't excel at Taiwanese cooking." Hong-Wei sipped at the water he'd poured for himself, refusing alcohol because he'd pointed out he was now on call. "I can make it, but I'm nothing compared to my sister, so I always end up frustrated."

That was disappointing, because Simon wouldn't mind trying some more dishes like the one he'd had. "I take it your sister is a good cook?"

"My sister is a *phenomenal* cook." Hong-Wei sliced angrily into his chicken as he said this. Owen chuckled into his wine.

Simon sighed. *Why* were they all so competitive?

The end of the meal didn't bring a cease-fire, either. When it came time to decide who was doing dishes, Jared told Owen it was his turn, Owen made a wry remark baiting Hong-Wei about who did dishes better, and before it could start up again, Simon rose, swiped everyone's plates in a stack, and headed out of the room.

"*I'm* doing the dishes," he called over his shoulder.

He wasn't surprised when someone came into the kitchen with the glasses and took up a dishtowel to dry, but he didn't expect that person to be Hong-Wei. Simon faltered, realizing this was their first time alone since Hong-Wei had kissed him.

"Sorry," Hong-Wei said at last.

Simon dropped the dish he was loading into the dishwasher, then fumbled, red-faced, with shaking hands, to right it. *What are you apologizing for, exactly?*

"I'm sorry for the way we were all behaving when you got home, and through dinner, and now." When Simon still struggled with the dish, Hong-Wei came around the other side of the dishwasher and reached down to fit the plate in the slats, and when their gazes met, his smile made a different kind of heat diffuse through Simon. "I'm not apologizing for the kiss."

Simon stood and busied himself with filling the sink. *That can't happen again* is what he needed to say. It wasn't what he wanted to say, however, and he discovered at this particular moment he couldn't say anything at all.

Hong-Wei resumed drying as if he hadn't rendered Simon mute. "I hope I didn't put you out too much, the way today's events must have jumbled your schedule. I'm almost glad Orth is out of the picture, but I understand it's put a strain on the staff."

It was so much easier to talk about work. "Oh—no, it's fine. Honestly, we're used to chaos. No one's going to think anything of it. Besides, you're so much nicer than Dr. Orth. The surgical team all said so."

"Really? I thought they might find me strict."

"Yes, but you were efficient too, and you took care of us as well as the patient, and we appreciate it. We've had a lot of erosion on the staff, but by some miracle our surgical team has survived despite everything, and it's a good crew. We've been waiting for—" He almost said *someone decent* and stopped himself. "We're glad to have someone like you, let's leave it at that."

"The feeling is mutual. I've worked with internationally famous doctors and their nurses, and I didn't feel at all unsupported today."

Now Simon was glowing. He'd been the one who'd moved heaven and earth to keep the team together on the wish and hope that someday their dream surgeon would come. It felt good to know the dream surgeon felt the same way. "I wanted to tell you, I enjoyed the music during surgery. I've never had any doctor do that before, but it was quite pleasant. It kept me calm and made everything go so much faster."

"My first supervising physician had a thing about doing surgery to music. Most people gave him grief about it, but I discovered it helped me focus. When we got to the point we could take lead, he wouldn't let us use it for the longest time, saying he didn't want us to be unable to operate without it. Now that I work on my own, I play music during my surgeries whenever I have the option. It helps me cut through the noise. An operating room has so many beeps and blips—it's nice to have something with more tonal quality."

"Do you always use classical music?"

Hong-Wei hesitated with the towel poised over a plate. "Yes."

He seemed to have more to say, but he also clearly didn't want to say it. Since Simon had spent the evening not wanting to say things, he didn't push the man.

Simon braced for another battle over who would take Hong-Wei home—his car wasn't due to arrive for another few weeks—but Hong-Wei insisted he didn't need one. "It's barely a mile to my house. The walk will feel nice."

He waved to them as he left, winking at Simon.

Simon went to bed confused and agitated, feeling somehow the events of the day had gotten away from him. He'd wanted to confront Hong-Wei about the kiss and be firm in his resolve it couldn't happen again, but instead he'd had dinner with the man. Dinner with Owen and Jared as well, granted, but still, it wasn't what he'd intended. He supposed so long as things stayed professional, that was enough, but he decided he had to remain on guard all the same.

His guard turned out to be unnecessary, because over the next few days nothing else happened. The two of them continued to work together, navigating the fractured surgical schedule, smoothing over nervous patients who had somehow liked Dr. Orth and were suspicious of this outsider. The worst was when an old man swore at Hong-Wei and said, "No way in hell is some Chinaman working on me."

Hong-Wei didn't bat an eye. "None will, Mr. Wilson. I was born in Taiwan, but I've lived in the US most of my life and did all my education here. To be blunt, I'm better and more educated than any surgeon you'll see within your insurance plan. None of this matters, however. If you don't have this temporal artery biopsy today, I won't be able to put you back on your corticosteroids until you reschedule, which will need to be at another hospital. Or you can let me do my job, which will take barely any time at all, and then you'll be on your medication and taking treatment for anything we find today. The choice, of course, is entirely up to you. If you want, my nurse can check the surgical schedule at Eau Claire for you. I believe the wait time at this moment is six weeks, but perhaps you'll be lucky and it will be five."

Simon didn't have to make any phone calls. Mr. Wilson underwent his surgery, and when he was in postsurgical care and Hong-Wei didn't like the edema in his legs, after a check of the patient's heart, Hong-Wei ordered a med change and referred him to a cardiac specialist. The patient left the hospital singing Hong-Wei's praises and proudly telling his children, who came to pick him up, that he got the best doctor in the whole of Wisconsin to care for him.

Mrs. Mueller returned to the hospital as well, as predicted. She wasn't a surgical patient, but when Hong-Wei heard she was back, he did an exam, consulted her admitting physician, and explained that after reading her chart, he was convinced her surgery was not only possible but might alleviate several other symptoms she was having. Sadly they couldn't reverse her dementia, but her quality of life could be restored significantly. Within three days they had

Medicaid approval, and two days after the surgery, everyone who knew her—which was pretty much the town of Copper Point—said she hadn't been this close to her old self in years. Despite Hong-Wei's warning she likely wouldn't improve, Mrs. Mueller seemed to better remember some people, and she didn't look for her wretched ex-husband anymore.

Word of Hong-Wei's miracles spread through the town like wildfire, and the surgery schedule filled up quickly.

Naturally, Andreas and Beckert loved this development and tried to take Hong-Wei to lunch in thanks, but Hong-Wei declined, saying he needed to meet with Simon instead. "We have cases to go over, but thank you." He took Simon into the doctors' lounge, where every head turned at the sight of a nurse where he shouldn't be. Hong-Wei ignored them and pulled out a file.

"Sorry, I wanted our food to be here already, but I sent for it late. Unfortunately I'm the only one who can place the order. I told the front desk to call me when they arrived. Is it all right if we work until then?"

Simon could feel the rest of the room staring at them, but Hong-Wei didn't seem interested in engaging with them, so Simon did his best to ignore them as well. "Sure. What did you need to discuss?"

It turned out Hong-Wei had several patient files he wanted Simon to follow up on. Apparently he'd reviewed every patient Dr. Orth and the other fill-in surgeons had seen, and whenever he didn't care for their diagnosis and treatment plan, he'd gone over things a second time and triaged patients according to ones he simply wanted to monitor and ones he wanted to bring in.

"Obviously the hospital legal department has feelings on some of these cases, which is frustrating but understandable, so I began sorting them by severity and practicality."

Simon practically fluttered with excitement. Hong-Wei truly was the dream doctor he'd always wanted to work for. Part of him was disappointed he hadn't made any more romantic overtures since that day in the closet, but perhaps it was for the best. "I'll phone the patients right away."

"Oh." Hong-Wei pulled out his phone. "That's our lunch. Do you want to wait here or come with me to pick it up?"

No way in hell Simon was sitting here while everyone glared at him without Hong-Wei as a buffer. "I'll come along."

An older man who was unmistakably from China Garden stood by the main reception desk. The elderly volunteer whose job it was to shuttle people to appointments was speaking to him with a frustrated look on her face. As they approached she kept saying, "Sir, I've paged him for you," but the man continued inclining his head and repeating, "Doc-tor Wu, please, thank you," in incredibly hesitant English.

Then the man saw Hong-Wei, and everything about the scene changed.

Smile widening, the man turned to face Hong-Wei, laughing as he presented the paper bag of takeout, speaking rapidly in Mandarin. It sounded to Simon as if the man making the delivery was teasing, and he must have been, because Hong-Wei blinked, laughed as well, then replied in the same light tone as he accepted the bag with a gracious incline of his head.

They spoke like old friends for several minutes—the man clearly had deep affection for Hong-Wei. Simon enjoyed watching them talk to one another almost as much as he enjoyed watching the white people in the lobby with their jaws on the floor, gawking.

Then he realized he was one of the white people too, and blushed.

Abruptly, Hong-Wei stopped speaking and pointed to the older man's hand, where Simon saw a rather crude bandage wrapped around his palm and wrist. The older man waved the injured hand dismissively, but Hong-Wei grew serious, and Simon didn't need to know Mandarin to understand what he was saying. *Let me see that.* The older man shook his head, laughed, and wagged a finger at Hong-Wei. *Nope, not going to let you.*

Not looking happy, Hong-Wei handed the man several bills, and then the man left.

Hong-Wei still frowned as he approached Simon, clutching the bag.

"Something wrong?" Simon asked.

Hong-Wei grimaced. "Probably just my ego. He wouldn't let me see the cut on his hand. Told me it was no big deal, he'd put medicine on it. Also teased me again because I didn't know Chinese medicine."

"I've heard Chinese medicine is quite something, though I admit I don't have any real experience with it."

"Yes, well, Chinese hospitals utilize a combination of modern medicine of all disciplines. I'm afraid he's using nothing but *folk* medicine, which isn't the Eastern medicine he's so proud of so much as medieval hocus pocus. When I tried to look at his wound, though, he called me a nice young man and said he'd make me some more soup if I went to see him again."

Simon leaned in as surreptitiously as possible and got a whiff of the bag. "Is that what we're eating today?"

"Yes. Taiwanese chicken soup, with rice on the side." He opened the top and peered inside, his face lighting up. "Oh, that rascal. He added some Chinese pickled cucumbers. He's trying to spoil me."

"Who was it that made the delivery?"

"The owner of China Garden, Mr. Zhang. Though I think these are his wife's pickles. He was bragging about them the last time I stopped by." Hong-Wei cast Simon a guilty side glance. "I may have been making a few too many special orders to China Garden in the evenings. I miss my sister's cooking."

"I think you miss your sister."

Simon wasn't prepared for the flash of vulnerability on Hong-Wei's face. Gone was the cool surgeon, the playful flirt—Hong-Wei looked ten years younger, frightened, lost, and alone.

Simon wanted to wrap him in his arms and tell him everything was all right.

Then the look was gone, and Hong-Wei smiled a jaded smile that could rival Owen's. "Ah, come on. This soup's best when it's piping hot."

The soup was excellent, and even without Simon's foodgasms, the smells alone drove the rest of the room crazy with jealousy, everyone wanting to know where they'd found such great food. Hong-Wei explained what it was and how to order it at China Garden, warning them they needed to give Mr. Zhang plenty of notice and to be polite about those requests, since it was a special thing.

"Will it put him in a bind, so many people coming?" Simon asked when they were alone, on the way back to the clinic.

Hong-Wei laughed. "Are you kidding? He's going to be over the moon if it brings him extra customers. Also, if enough people start ordering Taiwanese food, he'll put it on the menu, and I won't have to coax him into making it. I think you and I need to start eating in the cafeteria together with special orders to drum up even more business."

It was still flirting, but it was light flirting, and… well, Simon didn't think he minded. He couldn't exactly complain when Hong-Wei wasn't doing anything more than buying him lunch.

That, and touching his elbow.

It was subtle, and it didn't happen often, but it occurred enough Simon had begun to anticipate it, almost hoping for it. If they were in the elevator together and Simon had his arms full of charts, Hong-Wei would cup Simon's elbow and reach around him to press the button, meaning for the briefest of seconds Hong-Wei's whole body brushed against him, his face and subtle scent passing right before Simon's face.

He was ashamed to admit he'd begun to make sure he went into elevators with his arms full in case Hong-Wei got on with him.

They did start eating in the cafeteria together, but they didn't always order takeout, and when they went through the line, Hong-Wei sometimes reached around Simon to grab a bowl of vanilla pudding with a dab of whipped cream, his self-confessed weakness.

He always seemed to need to pass by Simon to do it, and the elbow touch would happen then.

Simon began to feel fondly about vanilla pudding as well.

He received only a few rogue elbow touches, in the halls when a patient bed was coming by and Hong-Wei moved Simon out of the way, and another time when Simon was taking patient history and Hong-Wei had interrupted to let him know he intended to move into surgery faster based on some test results—there had been an elbow touch then, letting Simon know Hong-Wei wanted to see him in the hall.

He'd received nothing *more* than elbow touches, though. Hong-Wei hadn't so much as looked at Simon's mouth.

Which was good, yes? This was what he'd asked for. He'd specifically told Hong-Wei *just this once*. It needed to stay just the once too. There wasn't a problem here at all.

No problem except every time Hong-Wei walked into a room, Simon's heart skipped three beats.

Hong-Wei came over often for dinner or went out with them to eat, but it was never Simon and Hong-Wei alone. Sometimes they ate at the house, Hong-Wei, Owen, or Jared cooking, or sometimes they went out or brought takeout to the hospital. Simon couldn't remember when he'd last eaten so well. Every night was a cook-off—lasagna, steaks, burgers, soups, pasta dishes—until he was beginning to fear his scrubs would be tight.

One night when Owen declared it was time for a cooking rematch, him and Hong-Wei head-to-head, Hong-Wei pleaded for a stay and asked if they could go to China Garden instead. "I haven't been able to go in person, and Mr. Zhang hasn't been making deliveries."

When Owen and Jared frowned in confusion, Simon explained. "Mr. Zhang is the owner. Hong-Wei wants to check on an injury on his hand."

Jared shrugged. "I'm down for Chinese. Or are we going to have something from Wu's secret Taiwanese menu?"

Hong-Wei gave Jared a look that said, *Please, what do you take me for?*

China Garden was busy when they arrived, but as soon as the waitstaff saw Hong-Wei, they spoke animatedly to him in Mandarin, magicking a table out of thin air as Mr. Zhang himself came out to expansively greet them. He bowed and said, "Welcome, welcome," to Simon and the others, but he addressed Hong-Wei in their shared language, laughing, teasing, and from the looks of things, refusing to let Hong-Wei see his still-bandaged hand, assuring him he was fine.

"What's going on, do you know?" Jared asked as the three of them sat but Hong-Wei remained standing, arguing.

Simon explained about the cut, the possible folk remedies, and Hong-Wei's concerns.

Owen shook his head, hypnotized by their exchange. "Goddamn, but I want to know what they're saying."

Jared shrugged as he watched the argument like a tennis match. "I dunno. Seems clear to me. 'Let me do this.' 'No, thank you, I'm fine.' 'No, let me do this.' 'You're quite persistent, young man, but I don't think so. Why don't you sit and order with your friends? There's a good boy.'"

Simon had to press his lips together to keep his laughter in.

Owen didn't laugh, still mesmerized. "Obviously I was aware Jack knew another language, but it's something else to hear him rattle it off like this. How dumb are we, anyway, Americans, only knowing one language? I mean, I've already forgotten my two years of high school Spanish. This guy could probably practice medicine in Mandarin and English both. Dammit. I'm never catching up to him."

Jared raised an eyebrow at him. "Well, no. Not in the foreign language department, you're not. I hate to break it to you, but he'd beat you in surgery as well."

Owen was lost to his own world now. "And what is this with him having to pick a Western name? Why can't he just be Hong-Wei? Why does he have to be Jack? Why are we so precious we can't learn his given name?" He scowled at Hong-Wei's back. "And why is Simon the only one who gets to use it, dammit?"

"Owen, what in the world are you carrying on about?"

They all turned as Kathryn came over to their table, her wife Rebecca close behind her. Relieved for the distraction from Owen's diatribe, Simon smiled at them in welcome. "Hey, what are you guys doing here? I thought you had a full night in OB, Kathryn."

Rebecca looped her arm through her wife's elbow. "I stole her away on the promise I'd return her if anyone dilated past seven centimeters."

Kathryn patted Rebecca's shoulder as she raised an eyebrow at Owen. "Look at you, enjoying yourself as you leave me with a borrowed anesthetist all weekend long."

Owen showed no shred of guilt. "I'll relish every moment. I've spent, what, the last four weekends on call? And don't tell me how long it's been for you. It's your choice to play Saint Kathryn of All the Babies. Why don't you let the hotshot surgeon here handle some of your weekend cesareans?"

Kathryn sighed. "I will, eventually. *He* is the one working the craziest hours right now. I think the man is a machine."

"Nah, just recently off residency." Owen yawned, stretching. "He'll get over himself."

Rebecca glanced over her shoulder. "Honey, it's so busy in here tonight. I worry if our table will be ready in time. Should we go somewhere else?"

Simon rose. "Hold on." He crossed to where Hong-Wei stood locked in his polite battle with Zhang. "Excuse me," he said, bowing awkwardly, yet feeling as if it would be worse if he didn't do that much. Then he explained the situation with Kathryn to Hong-Wei as briefly as he could. "Do you think it would be possible to add two chairs to our table?"

Hong-Wei turned to Zhang and launched into Mandarin, gesturing at Kathryn, the table, and the direction of the hospital. Zhang stopped looking like the uncle who wasn't having any of this youngster's nonsense and more like the businessman who wanted to please his favorite customer, and seconds later there were two more chairs, glasses of water for everyone, and hot tea.

"My goodness, you're the man to know." Rebecca raised her eyebrows at Hong-Wei as she tucked her napkin into her lap. "Now, does this mean we get to eat your secret menu too I keep hearing about? The owner at my firm tried to order from it the other day, but he didn't know what he was doing and ended up with a regular stir-fry."

Hong-Wei blinked at her. "Goodness. It's gone that far?"

"Of course it has. Why do you think it's so crowded in here? Also, do you understand how many people are watching this table? I feel like a celebrity." Rebecca fluffed her hair and winked at her wife.

Kathryn bopped Rebecca on the nose with her napkin and turned to Hong-Wei. "All right, secret menu man. What are we eating?"

Hong-Wei had them eat Taiwan-style hot pot, which meant there was a large pot in the center of the table on a butane burner making their soup bubble as they cooked their own meat and vegetables inside. They also had rice, Chinese pickles, and because Rebecca whispered a request to Hong-Wei for her wife, the traditional crab Rangoons, which Simon now wondered how traditionally Chinese they were at all.

"So how is this Taiwan-style instead of Chinese?" Kathryn asked as they sipped the soup at the end, their bellies full and sated.

"Slight difference of flavors. To be honest this isn't much like my sister makes it. It's more standard Chinese hot pot, which is fine."

Owen popped a pickle into his mouth. "I need to meet this sister."

Simon wanted to meet her too, though he didn't say so, only glanced at Hong-Wei to make sure this comment didn't gut him this time. He seemed okay, but he was definitely walling himself off.

Jared leaned on his elbow as he poked at the dregs of the pot. "Didn't you say you lived with your grandparents and your parents? It's interesting how you always miss your sister's cooking, not any of theirs."

Hong-Wei sipped his tea. "My mother was too busy working to cook, but even if she hadn't been, it was never her strength. My grandmother's cooking is exceptional, but it came with lectures. My sister's cooking is the same as hers, and I had it the most since I lived with her, but…." There it was again, a flash of vulnerability, and then a wry smile. "Well. She lectures, I guess, but it's different. Also my grandmother is getting a little old to cook the way she used to. Though don't tell her that."

Kathryn looked sad. "It must be difficult, to be so far away from them. You sound like you miss your sister in particular quite a bit. I didn't realize you lived with her."

Hong-Wei's walls went up so fast Simon almost startled. "I lived with Sara, yes, during graduate school and my residency." Vulnerability gone, now he wore his *do not engage* smile. "I miss my family of course, but I'm all right. Thank you for your concern. Should we wrap this up so you can get back to the hospital, Doctor?"

Their evening ended shortly after, and though Jared tried to convince Hong-Wei to come back to the house with them, he declined. Simon was sure it had something to do with discussing his family so much. Jared seemed to agree, bringing up the topic as the two of them settled in to watch TV while Owen argued with people on the internet.

"He's sensitive about his family, isn't he?"

"Yeah." Simon hugged the giant bowl of popcorn, more out of a sense of comfort than because he thought he'd ever be able to eat again after their huge meal. Hong-Wei had a sister named Sara. Except he doubted that was her real name. Probably a Western name again. He wondered if he could ask what Sara's Taiwanese name was or if that would be considered rude.

"Your doctor sure likes his secrets." Jared took a handful of corn and nodded at the screen. "Now, what is this we're watching? I feel as if I've seen this already."

"*They Kiss Again*."

Jared shook his head. "Yeah, that was a dumb question. Let me rephrase. Have I watched this with you before?"

Simon resisted the urge to sigh. "Yes, but you never remember anything."

"You're right, but this really does seem familiar. Oh, hey, they're in a hospital. Wait, is this a doctor-nurse romance?" He elbowed Simon with a grin.

Simon swatted him. "*Stop*. It's my favorite show, all right? I love a lot of Asian dramas, but this one's the best. This and *It Started With a Kiss*, the first installment in the series. I don't expect you to remember either title for five minutes or for you to understand why I like this, but if you could sit here and pretend to care without mocking me, I'd appreciate it."

"Don't get upset, I'm not going to tease you. I was surprised, is all. I thought you were insisting you weren't going to have anything to do with this, since it threatened your job."

"I'm *not* having anything to do with it." Except Jared was right, he'd skipped the first half of the series where the hero and heroine were in high school and went right to the part where they worked in a hospital together. There was definitely something subliminal at work. Simon sighed. "It doesn't matter. I think he's lost interest."

Jared snorted. "No chance."

"He hasn't done anything but touch my damn elbow since—"

Jared raised interested eyebrows. "Since what?"

Simon fixed his gaze on the TV. "Like you said, it threatens my job, so I can't do anything. So I'm sticking with Asian dramas."

"You do know the no-dating policy is the number-one thing Owen argues with Andreas about, don't you? Not only for you, so don't give me that look. It's for the principle of the thing. Also I think he simply likes arguing with the man."

"I know Andreas is good for St. Ann's, but he's terrifying. I never feared losing my job until he showed up, and now every time he walks into a room I'm afraid it's to hand me my notice."

"Trust me, if it happens, a whole bunch of doctors will be down the man's throat over it, and a certain surgeon will be at the front of the line." Jared leaned over to murmur in Simon's ear as he went for more popcorn. "He wants to do a lot more than touch your elbow."

"Well, he's not touching anything else."

"Then you touch other stuff first."

Simon's body temperature rose several degrees, sending heat flooding from the tips of his hair to his toes. "I can't do that."

Jared laughed. "Okay, then *signal* you're open to him touching first. And maybe don't do it at work. Go over to see him. Put some K-pop on or one of your dramas, and bat your eyelashes. The rest should take care of itself."

"I am *not* playing K-pop or Asian dramas for Hong-Wei."

"Why in the world not? Of all the people you could share them with—"

"Oh my God, *don't*. Just because he's Asian doesn't mean he automatically likes K-pop and cheesy dramas."

"For crying out loud. *Obviously*. But he likes you, a lot, and so even if he doesn't care for them, I bet he'd be willing to learn. I mean, do you think Owen and I know anything about this stuff because we enjoy it?"

"You don't know anything. You forget everything I tell you, and what you do remember, you mock."

"My point is we watch them with you because we enjoy *you*. And who knows, *maybe* he does like the same stuff as you. Just as a radical thought, since this stuff is from Asian cultures, and he is also from an Asian culture, there's a shot he thinks they're as cool as you do. Or not. Possibly he'll fake it to get you into bed. Do you lose here?"

Simon had slumped so low into the bowl his face was practically planted in it. "I don't want to mess up what we have going. I don't want it to be awkward at work. Sometimes I wonder if Andreas is right. Maybe this is why he made the policy."

"I'm going to tell Owen you said that."

Simon yelped and practically tossed the popcorn into the air.

CHAPTER SIX

HONG-WEI WAS in his office, trying to decide if he could dream up a decent excuse to take Simon to lunch or if he had to concede today was a wash, when Kathryn stuck her head through the door.

"There you are. This is your first time getting to see the show live, isn't it? Come on, if we don't hurry, you're going to miss it."

"Show?" Realization dawned, and Hong-Wei rose. "Is this the thing the three of them do when Kumpel dismisses a patient?"

"When Jared does, yes. Honestly, call people by their first names already." She grabbed his wrist and tugged him into the hall. "We have to hurry. It's already going to be hell to get a spot. But it's just as well we'll be in the back. I heard a rumor Simon is nervous about you seeing it."

"Why doesn't he want me to see them put on a show for Kumpel—Jared's patient?"

Kathryn gave him a knowing look. "I don't *know*, Jack, why might that be?"

Hong-Wei's blood ran cold, and he glanced around. He thought he'd been careful, but if Kathryn was onto them….

She gentled and patted his hand. "Don't worry. I only figured it out because I watched the two of you at dinner. You're not like that at work. I mean, it's clear the two of you are close, but it wasn't until I saw you interact that night I put it all together." She leaned in close and lowered her voice. "Be super careful in the future. This town loves gossip, and Andreas is as serious as a heart attack about this idiot policy of his. He fired one of my nurses last week for dating someone in records. They've been together for five years."

Hong-Wei stopped short. "That's inhuman."

Kathryn nodded. "They were planning on getting married. Now they're both out of jobs."

"Would they have been safe if they were married?"

"Unclear. Becca says it would be some interesting waters, because if someone showed up to work married and then the administration made hay over it, what are they going to do about the other married work couples, fire them all? Which only underscores the foolishness of this policy, especially when we're so understaffed. I went to Erin and pled my case, but I got nowhere." She shook her head. "It makes no sense to me. I knew Erin when we were younger. He didn't go to Copper Point High—his parents put him in a private school in Sault St. Marie—but we ended up in a lot of the same extracurriculars: church camps, sports, and country club activities. I saw him as a quiet but kind young man. Once you got him to open up, he laughed, and he cared about people. He was always so interested in learning about everything. Now he's a corporate robot. It makes me think this isn't his will at all, or Nick's. This is someone on the hospital board pushing some sort of punishing agenda for their own sick purposes. Probably Erin's dad."

"Would the board be able to do that?"

"You haven't lived in a small town before, have you?" They were at the cafeteria doors now, and she waved her hands excitedly, also shushing him at the same time. "Okay, we're here. Remember, try not to let Simon see you. I'm so psyched. I think this is going to be a good one. Owen said they were practicing last night for like an hour."

Hong-Wei followed her into the cafeteria, which was indeed packed with people, and none of them were eating food. All the chairs faced an area designated as a stage. Sitting before it was a girl who looked to be around ten years old, bouncing excitedly in her chair.

The cafeteria lights lowered, music started from somewhere near the front, and Simon, Owen, and Jared appeared from the swinging doors of the kitchen.

It took Hong-Wei a minute to comprehend what he was hearing. He understood the three of them were lip-synching and doing a dance number to pop music—it was cute, if you liked pop music, which he didn't—but as he listened more closely he realized he didn't understand the words being sung. It wasn't English, but it was… something Asian, though not Mandarin. And now that he considered it, he thought he'd heard this song.

Oh God. Hong-Su had played this. This was Korean. This was… *K-pop*.

He covered his mouth and nose with his hand.

Kathryn, mistaking his reaction, elbowed his ribs and grinned. "I know, right? They're kind of a mess, but they're so cute. Okay, mostly Simon is cute. He can't get enough of this stuff. He knows every artist, and he learns all the words."

Yes. Hong-Wei could believe it. *Sweet Jesus.* Hong-Su could never hear of this.

Kathryn was practically a groupie at a concert, waving and cheering. "Look at them having so much fun, even Owen. I want to join them, but my knee would never forgive me. They watch the dances online and then practice them, or something—Simon learns the choreography, then teaches the others. Isn't it great?"

It was cute, but it was also, aesthetically, godawful. The song itself was as banal and painful as the rest of the bubblegum garbage his sister had inflicted upon him when they'd lived together. Their dancing, however, was nothing like K-pop dancing, which he also knew about because Hong-Su forced him to watch it with her, convinced if he saw them moving, it would change his mind about the quality of their work. Simon wasn't bad, but the other two were almost insulting.

Yet the room cheered them as if this was some sort of incredible thing. Good grief. What a nightmare.

When the atrocity ended, though, he clapped along, and when the people next to him remarked, "Aren't they something?" Hong-Wei nodded and said, "Yes, they certainly are," and he wasn't lying, they were something all right. It was his intent to slip out before Simon found him, which he thought would be best for all parties, but despite her saying they shouldn't be seen, Kathryn wouldn't let him leave.

"Where are you going, silly? We have to go up and tell them what a good job they did."

Part of him honestly wondered if Hong-Su hadn't orchestrated this somehow to torture him. *She* would have loved every second of this, bad dancing and all. Except when Simon saw them approaching, it didn't look like Hong-Wei was the one being tortured.

Simon startled as he saw Hong-Wei, and Hong-Wei knew it was bad because for the first time, Simon blanched instead of blushed. He wouldn't meet Hong-Wei's gaze as Kathryn praised the three of them either. It wasn't until Hong-Wei took Simon's arm and drew him into an alcove near the dish return area that he managed to get him to speak. "Are you all right?"

Simon still couldn't look at Hong-Wei, but he managed to focus on the shoulder of Hong-Wei's lab coat. "I didn't want you to see."

"Why not? You were pretty cute up there." It was true. He was. Quite adorable. It was the song that was godawful.

Simon dared a cautious glance at him. "Do… do you listen to K-pop?"

"No, but I'm moderately familiar with it. My sister is an avid fan."

Somehow this only seemed to send Simon into his clouds of despair again. "I'm sorry, then."

"But why? I honestly don't understand."

"Because we suck. I mean, I try, but I don't have any dance training. I'm simply copying what I see online. Jared and Owen are nothing but hams. I keep telling them we should do something other than K-pop, but they think the dances are fun. Which they are. It always felt okay because I'm pretty sure I'm the only person in northern Wisconsin listening to the genre. I've always dreaded someone who knows about it seeing us do this and realizing how stupid we look. Or finding our efforts offensive." His shoulders sagged, and he sighed. "I'm sorry."

Hong-Wei didn't know quite what to say. If he hadn't developed a callus to white people cluelessly making a hash of other people's cultures at this point, he didn't know how he'd have survived his life. Was that what Simon was worried about? Or did he think Hong-Wei cared about K-pop and was offended by the way they'd failed to replicate dance moves? How was he supposed to respond?

He seriously didn't remember flirting being this complicated.

Hong-Wei decided to play the middle. "I'm not offended. Why don't the three of you expand your repertoire, though?"

More wilting. "See, you *are* offended, and you're only being nice."

"I'm going to let you in on a secret." Hong-Wei leaned in close as he pitched his voice low. "I respect the right of others to enjoy it, but I don't care for K-pop." When Simon shivered, Hong-Wei drew back, concerned, and this time Simon blushed.

"I— Sorry. It gets me when you put your hand on my elbow. Then you whispered in my ear this time too, and it shorted my circuits."

Hong-Wei blinked at him. "I put my hand on your elbow?" He glanced down, saw Simon was right, and let go. "I'm so sorry. Do I do this often?"

Simon touched the hem of his shirt. "Yes. But I didn't say you should stop."

Kathryn's warning echoed in his head... then died under the heat in Simon's gaze. Hong-Wei gave him a half smile. "Mr. Lane. How forward of you. Right here at work?"

"It's just an elbow."

The spell of the moment was tangible between them, the air heavy with desire. On the other side of the wall, the cafeteria buzzed with people still talking about the K-pop dance, but here in their corner, Hong-Wei and Simon were alone, and for the first time Simon wasn't hesitating, wasn't running.

Don't let him get away.

Hong-Wei lifted his hand, this time to take Simon's arm deliberately. To caress him with his thumb, feel his pulse at the crook of his elbow, make him tremble as he ghosted his fingers to Simon's wrist and—

"Dr. Wu?"

The flash of fear in Simon's eye triggered something primal in Hong-Wei. Even before his brain recognized the speaker was Andreas, Hong-Wei had taken Simon's arm, yes, but to put him behind his body and shove him gently toward the fake ficus at the back exit of the cafeteria. He stepped forward on wooden legs, his mind screaming at him, *That was too close, you were almost seen making love to Simon's hand in the cafeteria by the one man you can never let see you making out with Simon's anything.* The next thing he knew, he was staring at Andreas, pasting on the kind of smile he used on doctors and administrators at Baylor when he'd been in residency pulling three-day shifts and slowly going out of his mind, but didn't want them to know.

Inside, he acknowledged the truth. He was falling for Simon, more so every day, and he didn't want to go slowly anymore. Unfortunately, as he stared down Erin Andreas, he realized he might already be too late.

ANDREAS NEARLY caught us.

The thought rang through Simon as he fled the cafeteria, wandering aimlessly through the halls on unsteady feet. If Hong-Wei hadn't been so quick to react and send Simon away, Simon would have stood there looking guilty and terrified as Andreas rounded the corner.

He made his way to the elevator and stumbled toward the nurses' station, avoiding people who had been to the show. After locking himself in the patient shower area and sitting in the corner, he hugged his legs to his body, drew shuddering breaths, and attempted to calm himself.

It was a sign. He'd considered for two seconds giving in to this, letting his heart drive instead of his head, and it had nearly ended in disaster.

Except… it had felt *so good*. He shut his eyes, remembering the moment Hong-Wei had smiled at him, the way he'd drawn him aside. He'd touched Simon's elbow subconsciously. It hadn't been him making a move. He had simply reached naturally for Simon.

If it wasn't for my job, I would leap into this. He knew that now, no question. Fear aside, hesitation be damned. Except Simon did have a job, one he loved.

One he *needed*. If he didn't work at the hospital, he'd have to apply at the care center or move. Or commute, possibly a crazy distance.

Obviously he wouldn't quit his job for a relationship, but how was he supposed to work so closely with a man he so desperately wanted to have a relationship *with*?

His phone buzzed in his pocket, and he pulled it out, worried it was the charge nurse asking where the hell he was. It wasn't the charge nurse or anyone at the hospital, though.

"Hey, Mom." He cleared his throat, trying to sound as if he wasn't huddled in fear in a bathroom. "What's going on?"

"Sorry to call you at work, hon. I'll keep this brief. I wanted to remind you about the fundraiser meeting tonight."

Simon could barely focus on what she was saying. "There's a meeting?"

"Yes, dear. You remember, you agreed to be on the committee? The first meeting is tonight at seven. Your sister can't make it, so I'm counting on you to go. I'd asked you to make sure your schedule was free, and I'm hoping it's still the case. They need to start planning now if they're going to get anywhere by the Founder's Day festival. And then you have to work at the fundraiser tomorrow as well."

Simon didn't remember any of this. *You've been so wrapped up in Hong-Wei, that's why.* He shifted his body so his legs were to his side and sat up straighter. "I'm sorry. Yes, I'm free. I'll go to the fundraiser too. But I can't remember where the meeting is tonight. Also, do I need to bring anything?"

"It's at church. Probably a pencil and paper, I'd say. Just for heaven's sake, don't be late. I'll never hear the end of it."

"I won't be late, I promise." *I won't let destructive thoughts distract me anymore either.*

Simon left the bathroom and went to the nurses' station, where everyone smiled at him and told him what a great job they'd done with the performance, as usual. Amanda wanted to play some K-pop on Spotify at the desk to get Simon to give them another taste, but Simon flatly refused, reminding them it wasn't allowed and they needed to get to work.

He worried all afternoon he'd run into Hong-Wei, but Simon didn't see him. This was good, he decided. It made this easier.

He left the second his shift was over, ignoring texts from Jared and Owen asking why the hell he'd disappeared so fast after the performance. After a stop at the house to change, Simon went to the Main Street Cafe to eat dinner and read a book while he waited for the seven o'clock meeting.

At six, he got texts from Jared and Owen again, asking where he was. *A meeting my mother asked me to attend*, he replied, then stopped answering.

At six thirty Hong-Wei started texting.

Sorry, I had a late surgery after your shift. Emergency appendectomy. Rita assisted. I want to talk to you. Can we please meet?

Simon didn't answer.

It was cowardly, but he told himself it was the smartest approach.

The meeting was incredibly boring. His mother had volunteered him for a subcommittee of the city festival planning commission, and his group was in charge of the entertainment venues for the Founder's Day festival. This meant for the two hours he sat in the room, mostly everyone argued, and he checked his phone to see Hong-Wei's increasingly intense texts asking where he was and insisting they needed to speak.

Then Hong-Wei wrote, *Please. I need to speak to you, if only for a few minutes.*

Simon's shoulders slumped. He could have resisted pushy Hong-Wei, but those pleading texts made him fold all too fast. Besides, if he didn't give in, he could well imagine Hong-Wei wandering town like a madman, attempting to locate Simon to plead his case.

Still, he felt he should make one last effort to resist. Simon pulled his phone under the table and tapped out a text. *I'm in a meeting. I'll talk to you tomorrow.*

I'll wait until you're done. Where are you? I can come to you.

So much for resisting. Simon glanced around the room to see if anyone was paying attention to him, but his frantic texting was nothing compared to the scandal of three stages instead of four and one made of a hay wagon.

Simon slipped both hands under the table to text more efficiently. *I'm at the Presbyterian Church. Don't come in, because we're having a meeting. I have no idea when we'll be done.*

I'll wait in your car. Is it unlocked?

Of course it was unlocked. Who locked their car in Copper Point? Simon shut his eyes on a silent sigh. *Yes. But you don't need to come. I'd actually prefer you didn't.*

I know. I'm sorry. I promise it will be short.

Simon put the phone on top of the table, but as he set it down, one last text came through.

He didn't see anything.

Simon didn't reply to this, but those four words rattled in his head the rest of the meeting, banging against the fear and guilt he'd tried to pack down all afternoon. *He didn't see anything.* This was what Simon had secretly lived in terror of, that somehow because they hadn't been paying attention Andreas had witnessed their private moment. Simon didn't know what it took to be fired for breaking the policy—he wasn't dating Hong-Wei, and surely they couldn't do anything to him for simply gazing at the man with want—but the idea that now Andreas would be onto him, watching him like a hawk, made him feel ill. When he left the meeting and walked toward his car, he solidified his resolve to clarify he'd be happy to have an intimate *friendship* with Hong-Wei, and nothing more.

Hong-Wei indeed waited in Simon's car—in the driver's seat. Simon stopped short for a second in the middle of the parking lot, realized the other attendees of the meeting would be coming out soon, and hurried to the passenger side.

"What are you doing?" He fumbled angrily with his keys and tossed them at Hong-Wei. "Go before someone sees you."

"And what? Spreads a rumor that the surgeon took a drive with his nurse, who he's also friends with, the same as he is with his nurse's housemates? Relax."

No power on earth could make Simon relax right now. Face flushed, hands clammy, stomach doing flips, he fastened his seat belt and stared out the window. "Just drive."

Hong-Wei didn't, not immediately. He withdrew his phone, pulled out the earphones, and plugged it into Simon's stereo system. Soon music began to play over the car speakers—something classical and mournful, with strings and choral voices full of vibrato.

"It's Poulenc's *Stabat Mater*, the 'Dolorosa.' I was playing through the entire piece earlier." He put the car into drive and maneuvered out of the parking lot as he spoke. "This particular version is by the Estonia National Symphony Orchestra and the Estonian Philharmonic Choir."

"It's very... sad."

"It's Mary's lament as Christ is crucified on the cross, so yes."

Simon had been staring at the musical app on the phone, where a tiny album cover glowed against a black screen, but now he glanced at Hong-Wei. "Are you religious?"

"I guess. I'm Buddhist, though. You?"

"A little. Methodist." Simon went back to staring at the album cover. "Seems odd you knew about the *Stabat Mater* but I didn't, since I'm the Christian."

"I think it's more a Catholic thing, so we're both out. I know about it because I love classical music. In more than the operating room. I always have." He smiled wryly, his expression distant and melancholy. "I wanted to be a professional musician. I studied piano and violin all the way through high school, right up until I fought my father on what I wanted to major in. When he found out I was applying for music scholarships so I could be a music major, he threatened to take my violin away and sell the piano."

Simon looked up sharply, mouth open in shock. "That's *terrible*."

Hong-Wei shrugged. "I don't know. It was the only way to get me to listen. My sister intervened, convinced my father not to act so rashly, got me to use the music scholarship to get into a school with a strong science program and begin taking courses good for a premed major. You can go to medical school with any major, of course, but the more sciences the better. So I took some music courses, but also human anatomy and chemistry and so on, and I was in the orchestra. I ended up with a music minor, but I followed my father's path after all."

This was a side of Hong-Wei Simon had never imagined. "Why didn't you stick with music?"

"Because they were right. It was far tougher than I'd thought, and though I was good, I wasn't good enough, not to make a real living at it. At best I could have become a professor at a university, or taught high school, or been principal violin in a small city's symphony, and none of it was what I wanted. I dreamed of being on a major stage, but I was lost in a sea of talent, of people vying for the same dream as me. I gave it up, but I never stopped loving music."

Simon ached for him. "That makes me so sad."

"It's the reality of the world."

"But it's still sad. Do you not play at all now?"

His laugh was sharp and bitter. "When would I have the chance? When I wasn't putting in my residency hours, I was moonlighting or sleeping. My entire life was being a doctor. I'm a better doctor than musician anyway."

"Who said you had to be the best to do it? Besides, you have more time now. You're still busy, but you had time tonight to run all over town finding me. You could play violin now, for fun. You could get a piano—"

Simon yelped as the car stopped abruptly. They were in the middle of nowhere, near a stretch of forest heading out toward the lake. He put his hand on the dash and looked around for whatever wildlife had caused Hong-Wei to stop, but Hong-Wei only cut the engine, pocketed the keys, got out of the car, and came around to Simon's door.

"Come with me."

Simon allowed himself to be led out of the car and into the woods, but he couldn't help glancing around nervously. "Hong-Wei, this isn't the best place. There are *bears*—"

Then he couldn't say anything else, because Hong-Wei pressed him to a tree. When Simon gasped in surprise, lifting his arms to push at Hong-Wei, Hong-Wei captured Simon's hands—lightly, he could get away if he wanted—and held them against the bark.

Simon's knees went weak as Hong-Wei leaned in close, his earnest face lit by moonlight through the trees.

"I want to explain this to you, but you're not hearing me. All I've done since the day I gave up music is work. I told myself I'd become the best doctor in the country, the world, to make up for having to give up my dream."

"You *are* a wonderful doctor. You're the best I've ever worked with. What does it matter, though, if you beat everyone else or not? And I don't understand, why can't you play anymore? You're just like Owen and Jared, always having to top everyone. Why can't—"

"I'm *not* like Owen and Jared." His grip on Simon's hands slackened. "This isn't working. I can't get the words out right."

Simon slipped his hands out of Hong-Wei's grip and settled them on his chest. "It's okay."

"It's not." He leaned into the tree, into Simon. "I came to Copper Point because I was running away. I didn't know what I wanted anymore, but I knew it wasn't to be the best. I'd figured that much out, almost too late. I ran away as far as I could, hoping someplace quiet would let me sort things out. It worked too. I know what I want now."

His breath was on Simon's neck, tickling his skin, sending goose bumps across his flesh. "You do?"

"Yes." Hong-Wei lifted his head, his gaze level with Simon's, no longer sad, no longer lost, only fixed and determined and entirely focused. "I want you."

Simon tried to slide away from Hong-Wei's intensity, but he was fully flush to the tree. His knees had already sagged on him once, and the truth was, his heart wasn't in his escape. "Hong-Wei," he whispered.

Hong-Wei threaded fingers through Simon's hair. "Andreas didn't see us. I swear to you. We can keep our relationship secret. We'll be professional at work, but outside of work—"

"Outside of work we'll what? Meet in this forest? Send Owen and Jared on grocery runs? Do you think if we start this, we'll be able to control how we behave around one another?"

"Do you honestly think we can now?"

Simon's gut twisted in ache. "This is my *job* on the line. My *life*. I've never lived anywhere but here except when we were in Madison for school, and I was miserable the entire time. I watch dramas from around the world and dream of travel in exotic places—exotic to me is Chicago, for what it's worth—but I rarely get farther than Duluth. My dreams are simply dreams. My reality is I will live here, probably never get married or ever have a real relationship, and if Owen and Jared get serious about someone, I'll end up back with my parents. I've made peace—" His voice broke, and he had to gather himself before he could continue. "I'm not going to have an exciting life. I've made peace with it. It doesn't help me when you try to tear that peace down."

Hong-Wei captured Simon's hand and pressed it over his own beating heart. "Feel this, Simon. I'm not a fantasy. I'm standing right here in front of you. Begging you."

Simon was going to cry. In fact, his eyes were full of tears. "*Stop.*"

"I won't. I've tried to woo you slowly, to figure out the way to court you and win you over, to be the best. I've always had to be the best. It was the only way I've survived. Then today you looked at me, you smiled, you flirted, not hesitating, and it was as if everything shattered. I finally had a place I belonged. I didn't want to be the best anymore. I only wanted to be me."

Simon's breath hitched on a sob. "Don't *do this* to me."

Hong-Wei's laughter was bitter, sad. "What, you think I should be the only one to suffer?"

"I can't believe I did all this. You found this in yourself by getting away."

"By getting away I made things so quiet I felt panic pressing in around me everywhere I turned. Then you showed up and took me furniture shopping in the middle of the night, accepted me into your circle of friends, let me borrow your car, blushed when I bought you lunch, loved how it was my home country's food. You proved to be the most competent nurse I've ever partnered with—"

"—that's simply me doing my job—"

"—and then you got all flustered when Owen and Jared teased you, came to my defense when they teased me." His thumb grazed Simon's neck. "You kissed me back when I kissed you."

If Simon stayed here a second longer, he was going to give in. "I have to get home. It's late, and I have work in the morning."

"Dammit, Simon, all I'm asking is you give this a chance. Give *me* a chance."

Yes, and that was the most dangerous thing Simon could do. He turned away from Hong-Wei, intending to walk to the car.

Hong-Wei blocked him with his arms, trapping Simon between them, pressing his forehead to Simon's own.

If Simon tipped his face up, their lips would meet. If he let out the right sigh, Hong-Wei would kiss him. If he stayed still long enough, Hong-Wei would grow tired of waiting and take possession of his mouth, his body, his soul. He was convinced of it.

Why don't you let him, then?

Because it wasn't so simple. Because Simon had nowhere to go if this relationship didn't work out and he lost his job. Because he didn't want to face the humiliation of being fired.

Because he was scared of his fantasy coming true. Dreams were meant for the other side of the television screen. Pretending they'd work out in real life would only leave him disappointed.

Simon steeled himself and took a deep breath, letting it out with as much determination as he could. "I need to go."

He told himself it was a good thing when Hong-Wei's arms fell away and he stepped back, saying nothing more.

HONG-WEI STOOD in the entryway of his apartment and stared at the empty space, trying to calm the raging emotions inside him. He resisted the urge to dwell on the fact that he hadn't felt like this since college when he'd given up music. He was an adult now. He could handle this.

He couldn't handle this.

His phone was in his hand, but he didn't know who to call. Owen and Jared were out. Completely out. Were they out forever now? Had he lost the friends he'd made here as well as Simon? Had he ever had them, or were they extensions of Simon?

Should he call his sister? No. He wasn't ready. She'd either be annoying, or she'd be too helpful— he'd want to shout at her, or he'd miss her so much he'd crumble. Who was left?

That he went so far as to open his email, seeking the messages from his father, was a sign of his desperation. There were seven. Gut twisting, he opened the most recent one.

Hello, son. I hope you are well. We are thinking of you and hoping you are happy. Please remember if things don't work out, we'll help you find somewhere else to practice. Here are some of the most recent places who have offered for you. These are only a sampling.

We hope you are doing well. Please contact us soon. We miss you.

Love, Dad.

Hong-Wei ignored the plea to contact his family. He tried not to read the list of hospitals. He didn't make it.

You could run away....

He dropped his phone with a shaking hand.

When he left the house, he went without his mobile or his coat, but he went back, limbs stiff and heavy, and retrieved both. The coat was because it was stupidly cold in Wisconsin, and he was never getting used to it. He didn't want the phone. He wanted to flush it. But he was on call. Someone might need him.

Someone might need his hands and his degree, that is.

He supposed it wasn't surprising he ended up at China Garden. They were just starting to close, but when they saw him, they opened up and welcomed him as they always did, ushering him to the booth in the back nearest the kitchen, and within five minutes Mrs. Zhang was out with a pot of tea and a piping hot bowl of noodles.

"You're sad tonight. What happened?"

Hong-Wei shook his head and sipped at the tea. "Good evening, Auntie. I won't burden you with my troubles."

She clucked her tongue and swiped a scolding pat at his arm. "I'm asking to be burdened. You've brought us so much business. You come so much I should make you a bed."

That made him laugh a little, though he couldn't shake the sorrow on his heart. "It's an old, boring story. I'm unlucky in love and unsatisfied with my life. And selfish, I know. You don't need to tell me. My family has told me often enough."

"You're not selfish. You work long hours at the hospital. You ask us to make special meals to please your friends. You let my silly staff ask you so many medical questions when they aren't sick, and you charge them nothing. And you always ask after my husband."

Hong-Wei glanced around, realizing at last what was out of place in the restaurant. "Where *is* he?"

"He's tired tonight. A small fever from working too hard." When Hong-Wei rose, she waved him down. "Sit, sit, and eat your noodles. It's nothing. I've given him herbs."

Hong-Wei didn't sit. He felt sick with dread and guilt, because he'd stopped coming to ask about the owner. "Is his wound still not healed?"

"It's being fussy, but it will improve with time. I prayed for him this morning."

Prayers. Hong-Wei stood, made his body rigid, then bent in half in a bow, keeping his body in the submissive pose as he spoke. "Please, Auntie, please let me examine your husband."

He had to beg for almost a minute, but she eventually relented. He thought it might have been because he was attracting attention from the rest of the restaurant. He didn't care. His heart pounded at the top of his throat as he followed her up the stairs to the apartment where the workers slept.

Please let me be overreacting. Please let me be overreacting.

He wove past boxes, stepped over a line of sleeping mats, and pushed past a curtain leading to Zhang and his wife's private compartment, and there on a double mattress on the floor was Mr. Zhang.

Hong-Wei was not overreacting.

Mrs. Zhang was stunned by the sight of her husband. She crouched beside him. "He wasn't like this an hour ago." Touching his forehead, she gasped. "He's so hot!"

The man wasn't only hot, he was pale. Hong-Wei flipped on the light beside the bed and knelt beside his patient, assessing him visually as he took vitals. Elevated pulse, but stable. Fever was definitely not in a comfortable range. Breathing was erratic. "Uncle?" No response. "Uncle? Mr. Zhang?" he called out louder, but still, nothing.

Mrs. Zhang began to weep. "Yi Fu, Yi Fu!" Mr. Zhang didn't answer her either.

Hong-Wei lifted one of Mr. Zhang's eyelids, then swore and fumbled for his phone.

"911, what's your emergency?"

"This is Dr. Jack Wu of St. Ann's Medical Center. I'm currently in the upstairs apartment of the China Garden with an adult male, approximately age sixty-five, in need of immediate medical transport.

Patient is unresponsive with a high fever and sepsis from an infection, and his left hand is oozing purulent, puslike fluid." He rubbed soothing circles on the back of the now-weeping Mrs. Zhang and added, "Likely progressing to septic shock and organ failure."

CHAPTER SEVEN

SIMON WAS lying in bed, staring out the window and trying to sleep despite the hollow pit of guilt in his stomach, when the door to his room opened and Owen stuck his head inside. One look at him told Simon something was wrong.

He sat up, tossing his covers aside. "What is it? Code Orange?"

Owen already had on his coat, and as he spoke, he tossed scrubs at Simon. "No mass casualties, but Jack's calling some kind of four-alarm fire. Ran roughshod over the ER and is setting up his own team. He wants you on it."

"What?" Simon stumbled into his pants, his legs nothing but jelly.

"He said to pass on a message. 'Tell Simon we'll be working off the contingency plan.'"

Simon sat on the bed, his pants trapped at his knees. "Oh my God. Code Violet."

"I have no idea what you're talking about, but you can explain in the car. Jared's coming too. I don't know what good a pediatrician will do, but I have the feeling Jack's going to need all the friends he can round up tonight."

Simon left the house with his shoes untied, his coat unzipped. He did his best to explain Code Violet in the car, but his voice shook, and he stumbled over words. "Hong-Wei's thorough about his OR, but he has all these rules about patients too. I... I didn't ask questions because it's not my place. Except I didn't understand one section. It was as if he expected our surgery patients to end up in the ICU and we wouldn't have any ICU staff. I asked him what the section was for. He looked strange as he replied, like someone coming home from war, and he told me it was our contingency plan. When I asked him contingency for what, he told me it was just in case. So I laughed it off and gave it a nickname. I called it Code Violet, since we didn't have a code by that color, then said I certainly doubted we'd ever need this." Simon's stomach hurt. "Now here we are. What's going on?"

Owen stared grimly at the road and wiped his mouth. "I think your boyfriend has some serious secrets to share tonight."

Jared leaned forward from the back seat. "Why would he do this, though? Why not send whatever this is on to a bigger hospital? I mean, if this is a surgical case and he's on call, fine, but what's with calling Simon in and barging around like a bull?"

Owen shook his head. "They said he brought the patient in himself. I didn't get much more. Everybody was bananas. He's got the whole fucking place on fire. I swear, I will beat that boy's ass."

When they got to the hospital, Owen parked in the fire lane, tossed Jared the keys, and Simon rushed inside, Owen hot on his heels.

The ER was complete chaos, and at the center of it were Hong-Wei and Mr. Zhang.

Simon didn't get a chance to speak before he was swept up in the madness. "Dr. Wu, Simon Lane is here," someone shouted, and even before Hong-Wei barked, "Get him scrubbed," Simon was whisked toward a sink.

Susan, one of the CNAs, smiled nervously at Simon. She helped him into gloves and spoke over the din. "Patient is a sixty-five-year-old male with a high fever and probable infection of the hand. Breathing is unstable, as are blood pressure and heart rate, despite a norepinephrine drip. Liver and kidneys are in jeopardy. Dr. Wu is monitoring his vital signs and organ function. He hopes to take the patient to surgery to flush the infection once he's stable, but we're currently having difficulty."

Simon's breath caught, and he sagged against the sink as Susan tucked his fingers into the latex. "We aren't equipped to handle this."

"I wouldn't advise saying that to Dr. Wu." Susan helped Simon into the last glove. "We have the OR ready, and Rita has checked it to make sure it's the way Dr. Wu wants it, but if you end up in surgery, you might want to double-check because we're all a bit nervous. Dr. Wu got angry at pretty much every doctor in the hospital, and everyone is terrified of him right now. He yelled at Rita too, but she managed to keep from crying until she was out of the room. We were hoping you could handle him, since you seem to know him best."

Simon wanted to let out a long, black laugh. Yes, he did know Hong-Wei best. So well the man had spilled his guts to him and then he'd sent him away. To China Garden, apparently, where he'd discovered some sort of strange medical mystery in a man he had great affection for. The man who spoke no English and whose wife was weeping in the lobby with only one of the waitstaff to comfort her. Had anyone attempted to convey what was going on to them?

Too early for that. Far too early. He understood, though, why Hong-Wei had kept Mr. Zhang here, from an emotional perspective. But could they give him what he needed at St. Ann's?

Not your job to make that call, nurse. Your task is to follow your doctor.

"I'll do my best," Simon told Susan, and went to face the beast.

There were three exam areas in the St. Ann's ER, and Mr. Zhang was in the center one. Two nurses, three techs, and four angry doctors flanked Hong-Wei. As Simon approached, the nurses stepped back, the doctors glared, and Hong-Wei continued to stare at the monitor.

Simon went to his side. "Dr. Wu, I'm sorry I'm late. How can I help you?"

Hong-Wei didn't so much as glance at him, la-ser-focused on Zhang's vitals. "Have you been briefed on the patient's situation?"

"I have, Doctor."

"I've dispatched a courier to Ironwood for supplies and called for ambulances from Duluth and Eau Claire to bring specific medications we're missing. If you could appoint someone to be in charge of monitoring those transports, I would appreciate it." His lips thinned. "Everyone here has lost their heads."

"If I can make a suggestion, Dr. Kumpel is here."

Some of the tension bled off his shoulders. "Bring me Kumpel, STAT."

"Jesus, Jack, read a room." Owen's tone was light, but Simon knew him well enough to understand he was all business, suited up surgery-ready with his mask down, studying the monitor. His expression was as grim as Hong-Wei's. "Christ. What the hell happened? Do we know?"

"Fucking home remedies. Tried to treat an infection with grass, called it Eastern medicine when it damn well wasn't, wouldn't let me see it, and I didn't push hard enough to override him."

"Not your fault, man. Guy's still got free will."

"Yeah, and it landed him at the edge of organ failure and septic shock."

The monitors began to go crazy, and so did the ER. Hong-Wei called for the defibrillator, Simon prepped the machine, and the doctors who had lingered on the sides began murmuring. Everyone backed up as Hong-Wei shouted "Clear," and gave Zhang a shock to the chest. Once the patient's heart rate was under control, the doctors stepped forward, brows knit and chests puffed up.

"Now hold on, young man." This was Dr. Stallman, a general practitioner at St. Ann's since Simon was little. "You've done enough. This patient isn't going to make it if we don't send him to—"

Hong-Wei turned on the doctors, teeth bared, eyes lit with a fury that startled even Simon, and when he spoke, his voice was whispered ice. "I'm just getting started, and I'm not sending my patient anywhere. I'm a board-certified intensivist who had job offers from every hospital you had wet dreams of in medical school. If you're not going to assist, *get out of my ED*."

Owen drew back, eyes wide. For a moment he was as stunned as the others, though whereas they seemed confused—as was Simon—Owen apparently understood something the rest of them didn't. Owen swore under his breath as he wiped a hand over his mouth. "You heard the man. Suit up or go home. Oy. Jared, any word on those meds yet? Something tells me we're in for a ride. Get on the horn and put some fire in the couriers' bellies."

"Got it." Jared's voice was light, but Simon could tell he was shaken too. So Jared also understood what Hong-Wei had just said. It was only Simon, the other nurses, and old men who didn't get it.

Simon frowned as he put the paddles away, trying to figure it out, but he honestly had no idea. What in the world was an intensivist? What was going on here?

The doctors were still in the room, but they were grumbling in the corner now, whispering to one another in confusion. Hong-Wei called for a phenylephrine infusion, and as Simon changed the bag, Owen tilted his head at Hong-Wei in some kind of silent question. When Hong-Wei nodded, Owen cleared his throat, then began to speak, addressing the entire ER.

"All right. Since nobody here reads a journal anymore, apparently, let me update you on what goes on in the big wide world beyond our teeny-tiny hospital. As you're aware, when you specialize in surgery, you pick an area of specialization. General surgery is an area of specialization. But there are further specializations for those who board certify, and they've come up with some new specialties recently, especially for larger, more progressive hospitals. One of those new specialties is a critical care surgeon, also known as an intensivist." He cast a side glance at Hong-Wei, who was watching the monitor like a hawk as Simon hooked up the new bag. "Dr. Wu isn't supposed to remove gallbladders and appendixes and all our piddly nonsense at St. Ann's. He's trained to make quick decisions during high-stakes situations with little information. He's supposed to be bossing the bigwigs around in intensive care units and solving crises in ERs in major hospitals. Probably there's nobody outside of Mayo Clinic in our area who outranks him, and it sounds as if they'd be happy to hire him."

Hong-Wei didn't look up from his study of Zhang's monitors. "I didn't feel they were a good fit for me."

"Yes, but somehow you thought our moth-eaten outfit was? I am finding you some surgical coverage, and you and I are getting shitfaced once this is over so I can ask you ten million questions, wise guy."

"Let's focus on the patient first." Hong-Wei's lips went completely flat, and he grimaced. "I need those meds. I can't drain the infection until he's stabilized, but he's going to keep crashing until—"

On cue, the monitors went off again, but this time no one intervened, only let Hong-Wei do his job.

"The infection is chewing up his heart, not to mention his kidneys and liver, and I damn well know St. Ann's doesn't have the equipment he needs if this keeps up." Hong-Wei's gaze darted to Simon's. "Get a status on the medication from Eau Claire. Also someone call in the hospital pharmacist for me. I need help thinking outside this box."

Owen glanced up. "Who's on call?"

Susan looked up from the computer where she was typing notes. "I think it's Tony Hansen."

Owen curled his lip. "Absolutely not. Call Dan Newcomb and tell him I'm calling in my you-owe-me."

As Susan went to make the call, Owen returned his focus to Hong-Wei. "Trust me when I tell you if you're playing around with medication while you wait for the drugs you want, you want Dan, not Tony. He used to work at U-W at Madison, so he has more of the experience you're after. He lives close too, and he'll come without asking questions."

"Thanks."

Simon was pretty sure Owen was bantering to keep Hong-Wei level at this point, because he seemed to be reaching for conversation. "You said the medicine you wanted was on the ambulance from Eau Claire. What are the other couriers for?"

"Insurance." Hong-Wei wiped at his brow with his sleeve. "Has anyone checked on Mrs. Zhang? Does she still have an English-speaking interpreter with her?"

Rita popped off the wall. "I'll go check."

Mrs. Zhang was alone in the waiting room, rocking and weeping silently with her eyes closed. When Hong-Wei heard this, he had Rita hold up her smartphone so he could record a message in Mandarin. It sounded different than usual, more formal and rhythmic. When he finished, he told her to go and play it for the patient's wife. "Bring her hot tea. Green if you have it, or herbal, but bring her something. Don't ask. Just bring it. Someone sit with her. Hold her hand. You don't need to speak her language to comfort her. You simply have to be human. But play that recording for her as much as she wants to hear it."

Simon knew he should be quiet, but when Owen was busy and it was only the two of them monitoring the patient, he leaned close and asked, "What did you record?"

"Something to make her feel a little less alone." He kept his focus on Zhang's monitor, a tic forming in his cheek. "She probably sent the waitress back to give directions to the others to finish closing the restaurant, and because she didn't want the girl to see her worried. She doesn't have need of a translator right now. Either I'm going to come out at some point and tell her that her husband is alive, or I'm going to give her the news she's been dreading. Everything else is noise."

"They didn't close the restaurant?"

"The place could burn and they'd try to cook on the flames. You don't understand what those jobs mean to the people who work there."

No, Simon didn't. Which was some kind of irony, wasn't it, given the argument he'd had with Hong-Wei earlier?

Are you scared for your job, or your heart?

Or was it so noble? Was he simply only thinking of himself?

Jared stuck his head past the curtain into the room. "Ironwood courier almost here. About five minutes."

Hong-Wei nodded. "ETA on the others? Also where's the pharmacist?"

"Dan's in the parking lot. Duluth is an hour out. They're calling ahead to stop the pilot car, but the one-lane road is crap and they can't drive like bats out of hell."

"I don't need them as much anyway. What about Eau Claire?"

"You don't want to know. I called Andreas and Beckert and asked them to pull some strings. Maybe a chopper ride."

Owen shook his head. "They'll never approve the expense."

"He's going to die without the drug." Hong-Wei grimaced, staring at the monitor readouts, daring them to dip. "Of course, he might die with it."

Jared inclined his head. "What is it, if I might ask?"

"Brand-new high-powered antibiotic. We were lucky anyone had it." He rested his elbows on the rail of the bed, looking weary. "Dammit, I could do this if I had a cardiac unit. I'd have sent him to a better facility so he'd have had the option if I'd thought he'd survive a two-hour ambulance ride. But if I'd sent him to Duluth, they wouldn't have had the drug, and they wouldn't have known to call for it. They might not have called for it in Eau Claire. It's not something most people think of. It might as well be on the moon, though, if I can't get it in him before his organs fail. I've got to come up with some kind of stopgap in the meantime. I can't get an accurate account of what we *have*, though."

The door to the ER waiting room burst open and Dan Newcomb came through, face flushed, glasses askew, salt-and-pepper hair slightly mussed, as if someone had gotten him out of bed and he hadn't had a chance to put himself entirely to rights. He had on a pair of beige khakis and a plaid shirt, his usual work uniform, and he was sliding into his lab coat as he walked in. "Sorry it took me so long. How can I help?"

Hong-Wei gave him a quick rundown of the situation, stopping in the middle to adjust the flow of norepinephrine. "I can't stabilize him, and at the moment I can't even keep his heart going. I wanted to run through what you have in the pharmacy to get a better idea of my options until my drug of choice gets here, but I don't dare turn my attention away from him too long."

"Sure, sure." Dan pushed his glasses higher and settled on a stool in front of a monitor. "Let's start problem-solving."

It was something to listen to the two of them shoot back and forth, Hong-Wei seizing on drugs and theorizing doses and combinations, Dan nodding or shaking his head, adding commentary such as "I don't see a conflict if you keep the dose low," or sometimes "Considering the other drugs you've already administered, you're at a high risk for a bad outcome if you go that route," or "Sure, but it'll rule out the one you're waiting for." Simon always marveled at this interplay between doctor and pharmacist: one was a master strategist, the other a walking encyclopedia. Combine the two, and you had an incredible duo.

They decided to use the Ironwood drug in combination with another and a slight uptick in the flow of saline, and additional vasopressors, and as soon as the courier arrived, Dan had it compounded and ready for Hong-Wei to administer. Everyone held their breath as the drugs went in, but Zhang didn't crash, and his blood pressure and heart rate stabilized slightly. Not enough to get him into surgery, but enough to buy them some time.

Then Beckert and Andreas came through the doors, flanked by John Jean Andreas and two other members of the hospital board.

They lined up at the back of the room, near the ER doctor and other physicians who had been present at the onset of the crisis and hadn't left. The ER was practically packed to the gills now. Beckert came forward awkwardly. Erin Andreas stood beside his father, unusually silent.

"So." Beckert's smile was strained, and he looked as if wanted to be anywhere but where he was. "It sounds as if we've had a bit of excitement here tonight."

Owen faced them down before Hong-Wei could. "An emergency, more to the point. Is there something you needed, Beckert? Or did the old guard tattle, and you came here to check on us?"

John Jean fixed Owen with a quelling gaze. "That's quite a tone to take with your employer."

"There's been more than enough tone tossed around here this evening, so yes, I'm not in the mood. I can't believe you're lining up like a firing squad in front of a goddamn patient on the table."

"A patient who is unlikely to pay," one of the board members grumbled.

A collection of soft gasps filled the room. Erin Andreas shut his eyes on a painful wince. Hong-Wei's hands clenched around the rail.

Shifting his body to block the line of sight of the others, Simon closed his hand over Hong-Wei's.

"Oh, Mark Larsen." Owen's voice dripped with venom. "A roomful of witnesses just heard you say that. How do you get to be a board member and not understand it's illegal to refuse medical treatment to a patient, regardless of anything whatsoever? Wait, I know. You're *our* board member."

"Don't bother calling ICE." Hong-Wei's jaw was tight, but he linked his thumb with Simon's as he continued to face away from the board members. "Zhang and his wife have green cards. So do all their employees." His tone became incredibly bitter as he added, "I'm a citizen, since we're clearing the air."

The board member who'd spoken began to sputter. "I wasn't implying—"

"Stop talking, Mark." John Jean's voice was chilling. "You've put the entire hospital in legal jeopardy. I expect your resignation from the board in the morning. You may leave."

Larsen shuffled out, and as the room became a susurrus of whispers, John Jean spoke again. "Dr. Wu, you have my apologies if you felt anyone was questioning your citizenship or your right to treat your patient. However, you must allow this has all been an irregular evening, and now we're being asked to bring a costly and novel drug to the hospital in the most expensive way possible. It seemed most expedient for you to explain to us in person what was going on."

Hong-Wei let go of Simon's hand and rubbed his temple. Glancing around, he saw Jared and waved him over. "Watch the monitors for me. I'll give you a set of ranges, and if they move beyond those points, I want to know immediately. If he crashes, I'll handle the paddles, but I want you to prep them."

Jared saluted. "I can do that."

Hong-Wei faced the CEO and directors, and the oddly quiet Erin. "You saw my CV when I applied, and you know I had more experience than simply a general surgeon. I had a suspicion only a few of you, if any of you, fully understood what you were hiring. This is it. This is my experience. If you had a cardiac unit and a bit more equipment, whenever a critical case came through, I could keep it from being sent out. Strange critical cases are what I was trained for. I chose not to pursue that career path for my own reasons, and I haven't regretted working at St. Ann's, until tonight. What you need to know as a board is I'm saving this man's life. It would be an easy thing to do if I had a little more equipment and had worked longer with my staff." He gestured to Simon. "Having Simon Lane on my team is a significant asset. Having doctors such as Gagnon and Kumpel and PharmDs like Dr. Newcomb make all the difference as well. It's trickier to work under these conditions, but I can manage. The fact of the matter is, this patient would have died in the ambulance had I sent him on to another hospital. If I get the drug I'm seeking, he stands a good chance of living, once I can get him into surgery. If you have the means to get me the drug faster, it would make his odds better. If he crashes too many more times, there won't be any way to save him."

John Jean appeared thoughtful. "Are you saying you can do this for other patients in critical situations at St. Ann's?"

"Under specific conditions, yes. The lack of a cardiac unit is severely limiting. Having a second surgeon would also change the game a great deal."

"We're starting to get close to numbers you won't like, Jack," Jared called out.

Hong-Wei talked over his shoulder as he went back to his patient. "Right now everything you're discussing is theoretical and for another day. I need that medicine. Are you getting it for me, or not?"

Zhang destabilized a few seconds later, and Dan helped Hong-Wei invent another band-aid drug combination. By the time they'd finished, Erin Andreas came to the foot of the bed. "I'm happy to report a helicopter will have the drug to you within fifteen minutes."

The entire room sighed in relief.

Simon felt Hong-Wei's hand on his elbow. He glanced down, then up—Hong-Wei was looking right at him. Weary. Scared. Grateful.

Simon leaned into him as surreptitiously as he could. *I'm sorry*, he telegraphed with his gaze.

Hong-Wei squeezed his elbow harder, then turned back to his patient.

Everything happened quickly once the drug arrived. Simon helped administer the IV, and Hong-Wei watched the readouts as the medicine dripped into Mr. Zhang's bloodstream. It worked exactly as Hong-Wei had hoped it would, and quicker than Simon had thought possible—twenty minutes later, Zhang's vitals were stable, and within the hour, they were prepping for surgery.

Mrs. Zhang had to be brought in to give permission, Hong-Wei translating the form for her and showing her where to sign. She nodded tearfully as she signed, kissing her husband on the forehead and putting her hands together, bowing over him as he left. Hong-Wei spoke over his shoulder to her as they disappeared, and the last thing Simon saw was Mrs. Zhang alone in the ER, weeping silently.

After that it was simply another night in emergency surgery. Simon had assisted in draining infections before, though never ones with quite this much on the line. Hong-Wei had Rita scrub in as well, and she was Simon's second assistant, present in case of complications during surgery. Hong-Wei and Owen kept discussing scenarios, Owen pointing out they could still airlift him if need be, Hong-Wei shaking his head and saying it was this or nothing. But there weren't any complications, the surgery was fine, and soon Zhang was in recovery, waiting to come out of the anesthesia.

His fever was still high, meaning he was also nauseous and delirious. Normally surgeons weren't at patient bedsides in recovery, but Hong-Wei didn't leave, staying beside the tech as Simon and Rita finished postsurgery cleanup, conversing quietly to the patient in his native tongue. The surgeon's face was gentle but full of exhaustion.

Simon clutched the blanket he'd brought for Zhang, aching for Hong-Wei. He was at the center of all of this, and despite so many people around him, he'd borne the brunt of this alone. It was his decision to treat Zhang, to reveal the truth about his specialty. He'd stood alone in the ER and fought for the right to treat his patient, invented ways to save him while explaining what he was doing to those attempting to assist him.

How much of his career was like this before he'd come to St. Ann's? Doctors were arrogant everywhere. Owen made this intensivist thing sound like a rather new specialty. That meant Hong-Wei had been the young resident, fighting veteran doctors for the right to do his job. Every day. No wonder he had run away.

Except it wasn't St. Ann's that brought him peace, he'd said.

Feel this, Simon. I'm not a fantasy. I'm standing right here in front of you. Begging you.

Simon clapped a hand over his mouth.

What have I done? Why in the world did I turn him away?

Because I'm scared. Because I'm terrified to do anything that might be a risk, and because I've conditioned myself so well to doing nothing but what I'm supposed to do, even if I know it will never make me happy.

He stared at the man in front of him, finally understanding happiness—real happiness—had been offered to him and he had refused it.

Please, Hong-Wei, let me not be too late.

He brought the blanket to Zhang and spread it over him with trembling hands as Hong-Wei continued to attempt to soothe him in Mandarin. Hong-Wei stayed with them as they moved Zhang to the ICU, though on the way he sent a tech to collect Mrs. Zhang, and she arrived in the ICU room as they did, breaking into a sob as she rushed to her husband's side.

Hong-Wei spoke to her for some time, and a little to Mr. Zhang, though the patient was still slightly dazed. When Hong-Wei finished, he called in the ICU nursing staff and addressed them.

"I've explained to the Zhangs what will happen overnight, telling them to trust the staff and go along with what you ask as best as they can. They know some English, and Google Translate is going to help you out to some degree, though it's also going to be inaccurate."

One of the nurses raised her hand, wide-eyed and panicked. "But what language do they speak?" When Hong-Wei seemed briefly taken aback, she added, "I mean, you're from Taiwan, right? But you can speak to them? How are we going to talk to people when I don't know what language to use?"

"I'm speaking Mandarin. But look up Chinese on Google Translate because that's what they file it under. Both terms are correct." He put a hand on her shoulder. "It's all right, Bethany. Breathe. You can do this. You only need words like 'toilet' and 'water' and 'blood pressure' and 'breakfast.' If you don't know how to say it, show Mrs. Zhang the word and she'll figure it out. You'll probably end up teaching each other things. It'll be fine."

Once Hong-Wei got the nurses settled, he said one last goodbye to the Zhangs, who thanked him profusely—Mr. Zhang in a bit of a daze, Mrs. Zhang with tears—and then it was time to leave.

It was almost four in the morning at this point. If they stayed much longer, they'd greet the first nursing shift. Simon could have left after the surgery, and there was no need for him to have gone with Hong-Wei to the ICU, but the truth was, he wasn't supposed to be in the hospital at all, so he felt like the protocol was off anyway. He wasn't sure what to do with himself now. He wanted to talk to Hong-Wei, but he wasn't sure how to start.

The easiest route would be to give him a ride, to have Owen drop the two of them off, and it had been his original plan, but first he had to be able to get close enough to the man to offer. The second they left Zhang's room, Hong-Wei was beset by people—nurses, other doctors, even Owen and Jared. The board of directors hadn't left, and neither had Erin Andreas or Beckert. Everyone kept coming up to Hong-Wei, asking him questions about the surgery, about being an intensivist. They drew him down the hall, away from Simon and into a world he couldn't access, the elite world of doctors and administration.

As they disappeared around a corner, Simon heard Beckert say, "Your car still hasn't arrived, has it? Let me give you a ride home, Jack."

Too late, Simon. You're too late.

After he collected his coat, Simon roamed the halls, searching for Owen and Jared. He couldn't find them. He couldn't find anyone. The doctors and administrators must have taken Hong-Wei to some conference area. No way Simon was going in there.

Feeling weary and heavy with regret, he fired off a text to Owen. *I'll be in the locker room whenever you're ready to go.*

Simon pushed open the door and sat on one of the benches between the lockers, draping his coat beside him before cradling his face in his hands. If it wasn't so late and they didn't live quite so far, he'd walk home. He wanted to get to his bed so he could have a good, hard cry. He wanted to put this day behind him, to not have to stay here a second longer and think about how he screwed up, how he'd hurt Hong-Wei, how he'd turned away, quite possibly, a chance at the relationship he'd always dreamed of. It was probably proper penance, though, that he had to sit here alone and wallow in his mistake. Hong-Wei shouldn't be the only one to suffer. Simon deserved this, and so much more.

When the door to the locker room opened, Simon sat up and gathered himself as best he could. Either this was Owen come to collect him, or some other staff member, and in any event, he didn't want them seeing him in this state. He lifted his head to offer a friendly smile as best he could, tucking away his misery.

His smile fell away, replaced by shock. Hong-Wei stood at the edge of the lockers, wearing his lab coat. He looked so worn out he could barely function, but he was also lit by some kind of low-banked fire, and the flame, though weak, was aimed at Simon.

Hong-Wei leaned on the lockers, supporting his weight against his shoulder, his breath uneven as if he had rushed to arrive. He stared at Simon with a fevered intensity. "I know you told me you don't want me to disturb your peace. I'm trying not to. The problem is, I don't back down well, tonight being exhibit A. You turning me away led me to finding Mr. Zhang in time to save him, which I'm grateful for, but working beside you tonight, the way you knew just when to support me without being told, without words, the way you were the single person who never questioned me—I'm more inside out than I was when you walked away." His hands bunched into fists at his sides, his face a picture of misery. "I'm not going to lie when I say I want you—I want you so much I burn with it— but I'm willing to accept anything. How can they fire us for being close friends? My point is there are ways around this, and I want to find them, Simo—"

The rest of his sentence was lost as Simon rose, closed the distance between them, and stopped him with a kiss.

Simon threaded his fingers into Hong-Wei's hair, anchoring himself. *A second chance. This is my second chance. I can't waste it.* He opened his mouth over Hong-Wei's, pressed his body in close, telling himself, *Let go, just let go and give in to this, stop letting fear drive you*, but he couldn't stop shaking. The smell and taste of Hong-Wei enveloped him, filling his senses, but he couldn't escape his terror.

Hong-Wei broke the kiss, cradling Simon's face. "You don't have to do this. I told you, I'll do whatever you want."

"I *do* want this." Simon clung to Hong-Wei's shoulders, resting his forehead against Hong-Wei's. "I'm so afraid. It's not only the hospital policy. It's everything. I'm so ridiculous. I'm sorry. I can't—"

"I can." Hong-Wei stroked Simon's face, brushed his lips across Simon's in a gentle kiss. "You don't have to be strong, Simon. Let me be strong for you. Let me protect you. Let me take care of you and cherish you."

Simon felt weak in the knees. He swayed on his feet. "Hong-Wei."

"I can keep you safe. I promise." Hong-Wei kissed Simon's eyebrow, breath tickling Simon's skin.

"Just stay with me. I'll do everything else. Only say you'll keep me from feeling so alone."

Simon knew Hong-Wei's promise to keep him safe wasn't possible, however much he might yearn for it. Even if it were possible, he couldn't ask that of anyone, not with the kind of burden it would bring. That last plea, though, made him ache. Simon touched Hong-Wei's face, wishing he could draw his lover's loneliness out with his fingertips. The memory of how isolated Hong-Wei had looked in his command of the ER came back to Simon, filling him with a need to protect the man in his arms.

"You can't keep me safe. It's not what I need." Simon turned his face toward Hong-Wei's. "I'll keep you from feeling alone, though. Anytime that you want."

Hong-Wei cradled Simon's cheeks for a moment, then took him by the hand and led him through the locker room, past the toilets and sinks and around the corner into the separate room housing the showers, where Hong-Wei shut and locked the door.

"I don't want anyone to find us." He ran a hand over Simon's hair. "Or should we leave?"

They should leave, yes. They'd waited this long. What was a little longer? That was the proper reply Simon should give, the responsible one.

Except he absolutely didn't feel like being responsible.

I'm tired of being afraid.

He lifted his arms and looped his hands around Hong-Wei's neck, linking them to hide his trembling. "I don't want to wait."

Hong-Wei caught Simon's trembling wrist, stilling it gently. "Are you sure?"

Drawing a deep breath, Simon nodded. "The door is locked. It's fine." His thumb grazed Hong-Wei's hairline. "I want to leave with you too. But first…."

Don't be afraid.

He slid his fingers into Hong-Wei's hair.

Inside, in the damp and dark with the faint echo of faucets dripping around them, Hong-Wei pressed Simon to the tile with his body, opened his mouth over Simon's, and devoured him.

Simon moaned under the assault, and Hong-Wei plunged deeper, teasing his tongue alongside Simon's as he pinned his hands above his head. Shivering, Simon arched into Hong-Wei's grip as his fingers traveled down Simon's sides, mapping his ribs and muscles through his shirt, sliding to the small of his back where his fingers kneaded gently, coaxing Simon.

"Give yourself to me." Hong-Wei drew Simon's hands down so they rested on Hong-Wei's shoulders. He nuzzled Simon's nose and brushed his lips and cheeks with tender kisses, trailing nibbles along the evening stubble growing along his jaw. His knee nudged Simon's legs apart, urging him to sit on Hong-Wei's thigh as Simon's appendages turned to jelly. "Let go, Simon. Give me everything."

Let go. Simon wanted to. He wanted it to be like TV, where he didn't have to think, where the plot swept him away with a slight dramatic twist to a happy ever after. He couldn't trust that, though.

Could he trust Hong-Wei?

Simon gasped as Hong-Wei's mouth closed over his jugular, sucking lightly at the pulse. "I…I—" He shut his eyes and arched his back as Hong-Wei's hands settled on his sides, pinky grazing his rib, thumb finding Simon's nipple through his scrubs, languidly teasing it into an aching peak. The hands that had worked so hard to save Mr. Zhang now wrung pleasure from Simon with the same deliberation and confidence he had in the operating room.

Yes. I should be able to trust this.

Still, Simon struggled to surrender. They were in the locker room, in the hospital, where anyone could hear them. His coat was on the bench. People had seen Hong-Wei come in. What if they—?

Hong-Wei nipped at Simon's collarbone. "Stop panicking. I can feel your pulse rate rising."

A love affair with a surgeon is tricky. "I'm sorry. I'm trying. I really am."

Hong-Wei drew his index finger down to Simon's solar plexus. "Forget everything but me. Trust that I'll protect you."

"But you can't promise something like that. You can't keep another person safe. No one can keep anyone safe."

Hong-Wei lifted his head to gaze into Simon's eyes as he stroked his face. "You can't begin to imagine how much effort I'll make to protect you. From rumors, from the administration, from your own fears, if I can manage it. You're right, I can't guarantee anything. But if there's one thing I know I can do, it's work hard." He kissed Simon's chin. "I'll do everything in my power to keep you safe. For now, though, Simon, don't worry. Focus on me, give yourself to me, and let go."

The door opening in the locker room startled Simon, but Hong-Wei's stare held him captive. Simon gazed back at Hong-Wei, barely able to breathe.

"Someone saw Wu come in here, but I don't see him."

Hong-Wei's thumb grazed Simon's bottom lip, which was still swollen from his kiss.

"There's a coat here," another voice said.

"Not his, I don't think." It sounded like one of the board members.

Was this it? Were they about to get caught? Were they over before they began? Simon didn't know what to think. He was tired of trying to guess. Tired of being afraid. Tired—and a little angry—that every time he had a moment with Hong-Wei, some kind of signal went off and the administration came to stop them.

Focus on me.

"We should check the shower—maybe he's cleaning up."

Fear punched at Simon's gut.

Hong-Wei drew Simon closer. *Trust that I'll protect you.*

Simon shuddered, yearning to give in, certain he shouldn't. He shouldn't be able to embrace something that made him feel so wonderful. He couldn't really trust this. It couldn't be real. He should... he should....

I don't want to do anything but be with him.

The footsteps came closer to the door. Simon scarcely heard them. The only sound he was aware of was the beating of his heart, too fast, too irregular. He didn't need medicine to be cured, though.

He needed Hong-Wei.

Give yourself to me.

Simon shut his eyes.

When Hong-Wei's mouth crashed over his own, this time it carried him away on a warm, perfect sea, and he knew nothing else—only the warmth of his lover's touch and the safety of his embrace.

CHAPTER EIGHT

HONG-WEI WASN'T letting Simon change his mind.

Breaking the kiss for a moment, he kept one arm around Simon as he reached over the half wall to the showerhead next door, standing on tiptoe to turn the spray on full blast. Then he resumed kissing Simon, touching his face, running his hands over his body, pressing his knee between his legs to feel both the surrender of his muscles and the delicious heaviness of his desire.

In the other room, the footsteps stopped and the knob rattled. "Ah. Oh well. I suppose we'll catch him on Monday."

Hong-Wei took Simon's face in both hands, drawing slow, drugging kisses from his lips until they heard the door to the locker room close once more.

Maybe it wasn't a good idea to stay here after all. Simon had relaxed, had stopped fighting this—that was enough. He didn't really want to make love to Simon in a shower anyway. Pulling away far enough to press a kiss to Simon's nose, Hong-Wei stretched once again over the wall to turn off the water, then unlocked the door to the showers. "Come home with me."

He loved the way Simon clung absently to him. "How do we get out of the hospital? How do we leave the locker rooms?"

"You go first. Walk to the parking lot, then wait on the far side of the tall hedges. I'll come out in a few minutes."

Simon nodded, still leaning on him. "I need to tell Owen and Jared where I'm going. They think I'm waiting for a ride."

Smiling, Hong-Wei brushed his lips against Simon's ear. "Who do you think told me where you were?"

He worried Simon would fret, but it seemed when Simon let go, he let go. After one last kiss at the door, Simon exited the locker room without looking back, moving down the halls toward the parking lot. Once he was gone, Hong-Wei waited.

It was like being in school, though he'd never lingered for a lovers' tryst. He'd hidden in the locker room to escape his fellow students. When he'd first arrived from Taiwan, the bullying had been subtle but scary since he hadn't known anyone, and his English had been so poor. They goaded him into saying things they knew he'd pronounce incorrectly, and several boys had made a game of teaching him dirty or crude usage to get him in trouble. They'd laughed at the way he called his instructors "teacher" instead of Mr. or

Mrs. So-and-So, even though that was the way it was done in Taiwan.

Hong-Wei had learned to pick up on when his fellow students meant to lead him into trouble—"Jack, Jack, where are you, Jack? We want to talk to you…"—and he'd hide in the bathroom, or the locker room, or the janitor's closet. He went through a phase where he'd skip whole periods, copying the assignment from the board, taking his homework with him, sneaking back to turn it in. He'd steal out from his hiding spaces and erase his name from the attendance slips in the hall, then seek refuge in his private kingdom and work in peace. In his mind, it was the best solution for everyone. Unfortunately one teacher paid enough attention to notice she always marked him absent, yet somehow he was doing homework. Hong-Wei's parents were called in, which meant they had to take off of work, since his grandparents didn't speak enough English at that point to carry out the duty.

Oh, how he had been punished for his antics. Worse, he had to start attending class again. His grades took a downturn because he had to tune out the taunts and keep up with the pace the teacher set, not his own, and his parents became angrier.

He hadn't thought about it before, but it was probably then he'd begun to close off.

The old memories lingered as he left the locker room and wandered through the clinic, heading upstairs one last time to check on Mr. Zhang in the ICU. He couldn't remember most of it anymore, the coming over from Taiwan. He knew objectively it had been tough and had altered him irrevocably, but at the same time it felt far away and frothy when he thought about it, as if he had smoothed everything out until even the worst of it wasn't anything at all. He could imagine the ring of ten-year-olds staring at him as if he were a strange fish, remembered feeling terror and a deep yearning to leave, to go home to Taiwan, and yet it was so distant, as if it had happened to someone else, or as if it were simply a movie and wasn't real.

He had buried his feelings in his music, his outlet, his constant, his joy. When his father tried to take that away too, he feared the sucking void would be too much. Hong-Su had promised him he could come to love medicine the way he loved music. He'd learned to tolerate it, had mastered it, but he'd never found passion.

Not until tonight. Not until he'd been in the heat of the terror of not having what he needed, of giving aid to someone no one else could help, of being the only person who could do what needed to be done… and of having Simon and Owen and the others there to assist him.

Now he had Simon with him in other ways as well. Unless fear had gotten the better of him. Hong-Wei's heart seized at the thought, too raw from the day, too weary.

Please be there, Simon. Please don't have changed your mind.

Simon was at the hedge, waiting.

Clearly some of his nerves had returned, a few of his doubts, but he remained, and the sight of Hong-Wei apparently settled him, which didn't hurt Hong-Wei's ego in the slightest. Better still, when Hong-Wei closed the distance between them and ran a welcoming hand down his back, leaning in to press a kiss on the side of Simon's head, Simon didn't pull away or remark about anyone seeing.

That seemed odd, given how upset he'd been about it earlier. "Are you worried about people seeing us?"

Simon shrugged and kept his gaze focused straight ahead as they walked. "I am, but I don't want to be afraid. Besides, I decided I've either got to trust you to know how to hide us, or not."

Hong-Wei felt both the pride and weight of the flattery. "I have a lot of practice keeping secrets."

"Oh? When did you come out? Or is Owen right, that you didn't?"

He considered how to answer. "I didn't ever formally come out. In high school I was too terrified. In college I was too angry. In med school I was too busy. At some point my family stopped asking if I had a girlfriend and didn't offer to introduce me to nice girls any longer. I suspect my sister had a conversation with them, but maybe they figured it out another way."

"You did date, though, yes?"

"Date? No. Hooked up? Yes. Not often. In college I was still trying to avoid it, as if it were something I could put a lid on, and then in med school I was legitimately too busy. Plus I was always angry. Not really boyfriend material." He grimaced. "If you ask my sister, my broodiness made all the girls and some of the guys swoon over me. I didn't ask for that, and I didn't try to encourage it. I honestly didn't know it was going on. I was a mess."

"You sound like Jared before Owen got ahold of him." Simon smiled wistfully. "This was in middle school. Owen was our ringleader. Jared was one of the cool kids, angry and emo, but he says mostly he was terrified because he knew he was gay and wasn't sure how to come out. I was decidedly not cool, picked on and *called* gay even when I wasn't yet sure if I was. I was shorter then, and skinnier, and more concerned about whether or not my pimples would ever go away than who I wanted to ask me out. Anyway, one day the bullying was pretty bad, and I kind of freaked out. Then out of nowhere came Owen."

Hong-Wei could see it. "Was he all snarls and venom the same as now?"

"Oh, worse. He's calmed a lot. His home life was rough, and everyone was scared of him. He was a real thug. At first I thought he was going to beat me up. Imagine my surprise when he defended me instead, came out in front of the whole school, and said if they wanted to pick on a queer kid, they had to start with him."

Not the origin story he'd anticipated. "So how did Jared get involved?"

"Well, for a few days it was just the two of us, Owen walking beside me glaring at everyone. Then finally he goes up to Jared and gives him this long look, and the next thing I knew, Jared started walking with us. I guess it's been the three of us ever since in one way or another."

"And did *you* date?"

"I guess I've had a few relationships, but no one around here is interested in the things I am."

Hong-Wei raised his eyebrows. "Am I going to fail this test because I don't care for K-pop?"

"It's more… I don't know. It's hard to describe. I guess I feel like Belle in *Beauty and the Beast*. I'm not going to start singing about my provincial life or tell you about the books I keep rereading, but I definitely feel like the odd duck in the village. I don't want to leave the village, though, is my problem. I guess I want another odd duck to…." He stopped, frowning. "I'm losing my grip on this metaphor."

"To swim with you in the village pond?"

"See? You get it."

Did he ever. "I mean, not to brag, but I've been an odd duck since I was ten. Sometimes I feel as if every effort I make to assimilate, I only get odder."

"*Exactly*. I tried leaving—going to college, working away from home—and that wasn't right. I attempted to be the person my parents wanted me to be, the Simon Copper Point wanted. I hated myself. I focused on being a good nurse. I looked for local people to date I hadn't encountered yet. I tried not caring about dating. No matter what I do, I can't stop this crazy yearning for… something." One of his arms was still nestled alongside Hong-Wei's, but he tucked his other hand into his coat pocket. "The only thing I haven't done is travel. But it's like I told you before, I get overwhelmed by the idea."

"Maybe you should go with an escort."

Simon bumped him playfully with his shoulder. "Is this your not-at-all-subtle way of offering to travel with me?"

"It's my not-at-all-subtle way of offering to travel with you, yes."

"Well, where would *you* want to go?"

Hong-Wei would be happy to go anywhere with Simon, but he knew he had to give an answer. "To hear the Vienna Philharmonic. And the Berlin Philharmonic, and the London Symphony Orchestra. The Budapest Festival Orchestra too, but I wouldn't want to push things."

He glanced at Simon, expecting him to be wrinkling his nose or making fun, but he only looked thoughtful. "A symphony tour? Huh. It would make sense for you, since you love classical music so much."

"You'd hate it, though, right?"

"I didn't say that. They play in those gorgeous halls, right? With everyone dressed up? That means you'd go wearing something fancy too. Maybe a tux? If you're in a tuxedo in any of these events, hell yes, I'm going." While Hong-Wei laughed, Simon grew bashful and added, "The question is, would you go to a K-pop concert with me, if I went to a symphony with you?"

Hong-Wei imagined being in a throng of people, Simon clinging to his arm for fear he'd get lost, not knowing the language. That Hong-Wei didn't know Korean either didn't matter. He could learn. "Absolutely."

They walked in silence for a while, the companionable, easy kind allowing Hong-Wei to forget, for a moment, the crazy events of the evening. The air was spring-crisp, the trees whispered in the night breeze, and the few houses they passed were shuttered and dark, their occupants sleeping. Mostly they saw trees, because Hong-Wei had led them the long way to his place, past the golf course and patch of undeveloped land on the other side of the road, which in northern Wisconsin, Hong-Wei had learned, meant marsh or trees.

"You were incredible tonight." Simon leaned on Hong-Wei's shoulder briefly as they walked, putting a hand on his biceps. "That's what you're really trained to do, isn't it? I can't imagine how good at your job you'd be at a hospital with all the proper equipment."

"Excepting how terrifying it was to know it was Mr. Zhang who might die, the extra challenge of having

to solve the puzzle with fewer pieces was interesting."
Hong-Wei sighed. "Other than that, it was the same. People yelling at me, questioning whether or not I was doing my job properly, getting in my head, making it harder."

"Did you come here to escape?"

"I came here for a lot of reasons, but yes, that's one of them. I thought, maybe if I start over as a general surgeon somewhere quiet, it'll be fine."

Simon snorted. "I'm laughing at the idea of St. Ann's as somewhere quiet."

"It is, though. Medically. There are so few patients. I know the entire hospital staff on a first-name basis. The specialty clinics visit every few weeks. We send out more work than we keep."

"Don't think it doesn't drive the administration crazy."

"If they had a cardiology unit, it would change everything. They'd have more patients, more money, more doctors, and an entirely different kind of climate. The hospital should have one, by population density and the remoteness of their location."

"It's the expense. The county can't afford it, the state is a mess, and the hospital has been poorly run for too long."

Hong-Wei shook his head. "It's a shame. Do you think Beckert can turn it around?"

"I think Beckert and Andreas can. I used to think they were part of the problem, but after tonight, I've changed my mind. It seems as if the board might be the ones getting in their way."

"They have an opening now. Maybe someone new and exciting will be called up."

"Please. In this town?"

"Why not? It's an elected position, right?"

"Hospital board? When has anyone cared about a hospital board election?"

"Probably the last time other people asked them to care about a hospital board election."

"I suppose." Simon leaned on Hong-Wei's shoulder again. "I was going to say, I doubt what one person can do, but then I remembered watching you in the ER, and I realized I couldn't say that. Though so much of it, I swear, is you being you. I don't think I could take on the world the way you and Owen do. Your personalities are so big, so aggressive."

"It doesn't have to be about personality. When the world throws adversity at you long enough, at a point you decide you're going to confront it or let it wash over you. I've simply gotten good at confronting it."

"But see, I knew I could never confront it and win, so I let it wash over me. I'm not exactly bad at maneuvering underneath the wave."

"Yes, but are you happy?"

"Are *you*?"

Hong-Wei adjusted their entwined arms so they could hold hands, linking their fingers. "I am tonight."

His condominium was visible through the trees. They'd approached it from the back, and they wove their way silently around the sidewalk from the parking garage to the entrance, where Hong-Wei fumbled with the key.

"I never thought I'd know anyone fancy enough to live in this building." Simon glanced around at the darkened windows, his voice hushed. "Are your neighbors nice?"

"They're quiet. I don't know all of them, but I think there's a lawyer, a professor, and someone who works at the mine."

Hong-Wei opened the door.

Simon's eyes widened as he stepped inside. "Oh my goodness, it's so different from the last time. You have stuff, for one thing. But it's so beautifully arranged as well."

"Thanks to the decorator. But everything's not all here yet, either. I'm waiting for my stereo system and the cabinet. Here, leave your shoes on this mat. I have slippers you can borrow in this bag."

Simon removed his shoes and put on the slippers, then followed Hong-Wei into his house, still marveling. "The furniture looks so good all put together. But it hardly seems like anyone lives here. It's as if this is something out of a magazine."

Probably this was because Hong-Wei couldn't stand to be at home. Mostly he paced, then ended up at the hospital, working, in some kind of default mode. "I leave out dirty dishes. And look, there's my laptop on the coffee table."

"Yes, beside a neat stack of books and a perfectly folded blanket and gathering of throw pillows." Simon poked him lightly in the chest. "Do you do *anything* halfway?"

Hong-Wei captured Simon's finger and wrapped their palms together, drawing Simon closer. He liked the way Simon softened as Hong-Wei pulled him into his orbit, no more resistance in him at all. "No. I don't."

"So what comes next?" Simon fitted himself against Hong-Wei's body. "I mean beyond tonight. Or am I ruining things by thinking ahead?"

"I'd like to date you. To get to know you better."

"Yes, but how can we do that without getting caught? There will already be rumors if anyone saw me come in your door. What happens if we're seen?"

"We'll be careful."

"You don't understand this town. If one person gets the wrong idea, if anyone decides they know what we're doing, if they tell Andreas—"

Hong-Wei took Simon's hand and led him to the couch. He turned on the speaker as he passed it, then fiddled with his phone.

Simon touched the couch, momentarily distracted. "This really is nice furniture."

"It is." Hong-Wei connected the phone, started an app, and a piano ballad began to play.

Simon glanced sideways at him. "This sounds suspiciously like pop music. I didn't think that was your style."

"Most of it isn't. I have a few guilty pleasures, though, and JJ Lin is one of them."

The singer appeared in the song as if on cue, and Simon's eyes widened. "Oh—this is in Chinese." He listened for a moment, shutting his eyes, smiling. "This is quite lovely."

"Yes. There are a number of wonderful Chinese language artists, but they get outshone by K-pop and J-pop." He sighed. "Though my sister likes them all."

"I wish I knew what he was saying. It sounds sad. Is it?"

Hong-Wei ducked his head to hide a smile as he translated. "He's singing about his regrets. The English translation of the title is generally accepted to be 'If Only,' but it's not quite so simple. It's almost more accurately translated *sorry, there's no if*, or *unfortunately, if only*. He's saying he should have spoken when it was needed, should have been brave, should have been more understanding. There were so many ifs, but now all they have left is the consequence."

"All right. Point taken. I'm still nervous, but you're right." Simon leaned into Hong-Wei's shoulder. "Play me something else?"

Hong-Wei scrolled through his options. "More Mandopop?"

"Whatever you choose."

It felt like a trick question, so Hong-Wei went for more JJ Lin. "This one is called 'Twilight, the song which was not written for anyone.' He says it's the song for unsung heroes and the people who help you get to where you are."

Simon nestled closer. "This is beautiful. I feel as if it should be playing over an emotional moment in an Asian drama."

Hong-Wei glanced at the top of Simon's head. "That's right, you told me you watched Asian dramas before."

Simon shifted so he could meet Hong-Wei's gaze. "I do. A lot. When I met you, I thought you looked like Aaron Yan."

"I have no idea who that is." He was fairly sure his sister would, though.

Simon smiled shyly. "He's a handsome Taiwanese actor. One of my favorites."

Hong-Wei tweaked Simon's nose. "Simon Lane. Do you have an Asian fetish?"

He loved watching Simon sputter. "It's not a *fe-tish*. I simply appreciate Asian pop culture. Music and television."

"Anime too, I suppose?"

Simon grimaced. "Not really."

Hong-Wei thanked his ancestors for small miracles.

He played Simon some Jay Chou, "Dream" and "Love Confession," and he was pleased to see Simon sparkle with enthusiasm for a new vein of music. Simon had no idea what a balm it was for Hong-Wei to watch someone be so eager, so impressed, not once making the slightest joke about the language sounding funny to him. In fact, the only thing Simon said was how difficult it was going to be to sing along because he didn't want to sound foolish.

Hong-Wei flashed to the time in junior high when he'd stood rigid as a flock of students had passed around his headphones, laughing at the new Jay Chou song his sister had loaded for him, mocking it as they sang along. "*Ching-chaw, ching-chaw. Oh my God, is this what he actually thinks is music?*"

Simon had advanced it to "Lover From Previous Life," which had rap and a section that would have sent those kids into hysterics. Simon looked enraptured. "Wow. Does this have a music video?"

Hong-Wei wanted to kiss him. He didn't, but he did stroke Simon's back. "Yes, but it's more of a lyric video. The one for the title track of the album, 'Bed-time Stories,' is something to see."

"Can we watch it?"

They did—or rather Simon watched the screen of Hong-Wei's phone, and Hong-Wei watched Simon.

"Oh—" Simon turned to Hong-Wei, caught in a revelation. "This is Jay Chou? They reference him in my favorite drama. This is so great. Now I know why they wanted his tickets so badly."

Simon continued to listen, enraptured. When the video finished, Simon regarded Hong-Wei with shining eyes.

I want him.

I need him.

Hong-Wei decided there wasn't any reason not to have him.

He switched to a different playlist on the phone, and a piano played a few notes before a lovely soprano drifted over the room like a soft blanket, singing in English about the unrest inside her.

Simon glanced at the speaker, interested yet again. "What's this?"

"Dawn Upshaw. Celebrated American soprano. She can sing opera, folk, Baroque, contemporary— practically anything."

"It's pretty."

Hong-Wei stroked Simon's wrist, the perfection of Upshaw's voice soothing him as it always did. "I enjoy listening to her because I know what an accomplished artist she is, and in every piece she performs I can hear how much effort she puts into her work."

"Ah, I understand." Simon turned his arm over, giving Hong-Wei more skin. "Is that why you don't care for pop music? It doesn't have as much effort in your opinion?"

"It's more complicated than that. And sometimes more simple—it's mostly not my taste. Even JJ Lin and Jay Chou aren't my first listening choices any longer, though I appreciate them as Asian artists. But yes, I prefer classical works because of the exactness." A thought occurred to him, and he almost didn't say it, but he was staring at Simon's wrist, so open and exposed, and it spilled out. "I also like the way so few people listen to it or claim it as theirs. As if it makes it more my own."

Simon traced Hong-Wei's fingers with his other hand, making them a soft stack of fingers, palm, and wrist. "Play me your favorites? Share them with me?"

Hong-Wei shivered. He'd have been less unnerved if Simon had invited him to undress. "A lot of them aren't right for a romantic mood."

"But some of them are, I bet." Simon lifted his head. "Unless you don't want to. It's okay, if you'd rather not."

Hong-Wei could best Owen at his most confrontational, Jared at his bossiest, with the entire board trying to shut him down, but Simon's soft gauntlets, Hong-Wei acknowledged, would always bring him to his knees. He picked up the phone and searched for a song.

Soft, mournful strings echoed through the room, a single melody line arching, lifting through the violins and violas, then dying until it was picked up by the cellos and bass, then drawn back to the violins for one last note before a harp joined them in a sad pizzicato waltz beneath the soaring melody line.

Simon put a hand to his chest, his lips falling open as he stared ahead, breathless. "What's this?" His voice was barely a whisper, as if he might disturb the song if he spoke louder.

"'Solveig's Song' from the *Peer Gynt Suite*. *Peer Gynt* is originally a Norwegian play, which no one cares much about anymore because it's not great, but the music Grieg composed to go along with it was something incredible, and almost everything from the suite is well-known. You absolutely know 'In the Hall of the Mountain King.' This song, however, is from the end of the play, when the maiden Solveig is singing to Peer Gynt. He's run all around the world, and now he's disillusioned, sure he's a sinner and not worth anything, but she says he's not, and this is her lullaby to him as he dies."

Simon covered his lips with the tips of his fingers. "Oh, how sad."

"Yes, well, Gynt was mostly a jerk, and while it's noble for Solveig to have waited for him, she honestly could have done better."

Simon slapped his arm lightly. "Don't ruin such a beautiful moment."

Hong-Wei couldn't stop his smile. "You're a hopeless romantic, aren't you?"

"Yes. What about you?"

Hong-Wei's heart swelled, leapt, then darted shyly to the side. He stroked Simon's face. "Why don't you stay a while and see if you can figure it out?"

Simon shifted his position on the couch, leaned in closer, and pressed a soft kiss to Hong-Wei's lips.

Hong-Wei picked up the phone long enough to find a playlist, then drew Simon into his arms and kissed him back.

The light, lilting notes of Chopin's *Berceuse, Op. 57* wafted around them as Hong-Wei held Simon's face and drank softly, leisurely of those sweet lips. The kiss in the locker room had been passionate, but this one was all delicate worship, an unfolding. He let the master of piano lull Simon into the spell of the music, into Hong-Wei's embrace, and once Simon had surrendered, Hong-Wei invited him to dance. His draw on Simon's bottom lip was tender, the nuzzle of his nose slow and sensual. He stroked the downy hair along his jaw with deliberation before parting past his teeth to steal inside and startle his tongue, mating with it until Simon whimpered and sagged.

"*Hong-Wei.*"

Hong-Wei shivered, sliding his lips along Simon's chin, his neck, pressing a kiss on his lover's delicate throat. He'd become so fond of the way Simon said his name, to the point he longed for the sound now more than the sound of Hong-Su calling for him. He had three names in his life: Jack, the Western name his parents had given him, his family's private nickname for him, and Hong-Wei. His teachers and few friends, even the Asian ones he'd made in Houston, all called him Jack. Only at home and on trips to Taiwan was he Hong-Wei, the name wrapped in vowels Americans could barely hear, let alone pronounce. *Hung*-Wei would almost have been a more appropriate English spelling, but the true vowel was somewhere between *o* and *u*. Hong-Wei had always loved hearing his family call him by his name, like a secret they kept between themselves.

Now, though, there was Simon. Simon leaned on the *o* in *Hong*—*Hooong* Way, his American accent turning the *o* into a sort of foghorn, or the honk of a goose. If Hong-Wei corrected him, Simon would try to fix it, but Hong-Wei didn't want to.

Simon was the secret he would keep entirely for himself.

It thrilled him how compliant Simon was now, how readily he let Hong-Wei undress him, arranging him on the couch in nothing but his briefs, arms back, legs splayed to let Hong-Wei fit between them as he towered over Simon, admiring the view.

"You keep yourself fit." Hong-Wei ran his hands over Simon's chest, skimming over his nipples before caressing the hard planes of his abdomen. His gaze took in Simon's biceps as his hands roamed Simon's thighs. "I suspected you'd look lovely without your clothes, but your scrubs don't do you justice at all."

Simon shut his eyes as Hong-Wei continued to stroke him, but after a few moments of this he glanced up long enough to sear Hong-Wei with a steamy gaze. "I want to see you too."

Hong-Wei stripped out of his shirt. Simon's hungry look of approval filled him with pride, and he stepped off the couch to drop his pants, peeled off his socks, and his boxers too. He stood before Simon completely naked, Chopin cascading and ascending behind him, and waited.

Simon reacted like a starving man who had landed before a banquet. His nostrils all but flared as he raked Hong-Wei with his gaze, then let his hands trail where his eyes had blazed a path, as far as he could reach. "Oh my God, I've wanted this." His hand trembled as he reached for Hong-Wei's erect and bobbing cock.

Hong-Wei stopped his hand. "If you touch me there, Simon, we're going to explode."

Simon squeezed Hong-Wei's hand with a grip as firm as iron. "Then let's explode."

Hong-Wei picked up his phone, turned off the music, then caught Simon's other hand to lift him off the couch so they stood side by side.

"All right."

CHAPTER NINE

SIMON'S HEART beat a steady pulse in his ears as Hong-Wei took his hand and led him up the stairs. Vague details filtered through his awareness—four doors at the landing, one narrow, there appeared to be a closet and a bathroom on the right—then they were inside a bedroom, Hong-Wei's bedroom. The door closed. Hong-Wei pressed Simon against it, and the world fell away as Hong-Wei peeled off Simon's underwear, laced his arms over Hong-Wei's shoulders, and pushed their skin together.

Simon gasped, tilting his head as Hong-Wei kissed his neck, his skin prickling with goose bumps. *Thump, thump*, his pulse beat, growing stronger, louder. He felt as if he were in his own private dance club, pounding in his ears alone. Or perhaps the bedroom was their island, a private place where there was nothing else, only their bodies and their desires, and Simon's heartbeat was the drum.

Was it okay to escape like this, to forget everything and everyone and all the consequences being with Hong-Wei would bring? His conscience flared, interrupting the beat.

Hong-Wei's hands cupped his backside, tickling the downy hairs near his crack, and Simon's conscience evaporated in want and surrender.

"Mmm." A chuckle reverberated against Simon's chest before Hong-Wei smiled as he nuzzled Simon's chin. "You make the best noises."

He made noises? "What… noises?"

Hong-Wei's hands kept traveling over Simon's body, mapping the skin of his hips, ass, sides, back. He also continued to rain kisses along Simon's neck. "Little sighs and gasps."

Simon would have been embarrassed, except Hong-Wei was so… Hong-Wei. "I love your smile. It makes me dizzy."

Hong-Wei stroked Simon's cheek. "My sister nagged me that I never smiled anymore."

Simon's whole body was hot, an indistinguishable tangle of shyness and desire. "You smile at me all the time."

Hong-Wei cupped Simon's chin. "I know."

This kiss was carnal—slow, but deep and penetrating, the kind of kiss promising Simon he was about to be made love to like he'd never been made love to before. He tried to answer in kind, but mostly he was lost under Hong-Wei's assault the way he always was with this man.

In the end, all he could say in his kiss was, *I'm yours, I'm yours, do what you want with me*, over and over.

Hong-Wei seemed to know this without being told. He kept kissing Simon as he moved them toward the bed, tugging the sheets away with one hand, hitching one of Simon's legs around his thigh before laying him on his back, mouth closing over Simon's shoulder.

"Tell me what you want, what you don't want." Hong-Wei shifted Simon's other leg into the same position, opening him, then slid his hands up Simon's belly. "Tell me how to give you pleasure."

Simon could barely open his eyes or breathe, let alone form words. Everything came out as high-pitched sounds.

Hong-Wei's strokes slowed, and he kissed Simon's chest reverently. "Soft and sweet? Hard and rough? Which way do you want it?"

"Yes," Simon gasped, grasping for Hong-Wei, hands landing on his hair.

He laughed. "Which one?"

Simon threaded his fingers into the thickness. "Both."

More laughter as Hong-Wei hefted himself onto his elbows so he hovered over Simon's face. He traced Simon's forehead, nose, cheeks, and lips idly as he spoke, smiling. "I was last tested in January. Everything negative. Last partner was March. He told me he was clean, but of course, people lie." When Simon blinked at him and said nothing, Hong-Wei tweaked his nose. "You're a nurse. You of all people should know sexual health is important."

Simon shook himself out of his stupor, clamoring to recover so Hong-Wei didn't continue to misunderstand. "No—I know. I'm surprised, is all, because usually I'm the one trying to ask and then getting made fun of for it." He cleared his throat. "I was last tested in February. Negative as well. Last partner…." He blushed scarlet. "November."

"You're choosy as well as careful. Sexy." He stroked Simon's throat. "I'll get tested tomorrow for general STDs, since I haven't had the mandatory clinic test yet, but until then, we'll use condoms for blow jobs as well as sex." His fingers traced Simon's collarbone as he took Simon's earlobe between his teeth. "I want to keep you with me long enough for us to repeat the six-month AIDS test so we can ditch condoms altogether. I've never done that with anyone."

Simon fisted one hand in Hong-Wei's hair and clutched at his back with the other. "I never knew sexual history could be so erotic."

Grinning, Hong-Wei kissed his way down Simon's chest, lingering at his nipples. "I'd like to worship you, Simon Lane. Make you come apart so I can watch. I'll give it to you soft and sweet, with an edge of dirty." He ran a hand around Simon's hip. "Then when you're a shaking mess, when you're completely undone, I'll put you on your knees. You can hold on to the headboard while I give you a ride, until you can't hold on any longer. What do you think?"

Simon couldn't think at all. "Okay."

All right, he had *one* thought left, and it was that Hong-Wei had to be some sort of sex god come to life, that he had done a residency in Pleasing Your Partner, because somehow he kept kissing Simon's skin—legs, thighs, belly, hands, arms, fingers—while he produced lube from who knew where, warmed it in his hand, then slicked it over Simon's cock. The condom went on just as smoothly, and Simon gave Hong-Wei all the soft sounds he wanted as he spit on the outside and jacked him into a state of exquisite hardness. The only break in his sexual spell was when he began the blow job, then stopped, shuddering as he made a sound of disgust.

"Sorry. Clinic condoms. I'll get better ones tomorrow."

The mention of condoms and the alert of potential danger drew Simon out of his haze. "Don't buy in town. Get them online. From Amazon or somewhere that isn't going to say Condoms R Us on the label. Or I can ask Kathryn to get them."

"Ah, the lesbian condom decoy." Hong-Wei ran his thumb down Simon's perineum and dipped his head toward Simon's cock.

Simon arched toward him, clutching the sheets as Hong-Wei closed his mouth over Simon once more. Without slowing down, Hong-Wei kept up the blow job as he pushed a pillow under Simon's ass, hooking Simon's legs over his shoulders before working lubed fingers inside him. Hong-Wei's other hand roamed his thigh, stroking him reverently.

Breaking away from the blow job, Hong-Wei lifted his smoky gaze to Simon's. "Play with your nipples for me."

He waited for Simon to comply, his index finger deep inside Simon now, stretching him, teasing his prostate. Simon shivered and moved his hands, pinching his already erect nipples, unable to tear his gaze from Hong-Wei's.

"Beautiful. You're so sweet. Keep doing that for me. I want to look up while I suck your cock and finger you and see you playing with yourself." When Simon gasped *Oh* and turned scarlet, Hong-Wei's grin widened. "Sweet and dirty, as I promised you. This okay?"

Breathless, Simon nodded, and sailed away on a sea of desire as Hong-Wei lowered his head.

He'd never done anything like this. He'd had sex, yes; he'd played games, yes, had guys tell him to do things, but it hadn't ever felt this way. He'd never felt as if he were caught in a glass ball, spun into silk fibers and run through electricity, all while Hong-Wei smiled at him and told him he was beautiful. He felt like he could have come any second, but whenever he was close, Hong-Wei seemed to know and winked at him, whispering, "Wait for me, Simon," and Simon went back into his suspension of pink lust.

Worshipped. Yes. He felt worshipped. He'd never felt like this before in his life.

He didn't think he could have sex with anyone else again.

When Hong-Wei pulled out of him and turned him over, Simon wasn't sure how he was going to get on his knees or hold on to anything. He was a limp noodle. He'd been worshipped into a puddle. But then Hong-Wei lifted him enough to wrap arms around him, Simon felt the thick hardness of Hong-Wei's cock at his ass, and he began to reconsider his noodle-ness.

A hot kiss on the back of his neck sent electric shivers down his spine as fingers closed over his nipple. "Are you ready for your hard and rough?" Before Simon could try to form words, a hand gripped his hip, kneading, pumping heat into his blood. "You're so ready I can slide right inside you." He tugged at Simon once more, and when Simon gasped, he groaned. "God, your noises. They make me want to grab your shoulders, push you down, and claim you."

Yes. "Hong-Wei," Simon whispered.

He cried out as Hong-Wei bit his shoulder. "Yes. Say my name."

No one had ever bitten Simon before. If he didn't feel so underwater, he'd ask if Hong-Wei would do it again. All he could do right now, though, was what he was told to do.

"*Hong-Wei.*"

The next nip came at his back, accompanied by hot suction, and Simon answered the attack with a guttural moan. When Hong-Wei closed his mouth over him a third time, kneading his ass, Simon whimpered and pushed his hands to the bed. He was ready to get on his knees.

Hard and rough.

He shook as Hong-Wei helped him get into position, wrapping an arm around his waist as he lined himself up behind Simon. When he felt Hong-Wei's cock at his entrance, Simon hissed, flexing and pushing back, trying to take him in faster, but Hong-Wei eased himself inside.

"Too pretty of a view." He ran fingers down the bumps of Simon's spine as the last inches of his cock fit into Simon's ass. "I need a little more soft and sweet."

Simon ached with want and desperation. "Please, Hong-Wei."

Fingers grazed his shoulder, teased his nipple. "Again."

Simon's whole body shook. "*Please, Hong-Wei.*"

The thrusts were slow at first, but they were deep, and Hong-Wei hung on to Simon's waist with a rough grip that thrilled him. Simon clung to the wood, calling out, "More, please, more, Hong-Wei," until Hong-Wei had his hand beside Simon's, slamming Simon's body forward with each thrust.

Eventually Simon couldn't keep himself upright, and Hong-Wei supported him completely as Simon dissolved into pleas and sounds while he was fucked. When Hong-Wei grunted into Simon's ear, Simon came undone, shouting Hong-Wei's name over and over, filling the condom Hong-Wei hadn't ever taken off him, then stayed limp as Hong-Wei finished inside him.

When they were done, they collapsed onto the sheets together, a tangle of limbs, breath, and sweat.

Simon whimpered a complaint as Hong-Wei moved away, hissed as the condom was peeled from his body, then settled into peace as his lover spooned around him once more.

When Hong-Wei spoke, he sounded as drugged out as Simon felt. "If every time is like that, I'm going to have to start adding cardiac stress tests to my physicals."

Smiling, Simon lifted Hong-Wei's hand to his mouth and placed a weary kiss against his fingers.

WAKING UP next to Simon was almost as delicious as making love to him.

Hong-Wei vowed he would always wake up first when they slept together, because nothing was sweeter than Simon's face, softened and relaxed with sleep. For a half hour, Hong-Wei did nothing but lie on the pillow and stare at his lover. When Simon woke, he was almost as cute, blinking into wakefulness slowly, turning to Hong-Wei with a sleepy smile.

"Hey."

"Hey." Hong-Wei smoothed Simon's bedhead. He knew he was grinning like a fool, and he didn't care. "Sleep okay? As best you could get on four hours, I suppose."

"Amazing. I think your bed is a cloud. And it was a great four hours."

Hong-Wei couldn't stop touching Simon's face, hair, neck. "Hungry? I'll make breakfast."

Simon nodded, but he grabbed Hong-Wei's hand, kissing it and holding him in place. "When are you going into the hospital?"

"I want to check on Zhang by one. It's eleven now. I'll call and get a report while I cook. He's my only inpatient, though." Hong-Wei laced his fingers through Simon's. "Do you work this weekend?"

Simon shook his head. "Though my mother wanted me to go to something this afternoon for our church. Something she volunteered me for."

"Want company?" When Simon's eyes widened, Hong-Wei arched his eyebrows. "I'm not going to make out with you at the church picnic or whatever this is. I'll come as a regular attendee of the event and make a charitable donation."

"You don't know what it is. It's probably full of little old ladies."

"I'm a big hit with little old ladies."

He cajoled Simon until he relented, laughing, and then with a kiss Hong-Wei left him in bed and hurried to the kitchen, mentally mapping the best

morning-after breakfast he'd ever made. It wouldn't
be hard, since he couldn't remember making one before. What did Simon like, though? Of course, this
endeavor would be limited to the time he had and his
supplies. Which, given how long it had been since
he'd gone to the store, would be grim.

Had he bought flour? Please, let him have bought
flour.

No, he hadn't, but in one of the mountains of gift
baskets he hadn't opened there was, along with vanilla, a highly serviceable set of mixing bowls and a
whisk. After blessing the Presbyterian Women's Circle, Hong-Wei tied a towel around his waist—no one
had sent an apron, which was a shame—and set to
work. He had to step next door to beg a few things
from his neighbor, but when Simon came down the
stairs, he had coffee ready to plunge in the french
press and a stack of steaming pancakes waiting beside
a plate of bacon and scrambled eggs on the table.

The noises Simon made at the sight of the food
were almost as good as the ones he made during
sex. "Oh my God. Are you real? You're not real. I'm
dreaming I'm part of an Asian drama again, aren't I?"

Hong-Wei kissed the top of Simon's head as he
poured him some orange juice—not the brand he
would have preferred, but since it was borrowed, he
wasn't in much of a position to complain. "I wouldn't
know an Asian drama from a hole in the wall, so I
don't think so."

"Asian dramas are the best dramas. Nobody tells
more romantic stories. Hallmark would weep to be as
good."

"I'll take your word for it." Hong-Wei sat beside Simon and offered him the plate of pancakes. "I prefer to make them with buttermilk, but I didn't have it on hand. I was glad the neighbors had half-and-half and that the gift baskets had the right ingredients I needed to get most of the way there. I'll make them properly next time."

"You're telling me you made pancakes from *scratch*? My own *mother* doesn't make pancakes from scratch." Simon slathered a pancake in butter and syrup, folded it in half, and took a bite. He gasped. "Holy crap, I want to marry you." He dropped his fork, covering half his face with both hands now. "*Oh my God, I didn't mean to say that.*"

Laughing, Hong-Wei forked some of the egg and held it up to Simon's mouth. "Eggs are best hot."

"I promise not to propose after I eat them," Simon whispered.

"I promise to do better next time, then," Hong-Wei replied.

The entire breakfast went by in a delightful haze, until Hong-Wei glanced up and saw it was just after noon. Simon shooed him into the shower, promising to clean up and call Jared to collect him, and by the time Hong-Wei came downstairs at twelve thirty, Jared was in the kitchen, stealing the burnt remains of the bacon and making Simon blush. Jared didn't linger as soon as he saw Hong-Wei was ready, ushering him out to his car waiting on the curb.

"How's your patient doing this morning?" Jared asked as they pulled away.

"Fever's down a little. Mrs. Zhang is still there. The biggest issue right now is the language barrier.

When I called to check in this morning, the nurse said one of the women from the restaurant who speaks English had been by, but she had to get back to help prepare to open. The nursing staff is making do with pantomimes and Google Translate, from what I hear."

"Good, good." Jared rubbed his jaw. "I know this was a hot button last night, but seriously—is this hospital bill going to break them?"

"They'll have money, but nothing like what they need. Who does? It would break me without my insurance."

"The hospital will negotiate with them if they can make payments."

"It will probably be almost as hard to explain, the idea that they'll lower the bill and it's standard operating procedure, not a favor, insult, or something shady. It would be so fantastic if our country had a functional health care system."

"Didn't you know? We're the greatest in the world."

Hong-Wei smiled. "My parents think so."

Jared nearly drove off the road. "No way. You're pulling my leg."

"Oh, no. If my mother were here, she'd blister your ears for that sarcastic remark. She'd tell you all about the opportunity she and my family gained by coming here, how much she specifically received as a Taiwanese woman."

"Wow." Jared shook his head. "I guess that's something I've always considered my most prized privilege, to be able to rag on my own country when it's being stupid. Which I hate to say is often. It's not that I hate it, though. It's that I want it to be better."

"As a naturalized citizen—well, one raised by *my* parents—I understand where you're coming from, and there are times I agree with you, but I also can't disagree with my parents either." He shifted his gaze so Jared couldn't see his face, but his voice still grew thicker. "My family gave up a great deal both to bring my sister and me here and to make sure we had the education we did. There's no way I can ever pay that debt back."

"Well, you've done an amazing thing with the education they gave you. That has to count for something."

Bitterness threatened to choke Hong-Wei. "I threw away the celebrated career I trained for. How have I done an amazing thing?"

Jared took so long to reply Hong-Wei dared a glance at him to see what was wrong, and he was surprised at the intensity on his friend's face. Jared kept his gaze carefully out the windshield as he spoke, but the quiet passion in his voice resonated inside the confines of the vehicle. "Last night you saved the life of a man who would have died if you hadn't been a doctor here. I can rattle off at least seven surgeries and at least that many consultations you've done that have changed lives. And you've been here how long?" He pursed his lips. "I get that it looks fancier for you to be at Baylor or Mayo or somewhere with a better reputation. But a life is a life wherever you save it. Owen and Kathryn and I came back to Copper Point because we knew better than anyone how hard it was for somewhere this small and this remote to get good doctors. Simon chose to be a nurse here despite the fact that he could get paid better with stronger union protection in neighboring states. Maybe the people here don't always understand the gifts we're giving them, but we do. I was under the impression you did too."

Emotions overcoming him, Hong-Wei looked away again. "I do understand." A *but* formed in his mouth, but he didn't let it out.

He worried Jared would hear it anyway and chastise him again, but blessedly he changed the subject, his tone brightening. "It looks as if things went well with you and Simon?"

Though Hong-Wei's knee-jerk reaction was to tell Jared it wasn't his business, he certainly wasn't going to try to say so after such a dressing-down. "Yes. Thank you for your help."

"All we did was tell you where he was going to be. You kids figured the rest out yourselves." He glanced across the seat. "How are you going to play this?"

Hong-Wei frowned at him. "What play is there? We hide it, obviously."

"Glad you're thinking in terms of there being an *it* to hide."

Now Hong-Wei was annoyed. "Of course there's an *it*. Simon's not the kind of guy you fool around with."

"We're keeping you, Jack, you know that, right? I mean, Owen and I already basically had a meeting about it, but we're *really* keeping you." Jared sighed and squared his shoulders as he pulled into the hospital parking lot. "All right. I know we've already had the *it's a small town after all* discussion, but tonight you need to come over for a sleepover, and before you get to be handsy with our resident nurse, you need to come to a fully clear understanding of what *lying low in Copper Point* means."

Hong-Wei rolled his eyes. "Come on. You can't tell me people haven't had clandestine relationships in this town before. Don't give me that smug look either. Absolutely there are queer people here you don't know about."

"Oh, those are fighting words."

"Those are *arrogant* words. You were the three amigos who came out, yes? There were plenty who didn't."

"Yes, and I know who they are."

"You know who *some* of them are. That's the thing about secrets, Jared. By definition, they're things no one else knows. I get you think everyone here knows everyone else's business, but I promise you they don't."

Jared put the car into a parking spot and turned to face Hong-Wei, eyebrow raised. "Is this your way of telling me you have bigger secrets than the fact that you're a board-certified intensivist?"

Hong-Wei pinched the bridge of his nose. "It's so clear to me now why Simon didn't want to date you. The friend part is still a bit of a strain, to be honest."

With a snort, Jared punched Hong-Wei in the arm and got out of the car. "I have three patients to see, but I suspect they'll take me half the time you'll end up spending with yours. Text me when you're ready to go, okay?"

Mr. Zhang was awake when Hong-Wei arrived, bleary but able to answer a few questions. It was difficult to tell if he was slightly delirious still from his fever or if he was being effusive in his thanks to Hong-Wei because he'd nearly died. In any event, his vitals were good, Hong-Wei liked how things were progressing, and most of his job was being present with his patient and his family. Mrs. Zhang didn't ask many questions, but she listened intently, agreeing with every instruction Hong-Wei gave her about what Mr. Zhang should and shouldn't be allowed to do for the near future. She didn't fight him on how long the hospital stay would end up being, which was good. He hoped she wasn't planning on being polite to his face and slipping out quietly when he wasn't paying attention. Of course, right now Zhang would have difficulty slipping anywhere but the floor.

The nurses were less skittish about dealing with a patient and family who didn't speak English than they'd been the night before. Kevin, the nurse working ICU, grinned when Hong-Wei asked how communication was going.

"Mrs. Zhang actually knows a few words here and there, more than she lets on. I think she's mostly embarrassed at how poor her English is, but once she hears us try to butcher Mandarin, she changes her tune pretty quickly." Kevin shook his head, holding up his hands. "Man, my hat is off. I listened to the Google Translate lady say some of those words twenty times, and I still couldn't make some of those sounds."

"Every human baby is born with the capability for all language, but as we age, the brain shuts off things we don't need, so when we try to come back and learn them later, it feels impossible. You should hear my grandmother try to say anything with a *th*."

"Yeah, but you have almost no accent whatsoever. You're from Houston, but you sound like a news anchor. You absolutely don't sound Southern."

Hong-Wei shrugged. "We worked hard to fit in, to sound like our peers."

"Still, this is crazy, us waiting until we're in high school to start learning languages in the US." Kevin leaned on the counter. "Anyway, I'm having fun trying to figure it out, and Mrs. Zhang is patient. Also, the hostess who speaks English is sweet. I keep trying to find out if she's single."

Hong-Wei wasn't getting involved in that one. "Keep me informed if anything changes."

Jared took him home, though he wanted to take him straight to the house the three of them shared. Hong-Wei refused. "I need a quick nap before I go to this thing with Simon. He's coming to get me at five."

Unsurprisingly, this got Jared's back up. "*Where* are you going with Simon at five?"

When he heard it was a church social function, Jared started on his rant about exposure in small towns again, but thankfully they were at Hong-Wei's condo by then, so he simply got out of the car and walked up the steps, yawning. He set an alarm with enough time to get ready and passed out on the couch with Benjamin Britten playing in the background.

By the time Simon arrived to collect him, Hong-Wei was rested and dressed in what he hoped was suitably casual and yet not too casual for whatever this was they were going to. He had only vague memories of the church functions his family had attended during what his sister called the family Bible Beater phase, having done his best to block them out, but the one tidbit he recalled about dress code was that it seemed to involve khaki pants and a button-down shirt. Since it was chilly, he added a light blazer, and a bit of cologne because he wanted to intoxicate his date. He hoped it was an adequate presentation.

The way Simon's eyes widened and raked Hong-Wei head to toe when he opened the door told him he'd chosen well. Maybe a little too well, since Simon ran his hand longingly down Hong-Wei's arm after he closed the door, gaze lingering on his waist. "I wish we could bow out of this, but I really can't. My mother would guilt-lecture me for a week straight."

"It's fine. I haven't met many people outside of the hospital, so I'm hoping this will give me a chance to change that."

"Oh, it should. There's not a lot of options for things to do in town unless the college has something going on, which they don't this weekend, so it's whatever's showing on the two movie screens and our fundraiser. You should meet a decent cross section of residents."

Hong-Wei brushed a kiss on Simon's cheek. "Shall we get going?"

Simon held on to Hong-Wei's shoulders, leaned into his neck to inhale deeply, and shuddered. "God, you smell good."

The church parking lot was indeed packed when they arrived, as was what Simon called the fellowship hall, a large public meeting and socializing area beside the main sanctuary. It was full of people mingling over punch and cookies as they placed bids on silent auction items, the sale of which would help an Indonesian village that had been devastated by flooding. A quick glance around the room told Hong-Wei his memory of what to wear to a church had been correct.

Being in a Christian church for the first time in so long, even simply for a social occasion, affected him more than he'd bargained for. He truly thought he'd buried those old memories deep enough they'd never resurface, but here he was, thirty-two years old and sweating as if he were still twelve and waiting to be found out for being gay. He did his best to talk himself out of the irrational feelings, pointing out if he avoided images of the crosses, it looked like any other meeting area, almost. There weren't that many in the fellowship hall, which was a relief, and honestly there were so many people, he could easily focus on faces instead of religious symbols. To his surprise and delight, a few of the women wore hijabs. Did this mean Copper Point was more diverse than he'd known?

This joy turned out to be short-lived, as when he approached the group they belonged to, he learned the women were visiting artists-in-residence at the college, staying only another two weeks. They were musicians, members of a traveling chamber orchestra to be precise, guests of the director of music at Bayview University.

He was Indian-American.

"You must be the Dr. Wu we keep hearing so much about." The man, who couldn't be more than thirty, smiled politely as he shook Hong-Wei's hand. "It's a pleasure to meet you. I'm Ram Rao."

"Please, call me Jack." Hong-Wei nodded to the members of the chamber orchestra mingling with other community members. "Are your guests scheduled to have a concert? I'd love to attend if I'm able."

Ram brightened. "Yes, tomorrow afternoon. I'll get you a ticket."

Hong-Wei almost asked for one more for Simon, then thought of Jared's warning. "Can I get a few extra? I'm happy to pay, of course." He hoped Owen and Jared were busy and wouldn't be able to come along.

"Absolutely not." Ram's cheeks were flushed with excitement. "Think of them as my welcoming present. Also, I'll admit, I'm hoping they can be a bribe. I'm our band director at the college, but I'm also trying to get a community quartet going." He rubbed his cheek ruefully. "Recruitment hasn't gone as well as I'd like. I know you're friends with Owen and Jared, who both played in high school in the last gasps of our school orchestra. Jared was a cellist, but I already have a cellist, a violist, and one violinist, but I'm missing the other. I'm one of the violinists. Owen was a fairly decent violin player, from what I've been told, but I can't get him to join."

Ah, but sometimes victory was sweet. Hong-Wei hid a smug smile in his Styrofoam cup of terrible coffee. "No need. I'd bet my new car I'm a better violinist than Owen is."

Hong-Wei could practically *see* the stars forming in Ram's eyes. "Please tell me that's not a joke."

"Not in the slightest. I nearly majored in music instead of medicine, but… well, first-generation immigrant parents."

Ram held up his hands in a say-no-more gesture. "I have to sit in the car for a good twenty minutes every time before I go to a major family gathering, getting my courage together because I know everyone's going to make comments about how I didn't go into law as I was supposed to, and now I'm teaching at such a small college in the middle of nowhere. I know

they mean well, but still. I spent a lot of time in high
school wishing I were a blond quarterback named Da-
kota with parents who looked the other way while I
went out drinking."

Hong-Wei could have kidnapped Ram then and
there and spent the night getting to know the man. Instead, he gave him his business card from the hospital,
wrote his personal cell phone number on the back, and
encouraged him to get in touch about his quartet or
anything else as soon as possible.

Simon came up to him as he was leaving the musicians. He smiled, but the gesture didn't quite reach
his eyes, and he looked as if he wanted to lead Hong-
Wei away by the arm but knew he couldn't. He indicated the hallway with his head, and Hong-Wei followed him, though he was taken aback when Simon
took him into the sanctuary.

Hong-Wei's heart tripped a beat, and not in a
good way. "Why are we going in here?"

"Because I want to talk to you in private, and this
is the one place nobody is."

"But this is *the church*." Hong-Wei truly hoped
that didn't come out like *the death pit*, but Simon
seemed too distracted to notice.

He glanced around, then yanked Hong-Wei inside
by the hand, letting the doors close behind them. "It's
no big deal. Nobody's in here, and there's no service
or anything right now. I want to talk to you."

It was a pretty big deal to Hong-Wei. The room
was dark, except for the altar, which glowed haunt-
ingly from the front of the room as Simon drew Hong-
Wei away from the door. Hong-Wei tried to turn away
from the huge backlit cross, but it somehow felt better

to keep his gaze *on* the damn thing, lest some night-mare spring out of it. "I'm really not comfortable in here. Can we leave?"

Simon stopped looking borderline annoyed and drew away, blinking. "Are you... sweating?"

He was, damn it. Hong-Wei wiped at his brow. "I *don't want* to be in here, I said."

Still surprised, but subdued, Simon nodded, taking his hand. "All right. Let's go outside. Do you want your coat?"

No, the cool air would feel wonderful right now. "I'm fine."

Simon led Hong-Wei out of the sanctuary, and after a trip down a hallway, he took them out a side door to stand on a cement landing beside some bushes. Hong-Wei let out a sigh of relief, and Simon turned to him.

"You were really nervous. You weren't being polite about a church sanctuary or reverential or anything. You were scared."

Hong-Wei hadn't wanted to have this conversation—ever—but they were here now. He stared into the inky shadows of the church's playground, trying to find the place to start the story. "When we first moved to Houston, my parents joined an evangelical church to better fit in. It was one with a number of other Asian members, which was the only real reason we went. I found it jarring, though, and since I was just figuring out I was gay while having recently moved to a new country, the whole experience is a kind of horror film in my memory. I don't know what was worse, the feeling that I was being indoctrinated into a cult I didn't believe in, a religion I'd never subscribed to in any way before at all, or having to swallow their antigay sermons. They told us how we were going to hell if we weren't saved, that people who didn't believe would be burned in fire. I didn't understand how rational-thinking people willingly went to such places or why my parents had us attend. My grandparents eventually put their foot down and had us quit, because they felt we should remain Buddhist, but we went long enough I got a few mental scars. I don't care for Christian churches much. Usually I simply avoid them, and I didn't think it would be a big deal to come here, but the sanctuary in the dark was a little more than I could take."

"Oh. Wow." Simon seemed at a loss for words, which made Hong-Wei regret even more that this whole thing had come up. "I mean—I'm so sorry that happened. I can't imagine."

Hong-Wei was pretty sure Simon couldn't, which was fine. He didn't want Simon to know. *He* didn't want to know, to remember, to talk about it, not for another minute. "What was it you wanted to tell me?"

Simon wasn't done, unfortunately. "You don't have to worry—this isn't that kind of church."

Hong-Wei thought about letting it slide, he really did. Except Jared was right about one thing. Copper Point was a small town, and this sort of thing was going to be an issue again. In the end Hong-Wei decided if he wanted to be with Simon, they might as well face this demon now. "I do understand not all Christian churches are the same. You'll have to forgive me, though, for not being interested in the differences at this point. I still have nightmares about those years sometimes."

He braced for Simon to be sad or defensive, but he only nodded, looking weary. "I'm sorry. I have the feeling all your bullying stories are ten times more intense than mine, now that I think about it, and it makes me feel… sorry. Angry, helpless, ridiculous, and mostly sorry."

"It's not a contest, you know."

"Obviously it's not. But…." He sighed and tucked his hands in his pants pockets, fixing his gaze on the light above the door. "Well, I feel like a complete idiot for hauling you away from the fundraiser to be jealous of Ram."

Hong-Wei did a double take. "Ram? Why—because I was talking to him? But we were discussing the artists-in-residence and his community quartet."

"Yes, but Ram is cute, and my ex." Simon's cheeks were red from more than the cold. "I saw you give him your number."

Hong-Wei laughed, warmth blooming and spreading through him despite the cool air. "You think I'd cheat on you on our first date?"

"Of course *you* wouldn't, but Ram—"

"Doesn't stand a chance."

Simon stared at Hong-Wei for a long, hungry second before speaking. "I sincerely wish I didn't have to help my mother for another hour. I truly don't."

Hong-Wei wished he dared kiss Simon's knuckles. "How did you get away from your post?"

"I bribed my sister. I need to get back, though, because she left her kids to mind my refreshment station, and I'm going to catch the devil from her."

"Then by all means, let's get you inside."

Simon closed his hand over Hong-Wei's. "Are you okay? I won't be upset if you need to leave."

"I'm fine. I promise." Hong-Wei glanced at the little window in the door. "Do we need to stagger ourselves one at a time? I don't want to get a lecture from Jared and Owen."

"This is a pretty remote section of the church. If someone does see us, we can say we were discussing Mr. Zhang and needed privacy to make sure we didn't have any HIPPA violations."

Hong-Wei was a little surprised at Simon's change of heart, but he didn't question it, glad Simon had embraced their relationship and heartened that he too didn't think there would be that many barriers. This was an auspicious beginning.

When they entered the hallway, a short, pretty, slightly plump blonde woman stood waiting with her arms folded, and when she saw Simon, she pursed her lips and arched an eyebrow.

Decidedly pale, Simon turned to Hong-Wei. "Dr. Wu. I'd like to introduce you to my mother, Madeline Lane."

CHAPTER TEN

SIMON TOLD himself he had no reason to panic. Or rather, if there was, it was because his mother was angry with him for leaving his post and forcing his job on his sister.

Except something about her expression told him somehow she'd done exactly what Hong-Wei had said was impossible. She'd taken one look at the two of them coming through the door and known exactly who they were to one another.

He wondered if Hong-Wei had sensed the danger too, because he was playing it smooth, wearing a fourteen-karat smile as he bent over Simon's mother's hand. "Forgive me for stealing your son. I had a small work matter I needed to discuss with him in private, and then I got to talking with him. My apologies if I've held up the fundraiser."

Maddy's cheeks flushed as she reclaimed her hand. "It's quite all right, though yes, I do need Simon back. His sister needs to take the kids home. One of them is coming down with a fever, I think."

Now Simon felt terrible. "Oh no. Does she need anything?"

Hong-Wei also looked concerned. "Does she need a doctor?"

Maddy patted their shoulders. "Naomi's fine, and the kids will be too. Dr. Kumpel gave Ollie an examination, and he says it's a regular cold, but she needs to get him home and into bed."

Simon put a hand on Hong-Wei's arm, realized it might look bad, then lowered it. "I'll… catch up with you later." Leaving his mother and Hong-Wei in the hallway, he hurried to the fellowship hall, ready to apologize to his sister. He could only hope his mom didn't give Hong-Wei the third degree in his absence.

Naomi was already gone, someone filling in for her until Simon could return. After an apology for his prolonged absence, Simon resumed his task of handing out punch, but he was distracted, thinking about what Hong-Wei had confessed about his old church and worrying about what his mother had said.

She hadn't guessed they were dating, had she? How? All they'd done was walk through a door together. Literally. They did it all the time. Hong-Wei even had a good lie.

And then there was the insanity about Hong-Wei's Texas church. Simon could tell there was a lot more to the story, though the bit Simon had heard had hollowed him out. Should Simon ask about it, or would that be prying and he should leave it alone? Simon couldn't decide. The idea of a church telling a child they would go to hell was so horrifying to Simon, and yet Hong-Wei had spoken so calmly about it, as if it wasn't a big deal.

Maybe it wasn't to him. Maybe that wasn't the worst thing that had happened to him.

Your doctor sure likes his secrets.

"Simon?"

Simon jolted out of his thoughts and saw Rebecca and Kathryn standing in front of him, waiting for punch. "Oh. I'm sorry. I was lost in thought." He ladled them each a cup of punch and handed them over, trying to get his cheerful host expression back. "You have the evening off, Kathryn?"

"So far." She sipped at her punch, then all but pouted as Rebecca gave her a knowing glare. "*Stop.* Don't give me that look."

Simon glanced between them. "What's going on?"

Rebecca shook her head with a weary smile. "I want her to ask Hong-Wei to cover her call for a weekend. Just one weekend."

Kathryn set down her punch. "I keep telling you, it's not so simple. He has surgical call. He'd have to hand over regular call to take mine. Or we'd have to have a better system in place for someone to be on both surgical and OB call at once."

Simon ladled punch for another guest while he considered. "We used to do it, though. I don't think H—Dr. Wu would be against it."

"See?" Rebecca shook a finger at her wife.

Kathryn sighed. "I know, but I don't want to ask him right now. I was about to, and then he had the whole thing come up with Mr. Zhang. Now the board—" She glanced around and lowered her voice. "I should shut up."

Simon leaned forward. "The board what?"

Kathryn spoke so only he and Rebecca could hear. "I heard the board is all excited about him being an intensivist, and they want to capitalize on it. I don't know how much call he'll be able to take."

Rebecca grumbled and drank her punch.

Simon frowned. He hadn't heard any of this. Something told him Hong-Wei hadn't either, and he wasn't going to like it.

He thought about how to bring it up to his boyfriend all through the rest of the evening, and he was still pondering it as the event closed down and his mother approached his table. "Simon, honey, help me load some things into my car."

Catching sight of Hong-Wei across the room, he waved a *be right back* before following his mother into the kitchen, where she stacked boxes into his arms. "Did the fundraiser do well?"

"It did fine."

Okay, she seemed a little curt.

Doing his best to keep up a brave front, Simon forced a smile as he followed her from the kitchen to the car. "Well, I'm glad to hear it. It was a nice turnout. I'm sure the committee—"

"Simon, sit in the front seat with me for a second, please."

Simon stopped short and stared at his mother, but since she was getting into the car, there was nothing to do but follow suit. Once the doors were closed, he faced her, ready to ask what was going on, but before he had a chance to so much as open his mouth, his mother spoke.

"If you're seeing that surgeon the way I think you are, you need to be a lot more careful."

Simon couldn't breathe.

His mother stared straight ahead at the dashboard. "I suspect you thought you were being cautious, but you're a terrible liar, honey. You always have been. People already whisper because Dr. Wu hangs out with the three of you so much, and since you're all gay, they assume he must be too. Don't lecture me about that assumption being ridiculous. This town is ridiculous most of the time. I thought maybe you just had a crush on him. Then I watched the way you reacted when he talked with Ram, and at this point it's clear you're either dating him, or you think you have a shot. I don't know who else got an eyeful, but you need to mind yourself. I don't want you to lose your job."

Simon melted into his seat. "I thought I was being careful."

"I'm telling you it's not enough." She sighed and leaned back, rubbing her cheeks. "Somewhere in heaven, your grandmother is laughing so hard right now."

"It's this stupid rule. Why can't we date people at the hospital? And why would Grandma laugh at this?"

"The hospital-wide edict is a bit strict, but it's not bad to say people shouldn't have superiority over each other and be romantically involved. Such policies are common in a lot of workplaces."

"We do fine." That was a bit of a lie. They hadn't dated twenty-four hours yet. "You still didn't answer my question about Grandma."

She turned in her seat to better face him, clearly gearing up for an unpleasant conversation. "Because I'm having the same talk with you as she did with me when I was having an affair with your father while he was still married."

Simon's eyes bugged. "She—you—he... *what*?"

"You heard me right. Your father was still married when we met. He was in the process of getting a divorce, but it was messy because of the kids and the business, and Grandpa Lane was angry because he felt your dad should have tried harder to save his family. Here I was a secretary at the accounting firm to boot. Grandma Petersen told me to quit and come work for the furniture store, or we'd get found out for sure. Eventually we both quit the firm, but we didn't make our relationship public until his divorce was final. A lot of people suspected, but they let us have our fiction because we'd played by the rules."

Simon felt as if he'd had the wind knocked out of him. "I had no idea. Literally no idea. Does Naomi? Rob? Lia?" He tried to think if his siblings had ever dropped any clues about this that he'd naively missed, but he couldn't come up with a thing.

"No one knows but your father, Grandma, and you, and since Grandma's not with us, now it's just you, your father, and me. Well, and as I said, the people who suspected us." She patted his leg. "I became quite good at hiding how I felt for your father in public. Now I'm going to teach you how to do the same."

By the time she let him out of the car, everyone had left except for Hong-Wei, Jared, and Owen. The three of them stood by Jared's car, talking about when Hong-Wei's vehicle was due to arrive, and when they saw Simon approaching, they waved. Simon waved back, still dazed. He wasn't sure where to look or what his face gave away, so he avoided making eye contact with Hong-Wei as much as possible.

"We're all going to the house." Jared aimed a finger at Hong-Wei. "Don't think you can weasel out of our conversation, either."

"Wouldn't dream of it." Hong-Wei stood beside Simon, not touching him, but Simon could feel his body heat. "We'll catch up with you."

Owen frowned at Simon. "You feeling okay?"

His mother was right. His face was an open book. Simon did his best to school himself. "Fine. Just tired. It was a long night."

Winking at him, Owen opened the door of Jared's car. "We'll be sure to put you to bed early, then."

Simon did his best not to panic as they walked across the gravel. No one else was around. No cars were left. It was only the two of them. Still, when Hong-Wei touched his elbow, he startled and stepped to the side.

"Simon?" Hong-Wei stood in front of him, calm but serious. "What happened? Talk to me."

"Can we get in the car?"

Hong-Wei stopped him as he headed for the driver's side, taking firm hold of his forearm. "Give me the keys. You're shaking life a leaf."

Simon handed them over without a word. In fact, he didn't say anything even once they were both inside, and Hong-Wei didn't press him. He also didn't take them to Simon's house, instead meandering a long path around the edge of town until they were driving out toward Arastra Park. Still neither of them spoke a word, not until Simon's phone sitting in the cupholder rang and the caller ID showed it was Owen.

"Leave it," Hong-Wei said when Simon started to answer. "They're just being busybodies. They know we're together, and they saw your face too. You don't have to force yourself, though. If you want to talk, talk, and if you want me to keep them off your back instead, let me know."

Hong-Wei calm was what undid Simon. Until then, Simon had been enthralled by Hong-Wei, swept up in their new romance. He admired him as a medical professional and as someone who had clearly overcome so much in life and done such amazing things. His casual vow, though, tipped Simon over. Such a small thing, Hong-Wei taking the keys because he'd noticed he was upset, making sure other people didn't bother him, promising to leave Simon alone if that was what he wanted—such a simple gesture, and yet this was the moment, Simon knew, that he'd begun to fall in love.

Which was likely why his voice wavered as he replied.

"My mom says she could tell we were dating right away, that I need to be more careful. She gave me some pointers on how to meet secretly with my lover without getting caught in Copper Point, which she has some authority on, it turns out, because she revealed to me for the first time she had an affair with my dad when he was still married to his first wife." Simon's gut clenched, and he tried to laugh, but the sound came out hollow. "Nobody knows that, so keep it to yourself."

Hong-Wei laced their fingers together. "Is the affair what's upsetting you?"

"No. It's a bit of a shock, but it was a long time ago." Simon loved the warm feel of Hong-Wei's hand. He squeezed it tight. "I can't put my finger on why I'm upset. Or if I'm scared or angry or what. Both, I think. And ashamed."

"Why ashamed?"

"I almost gave us away on the first day, and I was being petty when I did it."

"You were being *possessive*. I approve of this, for the record. I've never had anyone drag me away from another man before. It was thrilling. I love you thinking of me being yours. I thought I was the only one who felt that way."

His remark interrupted Simon's spiral of dark feelings. "You feel possessive of me too? But who in the world would try to steal me away?"

Hong-Wei grunted and lifted Simon's hand to kiss it. "Who or what are you angry at? Are you upset with your parents?"

"No. With this policy. But I can't do anything about it, which is why I'm scared." He stared out the window. "It dawned on me while my mother was talking to me how much work it's going to be to hide. How much we'll have to *lie*. I'm a terrible liar. I'll have to act like I don't have feelings for you when I do. When women or even other men flirt with you, I *can't* be possessive. I have to stand there and take it."

"Do you think I enjoy being flirted with by anyone but you?"

"Not the point."

"I know." Hong-Wei stroked Simon's hand with his thumb.

Simon tangled his thumb with Hong-Wei's. "This is making me realize how spoiled we are. Hiding like this, being afraid—this is how it used to be for all queer people. How it still is for plenty of them. Which is also why I'm ashamed, because it's finally hitting me this policy isn't going anywhere, so I don't know how—"

Simon cut himself off and shut his eyes.

Hong-Wei tapped Simon's wrist. "Don't back out. Finish what you were saying."

Simon didn't want to. *What if it's too bold?* He already felt tired and lost. When Hong-Wei stopped the car, turning to him and waiting with the same patience with which he'd begun driving, Simon caved and plowed ahead, accepting his fate.

"With this no-dating policy at the hospital, I don't know how our relationship is supposed to go anywhere." Panic made Simon scramble. "I don't expect you to feel the same way—"

Hong-Wei stopped him with a kiss, soft and tender on the lips. He lingered close as he spoke quietly. "We just got started, which is what makes it unfair to have such an unnatural roadblock to consider in advance, making us alter our behavior in a way that could affect the natural course of our relationship if it weren't present. Is that what you were going to say?"

A tear escaped down Simon's cheek, and he hurried to wipe it away. "Stop being so perfect and making me like you more, making me think about how much I want to be with you instead of how I should be smart. It isn't fair."

"Who said this was going to be fair?" Hong-Wei smoothed the hair around Simon's ear. "Besides, if I can't think straight around you, I think turnabout is simple justice."

With a sigh, Simon leaned against Hong-Wei's forehead, not stopping the tears as they slipped out this time. "I don't want to lose my job."

"I won't let you lose your job."

"It's not something you control."

Hong-Wei took hold of Simon's face, cradling him gently as he looked directly into Simon's eyes.

"I'll take care of you, Simon. I swear to you. No matter what happens. I'll keep you safe, as best I can." He stroked Simon's tears away with his thumbs. "And despite knowing you only see them as friends, every time you smile at Owen and Jared, I'll always keep a hot coal of jealousy roasting inside."

Simon really wasn't sure if he was crying in sorrow, fear, happiness, or relief anymore. All he did know was though his phone buzzed insistently for the next fifteen minutes, he wasn't breaking their kiss for anything.

By THE time Hong-Wei and Simon arrived at the house, Owen and Jared paced the floor of their living room, ready to light into Hong-Wei, but once they got a better look at Simon's weary and still-scared expression, their fury melted away and they became doting mother hens instead.

The four of them stayed up another hour together, discussing strategy going forward. Hong-Wei had originally harbored plans of making love to Simon, but it was clear his boyfriend was too wrung out to do much but be embraced in bed. While Simon found sleep easily, Hong-Wei was awake long after, and he wandered downstairs, thinking a glass of water might help him.

He discovered Owen with a bottle of expensive vodka instead.

Hong-Wei stopped in the doorway. Owen glanced up and smiled wryly.

"Don't worry. I'm only eyeing it fondly, wishing we had a second anesthesiologist or a nurse anesthetist so I could ask them to take call. I seriously thought about calling over to Ironwood and asking if they'd back us up with a surgeon and anesthetist if something came through so I could get wasted. Then I decided I'd stare at this label as a compromise." Owen waved the bottle at him. "Care to join me?"

Hong-Wei didn't know what he wanted to do. He was fairly sure his only real option was to sit in the kitchen and listen to whatever Owen was going to say.

Owen set the bottle down and reached for mineral water from the fridge. "This do you? Or you want something else? Simon always drinks tea."

"Water is fine."

Owen poured them each a glass. "A few years ago the union would have been all over this dating rule. Of course, thanks to all the bullshit politics going on in our state, the unions are toothless now."

Hong-Wei wasn't certain how to respond, so he drank his water.

"It's as if I'm fourteen all over again, except this time I honestly have no idea how to stop the bullies." He shoved his glass away from him, abruptly angry in a tight, controlled way that made Hong-Wei go still. "This is damn Andreas and his fucking prep school ideas. I want to punch his smug face in."

Hong-Wei understood for the first time when Owen said things like that, he wasn't being metaphorical. He really did want to punch people out, and probably had. Clearly Hong-Wei's role here was to calm the man down, even though it was *his* relationship on the line, not Owen's. "Erin Andreas might well be the mouthpiece for the policy, but he can't be its author. Or rather, if he came up with it, which isn't proven, it has to be rubber-stamped. He's the HR *director*. The CEO and the board are the ones making policy. Though it does seem like it's mostly the board."

Owen calmed somewhat, still furious but slightly thoughtful. "You're right. Ever since he and Nick took over, they've made this big show about the two of them being in charge of everything, but the truth is, the board calls all the shots. It's unlikely those old farts suddenly let two new guys run the place."

"Especially since one of them is a black man and the other is the president's son. Though it certainly looks good if they act as if it's a brand-new hospital."

Hong-Wei tapped the side of his glass. Owen stared at the ceiling. After a period of thoughtful silence, Hong-Wei spoke again.

"We should do some digging and see what we find out."

"Exactly what I was thinking. I'll poke at Andreas on Monday."

Good Lord. "I'll handle the digging, especially around Andreas. You only annoy the man. Besides, they're going to be up my nose about last night anyway."

Owen leaned over to grab a bag of potato chips out of a cupboard, straining his muscles against his

T-shirt. "They're totally going to try to get you to be an intensivist at St. Ann's."

This wasn't news to Hong-Wei, though he was realizing now the ways he could use this interest to his advantage. He reached into the bag absently when Owen held it out to him. "It's not practical at such a small hospital. Even if they could manage it, I wouldn't want to practice as an intensivist. The pressure of it was too much, which was why I stopped."

"Even though you were apparently so good God himself wanted you as his surgeon."

"I *am* that good, but this was part of the problem. All I wanted to do was practice, but it's not so simple. You saw how the other doctors reacted. They don't like being questioned. The competition is too insane, and I can't take it."

Owen snorted and threw chips at Hong-Wei's head. "What a load of crap. You're more competitive than I am."

"I am, but this was a whole other level. When I'm with a patient, I don't care about anything else, and I don't want to compete any longer. I can't handle trying to save someone, all while dodging hoops from jealous colleagues. I almost lost a little girl once because of it. My sister had to get me a Xanax prescription and an appointment with a psychiatrist not connected to Baylor. All I could think of, though, was how many times this was going to happen again."

"Okay, I'll grant you, that's trash, and it shouldn't have happened to you."

Hearing that made Hong-Wei feel a little better. He relaxed as he pressed on. "I didn't feel like I could be the doctor my patients needed. I hated admitting that. I hated letting the people who pressured me win, hated letting my patients and my family down, but I couldn't help it."

Owen frowned. "Wait. What do you mean, let your family down?"

"My family put me through college and medical school, and high school at that, since we went to a private school. I had tutors too, to help me with my English and to make sure I had the best SAT scores possible. I lived with my sister until I came here, and though I contributed to the rent, she still paid most of the expenses and made most of our food, including a lunch for me every day. I let them down with my failure." He shut his eyes, shame rolling over him. "What's worse is they won't say out loud that they blame me."

"Hold up. I don't get it. How is that worse?"

Hong-Wei knew Owen wasn't going to understand, but he kept talking anyway, mostly because he couldn't stop now. "Because I *failed*. I let them down. They should be scolding me, telling me to live up to their expectations, but they're so quiet. They're not even telling me to get married."

Owen shook his head. "I gotta admit, you've completely lost me here."

This wasn't about explaining to Owen anymore, only about confessing for the sake of his own heavy burdens. "It's an Asian family thing. I don't expect you to understand."

Nodding, Owen tapped his fingers thoughtfully on the tabletop. "Fair enough. I'm going to keep trying, though. Are you able to tell them any of this? Because it's clear you want them in your life."

"I wouldn't know how to start. And of course I want them in my life." Hong-Wei tipped his head back and stared at the ceiling. "My sister still contacts me regularly. Sara's the one who told me to focus on what made me happy, who helped me move here. I decided what mattered to me most was patient care, so I looked for a small hospital far away from Houston, somewhere unlike any practice I'd ever known. I wanted to go somewhere I couldn't imagine practicing as an intensivist again. That's how I ended up here." He clutched his glass, feeling almost cold. "I hadn't meant to say so much. I'm sorry if I burdened you."

"You didn't burden me, you goof. It's not your fault, though. I brought out the strong stuff for you. You didn't have any choice but to talk, drinking like this." Owen poured him more mineral water. "You have no one to compete with you here. For all the shit I give you, you laid down some world-class doctoring last night. I felt like I was back in my residency, and *you're* the one fresh out of school. About fifty times during that emergency, I barely knew what to do, and intellectually I understood you were scared shitless too, but you played the whole hospital like one of your operating room symphonies. The damn board loomed over you, and you faced them, all the while dealing with a crashing patient."

"Simon had just rejected me too." Hong-Wei narrowed his eyes at the bottle. "This *isn't* vodka, right?"

"Cheap sparkling water from Amazon. I buy it by the case." Owen cradled the bag of chips against his chest and eased back in his chair. "Look, I'm not going to tell you this thing with your family isn't important, but I will tell you I think you can make something of yourself in your own way here at St. Ann's. You just need to figure out what it is you want to do."

This was the same thing Jared had told him. "It can't be as simple as that."

"Well, I imagine fine-tuning the definition of the kind of doctor you want to be will take some time and focus, but I think you're on the right track, from what I've observed. As for the hospital, you're not going to have any opposition here. Oh, you'll have a few more doctors puffing up like they did last night, but not for long, because absolutely no one can hold a candle to you here, and you're amassing quite a backup team. So after that it comes down to the administration, and they're not going to be a problem at all. They're going to give you whatever you want, so long as they have the funds. It was clear you didn't have the setup you needed to do your job correctly with Zhang, but you're already the talk of the town, as you heard tonight at the fundraiser, I'm sure. You're the talk of the *county*. The word is out if you have a major medical emergency, St. Ann's is the place to go for it, which let me tell you *isn't* something people have been in the habit of saying. The board's going to be hot to think of how they can turn that into dollar bills. You need to think about what you want in exchange."

The answer to that was easy. "Simon."

Owen stared at him as he chewed the wad of chips he'd stuffed into his mouth. "What if it doesn't work out? What if you get tired of him?"

"I won't."

"What if he gets tired of *you*?"

Hong-Wei disliked thinking about that, but it was a practical question. "Then I'd at least like to know it was because we had a decent chance to have a relationship."

"Fair enough. That's a tough ask, though. I mean, I would personally love to see you be the one to up-end their idiot policy, but they've been so draconian, I have my doubts even this can shift them."

"Don't forget, either, how hard they resisted me in the ED." Hong-Wei propped his feet on an opposite chair and sipped his water thoughtfully. "I still wonder why. Both the policy, and that."

"You saw them. Bunch of old men who think they run the world."

Hong-Wei tapped his toe against the chair. "I think I'll invite Erin Andreas to lunch on Monday."

"You could ask Beckert along and kill two birds with one stone."

"No, I'd like to isolate them one at a time. Oh, but speaking of engagements—the four of us are going to the concert tomorrow afternoon at the college. Ram gave me tickets."

Owen grimaced. "No, because he'll bother me to play violin for him again."

Did Owen look tense as he spoke about playing violin, or was that Hong-Wei's imagination? "No worries. I already told him I'd fill in the position."

"Of course. You play violin on top of it all."

Hong-Wei smiled into his glass. "Since you're not trying out, I won't show you up. Not until the first performance anyway."

Owen tossed down the bag of chips. "That's it. You and I. Outside."

Hong-Wei laughed. "Absolutely not. There's no way in the world you could afford the insurance on my hands."

CHAPTER ELEVEN

AFTER HONG-WEI paid a visit to Mr. Zhang, Owen and Jared tested Simon all Sunday morning, asking him to react casually to Hong-Wei as he walked into the room. When they caught him looking a bit too lovey, they called him out and coached him into a more neutral expression. They tested out their efforts at the concert, then came back to the house to critique the performance: the one between Hong-Wei and Simon, not the musicians.

Hong-Wei noted they could make the job easier by designing casual contact signs of affection. They already had the elbow touch, and Simon added placing a hand on Hong-Wei's forearm. Easy gestures they could make while working that simply seemed like friendly contact but which would have extra meaning for the two of them.

More importantly, though, was the pact between Owen, Jared, Hong-Wei, and Simon to always be seen as a group. They went to great lengths to take Hong-Wei and Simon out individually, and Owen in particular hung on Hong-Wei's arm to the point he started some red herring rumors. Sometimes all four of them went out. Sometimes they were a group of three. They always ate lunch together, either dragging Simon into the doctors' lounge or joining him in the main cafeteria and putting on a public performance of unity. As far as Copper Point was concerned, Hong-Wei had been firmly adopted. Seeing him at the house, or any of them at his, was as common as rain.

The most troublesome part was when Simon and Hong-Wei wanted time alone. On the rare occasions Owen worked and Hong-Wei and Simon didn't, Jared simply found himself something else to do out of the house. What they truly craved, however, was to be able to go to Hong-Wei's place and be left in peace, which took some serious orchestration. The solution they came up with was for Hong-Wei to begin borrowing Owen's car liberally—continuing the rumor he was dating him, not Simon—and Simon would get into the back seat and lie down until Hong-Wei parked in the garage underneath his condo and closed the door.

"What would we do if your garage wasn't attached to your house?" Simon asked one night as Hong-Wei opened the door for him and helped him out of the car.

"I'd move," Hong-Wei replied, and Simon couldn't tell if he was joking.

Outside of their dating being an undercover operation, Simon felt a lot calmer about the situation than he initially had. He didn't like it, and he still felt uneasy about the massive boulder sitting in the way of any real future they could ever hope to have, but he did his best to live in the moment and trust Hong-Wei when he promised, daily, everything would work out okay in the end.

"I haven't had a chance to get Erin Andreas alone yet," he said one morning as they sat eating breakfast together at his condo, "but the glad-handing from the board has given me enough to do I'm almost relieved we've had to wait. They have some interesting ideas of what this hospital should be like, and some fascinating alternate takes on reality."

Simon paused with his bite of omelet halfway to his mouth. "What do you mean?"

"To start, they think they have some kind of leverage over me because I accepted a sign-on bonus. Bonuses can be paid back. I'm not their indentured servant for five years, and they don't have a stranglehold on my license. I've barely touched the money they gave me—something I did on purpose—and what I'm missing I could borrow from my sister or get from another hospital's sign-on bonus if I chose to go."

Simon's heart went to his throat. "You aren't considering leaving, are you?"

"Of course not. The point is they think they can control people, even when they actually can't. I need to talk to Rebecca again about how legal this dating policy truly is and where the loopholes might be. At the same time, I feel like I'm peeling away the edge of a rotten wall. I don't know if we can solve our problem without exposing the entire putrid structure, which will have some interesting consequences."

The whole thing made Simon feel slightly ill. He pushed his plate away.

Hong-Wei captured his hand and kissed it. "Don't worry."

Simon did his best to mask his feelings in public, to use their signals to show his love and be content with meeting and loving in secret. But as time wore on, his patience did too. He began to see couples everywhere he looked, people touching, holding hands, laughing, and he longed to do that too with Hong-Wei. He wanted to be picked up and taken on a date, to go grocery shopping together, to go to a movie together.

He wanted so many things. What he didn't want, however, was the situation he was in: forced to hide his relationship while falling deeper in love with Hong-Wei every day.

The day Simon and Jared were to go with Hong-Wei to pick up his car in Duluth, Simon could barely contain his excitement during his shift. Though originally Hong-Wei had planned to have it delivered, he'd decided to go pick it up himself to get away with Simon for the day, far from prying eyes. They were leaving as soon as Simon got off work, rushing to the dealership before it closed, and then Simon and Hong-Wei would have the entire evening out of town together. Hong-Wei wouldn't have call either, since they'd found coverage. Simon felt like he was about to be released from prison as he finally ended his shift, which was why when Susan Cardwell, the director of nursing, asked him to stop by her office before he left, he had to mask his displeasure.

Please don't do or say anything to stop me from getting out of here on time.

Susan smiled at him as he entered, inviting him to sit. "Simon. Thanks for stopping. Go ahead and close the door."

Closing the door was never code for anything good. "Is everything okay?"

"I wanted to talk to you about a few things briefly, is all." Her smile had that quiet, strained quality of someone about to discuss something uncomfortable. "You've become quite close with Dr. Wu, I've noticed."

Simon's blood ran cold, and he wanted to flinch, but his mother's warnings and all of the training with the guys paid off. "Yes, we're good friends."

She laced her hands together over her desk. "As your director, I wanted to remind you of the hospital's new policy about dating, and to make sure you're aware of the consequences of what happens if you're caught doing so."

Sweat ran down Simon's neck, but he leaned on the replies he'd been coached to give. "What is it that makes you think I'm dating anyone right now?"

"I didn't say you were dating. I only wanted to remind you of the policy."

Now Simon was terrified *and* annoyed. So she'd brought him in here to scare him? "How could I be anything *but* aware? Every time I turn around someone—I'm sorry, someone who's not a doctor—is getting fired for this policy."

Susan looked tired. "I'm only bringing this to your attention. I neither created nor endorsed this policy."

That he'd been dragged in on *pre*suspicion charges was more than Simon could handle. "Am I being watched?"

She sighed. "Simon, we're *all* being watched."

He was in a foul mood when he met Jared and Hong-Wei in the locker room, but he didn't say anything about the meeting until they were in the car. Once there, he gave way to his frustration. "She was trying to *make* me paranoid. I can't believe it."

"They're after all of us." Jared was alone in the front seat so Hong-Wei and Simon could sit closer together in the back, and he glanced at them in the rearview mirror. "Andreas came by with more of his memos today. If it makes you feel better, even the doctors are getting repeat ones now."

Simon leaned on Hong-Wei's shoulder. "I can't take this anymore."

Hong-Wei soothed Simon out of his bad mood by giving him an update about Mr. Zhang, who had been released the day before on the promise he'd come back for all his follow-up appointments with his new primary care doctor. "It turns out he's been a US citizen for the past five years, and he even speaks some modest English. He and his wife are both citizens. They were able to use the age exemption because of how old they are and how long they've had their green cards, so they didn't have to take the English aptitude test, but they've been studying English with the hostesses."

Simon frowned. "Wait, I thought you said he had a green card before. You sounded so certain."

Hong-Wei tweaked his nose. "I was lying to the board in case they had ideas about calling ICE, which they absolutely could have done. I had a *feeling* he had papers, but I didn't know for sure. I'm glad everything is fine, though. I'm trying to have Ram hook them up with someone at the college who can coach them more regularly." When Simon poked him in his side, Hong-Wei smiled and kissed him. "Ram isn't my type at all, but please keep being jealous."

"Oh my God, I can't wait to deposit the two of you in Duluth so I don't have to watch this," Jared grumbled.

Hong-Wei's car was indeed waiting for them, and Simon was impressed. It was a dark blue-gray, which the dealer called *gray mica*, and the interior was light gray with black accents. It felt decadent and luxurious to sit inside of it, running his hand over the dashboard and side panels as Hong-Wei signed papers and shook hands with the dealer. Soon enough, they were off, driving through Duluth with the in-car navigation system helping them on their way to the restaurant, which Hong-Wei insisted had to be the same one they'd eaten at the day they'd first met.

"I liked the food, plus it has sentimental value. It was our first date."

Simon laughed. "How was it a date? I was only picking you up from the airport."

"But you were enchanting from the minute I saw you."

"Now you're simply feeding me lines. You were annoyed with me when we first met. Don't try to tell me otherwise. You were so cold I almost couldn't bear it."

Hong-Wei looked slightly sheepish. "I was rattled, and frankly terrified. I couldn't believe the administration hadn't come. I worried you were there to insult me. But then all you did was charm me. I was glad no one else had come. I'd already decided I wanted to pursue you."

Simon put a hand over his mouth and stared at Hong-Wei as he navigated onto the highway. "You *didn't*."

"I *did*."

The idea that Hong-Wei had thought of dating Simon since the first day shook his entire world, and he was still preoccupied with the thought as they sat down to order. "You mean the last time we were sitting in this restaurant, you were thinking about how to ask me out?"

Hong-Wei smiled enigmatically. "I hadn't gone that far, but I wanted to get to know you better, yes. I thought it was convenient you would be my nurse, until I discovered the no-dating policy. Though I've always found it an annoyance rather than a reason to stop trying to win you."

Simon flushed. "You always talk about me as if I'm a prize."

"But you are, Simon. You're *my* prize."

Hong-Wei teased him throughout the entire meal, making Simon blush and laugh. They sat at a table, next to, not across from, each other, and they held hands, their knees touching, ankles flirting. Their waitress beamed at them, asking how long they'd been together, and before Simon could stammer out an answer, Hong-Wei explained how Simon had picked him up at the airport and brought him to eat at this very restaurant, and now here they were. She was so charmed she tried to give them free drinks, but when Hong-Wei explained they had a long drive ahead, she got them a dessert instead, which they ate together with a shared spoon.

Simon was fairly sure the waitress snuck a picture of them.

"You're in a better mood," Hong-Wei re
as they took a walk along the lake afterward. They had
to get going back to Copper Point soon, but it was a
beautiful evening, and both of them wanted to linger.

Simon leaned against Hong-Wei. "It's nice to get
away sometimes."

"Do you ever think about leaving? For good, I
mean. Moving away."

"No, I told you. At nursing school, all I could
think of was coming home. Which has always made
me feel so lame, but I can't change who I am."

"It's not the same, though. You were there for
school, and then you were waiting for Jared and Owen
to graduate. You weren't trying to put down roots. If
you wanted to go somewhere, you could do it. It's terrifying, yes, but once you get past the fear, you discover things about yourself you didn't know were there."

Certainly Hong-Wei had to be the authority on
that subject. "Do you ever think about how your life
would have turned out if your family had stayed in
Taiwan?"

"I can't imagine. My memory of growing up
there feels like a fairy tale or a dream. When we go
to visit, sometimes things are familiar, but it doesn't
feel like home. I'm not as close to the family that has
remained there, and it always feels like a strain, everyone so aware of how much money everyone else has
made, whose child is in what college, who has what
job." He grimaced. "Of course, Texas has never felt
like somewhere I belong either."

"That seems so lonely." Simon wrapped his arms
tighter around himself. "Do you still talk to your family, at least?"

"My sister calls me regularly, and I call her. I email my father."

The more they discussed his family, the more Hong-Wei seemed to become uncomfortable. Simon wondered whether he should press the issue, but the pain on his lover's face made him want to understand what was causing his distress. "Why don't you speak on the phone with your parents? Are they upset you left Houston?"

"It's… difficult for me, talking to my family. I know I let them down by not taking an intensivist position at a prestigious hospital like I was meant to do. I feel ashamed, too ashamed to speak to them." He looked out over the water. "Owen and Jared have both said I'm looking at it the wrong way, that I can make something of myself here instead, that I'm doing good work here. I want to do more of that. I want to do what Owen and Jared said, to transform myself here into a doctor my family can be proud of. I want to fulfill their expectations of—"

Though Hong-Wei cut himself off, Simon would have sworn he was about to say *marriage*.

With a deep breath, Hong-Wei continued. "I want to show them I can find a partner to have a long-term relationship with, someone they would approve of being part of the family. I want to do everything they expect of me, because I want to show them I've become the person they wanted me to be, the person they sacrificed for me to be. But I can't seem to let go of my failure."

Simon stopped walking and turned to face Hong-Wei, catching his hands. "I don't think it's a failure to realize you need to change directions. And even if you must view it that way, even if it's a stumble and a fall, it's one that led you to us. I agree with the others. You're doing good work here. I can't imagine your family wouldn't be proud of you. I know I am."

Hong-Wei ran his hand over Simon's hair, brushed his thumb over his cheek. "In case it isn't clear, you're someone I would be proud to introduce to my family. I hope that's not too much too fast. You make me happy. I hope I make you happy too."

Simon's heart turned over. "It's not too much. You *do* make me happy."

They kissed beneath a streetlight, soft and lingering like a movie. When Simon pulled away, he felt breathless and dizzy, and he truly, *truly* wished Copper Point weren't so far away. He thought he'd cool down when he got in the car, but all he could think about was leaping over the console and into Hong-Wei's lap. He kept scanning roadsides, trying to decide if there was anywhere they could pull off and have sex, but everything mostly seemed a good spot to get arrested. He was working up the courage to ask if Hong-Wei wanted to make a quick stop at a hotel when Hong-Wei pulled into one, a small midlevel chain of the type families usually stayed in.

"Let's go." Hong-Wei grabbed his bag from the back seat, full of his change of clothes from the hospital, and when Simon sat stunned in the passenger seat too long, Hong-Wei came around to open his door. "Come on. You don't get to look at me as if I'm a second dessert for the past five miles and expect me to wait until we get home."

Simon trembled, he was so embarrassed, but Hong-Wei had no such difficulties. He led Simon inside, where he asked for a room—the quietest one possible, away from the rest of the guests, thank you—then led Simon to the elevator. They rode up two floors with a father and two girls coming back from the pool, but for the last stretch, they were alone. Still, Hong-Wei said nothing, only held tight to Simon's hand.

Once they were inside the room, things changed immediately.

The door was barely closed before Hong-Wei was on him, mouth latched on to Simon's as he undid his pants and got him out of his clothing, breaking the kiss only long enough to peel off Simon's shirt and strip free of his own. Simon whimpered when their chests grazed one another, when Hong-Wei's hands skimmed down his sides to finish shedding his jeans and underwear and socks.

No one had ever wanted him like this. Men had longed for his body, yes, but they hadn't pursued him the way Hong-Wei had, not by half. They hadn't hidden him in the backs of cars, taught him how to lie. They hadn't taken him to the restaurant where they'd first met and bragged about him to the point they got a free dessert. They hadn't kissed him under the stars. They certainly hadn't wanted him so badly they stopped the car and rented a room.

Hong-Wei's mouth was sliding south over Simon's skin toward an inevitable trajectory, but Simon drew his lover's face to his, trembling. "I love you, Hong-Wei."

Turning his face to kiss Simon's palm, Hong-Wei closed his eyes. Then he opened them again as he looked up at Simon. "I love you too."

What had begun as frenzied lovemaking became slower, sweeter, though to Simon it still had an edge of desperation. He needed to connect with Hong-Wei more than ever, to show him he meant what he'd said, there was no one else for him. That despite this stupid rule, he wanted to date Hong-Wei seriously. His words didn't seem nearly enough, so he told him with his kiss, his touch, his body, with his passion.

"*Hong-Wei.*" Limp, sweating, clinging to his lover's shoulders, Simon tipped his hips up to grind against him.

"I'm right here, Simon." Hong-Wei paused in his descent toward Simon's groin to press a kiss on his abdomen. "I'll take care of you."

Fumbling for one of Hong-Wei's hands, Simon drew it to his mouth. "I'll take care of you too."

SIMON'S LEGS were shaky as they exited the hotel out a side door, and he slept most of the way home, nestled on Hong-Wei's shoulder as he played one of his classical Spotify playlists. He didn't protest when Hong-Wei moved Jared's car to hide his in the garage in an intent to stay overnight, because it meant they were able to hold one another all night long and have breakfast together in the morning.

He did blush, though, when, while he was prepping the OR, Hong-Wei came in holding a pair of borrowed surgical scrubs and explained why he wanted Simon to put them on instead of the ones he was already wearing.

"These are an older style, with a higher neckline." He leaned in closer as he cupped Simon's elbow. "My apologies. I misjudged how high I was marking you last night."

His entire body so hot with shame he was sure he would have registered a fever, Simon rushed out of the room, clutching the scrubs and scrunching his shoulders to hide his neckline, but not before he caught a glimpse of Hong-Wei's face.

The man didn't look sorry at all, only proud, possessive—and utterly in love.

CHAPTER TWELVE

ALL THROUGH June, Hong-Wei played a strange game of chicken with the St. Ann's hospital board.

On the surface they kept asking him probing questions about what it meant to be an intensivist, what he'd need to perform adequately as one at St. Ann's, but Hong-Wei understood what was really happening: the board, especially John Jean, was trying to work out how to use him, how to control him. As much as they loved the idea of what his talents could bring to their hospital, his power to take those talents away as easily as he had brought them to their door scared them much more. They kept bringing up his sign-on bonus, calling the five-year agreement a contract. Hong-Wei couldn't decide if they were that stupid or they thought he was.

Their wheedling didn't bother him half as much as the fact that he could not for the life of him get Erin alone. He didn't know if the man was avoiding him or if the board was keeping Hong-Wei from him. The latter seemed a bit too conspiracy theory, but when he shared the thought with Simon, he only laughed and declared he was a true member of Copper Point now, if he was thinking like that.

Hong-Wei didn't know what that comment meant, and frankly he was a little afraid to ask.

In early July he had a small victory: he convinced the CEO to go to China Garden with him for lunch.

"I've been dying to try the secret menu." Beckert rubbed his hands together as Hong-Wei drove them out of the parking lot. "Also to get a ride in your car. This is a nice set of wheels."

"Thanks. Not the flashiest, but it gets me where I want to go."

Beckert eased into his seat, running his hand across the leather. "I need to get a new car sometime. Heard you bought this online? I should do that. I never have the time to get anywhere."

"Jared and Owen helped me sort out what I wanted. I'm sure they'd help you as well."

Hong-Wei was surprised Beckert stiffened. "Nah, I bet I can figure it out."

Interesting. He wondered which one of them inspired that reaction.

The restaurant had a line of people waiting to be seated that ran out the door. Beckert glanced at his watch. "Should we go somewhere else? I have a meeting at one."

"No worries." Hong-Wei led him inside, nodding and smiling at people he knew in line. He was surprised at how many people he recognized and how many people knew him. More knew Beckert, of course, and the two of them were quickly caught up in a social whirlwind Hong-Wei hadn't meant to encounter.

Then Mrs. Zhang found them, and everything changed.

To Hong-Wei she gave an effusive, joyful greeting full of love and demands he come to her and give him a hug and a kiss, which he did, asking his auntie how she was doing, inquiring after his uncle. She thanked him for coming, then patted his shoulders and insisted he must be hungry and he needed to come and eat right away. Everyone around them had gone quiet, watching their conversation.

Hong-Wei indicated Beckert and continued to speak in Mandarin. "This is Nicolas Beckert, the CEO of the hospital. He'll be eating with me today."

Mrs. Zhang covered her mouth for a moment, then came forward reverently to take Beckert's hand. "Thank you very much," she said in English, her words choppy and slow, but precise. She gestured to the restaurant. "Please, come eat."

She led them past the waiting throng to an area in the back where, as they approached, servers were bringing a table from a storage room and making a space for them in a semiprivate area. While this was being set up, a waitress who spoke nearly perfect English asked them politely to please wait, Dr. Wu and his guest, and they would be seated as quickly as possible.

Beckert shook his head, mystified. "Does this happen every time?"

Hong-Wei nodded. "I used to try to stand in the line, but she gets so upset, I stopped. We have arguments over whether or not I get to pay for my meal, and sometimes I win, but with you here, there's no chance. You should know too whatever we order, extra food is going to show up."

"But… why? I mean, I know you saved his life, but it's your job."

"Yes, but it was *his* life, and he didn't believe in doctors. Also, they think I had something to do with the bill being lowered."

"Oh, you mean writing a lot of it off? That's standard procedure. We already assume they can't pay what's left. That they're making payments so soon is impressive. She's been in twice insisting on giving us money. We had to hurry up and figure out a payment scheme to satisfy her."

"You don't understand. They're going to die trying to pay their bill. It's about family and honor."

Beckert rubbed his jaw, grimacing. "I really kick myself sometimes. I grew up here, always seething about the way nobody ever saw racial injustice in this town. Now I realize how many times I've come to China Garden, seeing Zhang, his wife, and their workers as fixtures, not people and members of my community. I didn't think I considered them as such, but in hindsight, I know that's the term that applies to my thinking. I guess I assumed they didn't engage with Copper Point because they didn't want to. Now I know them personally, and I feel like a fool for taking so long to start that relationship."

Hong-Wei clapped his hand on Beckert's shoulder. "It looks like they're ready for us. Shall we?"

It hadn't been part of Hong-Wei's plan, but the Zhangs turned out to be the perfect icebreaker on so many levels, because Beckert couldn't stop talking about them, which led to the topic Hong-Wei wanted to get to anyway.

"I would get the bill lowered further if I could, but the board...." Beckert trailed off.

Hong-Wei dipped a dumpling in sauce with his chopsticks, avoiding eye contact to keep things casual. "You came to your position not long before I arrived, am I correct? Is this your first administrative position, or did you work elsewhere?"

Several walls went up, slow partitions being raised. "I worked as director of a few area nursing homes and with a local health care organization, but yes, this is my first hospital administrative position."

Hong-Wei continued to focus on his food. "I'm impressed at all of you who come back to your home-town to work, especially since it's so small."

"I used to have negative feelings about Copper Point, until I went away to college. There's about a fif-ty-fifty split, really, of people who graduate and leave, and people who graduate and stay or return. I don't know what it is that pulls people here, but something does. The bay, perhaps, though with the way they built the downtown, you can barely see it—you have to drive to one of the beaches to experience it proper-ly. Honestly, sometimes I can't figure out why I came back. In any event, here I am. For better or for worse."

Hong-Wei decided to push. "What are your hopes and dreams for St. Ann's? I know you can't magically make everything happen as the CEO, but surely you came here with at least a few goals."

Beckert shuttered again, but before he did, Hong-Wei saw such pain in the man's countenance he nearly startled at the sight of it. Then Beckert's smile smoothed everything away, his expression calm as if nothing bothered him at all. "Oh, I have some dreams, but mostly I want to see the hospital do well."

Hong-Wei didn't get much else out of him, and by and large they simply had a pleasant lunch. He didn't feel it had been a worthless endeavor, though, because despite a lack of specific progress, he felt more certain of his initial conviction that Beckert wasn't as much aligned with the board as he was stuck with them. At the same time, unfortunately, Hong-Wei didn't think the CEO was going to be of much help to their cause.

What surprised him was that when he brought this up to Jared as they went for a jog together one night, his friend became bristly. "I wish I'd known you were trying to get information out of Nick. I could have saved you time and told you he wasn't going to give you anything."

Hong-Wei cast an interested side glance at Jared. He would never have guessed moving to Copper Point would have been like descending into a soap opera. "I take it you know him as more than your CEO?"

"We were friends, back in the day." Jared practically spat the words.

"Sounds like a good temperament for a CEO."

"He'll pick the safe and cautious road even if it costs him his own integrity." Jared grimaced. "All right, I'm being unfair. My point is, don't back that horse."

"I don't think he agrees with the board."

"Oh, I already knew he doesn't agree with the board, and he had nothing to do with the policy. Nick probably took the job thinking those old geezers would die off and he'd be left standing right where he's always wanted to be. He's chumming it up with Erin Andreas, trying to make a new alliance, but in the meantime Erin is dancing to his father's tune, and that boy has more baggage than Louis Vuitton."

Everything kept coming back to that man. "I want to get Erin alone, but it's impossible."

Jared raised his eyebrows. "You think a conversation with him is going to change the dating policy?"

"I think a conversation with him is going to help me figure out what's going on with this board. I need better leverage, both for the dating policy problem and for their attempts to use my position as an intensivist to fit me into their vision. I'd like to make them part of my plans instead."

Jared shook his head, grinning. "Owen is right. We thought we were control freaks, but as in so many things, it turns out we're nothing when compared to you."

Hong-Wei kept his gaze on the trail ahead of him, focusing on matching his pace to Jared's. "Well, I never had any friends until I met everyone here, so that's one thing you can be better at than me."

Jared laughed and shoved him lightly across the path.

He occasionally had weekends off now. They were still rare, but not as impossible anymore, thanks to the bimonthly call relief rotation from Eau Claire. Orth was never one of the surgeons, which was fine by Hong-Wei, but plenty of others came to fill the Friday-to-Monday rotation, taking over not only for Hong-Wei but Kathryn as well. Never at the same time, since Kathryn couldn't bear the idea of a mother needing an emergency cesarean while the general surgeon was already occupied, a policy Hong-Wei agreed with. The odds of a problem were low, but they were present, and one life was one too many. Still, he sometimes took an evening or afternoon call for her during his free weekends, letting her get away to Duluth. He'd delivered two babies now, since the deal was he'd *take* her call, not give it to the fill-in surgeon, so now when he was out and about in town, in addition to the usual waves and greetings he got, he also got shown baby pictures and was given updates on his deliveries. And hugs. So many hugs.

He'd never had anything remotely like this happen to him in Houston.

Kathryn treated him to lunch the week after his date with Beckert—this affair was held in her office, not a restaurant, and it was delivery pizza from the dive Simon had told him the college students favored.

"Don't you dare tell Becca." Kathryn passed him a slice on a napkin as he pushed the door shut. "She hates it when I eat junk food. Carries on about how a doctor should know better. Pulls the 'heal thyself' line on me."

Hong-Wei held up one hand as he accepted the food with the other. "Wouldn't dream of it, so long as you don't tell Simon."

She grinned as they took their seats and dug into their slices. "How's it going with the two of you, anyway? I can't really tell, because you're doing an incredible job of hiding it. I love the subterfuge with having everyone think you're dating Owen, by the way."

"Things are going fine. Simon's troubled that we can't be open about it, though. I keep looking for a way to end-run the administration, but I'm still coming up short."

Kathryn's eyes widened, and then she laughed. "You're serious? You think you're going to take on, what, the entire hospital board?"

Hong-Wei focused on his pizza. "I don't need to take them on, precisely. I only need to get them to let me doctor the way I want and date Simon. Beyond that, they can do whatever they please."

"Well, let me tell you, they're going to do whatever they please regardless." She reached for a second slice and folded it in half before biting into it. "Simon gets angry because they prioritize doctors over other staff, which is true, they do. But they treat us like their tin soldiers as well. It's the way this town has always been run."

"I truly hate that phrase."

"What, 'it's always been that way'? I can't say I care for it either. I didn't say I don't think it should change. It's Copper Point's favorite excuse. I smelled it when my family brought us here, and I was only seven. Change is difficult for these people."

"Change is essential. This hospital barely exists. I haven't seen the financials, but they have to be bleak."

"Oh, they're awful."

"Then they need to focus on things like new doctors and new strategies, not archaic plans." He put down his slice and stared out the window. "It doesn't make any sense. I understand all these institutions are slightly insane, but this goes beyond anything. This is against their own survival. I expect better of them, especially Beckert and Andreas."

"Nick probably wants to do better, but he's hamstrung by his own self-doubt." Kathryn sighed. "Erin… I don't know what's going on with Erin. But I suspect it all comes back to his father. It usually does, with him."

"Has the board always been focused on controlling the staff?"

She shook her head. "Used to be completely the opposite, in fact. I assumed all this crackdown was their way of compensating and swing the other way." She reached for a third slice, but instead of eating it, she waved it at Hong-Wei for emphasis. "Here's the thing my grandma told me, and I remember it whenever people make me furious. Nobody wants to be a bad person. Nobody's *trying* to be evil. Everybody making you bleed is either bleeding themselves as well, or they think they're stopping someone else from doing the same. Even when they speak out of hate, underneath it is fear. I counted that as the wisest thing anybody ever said to me, and I think of it when I'm so pissed off I want to deck someone. I think it a lot about this administration. I figure they're messed up in a lot of directions, but if you trace back to their roots, they're attempting to do the right thing." She curled her lip and tore into the pizza. "Of course, they're also a bunch of old white guys holding on to power, so Grandma Mae might only take us so far here."

Hong-Wei traced his finger across Kathryn's desktop. "My grandmother said something similar to me when I got picked on at school."

"Why *do* people have to be so mean to each other, anyway? Every time I do the first weight and well-baby check, when it's just me and the newborn, I lean over and whisper, 'You be one of the good ones, okay?' Except you know they're all going to break my heart as I watch them grow up. Becca tells me I'm the biggest sap she's ever seen."

Kathryn spoke so much about her wife over lunch that by the time Hong-Wei went to his section of the clinic to meet with patients, his heart ached to see Simon. Happily, his boyfriend was at the nurses' station, talking with one of his colleagues. He smiled as Hong-Wei approached, pausing his conversation.

"Hello, Dr. Wu. Did you have a good lunch with Dr. Lambert-Diaz?"

"I did." He nodded a greeting to the other nurse, then slipped a quick brush of Simon's elbow. "When you finish, can you come to my office? I want to go over the afternoon's schedule."

It didn't take Simon five minutes to knock on Hong-Wei's door, and the lock was barely turned before he was in Hong-Wei's arms.

"We shouldn't do this at work," Simon whispered before wrapping his arms around Hong-Wei's neck and sinking into the kiss.

"I miss you." Hong-Wei took hold of Simon's ass with both hands and drew him in closer. "Come over tonight."

Simon laughed against Hong-Wei's mouth. "You stayed at my place last night."

"I know. But I miss you when you aren't around."

Simon sagged into him, resting his forehead on his neck. "Hong-Wei."

Hong-Wei cradled him close, drawing him into the kiss, which fueled his resolve all the more to find a route out of this mess.

One way or another.

SIMON FREQUENTLY wondered what it would be like to date Hong-Wei in the open.

On so many levels, they were doing fine the way they were. What Owen called their hide-and-seek system of dating kept them safe and content, able to see each other practically every night and, if you stretched the definition, go out now and again. Of course, when Simon had dinner in public with Hong-Wei, he had to be careful not to touch his hand or look at him too fondly, and Hong-Wei had to go on buffer dates with Jared and Owen, especially Owen, their red herring. But their system worked and allowed the two of them to be together and keep their jobs.

In private, they were as open with each other as they wanted. Once they were alone in Simon's room or together at Hong-Wei's place, they touched each other as much as possible as they shared stories about their present, whispered hopes for their futures, and confessed the secrets of their past as they ate takeout from China Garden.

"I used to want to be a marine biologist," Simon confessed one night as they lay twined together on Hong-Wei's couch, enjoying the expansive sound of his custom stereo.

"Hmm." Hong-Wei toyed with Simon's hair with one hand as he used the other to feed them each a bite of noodles from the carton Simon held on his chest. "What changed your mind?"

Simon chewed before he replied. "I realized I'd need to move to an ocean. Owen said he'd move with me, but it seemed so terrifying to go that far away. When he and Jared started talking about being doctors, I considered that as well, but I thought it would be too intense. I liked the idea of being support staff more."

"Doctors couldn't perform without nurses. Your job may not be as celebrated by society, but without you, especially in the operating room, I'd be hamstrung." Hong-Wei reached over to the table and snagged a dumpling.

Simon whimpered. "Oh, give me one of those, please?"

Hong-Wei did, but he tweaked Simon's nose with the chopsticks first. "You need another chopsticks lesson."

"I've been practicing. I swear. And I could do it, if we weren't lying on the couch. Are you telling me you want me to sit up?"

Feeling wicked, Simon tried to leave Hong-Wei's arms, smiling to himself when Hong-Wei immediately tugged him back into place—and fed him a dumpling.

Simon wiped the crumbs from his lips. "I've been meaning to ask you something, but I don't know if it's rude or not."

Hong-Wei raised an eyebrow. "Ask, and I'll tell you if it was."

Blushing, Simon averted his gaze. "Can I ask you what your sister's Taiwanese name is?"

"Of course. That's not a rude question. Her Taiwanese name is Hong-Su."

"Hong-Su." Simon tried it out a few times, attempting to mimic Hong-Wei's pronunciation. "Is it deliberate, that her name is so similar to yours? Because it sounds like you have the same start to your first name."

"It's customary to use the same first character for siblings, though it's an old way of naming, and not everyone does it anymore. My mother wanted to have the second character have the same meaning but use different characters. I would have been Hong-Wei, and she would have been Su-Wei, but my grandparents didn't like it. They wanted us to have traditional names, and so we do. Both of our first characters, Hong, mean *enlarge*, *expand*, *great*. My second character means *great*, *robust*, *extraordinary*, and her second character means *simple and pure*."

"From the stories you told me of your sister, both of you have characters which describe you pretty accurately. What does Wu mean?"

"Military and martial."

"I hope that doesn't mean your family fights a lot."

Hong-Wei kissed the top of Simon's hair, letting his chin rest there. "We have a few too many generals sometimes."

"Tell me about Taiwan. I don't know much about it, despite having watched so much television made there. Does it rain as much as it seems to on the shows?"

"It rains constantly. Sometimes for weeks without stopping. The monsoons can be incredibly violent too. We had one right before we moved away that wreaked devastation on our neighborhood. I recall so little about our life there before we left, but I remember being trapped inside, listening to the wind shriek and the rain pound against the house as it shook for days on end."

Simon couldn't imagine. "How do people cope?"

"The same as people everywhere. Taiwan has a number of earthquakes too. But the island has some incredibly beautiful landscapes as well. That's what Formosa—the name the Portuguese sailors gave it—means. Beautiful island." He sighed. "It's never as cold there, though, as it is here, and neither is Texas.

Everyone keeps warning me about winter and how much snow we're going to get. Frankly, I'm terrified."

Simon patted his arm. "Don't worry. I'll keep you warm."

Hong-Wei shifted so he could kiss Simon's cheek.

Simon's whole body tingled at the contact. Part of him wanted to nudge Hong-Wei toward taking this snuggle up a notch, but part of him wanted to keep enjoying this moment, because it was so perfect. He enjoyed touching and sharing with Hong-Wei as much as he loved being made love to.

He decided he was in the mood to tease his boyfriend. "So we're only going to listen to your music, are we?"

Simon expected a groan of protest, even a playful one, but all Hong-Wei said was, "Hook up your phone. Play whatever you want."

Well, now Simon felt completely sheepish. "I was only kidding. I know you don't like my music."

"I can learn to appreciate your music the same way you've come to accept mine. Go ahead and put on something you wish I'd give a second listen to."

Simon was nothing but a bag of regrets now, feeling awkward as hell, but he couldn't do anything but lean over and fumble for the music app on his phone. "Are you taking it this far to mess with me? Because that's an Owen-level move."

A hand down his spine soothed him. "I'm not messing with you. I've been thinking of how to broach this subject for some time. I'm glad you brought it up. Though I wouldn't mind if you opened your horizons to some Mandopop too."

"Well, I've listened to Aaron Yan. He sings as well."

"Ah, yes. The one I resemble. I'll play you some Mandopop, but first, let's hear your top three K-pop songs." When Simon gave him a pained look, Hong-Wei laughed. "All right. Your top five? Ten?"

"I'll give you a general sampling without giving them a superlative order." Picking his phone up off the table, Simon settled against Hong-Wei.

Simon waded through his files, searching for the best song to play first. He had his favorites, of course, but he wanted to select the right song to lure Hong-Wei into his world. He ended up with "View" by SHINee.

"I mean, I know it's not anything special." Simon tensed, abruptly aware of each note of the song, of every movement and breath of the man behind him.

Hong-Wei ran his hands down Simon's arms. "It's fine. It's a pleasant pop song. Do you know what they're saying?"

Simon did his best to remember. It had been a while since he'd looked up the lyrics. "I know they talked about tasting the light and seeing the color of the music, or something like that. About sixth senses, how the listener shouldn't hide anymore because tonight is the night. It's okay if it's a little rough, because it's a beautiful view. Take them to the beautiful view, etc. There's stuff about oceans, skies, and promises to show you everything."

"All right, then. So they're not holding anything back."

"Well, they're a boy band, and their roles are to be everyone's princes on stage, so it fits. Though for SHINee the story is sad. Their lead singer committed suicide. The pressure the producers and managers put on these guys to maintain their roles and keep up their images is insane. It got to him, basically. He was a vo-cal supporter of LGBT rights too, and the trolls online went after him. The whole thing made me so upset."

Hong-Wei continued stroking him. "That *is* sad."

Feeling as if he'd brought down the mood, Simon went in an entirely different direction for his second choice. He played "Peek-A-Boo," and three notes hadn't played before Hong-Wei chuckled.

"My sister loves this group. I can't remember the name, but it's something like cake?"

"Red Velvet. I love them. All their stuff is so great."

"Yes. As I said, she'd watch your dramas with you as well."

Simon tipped his head back to give Hong-Wei pup-py-dog eyes. "Will *you* watch my dramas with me?"

Now Hong-Wei had the look of someone wanting to get out of the question. "You're going to hit me with both in one night? Here I thought I was being so cool with the K-pop."

"Well, one could argue you were *too* cool with the K-pop, and now I'm feeling bold." Simon shifted to sit sideways between Hong-Wei's legs and bit his lip to stop his smile as he added, "Jared and Owen watch them with me."

All Hong-Wei's reluctance evaporated. "Pick your favorite show. We're watching it now."

Soon after they had a bowl of popcorn, a bottle of wine, and *It Started With a Kiss* playing on the television.

"So let me get this straight." Hong-Wei sipped at his wine. "This is the Taiwanese version of this drama, the *original* Taiwanese version which came out in 2005, though recently they made a Taiwanese remake of this same show. But first this story was a Japanese manga and a Japanese drama, and between the two Taiwanese editions it's seen a second Japanese adaptation, a Korean version, and a Thai version, the Japanese one last and consisting of two seasons. And this version we're watching also has two seasons. Did I get it right?"

Simon beamed at him. "You got it *perfectly*, and in one try, with the show playing in the background and everything. Owen and Jared have seen it seven times, I've explained it a million ways, and they still say it doesn't make sense."

"It makes perfect sense." Hong-Wei reached for popcorn. "As for understanding what's going on while the drama plays, it's not difficult. I mean, I understand the language."

"That's why I picked this version. Well, and because it's the best one. I think it's pretty faithful to the manga. In the Japanese versions she's Kotoko, not Xiang Qin, and they make a few other cultural changes with each country's version. I love this one, though. I love so many Taiwanese dramas. Netflix has a lot, but there are *so* many more on DramaFever. I can leave my account logged into your TV." He blushed. "I mean, I know you don't really want to watch them except with me."

"I love the idea of sitting here and watching shows with you."

Simon gave him a hard glare. "You're only doing this because you want to one-up Owen and Jared. Which I admit, I used to lure you in, but now all I can think about is you're secretly hating this, and I regret it."

"You shouldn't. Maybe I took up the challenge because of it, but now that you're tucked up against me, cheeks flushed and excited as you explain things about a show in my native language…." He trailed off, and Simon was surprised to see how soft and almost shy Hong-Wei's expression had become. "Well, let's put it this way. If *you* moved into my house in high school because of an earthquake the way the heroine in this show did, watched Asian dramas with me, and gazed at me like that, I'd have fallen in love with you a long time ago."

Simon's heart stopped, fluttered, and flipped over. He pulled back, staring at Hong-Wei, the show forgotten. "What—what did you say?"

Hong-Wei looked truly abashed now. "You heard me."

Simon's chest swelled, and he could barely breathe. "You just told me you loved me. During *It Started With a Kiss*."

Hong-Wei's whole face was red, and he couldn't meet Simon's gaze. "Yes, and I believe I've said I loved you before, haven't I? Now stop. Your reaction is making me needlessly self-conscious."

He had said so already, yes, but Simon almost wished this had been the first time, because *this* was an Asian drama moment come to life. Of course, if he looked at it another way, he'd now received two beautiful confessions from Hong-Wei. Who cared what order they'd come in.

He leaned in and kissed Hong-Wei sweetly on the lips. "I love you too. And I want you to know if I'd gone to your high school, I absolutely would have been your Yuan Xiang Qin."

They ended up watching the show all night long, Simon dozing occasionally because he was exhausted.

Hong-Wei, however, stayed awake for the entire thing because he was hooked. "This is so charming. Ridiculous, but charming."

Simon sighed happily. "I know. Nothing makes me feel better after a terrible day than to put on this show. In this version he's so in love with her—subtly so, but it's clearly present in the way it isn't in any of the other versions. Plus they play with each other. The director obviously let them riff and then kept rolling and put it in the final version. None of the other ones do that. So watching this means it's like visiting family. Nothing against my actual family, but...." Simon wasn't sure how to phrase the rest without sounding offensive.

"I know exactly what you mean. It's like the perfect family in a bubble, with contained, controlled reactions. The conflict is measured out with spoons. And since it's a romantic comedy, you know the ending, you know how it will resolve, so it feels safe. I understand why you love this. I can't say I mind it either."

They watched a good chunk of the show that night, and as soon as Hong-Wei finished his rounds the next day, they dove right back in, Hong-Wei turning the television on as soon as he had his shoes off. They ate more takeout and snuggled together under a soft throw on the couch as the drama raced ever closer to its thrilling conclusion.

Simon's heart felt so swollen with love and happiness. *This is what I've waited for. Who I've been waiting for.* This kind of understanding and sharing of his joy was so much more than he'd ever hoped for, and yet here Hong-Wei was, right beside him. He wanted to hug Hong-Wei, to press him into the couch and kiss him so passionately he'd never recover.

But it was almost time for the kiss in the rain, so he kept quiet.

When the show was finished at four in the morning, they stumbled up the stairs together, exhausted.

"I can't believe we watched the whole thing," Hong-Wei murmured blearily. "But that ending was worth it."

"Wait until you see the sequel. It's even better than the first one. At the end of each episode while the credits roll, they dress up as elderly versions of themselves and watch the highlight reel of the preview for the next one. Their relationship is a lot more developed, as are the ones of the other characters, and they tie so many things together. The ending is so incredibly moving too—I cry my eyes out every time. It's tragic, though, because there was supposed to be a part three, but it never got made. Ariel Lin, the actress who plays Xiang Qin, had to bow out for health reasons."

"Oh, that's too bad."

"You'll really be aching when you see the second season and realize you could have had more and I tell you what it was supposed to be. But it's still good, and in a way, the open-ended nature of it is good too. Also, Aaron Yan is in this, by the way. He was in the one we just finished, but he has a more prominent role in the second installment."

Hong-Wei cast a side glance at Simon. "He's not a doctor, is he?"

"No, he's Chun Mei's boyfriend. Ah Bu. The rich guy. This is his first role. It's not his best, but it's his start."

Hong-Wei seemed to relax. "Good. Because I'm not competing with this guy."

Simon nuzzled his shoulder. "Aaron Yan doesn't hold a candle to you."

"You remember that." Hong-Wei kissed Simon's hair. "We'll start watching tomorrow. Maybe at a more sedate pace, though?" He smiled. "I can see why you enjoy these. They're heartwarming. And they make me proud, to know my home country made them."

"While Asian romance dramas all have this same spirit, I feel the Taiwanese ones have the most heart. I love them all, though. I enjoy the warm, fuzzy feelings they give me." Simon stroked Hong-Wei's bangs, his forehead, his cheeks. "But I like the warm, fuzzy feelings you give me best of all."

They fell into bed together, a tangle of weary limbs. It wasn't their most dramatic or cinematic lovemaking. In fact, they were almost too tired to carry themselves over the finish line. Even so, of all the times Hong-Wei had made love to him so far, the morning after binge-watching his favorite Asian drama with his boyfriend was forever Simon's favorite.

CHAPTER THIRTEEN

HONG-WEI WASN'T only falling in love with Simon. The rest of Copper Point was steadily seeping into his heart as well.

Simon's family, particularly his mother, charmed him by degrees, and by the end of July, when Maddy asked them over for dinner, he looked forward to it. The Lanes liked it when he brought takeout from China Garden, begging him to order from what everyone called his secret menu, despite Zhang formally printing it up and calling the section *Little Taipei*. It was with the Lane family Hong-Wei finally taught his boyfriend how to use chopsticks, in part because Simon's mother and his younger sister, Lia, who was home from college at the time, fussed with him until he became so annoyed Hong-Wei was pretty sure Simon got the knack of it to spite them. They cooked Taiwanese dishes for Hong-Wei too, always asking what he missed the most.

"It's beef noodle soup," he said when they wouldn't give up, "but I'm so picky, you shouldn't bother. I'm terribly spoiled and only like the version my grandmother and sister make."

They didn't attempt to make the soup, but they did learn how to make a decent oyster omelet, which he appreciated.

Hong-Wei even had a soft spot for the way Simon's father barely engaged with anyone and stayed in his chair reading the paper until someone lured him into the conversation, at which point he doled out words as if they were diamonds. It reminded Hong-Wei of his grandfather, and made him a little homesick.

Several times, in fact, he left the Lane household and sat in his condo with his phone in his hand, his father's contact information pulled up, his thumb ready to dial. As of yet, he couldn't bring himself to press the button. Whenever he failed to call, he took a walk along the bay and asked himself what else he needed to do before he was ready to reach out, what achievement would make him feel worthy again.

It wasn't only the Lanes occupying Hong-Wei's time, though. Ram Rao was always dragging him out for coffee, so much so that Hong-Wei usually had to schedule their appointments so he could see Simon after and soothe his jealous feathers. Ram had no romantic designs on him, this much Hong-Wei could tell. Ram was all about his potential quartet. At first they met to discuss theoretical plans, but once Hong-Su shipped his violin, Ram plotted in earnest, coming to meet Hong-Wei at the hospital cafeteria on his break.

"When do you think we should start practice?" Ram tapped the side of his paper cup with a mad look in his eye. "Do you think three times a week is too much?"

"Definitely. I'll be lucky if I can attend one rehearsal, only ever on the weekend, and if I get called in for an emergency surgery, we'll have to reschedule. I can keep up with practicing on my own. I'll play at Simon's—and Jared and Owen's house, so I don't bother my neighbors."

Ram sighed. "All right. Well, I guess we'll make do. I can hardly argue with the surgeon. That's grim, you never getting time off. You need backup."

"They're working on it. I have more than I did when I first started, though I'm also busier than I was then too." Hong-Wei smiled. "In any event I'm looking forward to the quartet. I'm a bit rusty, and I'd like more time to practice than I'll have, but I'll make it work."

"You're kidding, right? I still have goose bumps from when you picked up the student violin in my office and launched into that Mozart piece like you were onstage."

Now Hong-Wei was flustered. "I was warming up."

"Exactly my point. You totally could have gone into music, man." Ram patted him on the arm. "But I'm glad you're here as our doctor. Never know when we're going to have something so dire that we'll need you, and in the meantime, you can play."

They were interrupted by a commotion at the front of the cafeteria, and people began to pour into the room. Ram looked confused, but now Hong-Wei had learned to read the signs. He gestured to where Simon, Owen, and Jared were taking their places next to the portable stereo. "They're doing one of their performances. Jared must have a discharge."

Ram's eyes lit up. "Oh, I've heard about these. I'm excited to get to see one." The music began, the guys began to dance and lip-sync, and Ram wrinkled his nose, laughing. "Oh my God, they're kind of bad. I love it. This is Simon's K-pop stuff, right? They should do some Bollywood numbers. Really bring the house down."

That night Simon had to work, and though Owen and Jared tried to get Hong-Wei to come over, he declined, opting to sit at home instead. He thought a lot about what Ram had said—all the things he had said. About playing music and being a doctor especially, but also how much joy he'd had over the quartet and the silly performance in the cafeteria.

When his sister called, he was almost relieved. "This was a good move for you after all, wasn't it. You're exhausted the same as you always were, but you're happy now. That's new."

"I like it here." He didn't try to hide the vulnerability in his voice. "I know this isn't the sort of place everyone expected me to end up, and I found my way here in an unconventional manner, but… I think I'm glad this is where I landed."

Her tone was soothing, not the usual wry sarcasm. "Don't be scared. It's okay. I'm glad you're happy."

He was scared, but he decided it was time to take the first step, with Hong-Su. "I know I've let everyone down, but I'm working hard here in Copper Point to be the doctor the community needs. I'm doing good work. I can say that now with confidence. It's not as showy as what I was doing before, but it matters to the patients here." He gripped his phone tighter. "It matters to me."

The pause on the other end of the line was torture, but when she finally spoke, she didn't say what he expected her to. "You need to have this conversation with Mom and Dad more than you need to have it with me. But I'll tell you this much. Don't assume you know how they feel. Don't assume you know what I think about your situation either. I understand you were disappointed in yourself when you left, and I wasn't going to tell you not to be hard on yourself because I was raised in the same house as you, and I get it. At the same time, I get *you*, Hong-Wei. I know what our parents don't know, what our grandparents can't understand, what it was like to be thrown into this country and try to turn into all-American kids as quickly as possible, while still being good Asian kids too. Never mind figuring out you were gay all by yourself on top of it all. I just want—" Her voice broke, and it took her a moment to recover. "I just want you to be *happy*. I mean it. I know happy to you means succeeding, making them proud, making yourself proud. So I want you to be able to do that in whatever way works for you. What I want you to hear from me, though, is that *all I want* for you, all *I* want, is for you to be *happy*. And I'll always be here to help you find it, no matter how many times you fall down trying to find that happiness."

Hong-Wei shut his eyes, but the tears that had begun halfway through his sister's speech continued to fall. "Thank you."

She sniffled, then let out a long sigh. "All right. Enough of making ourselves a mess. Let me tell you this funny story that happened to me this afternoon."

He listened to her story, let her voice wash over him, soothing him, centering him the way it always did.

IT WAS the Firefighter's Pancake Breakfast, the annual fundraiser during the second weekend in August, and Simon was losing his patience.

Simon, Hong-Wei, Jared, and Owen had gone together with the intent of letting Hong-Wei and Simon split off, but when most of the board turned up as well, including John Jean Andreas, they decided it would be best to drift apart. Simon ended up sitting with his mother, watching Hong-Wei be flirted with by the entire town, including Ram.

"I've looked forward to this all week, and now I have to watch *this*." Simon stabbed an overboiled sausage and gnawed the tip ferociously as he glared at Ram.

Maddy bumped her son's arm. "Hush yourself. People have ears."

Simon was so sick of people's ears. "I don't think I can take this much longer, Mom."

Her cup of coffee halfway to her mouth, Maddy paused and regarded him solemnly. She spoke in a low tone the people around them couldn't hear. "What do you plan to do, then? End it? Quit?"

Simon's shoulders slumped. "I don't know. I don't want to do either. I suppose I could go work in Ironwood. I've thought about it a lot."

"I don't like you driving in the winter." She touched his shoulder. "Do you want to leave, go talk somewhere for a bit? We can. I don't mind."

"No, I'm fine."

Simon said it, but he really wasn't.

He gave up on his food and mingled with the crowd, ending up chatting with Rebecca and Kathryn and a group of people from the chamber of commerce. They were animatedly discussing the vacancy on the hospital board and wondering who would take the open seat.

"I mean, we know it's going to be another one of their cronies," said Jacob Moore, the owner of the bookstore on Main Street. "They don't have many left, though."

Simon felt Hong-Wei's familiar presence, smelled his aftershave as he approached. Hong-Wei touched Simon's elbow briefly before he spoke. "You do know someone else could run."

The rest of the group sputtered and protested, and as they did so, Hong-Wei leaned in close.

"Are you all right?"

What was Simon supposed to say? There was no reply he *could* make, not here. "I'm fine."

Hong-Wei squeezed his elbow again, and then they were apart once more.

Simon hated this. He wanted to lean on Hong-Wei the way Kathryn did with Rebecca. He wanted people to *know* Hong-Wei was his.

"You could run," Hong-Wei repeated over the murmurs of the others in the group. "Any of you could, except Kathryn, since she's a hospital employee. Why don't you? New blood would be good for the board."

August Taylor, who ran the coffee shop, nudged Rebecca. "*You're* the one who should run."

Rebecca laughed so hard she coughed. "Oh my God. *No.*"

Kathryn seemed intrigued. "Baby, Gus is right. You'd be amazing."

They continued to argue, but Hong-Wei motioned for Simon to follow him away from the group, and they ended up leaving the event entirely, walking outside to meander along the ridge overlooking the bay.

"I have a meeting with John Jean Andreas on Monday," Hong-Wei said as soon as they were out of earshot of the crowd.

Simon's eyes widened. "You do? Why?"

"Ostensibly it's to talk about how St. Ann's can better support me as an intensivist, but what I want to do is find a way to get out of this dating policy."

Simon stopped walking and faced him. "You're still fighting that? After all this time?"

Hong-Wei frowned. "Of course I am. It's taking a while, but I'll figure it out. I wish I could get Erin Andreas to meet with me one-on-one. It's been months now, and he still won't do it."

"But what do you think this is going to accomplish? Do you honestly believe you can change their minds?"

"I think I'm going to find a way to be with you and let us keep our jobs, yes."

Simon looked out over the bay, watching the wind kick at the waves. "They're not going to fire you."

"If they attempt to punish only you, I'm going to have a lot to say about it. And if they force you out, I won't stay."

The ground beneath Simon's feet shifted, and he had to shake his head to get his balance back. "But you can't do that. You signed an agreement to stay—"

"Agreements can be broken. All I have to do to leave here is pay a penalty. Tell me where you want to go, Simon, and we'll leave tomorrow." When Simon swayed, Hong-Wei took his arm. "It's all right. I know you don't want to go. I'm not actually suggesting we do it. I want another way. It's taking me so long because I have to be patient while I suss out a way to leverage the board. I have the feeling I only get one shot to make a demand, so I want to make sure I know how to phrase what I'm asking for."

Simon stared at Hong-Wei, so handsome, confident, and caring, standing against the backdrop of Copper Point's Main Street, a breeze gently whipping his hair. Simon brushed a hand along his arm. "It's moments like this that make me crazy. Because right now what I really want is to pull you close and kiss you senseless."

Hong-Wei smiled, the gesture tinged with regret. "Give me a little longer."

Simon gave in and ran a hand down the front of Hong-Wei's shirt, a brief touch, but he loved how it made his lover shiver. "Take as long as you need."

HONG-WEI HAD met with John Jean Andreas countless times since coming to Copper Point, though his dinner after the Firefighter's Breakfast was the first time he'd been alone with the man.

They went to the same steakhouse the administration had brought him to when he'd arrived at St. Ann's. Though he'd garnered plenty of stares that day, tonight he was received as a local celebrity. He had to shake several hands in the lobby area and admire many babies on the way to his table, hearing stories of former patients in recovery.

John Jean stood patiently as Hong-Wei waded through his admirers, and whenever he was addressed, usually in apology for making him wait, he always said not to worry, he understood St. Ann's star surgeon was in high demand.

Once they were seated and the server had brought their drinks, Hong-Wei inclined his head. "I'm sorry, Mr. Andreas. Thank you for your understanding as I greeted my patients."

As Hong-Wei had hoped, John Jean ate up this deference with a proud nod, acknowledging Hong-Wei with a gentle toast of his wineglass. "Not at all. It's good business for St. Ann's that you're so popular with the community. They think highly of you, both for your professional and pleasant demeanor and for your impressive skill as a physician. As do all of us in the administration and on the board, for the record."

How convenient they'd leapt right into the conversation Hong-Wei wanted to lead them to. "Outside of the incident with Mr. Zhang, my performance has been quite standard."

"Nonsense. You solved Mrs. Mueller's case as well, and several others that I have it on good authority no one else could do much with besides refer them beyond St. Ann's. I know you've consulted with clinic doctors on their cases, helping them send their patients to the proper specialists. If we had some of those specialists here at Copper Point, you'd be consulting with them as well, and we'd be keeping those dollars here."

Hong-Wei sipped his drink. "You keep a close eye on the hospital."

The server came to take their order, and Hong-Wei panicked, thinking he'd lost the moment. Once they were alone, however, John Jean stretched his arm across the back of the booth and began to speak.

"Have you heard much of the history of Copper Point?" When Hong-Wei said he hadn't, Andreas nodded and continued on, settling in for a story. "It was one of the first cities founded in the Wisconsin Territory, a settlement established by Spanish, French, and English explorers. Like so many places, it started as a fur trading outpost, but then they discovered the copper veins, and the boom began, lasting all the way to the Civil War. After the war, interest in mining declined, and the town nearly died out. The timber industry saved Copper Point in the late 1870s, but trees can be harvested faster than they grow, and clear-cutting devastated the industry and blighted the landscape by the 1960s. By the turn of the century, tourism began to replace the timber loss, but ironically enough, mining has made a comeback, this time for sandstone. Of course, that industry is at odds with tourism, and so which direction our economy will take for the next few decades isn't entirely secure."

Andreas smoothed his hand over the tabletop. "My family has been in Copper Point since the fur trading days, and we established the first hospital as soon as the first houses were set up in town. We were part of building what would become St. Ann's during the 1880s. We've been part of every incarnation of health care in this city, through fire, blizzards, and devastation. So yes, I make it my business to know what goes on. It's more than my duty as president of the board. It's my responsibility as head of the Andreas family."

Hong-Wei let the story ring in his ears a few moments longer, longing to find a museum with photos and relics of all those ages past. He swirled his wine gently in his glass. "My grandparents would like you."

This seemed to surprise Andreas. "Your grand-parents came with your family to America from Tai-wan, am I remembering correctly?"

"Yes." He hesitated, then decided this wasn't about politics right now. Something about this mo-ment was simply about sharing. "You told me the his-tory of Copper Point. Are you aware at all of Taiwan's history?"

John Jean folded his hands on the table, quietly curious. "I'm afraid I'm not. There's some conflict with whether or not China owns it now? Or China wants to?"

"People have fought over Taiwan since the thir-teenth century. Mainland China, Europe, Japan—every-one has had their hand on us at one point or another, all the way into the previous century. Those who were on Taiwan before the supporters of Sun Yat-Sen and Chi-ang Kai-Shek and other Nationalists fled to the island have a different cultural and economic background than the mainlanders, and that still affects the nation today."

John Jean nodded, listening intently. "I remember bits of this from history class. Of course, it's much more personal for your family, isn't it?"

"For my grandparents especially, yes. They've seen so much change, both in their country and their family. They're not mainlanders, so they grew up un-der Japanese rule, then had that exchanged for Na-tionalist rule where they were penalized for not being immigrants from China. Their method of coping was to keep to their ways. They always said the most im-portant thing was keeping traditions alive, keeping the memories. Keeping our family together. When we first arrived in Texas and she could barely speak English, my grandmother didn't blink, only took my sister's and my hands and went out to the grocery store, declaring we would figure it out between the three of us. We could do anything so long as we stuck together and were respectful to others."

John Jean smiled. "What a lovely story. And now here you are, so successful. Your family must be so proud."

It was a blow John Jean couldn't know struck him so deeply. Hong-Wei recovered with the encouragement Jared, Owen, and Simon had given him, and Hong-Su's vow. "I'm striving to show them coming to St. Ann's was a decision worth making."

There was no question John Jean hadn't meant his comment to be a barb, because he looked genuinely taken aback. "You're doing amazing work here for people who deserve to have a good surgeon, and you're making yourself at home within the community. What more could your family want for you?"

How could he possibly explain to someone who had just sat here telling him how his ancestors had taken over and held this land so long ago? "It's been some time since your family had immigrants in it, Mr. Andreas. I can tell you from firsthand experience, not only does the first generation work itself to the bone, it does so dreaming of the second generation reaching for the highest point of the brightest star."

"We consider you *our* star, Dr. Wu, and we're going to get you the specialty clinics and support teams you need to make your own highest point right here at St. Ann's." John Jean winked. "From what I hear, we need to make sure we keep Simon Lane on your team at all costs."

Hong-Wei stilled. Surely he was imagining things. Andreas hadn't intimated he and Simon...

Had he?

John Jean set down his wineglass and filled it from the bottle on the table, tipping some more into Hong-Wei's glass as well. "I'll admit, you had me distracted by Dr. Gagnon at first. You don't need to worry, though. While we're normally quite strict on the no-dating policy, we'll make an exception for our intensivist. Provided you continue to remain discreet, of course."

Hong-Wei's heart pounded in his ears. *How?* What had given them away? They'd been so careful. He tried to follow the plan, to resist the urge to panic, but John Jean was good.

He cleared his throat. "I'm sorry. Why exactly do you think I'm breaking some kind of policy?"

John Jean waved a hand at him. "Don't worry, like I told you. We're not going to enforce it with you or Mr. Lane. Continue to produce the wonderful results you're giving us, help us put the hospital on the right track, and there's nothing at all to worry about. Oh look, our food's here. Now let's talk about what specialty doctor you think we should recruit next. Did you have anyone particular in mind?"

Hong-Wei felt as if he were moving through a fog. He needed to press on John Jean, to ask him why they had this dating policy at all, to follow through with his whole reason for coming here. Except he couldn't say a word, could only watch this man who had lured the story of his grandparents out of him, then threatened Simon and smiled kindly at Hong-Wei as if he hadn't just pinned him to the wall.

John Jean had come to this dinner expressly for this purpose, Hong-Wei realized. He'd known all along about Simon, and he'd waited until now to drop the bomb because he was trying to show he had leverage.

By God, he damn well had it.

CHAPTER FOURTEEN

WHEN THE car pulled into the drive, Simon was at home, watching *Miss in Kiss*. Jared, who was washing the dishes in the kitchen, peered out the window. "Oh, it's Hong-Wei. I thought it was some possessed delivery kid, the way he was driving."

Simon looked up from the couch. "Is something wrong?"

Drying his hands, Jared grimaced. "I think so, given the way he's tearing up the steps."

After pausing the show, Simon rose and went to the door. He opened it as Hong-Wei appeared, and his heart stopped at the look on his boyfriend's face.

Then it dropped to his feet like lead as he said, "They know, Simon."

Battle mode engaged, Owen got up from his computer. "Come inside and close the door."

Simon could only stare at Hong-Wei, his body abruptly turning to jelly. "You mean they know… about us? The… the board knows?"

Hong-Wei nodded. He seemed lost, confused, and exhausted, as if he'd worked a twenty-four-hour shift full of surgeries that didn't make sense. "I still don't know how. I've racked my brain trying to figure it out, but I can't find any moment we gave it away."

Owen was still and laser-focused, quietly dangerous. "Did you confirm it to him?"

Hong-Wei grimaced. "No, but it doesn't matter. He doesn't play that kind of game. He basically said he won't fire Simon so long as we keep being discreet and I play lapdog surgeon."

Covering his mouth, Simon staggered backward.

Jared put a hand on his shoulder, then Hong-Wei's. "Everyone take a deep breath. Both of you need to sit." He marched them gently to the couch, then sat on the edge of the easy chair across from them. "Can you give us a recap of what happened, Jack?"

Hong-Wei ran a hand through his hair. "We went to the steakhouse. I got waylaid by patients all the way to our seats, so I apologized for that, but he said it was fine, that I was good for business. He did this thing where he talked about how Copper Point got formed and the Andreas family has always shepherded the hospital." He smiled miserably. "He was humble and human. He drew me in, got me to tell stories about my grandparents and Taiwan. I had my guard all the way down. For a moment I thought he might be the weak link, that I could talk to him openly. Then out of the blue he starts talking about Simon like he's my boyfriend. I was so stunned I didn't know what to do. Then he breezily let me know I didn't have to worry because I was St. Ann's star. I got special treatment, and my significant other did too, as long as I performed. It was so smooth and unexpected I didn't know how to respond. He played me the entire meal. He never raised his voice, never made a direct threat. He didn't have to."

This was exactly the sort of thing Hong-Wei had left Texas to get away from. Now here it was, uglier and magnified.

I'm the weapon they're using to manipulate Hong-Wei. Simon felt sick.

Seated on the edge of the coffee table, Owen looked ready to start punching people. "This has to be illegal. They can't prove Simon and Hong-Wei are dating. We need to get Rebecca. She has to know a legal loophole or something."

Jared shook his head. "They aren't actually firing them, though. And if they do, then Simon and Hong-Wei would have to sue to insist they're not dating. Which they are."

Owen threw up his hands. "What do we do, then? We can't let this stand. God*damn* I want the union right now."

Jared tapped his finger on his knee. "Calling Rebecca and Kathryn isn't a bad idea. I'm not sure how much there is for Rebecca to do as a lawyer at this point, but she's a cool head, and Kathryn is good in a crisis. In any event, friends are needed right now."

Swallowing the sick feeling in his stomach, Simon turned to Hong-Wei, though he couldn't quite bring himself to look his boyfriend in the eye. "I'm sorry."

Startling, Hong-Wei touched his leg. "Why are you sorry? I was sitting here trying to find the words to apologize to you."

"I'm the one who's trapped you. It's because of me the board is manipulating you."

"I'm the one who's failed to protect you the way I said I would. I went in overconfident like a fool and got slapped down so easily it's pathetic."

Shutting his eyes, Simon took Hong-Wei's hand and leaned into his shoulder. "I hate this."

Hong-Wei stroked his hair. "Me too."

Rebecca and Kathryn came over, and when they heard the story of what happened, they were shocked and appalled the same as everyone else. Kathryn was more worried about how Simon and Hong-Wei were doing, but Rebecca immediately turned lethal. She agreed with Jared's read on the situation, that there wasn't much legally to be done, but she was furious with the machinations of the board.

"They're completely out of hand. I'm absolutely done with them. I *am* running for the open seat, and I'm going to take it. I hope those wrinkled old misers are ready for a bitchy Dominican dyke to storm their fortress, because I'm coming in with an axe sharpened and ready."

Kathryn's eyes brightened at her wife's fiery display. "If only we could get a majority of people like you on the board, honey, we'd switch the policy."

Owen landed a fist on the table. "See, that's just it. The board members aren't the gods of the hospital. They're a damn advisory board, but they act like mob bosses. If Nick and Erin would do their damn jobs, none of this would be a problem."

The six of them sat up late into the night, complaining about the board and strategizing for Rebecca's run. Eventually they gave in and went to bed and went home, though Hong-Wei stayed with Simon. He didn't bother to hide his car anymore.

The next day at the hospital, Simon couldn't help but feel as if everyone was staring at him. He kept trying to figure out when and how John Jean Andreas could have discovered them. He analyzed his reactions to Hong-Wei to see if he was failing to follow his mother's advice.

Hong-Wei startled him at the nurses' station, running a hand down his back. Simon glanced around nervously. Other people were around, and they had to see what Hong-Wei was doing.

Hong-Wei didn't pull his hand away. "Stop worrying. We'll find a way through."

When Hong-Wei left to do his rounds, Simon turned to the others at the station, his heart pounding. To his shock, they didn't seem surprised at all.

Christie sighed and patted his shoulder. "Hon, everybody knows."

Thick panic spread through Simon's veins. "H-how?"

Dante gave him a sad smile. "The Firefighter's Breakfast. Neither of you hid it well. People started talking, and then someone overheard you guys outside, and the gossip took over from there."

Simon sat, his legs no longer strong enough to stand. "And none of you said anything?"

Christie looked appalled. "Why would we? We didn't want you fired. We're all shocked you're still here."

Dante snorted. "Are you kidding? They get rid of Simon, their golden goose will walk."

Ronnie looked up from the cart she was filling. "But they have the contract on him."

Dante shook his head. "Not a contract. The guy will leave if they screw with his man. You just watch."

Simon felt sick, but he'd feel worse if he stayed and listened to this. "I need to do hourly rounding."

He rose on unsteady feet and drifted down the hall, but each face seemed to belong to an enemy now.

Everyone knew. Not only that he was dating Hong-Wei, but that the only reason he still had a job was because of his lover.

This was about to be the longest day of his life—and all his days working would be this way.

He couldn't go on like this.

At his break, he escaped to the hospital courtyard and sat with his head in his hands. A hand on his back made him jump, but when he saw it was Owen who had come to find him, his emotions threatened to overwhelm him.

"Hey." Owen put an arm around Simon as he sat beside him. "It's going to be all right. I promise, we'll figure this out."

Simon settled against his friend's side, grateful for the support, but he still felt as if the world were slowly squeezing him in a vise. What a fool he'd been for thinking the worst thing would be to get fired. All that time being afraid, and he hadn't even anticipated the right fear.

He gripped the sleeve of Owen's scrubs. "I hate feeling so trapped. I hate that I can't do anything. I hate most of all that he was so happy, but my stupid town is screwing everything up. He's done so much for us, and this is how we pay him back?"

"For the record, Si, *you* deserve more from Copper Point too. You're the one who rode on that Founder's Day float. This isn't just where you grew up. This is the place where your roots go all the way down, as far as any white person's in this region can go. You have a right to be angry that they failed you too. That when you found *your* happiness, they used it to manipulate you and the one you loved. That's not your fault. That's an injustice."

Simon hadn't thought about Copper Point letting him down, not like Owen had said, though as he went to bed that night, he stared at the ceiling, his friend's words swimming in his head. He'd never considered himself some kind of son of Copper Point the way Erin Andreas was, but he supposed there wasn't a difference, if it came down to ancestry, except the Andreas family was showier about it. The Lanes and Petersens didn't exactly want for money, but they didn't live in a fancy mansion on the hill and open it for tours either. Grandpa Petersen wasn't on the hospital board, but he'd been on the city council, and one of the Lanes had been a mayor, Simon was fairly sure. His dad was active in the chamber of commerce too.

Yes, what *was* the difference between him and Erin? Simple perception? Was this because Simon was gay, because he'd been out all this time? No, he didn't think that was it. The only difference was that Simon had a different kind of family than Erin, and a different set of friends. He couldn't put his finger on exactly what those differences were, but it seemed to

mean, at the end of the day, that Copper Point protected Erin and not Simon.

Lying there in the dark, his heart breaking, Simon
acknowledged the town he'd stayed in because it was
safe had never truly been that town at all. The fears
that had kept him from exploring the world hadn't
given him safety in exchange, only meant he hadn't
experienced people and places that might not have betrayed him the way his hometown just had.

You're being overdramatic, he chided himself.
Not everyone in town has betrayed you.

That was true. Not everyone had. But the town
as a whole wasn't what he'd been pretending it was.
Maybe it wasn't the town's fault—maybe that was on
him. Maybe it was a little bit of both.

All he knew was that, with those chains broken, a
new possibility lay before him. He still wasn't sure he
was ready to open this door, but it was unlocked now,
and his hand was on the knob. He could ask himself
the question which, even a day ago, he couldn't have
begun to entertain.

If Copper Point was going to hurt him and Hong-
Wei so much, what was their reason to stay?

SIMON WAS upset, and Hong-Wei had no idea
how to make him happy.

He hated how Simon kept insisting their discov-
ery was somehow his fault, that it must have been him
at the picnic who gave something away. Never mind
that it was Hong-Wei who'd dragged his feet all this
time, not making any inroads with the board or using
his leverage, taking too long to read the situation until
it ended up closing in around him. It was his residency

all over again. The way the politics played out were different, the parts of the machine came together in new ways, but in the end everything was the same.

The irony was now he couldn't leave. Simon wouldn't want to, and the truth was, Hong-Wei wasn't sure he did either. He wasn't happy about the board trying to manipulate him, and the idea that John Jean thought he'd turned Hong-Wei into his puppet made him ill, but Hong-Wei truly did like living in Copper Point. It was more than Simon. It was Jared and Owen, and Kathryn and Rebecca. It was his first rehearsal with Ram's quartet coming up. It was the Zhangs and the staff at China Garden. It was the idea, outside of the machinations of the board, that he truly could be part of building a new future at St. Ann's, that it was here he could finally make a difference.

Copper Point had become his home.

The realization hit him one night at China Garden—he and Simon had no need for buffers on their dates any longer, but the two of them were both so depressed that their friends never left them alone, and so they ended up with a full table for hot pot, with Jared, Owen, Kathryn, Rebecca, Ram, and the rest of the quartet coming along. As Mrs. Zhang pressed her hand on his shoulder when she brought another tray of meat, Hong-Wei looked around the table and felt the warmth and love of everyone surrounding him.

He'd told himself he could always leave if things didn't go well. It had never occurred to him that for the first time in his life he'd become so enmeshed in a place, in the people, that he wouldn't *want* to go.

Simon came home with him that night, and as they sat facing one another on the couch, listening to

"Solveig's Song," Simon stroked Hong-Wei's hair, his face. "You seem troubled. More so than usual."

Hong-Wei ran his fingers slowly down Simon's arms. "I want so much better for you. For us. I'm aware the gossip is worse for you because you're the nurse and I'm the doctor. I want to make it stop, but I can't. I feel like I'm failing you."

It cost him so much to admit that, to acknowledge he was repeating his failures all over again. He didn't know what else to do, though. He couldn't run, and he couldn't do nothing and watch Simon suffer.

Simon pressed gentle fingers onto Hong-Wei's lips. "You haven't failed me. It's not your fault."

"It's not about fault. It's about responsibility. *You* are my responsibility. I *want* you to be my responsibility. I want to make you happy, to keep you safe. It's all I want to do. And I can't."

Simon kissed him, sliding his hands around Hong-Wei's neck as he shifted closer into Hong-Wei's lap. When he broke the kiss, he nuzzled Hong-Wei's nose, cheek, chin. "You *do* make me happy, and you do make me feel safe. But John Jean hanging this over your head isn't your fault, and you know what, it isn't mine either. It's our problem, together." He sighed, his face set in determination. "There's an easy solution, though, one we're both ignoring. It's time, I think, that we use it. We need to leave St. Ann's. We need to leave Copper Point."

Hong-Wei couldn't believe what he'd just heard. "You told me you couldn't bear to leave here. You never wanted to live or work anywhere else."

"I said that a long time ago, before we started dating. Before I fell in love with you." He took

Hong-Wei's face in his hands. "I love you, Hong-Wei. More than my job. More than Copper Point. If they make me choose between them and you, it's not a choice."

Hong-Wei stared at Simon, too stunned to speak. He touched his lover's face, his hair, his neck.

Simon bit his lip, looking uncertain, and caught one of Hong-Wei's hands. "Tell me you feel the same way?"

Hong-Wei let out his breath, a strangled sound escaping with it. Gathering his lover to him, Hong-Wei shut his eyes and buried his face in Simon's hair. "Of course I feel the same. I love you so much I can't breathe. I'm simply blown away by the idea that you would give up so much to be with me."

Simon wrapped his arms tighter around Hong-Wei. "I've thought about it a lot lately, to the point it's all I can think about. I'll miss Copper Point, yes. I'll miss St. Ann's, even with its aggravations. I'll miss my family. But I can't live without you, and I can't stand to stay here if this is how we have to live. I'd prefer to stay, but I want to be with you in a place where we can be happy. And I believe we can find the place where we can both make a difference and be happy together."

Hong-Wei laughed into the side of Simon's head, the sound becoming a half sob at the end. He felt so turned inside out, softened like butter in the sun, and all he could do was slide into Simon, to hold his face and kiss him, run his hands across his body.

They had made love so many times now, in every conceivable place in Hong-Wei's apartment, but as Hong-Wei led Simon up the stairs, it felt like it was the first time. A different kind of first time. Simon had just told him he not only loved him, but that he loved him more than anything. He'd change everything about his life to be with him.

If Hong-Wei ran away again, now someone wanted to come along.

Perhaps home wasn't Copper Point. Perhaps home was Simon Lane.

Simon stood naked before him now, trembling with want, but as Hong-Wei hesitated, he did too. "Hong-Wei? Are you all right?"

Hong-Wei stripped out of the last of his clothes and drew Simon into his arms, falling with him in a blissful heap onto the bed as he drew his lover tight to his heart. "I promise you, I've never been better."

CHAPTER FIFTEEN

THE NEXT morning Hong-Wei approached the music building at Bayview University bearing his violin and a heavy heart. His discussion with Simon over breakfast hadn't been about whether or not they should leave, only about where they should go. They planned to tell Jared and Owen that night, but Hong-Wei realized they had many people they'd need to tell. Ram was one of them.

The man had just found his missing violinist. Hong-Wei enjoyed *being* his violinist. It was a humble community quartet, so much less than his dreams, yet the thought of losing these rehearsals, of never being able to perform with his new friends—*his friends*—made Hong-Wei ache.

His quartet members were onto him too. He'd meant to keep everything secret, knowing telling Jared and Owen should come first, but somehow he'd become a man who couldn't hide his emotions anymore, or at least he'd become someone who couldn't hide his emotions from those he cared about.

Amanda Rodriguez, the violist and a chemistry professor, called him out first. "You seem down, Jack. Did something happen?"

Hong-Wei attempted to dismiss his mood, forcing a smile. "A lot on my mind, is all."

But then Ram talked about their upcoming performances. The pride with which he spoke of finally having a quartet to present at Founder's Day crushed Hong-Wei, and when Ram made a special point to brag that they'd be able to do extra-difficult pieces because of Hong-Wei's skill, he couldn't take it any longer. He covered his face with his hands.

Tim Lee, the cellist and world literature instructor, set his instrument aside and turned to him. "All right. Enough of this. What's going on? You need to tell us the truth before you explode."

Hong-Wei hadn't meant to, but he told them. Everything, every detail—about how long he'd wanted to date Simon, how hard he'd pursued him, how Simon had resisted at first because of his job, then agreed to see him in secret. About how John Jean Andreas had pinned him like a bug and tried to use Simon to keep him in line as part of his plan, and how now Simon had convinced him it would be best if they left together.

"I wasn't supposed to tell anyone any of this yet." Hong-Wei rested his elbows on his knees over the top of his violin and let his head fall into his hands. "We're telling Owen and Jared tonight. I don't know when Simon plans to tell his family. I don't know where we're going yet. I want to stay close for his sake, but he keeps insisting we find a good hospital for my career. My father would help us go to Texas in a heartbeat. I don't really know what I want. Except truth be told, I'd prefer not to leave."

Ram shifted the music stands so he could slide his chair closer to Hong-Wei's. "We don't want you to leave either. I feel comfortable speaking for everyone here, and to be honest, Copper Point." The others murmured and nodded in agreement before Ram continued. "Given your situation, I think I'd end up making the same decision. I'm stunned Simon wants to leave. He always swore he wouldn't. He dated a creative writing professor a few years ago who was hired on a grant, and they seemed to get along so well, but when the grant was finished and Marc had to go, Simon refused to consider relocating with him."

The passion with which Simon had insisted they leave, the way he'd told Hong-Wei he needed to be with him more than he needed to be in Copper Point, made his heart swell and ache all over again. "I wish I could make it work for us to stay."

Tim patted him on the back. "You can't control this situation. You can only run with it."

Hong-Wei understood this, intellectually. He just… hated it. "I'm going to find a way to make this a positive change. Duluth isn't far, and it seems like a nice city. Plus Minnesota doesn't have the same restrictive union issues, so Simon will be better protected." He sat up, took a deep breath, let it out. Part of him said he needed to keep some of these thoughts private. That part of him lost the argument, and he continued on. "Also, I think I should propose to him.

If we're going to alter our lives like this for one another, we should do it properly."

They erupted in shouts and cheers for him, taking his instrument from his lap so they could hug him in turns, and in Ram's case, ruffle his hair. They were all for him proposing, and they abandoned practice to help him brainstorm ideas how.

"It should be something romantic," Amanda suggested.

Ram snorted. "It's Simon Lane. It needs to be *incredibly* romantic. Dramatic as well. Something out of Bollywood or one of his Asian romances he loves so much."

Tim curled his lip. "I think you should do something in front of the whole town, so everyone is charmed and excited for the wedding, and when you end up leaving, they're pissed at the board."

Ram stood up, eyes wide, a slow grin spreading across his face. "Oh my God. I just had the best idea. I have no idea if you actually want to do it, Jack, but it's so perfect, I'm really hoping you do."

Hong-Wei glanced around the circle at the four of them, at their happy faces, so eager to help him and Simon.

How can I lose this part of my life?

He pushed past the pain in his heart and settled in his chair, giving Ram his best smile. "Let's hear it."

SIMON DIDN'T make it through the end of the day before he had to cave and confess to Owen.

His longtime friend had taken one look at him as he'd arrived at work and demanded to know what was wrong, and when Simon started his story at lunch,

Owen pulled them into an empty conference room and called Jared, telling him to get to the hospital, STAT. It was bad enough with Owen, but when the two of them bore down on him, Simon couldn't take it. He started crying.

"I don't want to leave, but I can't stay here and live like this. And I can't live without Hong-Wei."

He braced for them to yell, but neither of them did. Owen seemed more sad than furious for a change. He kept his hand on Simon's back, rubbing slow circles as he spoke. "Where are you going to go?"

"We don't know yet. We argue about it. He thinks we should stay close to Copper Point, but he's the one who's the incredible doctor, and he should go to a good hospital—"

Simon had to stop to draw breath, and Jared took his hand. "It's all right. You two will sort it out."

Hearing the two of them say the same thing he and Hong-Wei kept telling each other broke Simon. "I'm going to miss you so much."

Owen huffed and ruffled Simon's hair. "What do you mean, miss us? You think you're going to get rid of us so easily? If you leave, we're following you."

Simon was sure he was joking. Except he seemed entirely serious, and when Simon glanced at Jared, he held up his hands. "Don't look at me like that. We made a vow in middle school, remember? Pledged to be brothers for all time, to be together until the end no matter what happens. I'm with Owen. We came back to Copper Point because you wanted to come home, and we liked the idea of helping out the people here. But if they're going to drive the two of you out, it's not home anymore, and it's not worth staying. We're following you like a pair of bad pennies."

Simon covered his mouth, but he couldn't stop the sob. "You guys."

Owen grinned. "You think Jack will be annoyed we're following? I mean, I want him to be happy, but I want him to be at least a little pissed off as well."

Jared leaned against the table, propping himself on his elbows. "I just hope Nick shits himself when he realizes he's losing so much good staff. You think we could get Kathryn and Rebecca to walk with us too?"

Simon laugh-sobbed then, and they started crying too, and hugged him. He was late getting to his shift, but he felt so much better.

Somehow, despite him only telling Owen and Jared, people's whispers about him changed, and as he ended his shift, Susan asked him if it was true that he was leaving Copper Point. Too surprised to react properly, Simon mumbled noncommittally and made his escape, but a paramedic stopped him on the way to the parking lot and asked him the same question. Simon hurried over to Hong-Wei's apartment, concerned now, and a bit annoyed at Owen and Jared, because it wasn't like them to spread gossip.

When he shared the story with Hong-Wei, it turned out his boyfriend had been the leak.

"I'm so sorry." Hong-Wei looked sheepish as he sank into the couch. "The quartet pulled the story out of me. I told them to keep it quiet, but it sounds like they didn't."

"It's okay." Simon settled into Hong-Wei's side, tucking his feet onto the cushion. "It was probably Ram or Tim. They're both terrible gossips. No way it was Amanda. She'll take everything to the grave. This does mean I need to tell my mother as soon as possible, though."

Unfortunately, as Simon had feared, it was already too late. When he picked up his phone, he had a missed call from his mother, and when she answered, she started in immediately, asking him if the rumor was true, that he was leaving Copper Point with Jack. He apologized, saying he hadn't meant for her to find out this way, but yes, it was true.

He and Hong-Wei ended up going over there for a few hours to talk, which became interesting, since they still hadn't officially made their own plans.

"We honestly don't know where we're going yet." Simon glanced at Hong-Wei, who sat beside him at the table, sipping coffee with Simon's father. "I want Hong-Wei to go somewhere he feels comfortable as a doctor."

Hong-Wei cast a stern glare at Simon over the rim of his cup. "And I want Simon to stay close to his family."

"Listen to the two of you." Maddy sighed. "I wish the board would come to their senses so you didn't have to leave. I hate that Simon has finally found the right person for him and it comes to this. I swear I'm going to march over to John Jean and give him a piece of my mind."

"Don't," Simon's father said from behind his paper. "Nothing good will come from engaging that man."

Later, as they left, Simon's father pulled him aside and pressed a check for one thousand dollars into his hand.

"This is to get you started." His voice was gruff, more so than usual, and he couldn't look Simon in the eye as he patted him on the back. "You need more, you speak up, you hear?"

Simon cried all the way home.

He was weepy a lot over the next week, as people from the tapestry of his life came up to him, expressing their happiness for his relationship with Hong-Wei but their sorrow that he was leaving. They were upset about Hong-Wei as well, not liking that the town would be without a surgeon again, sad to see him as an individual going away.

When word got out Jared and Owen intended to leave as well, people's upset reached near-riot levels. The reality that they were about to lose their anesthesiologist didn't quite process, though it was the more critical problem, but every parent in town sent their child to Jared, except for the handful who were so conservative they feared an openly gay man might corrupt their offspring. The clinic doctors were already at critical mass with their patient load, and until Jared had come home with his degree, Copper Springs had never had its own pediatrician. The same had gone for Kathryn and her OB-GYN practice, and they'd begged for nurse anesthetists until Owen returned. Though Kathryn and Rebecca insisted they weren't going anywhere, the rumor began to spread they were leaving too, and the town was in a panic. People wrote letters to the editor and the hospital, and there were plans by some from the community to attend the next hospital board meeting and demand the hospital rescind the dating policy that had started all this in the first place.

Owen was particularly pleased with the chaos, sitting with the paper every night and grinning over the letters, reading them aloud and cackling at the parts he felt were particularly cunning. Jared focused on suggesting new locations. He had a three-ring binder full of tabs, and he liked to sit with Hong-Wei going over options for possible new hospitals and cities.

Simon was fairly sure Hong-Wei's heart wasn't in this move any more than his was.

None of them had given notice at St. Ann's, but the hospital behaved as if they were leaving tomorrow, everyone hugging Simon and getting teary, looking sadly at Hong-Wei and telling him they didn't know how they'd get along without him.

"The board members are in a panic," Hong-Wei told Simon one day as they ate lunch in his office—takeout from China Garden. The Zhangs had also heard the rumor they were leaving, and now when they ate in or carried out, their portions were more crazed than before. One takeout order became enough lunch for three days.

"I can only imagine." Simon poked his chopsticks into some noodles. "Have they tried to bargain with you at all?"

"No, which surprises me. I suspect John Jean thinks this is some kind of power move and is trying to stall. Or it's possible they truly don't know what to do with this." He nudged a dumpling.

Simon leaned across the desk and kissed his cheek.

As Jared's binder began to fill, Owen and Simon started looking at it too. After some debate, they decided to focus their efforts on a few hospitals in the Twin Cities area. They vowed it was the Four Musketeers policy: together or not at all.

Simon did his best to join in as well. He was glad, at least, he wouldn't lose his best friends. And he did laugh when Hong-Wei balked at Owen's assumption they were all four buying a house together, though something bloomed inside him as he realized Hong-Wei assumed the two of *them* would be sharing a residence.

He was daydreaming about what it would be like to live with Hong-Wei when he ran into Erin Andreas in the hall at work one day. Literally—he bumped into the HR director and sent his armful of files cascading across the tile.

"Oh, I'm so sorry." Blushing, Simon hurried to pick up the papers. "Here, let me get that for you."

"It's all right, I can get it." Erin crouched beside him, reaching for the folders as well.

His hands were shaking.

Simon glanced again at the director, regarding him more carefully. Erin looked wan, more so than usual, and he had bags under his eyes, as if he hadn't been sleeping well.

Simon focused on the papers. "I'm just off shift. I'm happy to help."

"It's a terrible mess. Everything's out of order, and I have a meeting in forty minutes."

Something was seriously wrong with Erin, there wasn't any question. It was the same sort of reply Erin would have given him on any other day, but *how* he said it, his voice too clipped and thin, the way he couldn't seem to look Simon in the eye…. The change was subtle, and Simon wondered if he'd have registered it if he'd still been ruled by fear of the man.

Now, kneeling here next to him, Simon regarded the man carefully, trying to ascertain what was wrong.

Erin looked, in fact, the way Hong-Wei had seemed when he returned from a single dinner with John Jean.

Erin lives with the man all the time.

Simon cleared his throat. "The conference room across the hall here is empty. Let's go in there, and if you tell me what to do, I'll help you sort these, and it'll go faster. It's the least I can do for causing the trouble in the first place."

He half expected Erin to refuse his offer, but to his surprise, Erin only nodded curtly. Simon focused on gathering up the remainder of the files and papers—he had the majority of them, since Erin was still trembling and unable to do much. The director followed Simon into the conference room, but he mostly stood by as Simon set the folders on the table.

On a hunch, Simon shut the door. It took about thirty seconds for Erin to start talking.

"I tried to warn you."

Simon, who had begun to sort the papers, glanced up. "Warn me of what?"

Holding on to the back of a chair, Erin stared at Simon, his expression flat. "I knew you were going to work in close quarters with Dr. Wu. I'd done research on him and had heard he'd had a few relationships with men, and I knew he was exactly the type of man you'd be interested in. This was why I handed you another copy of the memo the day you went to pick him up."

Oh. That… was unexpected. "I didn't realize." He paused, then added, "Thank you. I guess."

Erin snorted. "You didn't heed my warning, so it doesn't matter. You didn't heed it from *the beginning*. Neither of you. I suppose I should blame him more than you. I kept trying to find ways to get him to stop, but when he's determined, he's determined. It makes him a good surgeon, but it makes him difficult to direct."

Simon decided he didn't have anything to lose. "If you didn't try so hard to control him—and everyone here—we wouldn't have to leave."

Erin's gaze cut sharply to Simon. "So it's true. You really are leaving? This isn't a stunt?"

Simon blinked. "What do you mean, a stunt? This is my *life*. We're leaving because we want to live, not be controlled."

Erin rolled his eyes. "Everyone's controlled, everywhere you go."

"Not like this."

Erin was unraveling now. "My father told him he'd make an exception for the two of you—"

"Yes, so long as Hong-Wei was his puppet. Why in the world would he agree to it, Erin? He can get a job anywhere he wants, but he'd stay here to be manipulated by your father so I can stay in Copper Point? You think I'd let him do that? Even if I were selfish to allow it, how stupid are you to believe I'd be anything but ostracized by the rest of the hospital staff for being the one nurse who wasn't fired?"

Erin's grip on the chair was so tight his knuckles were white. "I told you, I tried to warn you—"

"I fell in love, okay?" Simon grimaced. "Why *did* you warn me, anyway? It's not like we're close. I don't know you at all. You're making it sound like you only warned me. Why?"

The conference room was silent as Erin met Simon's stare, saying nothing for almost half a minute.

When he finally spoke, his voice was brittle. "Since you're truly leaving, I suppose I can assume Dr. Gagnon and Dr. Kumpel are also serious about going along?"

Something about the way Erin spoke, his eyes a window of fury, betrayal, frustration, and deep sorrow, made Simon pause. Simon remembered all the times Erin and Owen had fought, *how* they'd fought. The way they seemed to seek each other out.

Oh.

Oh no.

What a mess this was. What a stupid, needless mess.

Simon pushed the pile of files forward on the table. "Can I ask who made the no-dating rule?"

Erin hesitated only a moment. "The board wanted to implement it because of the scandals, and Nick and the vice president agreed. But they basically do whatever the board says."

"And you do too, I suppose?"

Erin said nothing.

Simon kept his focus on the mess of paper. "Our nursing shortage was already critical since the unions were made toothless—why work here when you can easily move to Minnesota where the pay and benefits are better? But now it's awful because the word on the street is St. Ann's is a place where if you step out of line at all, you're sent away. We can't get doctors here because we're so small—and now you're about to lose three. I imagine the board thinks this is a threat, that we're hoping you'll back down so we can stay. I admit, I'd love if that happened. But we're assuming it won't, and we're planning to go. You're not a stupid man, Erin. You know if this keeps up, you'll keep bleeding people, and the hospital will founder. Kathryn will stay a long time because of her moms, but Rebecca will make her go if things get too bad."

Erin said nothing, but his fists tightened.

Simon laughed sadly and shook his head. "Hong-Wei was legitimately excited about building St. Ann's into a better place. He liked how small it was. He loved the idea of being his own version of an intensivist here. You don't know it, but until this happened, he'd been emailing friends of his to see if they'd potentially be interested in relocating. You almost had a cardiologist. But then you decided you'd rather have this policy."

"It's not me who wants it."

"But it is, Erin. Because you're the one focused on trying to control me instead of the board. Because this hospital, this town, has decided this is the vision it wants, instead of the one the four of us have been trying to help you build." Simon stepped away from the table. "You know, I'm sorry. I think you're going to have to sort this mess out on your own after all. Good luck."

He left Erin alone in the room, heavy in heart and lighter in spirit at once. He felt as if he'd let go of something he truly needed to set free.

That night he sat with the rest of them as they thumbed through Jared's binder, and this time he had Owen's laptop out, looking for places to rent.

Leaving Copper Point wasn't the future he wanted, exactly—but he was going to find a way to make it the best future possible.

CHAPTER SIXTEEN

By THE time the Founder's Day festival came around, Hong-Wei had serious offers from six different hospitals in the Twin Cities area, one he hadn't even applied to. Hong-Wei wanted a smaller hospital where they had more of a chance to work together and see one another the way they did at St. Ann's. The front-runner was a midsize hospital in a southern suburb of the Twin Cities. Owen spent a lot of time showing Simon all the things they could do in a city like Minneapolis. Simon was starting to get excited.

Only a little, but he told himself it would get better once they moved.

The festival distracted him—it saddened him too, reminding him of what he was about to leave, but in the here and now, he had his family and longtime friends with him. Founders Day was always a highlight of the year for Simon, this time all the more so since he'd helped plan it. He took pride in walking around the booths along Main Street, perched on the long stretch of greenbelt overlooking the bay. He'd been a part of this. It felt appropriate somehow, like he was giving Copper Point a goodbye in a way only he could do.

Copper Point was giving back to him as well—and so was Hong-Wei. In the city gazebo near the China Garden booth, the newly formed Copper Point Quartet played for the guests as they milled about. They performed several classical numbers, but they had pop pieces in their repertoire too, which pleased the crowd. They were quite talented, all four of them, but Simon couldn't help beaming with pride because Hong-Wei wasn't simply good. He was exceptional.

He was also incredibly handsome in his tuxedo. They all wore their tuxedos well, especially Amanda, but Hong-Wei, in Simon's eyes, made everyone else look slightly shabby.

Simon told him so when the quartet took a break, and Hong-Wei smiled and kissed him on the cheek.

Simon inhaled a heady whiff of Hong-Wei and ran a hand over his broad back. "You play beautifully as well. All of you."

"I'm glad you're enjoying it. I'm having fun."

Simon almost said something about how he hated that Hong-Wei would have to give this up, but he decided this wasn't the day for such things. He focused on the positive instead. "Are you going to keep performing after lunch? I know there's a group scheduled here later, but there's a gap in the schedule after the lunch break."

A mysterious smile spread across Hong-Wei's face. "Ah, well. We're going to do a few more numbers. Something special. I want you to stay and watch. Will you promise?"

"Of course." Simon eyed him carefully. "You're up to something, aren't you?"

With a wink, Hong-Wei kissed Simon on the lips and went off to join the others.

Owen and Jared found Simon then—Owen had a corn dog, and Jared was munching on a bag of kettle corn. Jared nudged Simon with his elbow. "So. You ready to see their performance? I hear the quartet thinks they're going to show us up."

Simon frowned. "Show us up? What do you mean?"

Owen's lip curled as he gnawed on his corn dog. "They're doing lip-synching and dancing like we do for the kids at the hospital. Except I heard a rumor they might actually sing, so it's a karaoke version."

Eyes wide, Simon took a better look at the gazebo. The chairs and stands from the quartet were gone, as were the instruments. The quartet members, still in their tuxedos, stood at the front of the stage, heads down, each of them wearing a wireless microphone.

As the audience began to murmur, Ram lifted his head. "Good afternoon, ladies and gentlemen. We hope you enjoyed our concert this morning, and as we take you into the afternoon, we're going to give you something different. Also, I have a message from one of our group to a member of the audience." Ram looked at Owen and blew a kiss. "Jack says follow this if you can."

The music began, and Hong-Wei sang in Korean. Simon's breath caught. He was so good! And he knew this song. It was SHINee's "Lucifer," a K-pop classic.

Having his boyfriend look him in the eye, belting out "Lucifer," and copying the K-pop group's dance moves—while sliding out of a tuxedo jacket—was something out of dark fantasies Simon didn't even whisper to his own subconscious.

Tim sang the verses too—to Simon's knowledge he'd been born in California and so had his parents, but he was Korean by heritage. Whether or not he actually knew any Korean, Simon couldn't say. He certainly sang it well, and Ram and Andrea didn't do too badly either. Their dance moves were *incredible*, right out of the music video. Simon couldn't help tapping his foot and shifting his body along to the beat, singing under his breath.

"Traitor," Jared murmured.

"They're fantastic," Simon replied.

When the song finished, everyone cheered, and Simon was one of the loudest, adding a wolf whistle for good measure. It turned out they weren't done performing, however. They held the final pose through the applause, but before it died away, new music started. Simon recognized it immediately as "Despacito," and he assumed Amanda would lead this one, since she was fluent in Spanish. Except to his surprise, *Hong-Wei* took the opening—and sang it in Mandarin. Amanda joined him eventually in Spanish, and they traded back and forth as the others sang backup and everyone danced. It was incredible.

The crowd went wild. The entire staff of China Garden had come out of their booth to dance, and the staff from Mexican restaurant. They ended up dancing with one another.

Owen groaned. "We will *never* live this down, ever."

At this point Simon was convinced there was no way there wasn't a third song, and he was right. With barely a pause this time, "Despacito" bled into something that sounded as if it were right out of a Bollywood movie, which knowing Ram, it probably was. It had lots of drums and filled the street with pulse and life, and for a moment as Ram sang and moved his hips, getting the entire town to shout *hey*, *hey*, *hey* with him, Simon remembered why they'd dated.

The cheering was intense as the song ended, because it felt like a finale. Everyone, including Simon, assumed it was. But after a bit of bowing, the quartet members shifted places once more. Ram waved for silence.

"We have one last song, and this one's the most important of all."

To Simon's surprise, Ram came into the audience.

Hong-Wei, Andrea, and Tim remained on the stage, Hong-Wei in the center. A slow song played, and Andrea and Tim started to sway. Hong-Wei sang in Mandarin again, so heartfelt and passionate, it made Simon shiver. Especially since Hong-Wei sang right at him.

Out of nowhere someone grabbed his hand—it was Ram. "Come on." Ram tugged Simon toward the gazebo. "We need you for this one."

Simon had no time to protest. Ram hurried him forward, through the crowd and up the stairs. Simon wanted to ask what was going on, but as the words formed on his lips, suddenly he was in front of Hong-Wei, who was still singing in Mandarin, looking right at him and nowhere else. Simon was hypnotized, unable to do anything but gaze back.

Out of the sea of words in the song he didn't understand came three in English. "Just follow me." Then the words Simon understood were gone again, Hong-Wei singing in Mandarin once more, but every so often in the chorus they would return, like an anchor. *Just follow me. Just follow me.*

The other quartet members kept dancing around them, but Hong-Wei did nothing else but hold Simon's hands and sing to him. Simon felt hot all over. Being sung to like this was so intense, and to have it happen in front of everyone he'd ever known… he could barely breathe.

Just follow me. Just follow me. He wanted to tell Hong-Wei yes, he would follow him anywhere. Everywhere. Forever.

The song ended, and though the crowd began to clap, Ram and the others quickly silenced them with a wave as Hong-Wei got on one knee and withdrew a small box from the pocket of his coat.

Tears springing to his eyes, Simon covered his mouth with his hands.

Hong-Wei captured one of them and drew it to his lips. "Please promise you'll follow me everywhere, Simon Lane. Because I'm already determined to stay with you wherever you go for the rest of your life, if you'll allow me to do so."

Simon scarcely managed a yes before he crouched to cup Hong-Wei's face and sealed his vow with a kiss.

As he rose to his feet, wearing a ring, his hand firmly laced in Hong-Wei's, he smiled out at the cheering crowd. He thought he saw a glimpse of Erin Andreas, who looked even more miserable than the day Simon had encountered him in the conference room.

Then Erin was gone, leaving only the joy of Copper Point in Simon's vision as the people of the town wished him and his fiancé well, wherever their life would take them.

THE MONDAY after the festival was one of the most bittersweet days for Hong-Wei at St. Ann's. Everyone made a point to come up to him and wish him and Simon congratulations, but they also began to tell him goodbye. They stopped trying to convince him to change his mind or tell him about the letters they were going to write. They simply shook his hand, gave him a hug and a sad smile, and wished him well. His surgery schedule, however, was completely filled, as far out as he allowed the receptionist to schedule him. When they went to dinner that night at China Garden, several people with appointments came up to give him their best, but they also worriedly confirmed he wasn't leaving *yet*.

Owen tapped his fork on the table as he leaned in to speak sotto voce to Simon and Hong-Wei. "I hope the board is pissing itself. We're leaving, creating a huge series of holes they have no hope of filling, and now Rebecca is ten times more favored for the open seat than the old fogey John Jean had step up. Of course, they're still too proud to so much as ask us to reconsider."

Jared flattened his lips before taking a sip of beer. "I asked Nick, thinking naively I could get him to listen to reason. He told me I wouldn't understand and walked away from me."

Simon forced a smile, the same false brightness he always had on this topic, which made Hong-Wei sad inside. "Don't worry. Let's focus on our evening and be happy about the time we have left in Copper Point."

Hong-Wei did his best to follow Simon's advice. Mostly he was grateful for Simon. They spent every evening together, alternating between houses still, though leaning a great deal on Hong-Wei's place. They cooked together, did laundry together, made love together, but a lot of the time simply shared space. Already coming home to Simon had become an integral part of Hong-Wei's existence. On the nights Simon had to work and he didn't, Hong-Wei watched the door, waiting for the moment when he came back, and when Simon arrived, it was as if light came with him.

For the rest of our lives. He'll come home to me like this for the rest of our lives.

The only task that remained for Hong-Wei that he didn't know how to prepare for was telling his family about the move.

He had so much to tell them—about Simon, about what he'd done in Copper Point, and what he'd lost once again. Part of him wished he'd said something sooner, before it had come to this. In so many ways, he was in the same place he'd been when he'd left Houston. Except this time, his heart was changed.

For days he thought of how he wanted to begin the conversation, and he even drafted a kind of speech on his laptop, though in the end he sat in front of the camera waiting for Skype to load with no notes before him, only the steady beating of his heart to guide him.

When the monitor began ringing, he clicked on the button to answer with a shaking hand.

The screen was black for a moment, and then there was his father, staring back at him.

His father looked the same. Handsome in his salt-and-pepper hair, his eyes bright and strong, though they were surrounded by wrinkles and a few age spots. He greeted Hong-Wei with the small, contained gesture he always had, no matter how long and arduous the man's day had been, whether Hong-Wei had disappointed him or not. As Hong-Wei had grown older, he'd learned to understand the weight his father carried behind that smile, and it had become his goal in life to lessen that burden, not add to it.

Drawing a slow breath, he said a prayer he would be able to live up to that vow now.

"Hi, Dad," he said in Mandarin.

His father kept smiling. "Hello, Hong-Wei. It's good to hear from you at last. Your mother and grandmother have worried how you have been. I have as well."

Hong-Wei inclined his head, as low as he could go without disappearing from the frame. "I'm very sorry for making you worry. I should have been in contact sooner." He lifted his head but not his gaze. "I was too ashamed to face you, too caught up in my failure. I know I let you down. I'm sorry for that. I'm sorry I'm not the son you deserve. I'm working hard to be better."

"Little Bun." His father's voice turned aching. "When did I ever tell you I wasn't proud of you?"

Hearing his father use his family nickname made Hong-Wei's eyes close, and he fought to keep threatening tears at bay. "How can you be proud of a failure?"

"I'm proud of a son whose sister tells me is doing good work in his new job, helping people in a remote place."

"Yes, well, I have to leave that place now." He felt sick, but he pressed on. "Because the administration isn't interested in helping people. They only want to blackmail me into being one of their puppets." When his father only frowned at him, Hong-Wei steadied himself and dove into the last confession. "There's someone I love, Dad. Someone I want to marry. Someone I want you and the family to meet, because I want them to join our family." He lifted his gaze to his father's, not looking away. "I want *him* to join our family."

Hong-Wei waited, his heartbeat quick against his chest.

His father's confusion faded to surprise, and then, at last, to warmth. "Is he a good person?"

The tears began to fall now, beyond Hong-Wei's control. "He's wonderful. He's a nurse. He's conscientious, kind, gentle, and bright. He helped me find my way to be the kind of doctor I always wanted to be, and introduced me to so many friends. He showed me a place I could fall in love with."

"That sounds wonderful. I don't understand, though, why you have to leave."

Hong-Wei explained, giving his father a brief summary of the policy, of the board and their history of control, of what he'd been trying to do with the new specialists and clinics and what he feared would happen now that the board considered him their pawn. "I can't work like that. I can't live like that. Especially since they won't let Simon and me live openly together. We'd have to be forever in secret."

Sighing, his father nodded. "I understand. I hope, then, this next hospital will be the right fit for you at last. I hope wherever you find yourself, you will be happy, Hong-Wei. And we all hope you will come home to see us soon."

Heart full, no longer heavy, Hong-Wei smiled at his father. "I will. I'll bring Simon too."

This time his father's smile wasn't small at all. "We would like that very much."

THE DAY before Hong-Wei and Simon were to leave for their interview, a new memo arrived.

Hong-Wei first realized something was wrong when he walked in the doors. Usually staff walked up and down the halls, doing their work, pausing to nod or wave as he walked by, but today they were huddled in groups, whispering to one another with wide eyes. Everyone in the building was behaving this way, and when they saw Hong-Wei, they glanced at him with a strange expression.

Instead of going to his office, Hong-Wei went to the OR to find Simon to see if he knew what was going on. Except Simon wasn't there. He was at the nurses' station, surrounded by people. They parted when they saw Hong-Wei. Red-cheeked, Simon came forward, holding a piece of paper at his side.

Hong-Wei pulled Simon aside, speaking quietly because he was aware everyone was staring at him. "Do you know what's going on?"

"Not exactly. I take it you haven't been to your mailbox yet?" He passed the paper to Hong-Wei. "This will be waiting for you inside."

Hong-Wei held the paper up and skimmed it. Eyes wide, he slowed and read it more carefully.

Memorandum

From: Erin Andreas
To: All Hospital Staff
RE: Policy Changes

Effective immediately, the dating policy forbidding relationships between hospital employees has been suspended indefinitely. Further changes regarding other policies should be anticipated to help retain employees and stimulate positive growth for St. Ann's in the future.

Any questions you have regarding this or any policy should be addressed to me. Thank you for your attention to this matter.

After reading it through for the third time, Hong-Wei looked up at Simon. "Is this real?"

"It seems to be, but no one quite knows. There's a rumor Erin is in the cafeteria, as if he's waiting for someone to come up and talk to him. So far, though, no one's been brave enough to."

Grabbing Simon's hand and clutching the paper in his other, Hong-Wei headed down the hall. "Let's be the first to break the trend."

Sure enough, Erin was indeed sitting in the middle of the cafeteria, all alone at one of the round tables. He had a pile of folders around him as he worked at his laptop, and he was sipping a cup of coffee from a paper cup.

Simon worried his bottom lip. "He still looks pale, but he's better than the day we talked."

Hong-Wei turned to Simon, surprised. "You spoke to Erin? You never told me."

Simon smiled coyly. "Yes, well, it's a long story. Though from the sound of things, it might have a happy ending."

They walked up to Erin together, somewhat tentatively, but when Erin saw them, he closed his laptop. "Ah. I expected the two of you."

Hong-Wei waved the memo in the air between them. "Is this serious? The policy is dead?"

"Of course it's serious. The policy needs to be reconsidered. It's far too vague and broad as it stands."

Hong-Wei raised an eyebrow. "And the board okayed this change?"

"The hospital has decided to pause the policy. That's all you need to know."

Except Hong-Wei could see the perspiration on Erin's brow. Hong-Wei had all he needed to know, all right. Erin had acted alone on this. He'd gone completely cowboy the day before Hong-Wei and Simon were taking the first concrete step toward leaving, and forced the hospital's hand. Now he was sitting in the cafeteria, waiting.

But not, Hong-Wei realized, waiting for the two of them, or anyone else on the hospital staff.

Hong-Wei put his hand on Simon's shoulder. "Go to reception and cancel all our surgeries for today. Give our patients my apologies. Then come back here."

Simon looked at him like he'd lost his head. "What?"

"As quickly as possible, please. On your way, if you can, grab my laptop so we can get some work done. Otherwise, don't let anyone detain you. Simply get out the order to cancel and get here as fast as you can."

Still confused, Simon left. Erin didn't glance up, but Hong-Wei thought he might be sweating a little less.

Hong-Wei stayed in the cafeteria, but he stepped to the side and called Owen, whom he knew would be on his way to work or nearly so.

"Get to St. Ann's immediately," he told him, "and drag everyone you possibly can into the cafeteria. Staff preferred, but I'll take anyone with a spine I can get right now."

"What in the hell?"

"Erin just rescinded the policy. Entirely on his own. Now he's waiting in the cafeteria for his father to come and eat him alive."

"*Shit*. I'll be there in seven."

He was there in five, his voice heard bellowing in the halls demanding everyone go to the cafeteria. At first the people who gathered were confused, but as Jared—who'd cancelled his clinic patients—arrived and whispered instruction, they simply took their seats and waited patiently.

Soon the room was full to bursting, and people kept coming. Community members came as well as staff—Maddy was there, and Rebecca with half her firm, and several other business leaders from Main Street. Ram came with Tim and Andrea and a number of professors and students from the university. Even the CEO of the sandstone mine showed up, standing off to the side with Kathryn and several of the other doctors. There were so many people now that when the fire marshal came—as an interested party—he made them file into the common areas outside the cafeteria.

In the middle of this shuffling of bodies, John Jean Andreas and the board arrived.

John Jean strode into the building as if it *wasn't* teeming with people who had shown up to silently support his son's rebellion. Erin remained where he was, fixated on his laptop as the board approached.

When his father stood in front of him, he closed the computer and looked up. Waiting.

John Jean smiled the smile he'd given Hong-Wei right before he'd upended his world. "I'd like to speak with you privately, please."

The room collectively held its breath.

Erin continued to exhibit calm, despite the fact Hong-Wei knew the man was terrified. "I believe we'll speak right here."

The only thing giving John Jean away was the barest flicker of flint in his gaze before he smoothed his expression back in place. "Very well. Where is our president? I don't see him in your little… collective."

"I'm here."

Nick stood in the doorway of the cafeteria, Jared at his elbow. Nick looked as wan as Erin, but he too was composed in the kind of way men were when resigned to their death. Nick said something to Jared, then waded through the throng to stand behind Erin.

John Jean turned on the CEO. "Are you part of today's shenanigans?"

Nick's expression remained calm. "I stand by rescinding the policy and the position of looking for ways to retain employees, yes."

The fact that he couldn't control the situation was clearly irking John Jean, and he wasn't able to hide his ire under his usual veneer. "Since you acted without consulting us, I assume this means the two of you are content with being removed from your positions?"

"If you remove them, we're removing *you*."

Hong-Wei didn't know who called the threat—the voice sounded familiar, but that made sense since he knew pretty much everyone in the room—and before he could attempt to place the first speaker, other calls joined in. It took less than fifteen seconds for the throng to tip toward being out of control, but then Rebecca's sharp voice cut across the room, via the microphone the cook used to call out special orders.

"Ladies and gentlemen who have come out here today in concern for your hospital—thank you. To the human resources director and CEO who saw this clearly important need and took it upon themselves to act—thank you. And to the longtime members of the St. Ann's board who have worked so hard for so many years to make this hospital the great institution it is today, who had the wisdom and vision to hire people such as Nick Beckert and Erin Andreas and to recruit doctors such as Dr. Wu, who made this hospital a place people like my wife and Dr. Gagnon and Dr. Kumpel and Simon Lane would come home to instead of taking their talents away from Copper Point—to this board I give my most heartfelt thanks, because without this foundation, we couldn't stand here today. A round of applause, please, for all these people."

The room became a thunderous echo of people clapping, except for Nick, Erin, and the board, who stood in stony silence. John Jean shifted his glare to Rebecca.

Hong-Wei bit his lip to stop his grin.

Rebecca continued looking so smooth and professional in her suit and wine-red lipstick, her dark hair and brown skin and her youth a beautiful contrast to the white hair and wrinkled pale skin of the board members who had come out in their old-man khakis and golf shirts. "We've had our rocky moments at St. Ann's and in Copper Point. But together, I know we can make this a great future." Smiling a smile that could eat John Jean's for breakfast, she met the president of the board's gaze head-on. "We don't need to talk about firing anyone or driving any of our doctors away. And so long as we can all agree to work together, for the future, for each other, there's no need to talk of voting anyone out."

"But we're all voting for you," someone called from the back, and the room erupted into applause again.

Rebecca put a hand on her chest as if that was the last thing she'd been thinking of. "I do appreciate the thought. But I'm not campaigning here today. I only wanted to speak up for my wife's place of employment, and for the town I love so much."

John Jean murmured something to the rest of the board, and they quietly filed out of the room, past at least fifteen smartphones that had been streaming Rebecca's speech live to different social media outlets. As the room became a blur of sound and chatter and people closed in on them, Owen leaned in to speak in Hong-Wei's ear.

"I'm pretty sure you could reschedule those surgeries you cancelled for tomorrow, because I'm thinking you don't need that interview any longer."

Hong-Wei drew Simon to his side and kissed his cheek, shutting his eyes as he inhaled in a breath of his scent. "No. I really don't."

CHAPTER SEVENTEEN

December

SIMON WAS in the kitchen, lifting the lid to his pot and biting his lip as he worried over the contents, when Hong-Wei opened the door to their apartment, took one whiff, and groaned aloud.

"*Oh my God*." He hung up his coat, kicked off his shoes, and stepped into his slippers before stumbling across the floor to the kitchen as if in a drugged haze. "That's beef noodle soup. That's *my grandmother's* beef noodle soup."

Simon's heart beat faster when Hong-Wei came up beside him, hovering over Simon's shoulder as he peered into the pot. "It is. She gave me the recipe when we visited, and while you were out with your parents, Hong-Su and your grandmother gave me some tips on how to make it. We didn't have time to go through it ourselves, but Hong-Su Skyped with me as I did test batches at Kathryn and Rebecca's house. I can't promise it's exactly right, but I've done the best I can, and I'll keep trying to do better."

"You did test batches?" Hong-Wei stuck his face deeper into the pot. "Oh, it *smells* exactly right. Let me have some."

Simon swatted him away and put the lid back on the pot. "It's not ready yet, and besides, we need to wait for the others to get here."

Hong-Wei looked horrified. "You mean I have to *share*?"

Simon gestured to the twenty-four-quart stockpot. "We have more than enough."

"You seriously underestimate how much of that soup I can eat." Hong-Wei drew Simon into his embrace, looping his arms around Simon's waist. "Fine, but I'm not sharing you."

Simon draped his arms around Hong-Wei's neck and kissed his lips. "How was practice?"

"Good. Ram is all excited because he found some competition he thinks we can clean up in. I'm going to have to find surgical coverage, but if they hire a second surgeon in time, it'll be easy."

"Sounds like fun. Did you find a time when we can have the quartet over?"

"Probably not until after the first of the year. Ram has to be with his family over break, and Andrea is traveling too. They all have finals coming up as well, and end-of-semester grading."

"Well, keep telling them to find open weekends, and we'll cook something."

Hong-Wei peered over Simon's shoulder at the pot, a look of yearning on his face. "I still can't believe you made beef noodle soup."

"Of course I did. You've been craving it since I met you. I only hope it lives up to your expectations."

Hong-Wei smiled and stroked Simon's cheek. "It's coming from you. That's more than enough."

They set the table together and selected the wine, though Simon had to keep a close eye on the kitchen because Hong-Wei was determined to sneak a bite of the soup. Simon had bread warming in the oven as well, and a salad tossed and waiting in the fridge. Hong-Su had suggested the recipes for both, saying they went well with the soup.

"I ran into Rebecca at the grocery store." Simon set a spoon beside a knife. "She says the board meeting was almost boring this time. Not even one of them murmured *well, I never*. I think she was disappointed."

"They don't know what to do with a self-possessed woman. They haven't seen one in the flesh, only read about them in scary stories."

"They have one living among them now. I think she's trying to get Amanda to run for the seat opening up in six months. They're terrified."

"Oh, my. *Two* women, both of color. Whatever will they do?"

"Sit back and take it." Simon sighed. "I invited Erin to dinner, but he declined again."

Hong-Wei tweaked his nose. "Wear him down like water on a stone. It's how I won you, after all."

Simon snorted and kissed Hong-Wei's chin. "No, you came after me like a CEO in an Asian drama."

The doorbell rang in the middle of their kiss, and Simon pulled away reluctantly, shaking an admonishing finger at his fiancé. "Keep setting the table. *Leave my soup alone.*"

Hong-Wei glowered and continued to lay out plates. Simon watched him all the way to the door.

He was swept up in Owen's embrace as soon as he opened it, and when he was done yelping to be put down, he had to nag Owen and Jared to remove their shoes. He was in the middle of handing them the guest slippers when he heard the clatter of metal and the sound of Hong-Wei's moan from the kitchen. As soon as he turned around, he saw Hong-Wei with a spoon dangling from his hand as he sank against the side of the counter, an expression of ecstasy on his face.

Simon dropped the slippers and stalked back to the kitchen. "*Wu Hong-Wei*, I asked you to *wait*!"

Ignoring this burst of outrage, Hong-Wei set aside the dish and took hold of both of Simon's hands. "Simon Lane, will you marry me?"

Simon huffed. "Yes, in June." Unable to stand it any longer, he let out a hesitant breath. "So… how was it?"

"You take incredible notes. If you make it a few more times at my grandmother's elbow, I'll never know the difference."

Simon blushed from his head to his toes. "Now stop, don't feed me lies."

"It's nothing but the truth. This soup seals the deal. You're the man for me. The *only* man for me."

As Simon beamed with pride, Hong-Wei caught Simon in his arms and swept him off his feet, dipping him gracefully to the side. Simon looped his hands behind Hong-Wei's head, ignoring the catcalls of his best friends, enjoying yet another romantic moment with his perfect hero.

His man, his one and only. Forever.

THE DOCTOR'S DATE

The hospital's least eligible bachelor and its aloof administrator hate each other… so why are they pretending to date?

Dr. Owen Gagnon and HR director Erin Andreas are infamous for their hospital hallway shouting matches. So imagine the town's surprise when Erin bids an obscene amount of money to win Owen in the hospital bachelor auction—and Owen ups the ante by insisting Erin move in with him.

Copper Point may not know what's going on, but neither do Erin and Owen. Erin intends his gesture to let Owen know he's interested. Owen, on the other hand, suspects ulterior motives—that Erin wants a fake relationship as a refuge from his overbearing father.

With Erin suddenly heading a messy internal investigation, Owen wants to step up and be the hero Erin's never had. Too bad Erin would rather spend his energy trying to rescue Owen from the shadows of a past he doesn't talk about.

This relationship may be fake, but the feelings aren't. Still, what Erin and Owen have won't last unless they put their respective demons to rest. To do that, they'll have to do more than work together—they'll have to trust they can heal each other's hearts.

www.dreamspinnerpress.com

CHAPTER ONE

WHEN OWEN Gagnon's friend Simon came by his house and asked him to be part of the hospital bachelor auction Valentine's Day fundraiser, he simply snorted and resumed arguing on an online political board.

Unfortunately Simon wasn't easily deterred. "Come on. We're short so many volunteers, and it's for a good cause. We *need* this cardiac unit."

Owen continued to type. "Then you and loverboy sign up."

"Hong-Wei and I can't. They want unmarried men."

"You and Jack aren't married yet." Owen waggled his eyebrows. "Get on the stage, and *I'll* bid for you."

Simon swatted him. "They don't want married *or* engaged men. Jared's already said yes. I need one more volunteer and I'll have met my quota for the committee."

"This is sexist as hell, only asking men. Why can't they do a gender-neutral auction?"

With a sigh, Simon sat beside him. "I know, but I've about sprained my back trying to yank the rudder on this ship so we stay away from insensitive areas. You wouldn't believe some of the racist, sexist, homophobic things these people wanted to do for a fundraiser."

"I would absolutely believe it." Owen ran a finger down Simon's nose. "Which is why I'm steering clear."

"*Please, Owen*. I didn't ask you to be part of the entertainment committee like I did Hong-Wei. I just need you to stand on stage for ten minutes while people bid on a date with you for charity."

Owen closed the laptop. "First of all, Jack loves performing, so it's no hardship. I assume your fiancé is playing with his damn quartet?"

"*You* could be in the quartet too. Ram keeps saying he'd make it a quintet if you came in as the other violin. He can play cello and double bass too." Simon bit his lip. "I don't know the whole story on why you don't want to play anymore, but it *has* been a long time—".

Owen held up a hand, unwilling to let Simon see how the simple mention of the violin made him queasy. "I'm not joining Ram's strings club, and I won't be auctioned off for a date. Don't start a sob story about the cardiac unit either. No one is going to bid on me if you put me on the block."

Simon's blush said this hiccup had occurred to him. "It's not only for dates. People can ask for favors or things. Plus I have a plan."

Oh hell. "Absolutely not. I'm not standing on stage so you and Jack can pity bid on me or so some nurse's aide can get revenge."

"*Owen—*"

Rising, Owen went for the door, grabbing his coat on the way. "I'm going to work."

"But we don't have surgery until ten today."

"I'm going to sit in the lounge and glare at people until your hubby needs me."

This was exactly what Owen ended up doing. The house he shared with Jared—which he used to share with Simon and Jared, before Simon went and fell and love—was only a mile from St. Ann's Medical Center, and three-quarters of a mile from the condo where Jack and Simon lived. It had snowed again the night before, bringing the on-the-ground total to a foot and a half. Damn lake effect snow anyway. The temperature was in the midtwenties, which for the end of January in northern Wisconsin was practically balmy. He considered walking, but since half the sidewalks were undoubtedly still not cleared, he drove.

He met Simon's fiancé, Dr. Wu—Hong-Wei to Simon, Jack to everyone else—in the parking lot. Jack was huddled into his hat and scarf and shivering. "Owen, how are you not freezing?"

"Because this isn't cold."

Jack, born in Taiwan and living in Houston until last year, grunted as he hustled to the door. He held it for Owen, which was nice of him.

It was also suspicious.

Owen cast a side glance at him. "You're here early for Monday. Since you didn't have call this weekend, you don't have any patients to see in rounds."

"Need to go over a few files before surgery."

Something fishy was definitely going on, and Owen was sure Jack was here because Simon had sent him to fulfill the mission he'd failed on. "I'm killing some time before surgery, so I guess I'll see you later."

Jack waved as they parted ways, Owen heading for the elevator, Jack the clinic entrance.

In the lounge, Owen surveyed the paper over coffee, reading the minutes of the most recent hospital board meeting, scanning an editorial that questioned where the funding had gone for the proposed cardiac program. Two of the visiting specialists were in the room with him, the speech therapist and the podiatrist. They were having a pleasant chat near the soda machine, but after a glare from Owen, they changed it to a hushed conversation. Two family medicine doctors entered, guffawing about something; then one of them shushed the other. "Gagnon's here."

Owen smiled behind his paper. He enjoyed his reputation as the resident pariah. It allowed him to live his life in peace.

The door opened again, and this time Jack entered. Owen groaned and slid deeper behind his paper.

Jack waved at the other doctors and returned their polite greetings before settling beside Owen. "Don't mind me." He tugged at the edge of the local news section. "Anything good?"

"The usual nonsense. Someone is up in arms about the cardiac unit, convinced the fundraiser won't bring in enough money because there's some kind of backroom conspiracy. Someone wrote a letter to the editor about the mine ruining the environment, and someone else wrote how we need more jobs. Then there's one complaining about whoever is kicking over his garbage cans."

Jack looked bemused. "I'll never get over small towns."

Owen pretended to read the paper a little longer, then folded it. "I'm tired of waiting. Ask me to take part in the auction so I can tell you no."

Jack stared back implacably. "I wasn't going to ask because I knew you'd say no."

"Seriously, you can stand down. Obviously I'm not going to participate, but I'll help Si find someone to fill his quota."

Jack shrugged. "Don't worry. I'm looking."

"You don't need to. I can do it, I said."

Jack glanced around the room at the other doctors, who regarded Owen with unease and Jack with respect bordering on awe. "I think it'll be better if you leave it to me."

Oh, now Owen was going to find Simon's last person *for sure*.

He left the lounge and wandered the halls, ignoring the way the nursing staff scuttled away from him. That was nothing new. He scanned every man he encountered, doctors and nurses both, for potential bachelor auction candidates. He was immediately hampered, though, by several factors. Jack was right, his pariah status did him no favors. Also, he had no idea who was already roped into the thing or who was working the night of the fundraiser and therefore was out of commission.

The thought of Jack's knowing smirk sent Owen grumbling to the third floor and the administration offices, where he tried the most obvious and therefore clearly stupid get, the hospital CEO, Nick Beckert.

Beckert was in his office, and he happily waved Owen inside. He grinned sadly when Owen asked if he could pin him down for the auction. "I was the first one they put on the list, I hate to tell you. But why are *you* asking me? I didn't think you were on the recruiting committee."

"I'm not. I was recruited, and I'm trying to find a replacement."

Nick lifted his eyebrows and whistled low. "Good luck. From what I hear, everyone else has either been called up, is on shift, or is ineligible."

Good grief. "How is that possible? Also, why is this limited only to men, by the way?"

"Because the planning committee is short on imagination and big on words like *traditional values*. If I'd known you were this invested, I would've put you on the team."

Owen held up his hands. "I'm fine helping find the last victim, thanks. There's got to be at least one single male who isn't on shift. I need to know who's already signed up and who isn't eligible."

"You'll need to talk to Erin."

"Speaking of Andreas, how come he's not on the list?"

"Ineligible."

"On what grounds?" Owen sat up straighter. "His father didn't finally coerce him into an engagement, did he?"

"No. But he's recused as a committee member."

Owen eased back, annoyed at his heart for kicking up a notch at the idea of Erin engaged. "That's ridiculous. Why can't committee members be on the auction block?"

"I did tell you this was an interesting group. The only rudders we had were Erin and Simon, and Erin wasn't supposed to participate, simply ensure the evening ran smoothly." Nick grimaced. "Between you and me, it's just as well he couldn't be asked to be auctioned off. His father would have arranged for something uncomfortable."

True. After all they owed Erin for, Owen would have ended up bidding on him to get him out of his father's clutches, which would've made Erin furious.

Actually, now Owen was mad he couldn't do this.

Owen sighed. "This whole Valentine's Day fund-raiser is ridiculous. Why aren't they doing a tired old dinner on a random weekend in March the way they usually do?"

"Because *someone* stood up in front of the board and declared we were going to do things differently. And now we're doing things differently. All of the things. Incredibly differently." Nick pushed his glasses higher on his nose. "Now if you'll excuse me, I have a mountain of work to finish before the board meeting."

Owen wanted to sit and argue with Nick longer, but he knew he'd get nowhere. The hospital CEO was cautious, though Owen understood why. He'd been brought on after the former president embezzled money from the hospital, but his predecessor had been chummy with the present hospital board, so they resented Nick at every turn. Additionally, his family had moved to Copper Point when he was young, and his father had joined and left the board in a scandal in the nineties. Though Nick had done everything he could to prove himself, plenty of people in town still saw him as a member of an enemy camp. Nick couldn't help Owen. He had enough work to do helping himself.

Owen could feel the writing on the wall about this stupid fundraiser. He was annoyed, and he wanted to argue. He wanted to snarl at someone without having to worry about being polite. If he was called a demon or a dragon or a devil or a monster or an ogre, he wanted it to be done with a glint in his accuser's eye, not a tinge of fear.

In short, he wanted to spar, and he knew exactly who he needed to see.

Simply pushing his way into Erin Andreas's office, taking in the ridiculously neat room, gave Owen a satisfying rush of annoyance. Nick's office was tidy, but it had a reasonable amount of lived-in clutter: overflowing inboxes, forgotten coffee cups, unopened mail in piles on filing cabinets, yesterday's blazer folded in a casual heap over the arm of a chair. Not Erin's workspace. It looked as if someone had gone across the bookshelves with a ruler and made sure the books and binders lined up, not a single one of them sticking out farther than the other, the decorative knickknacks on top drab and soulless, yanked from some design catalog—but perfectly arranged. There were three plants in the window spaced evenly across, neatly trimmed, not a dead leaf among them. The desk was clear of everything but Erin's ubiquitous laptop and a wire pencil holder—containing only crisply sharpened pencils—a pencil sharpener devoid of shavings, a desk lamp tilted at a ninety-degree angle, and of course his inbox.

The papers and files inside of it were stacked in such incredible alignment they looked like a single unit.

In the middle of the scene was the man himself, Erin Andreas, human resources director. He'd arrived almost two years ago to work at St. Ann's, but in the mindset of Copper Point, he was still *new*, especially since the previous HR director had held the position for twenty-five years. Erin wore the same prim heather gray suit he always did, with the same pristine white shirt. Only the tie changed, and not much. Today it was dark gray, almost black. It didn't suit him at all, though it did match the desk. The suit choked Erin's petite frame and made most of his body blend into his desk chair, giving the illusion he'd been strapped into it by invisible threads.

The only thing about the man that didn't fit the corporate image was his hair, which was curly and too long, resting in unruly ringlets around his ears and brushing his collar. The ringlets shone in the fluorescent overhead lighting, and as always Owen had the juvenile urge to tug at one and make it bounce. He managed to refrain, but his gaze trailed them, and he knew a whisper of delight as one caught the edge of Erin's collar and another *boinged* against his eyebrows as he lifted his head.

A kick hit Owen in his belly as his opponent's eyes ignited with fire. *Finally.*

Erin pursed his lips. "Is there any hope you will ever learn to knock?"

Owen shut the door and plunked with deliberate heaviness in the chair opposite Erin's desk, knocking it out of its careful alignment. He purred inwardly as Erin's annoyance ticked up a notch.

He kept his pleasure from his face as he laced his fingers over his chest. "What's going to change if I rap my knuckles on the door?"

"I'll tell you to go away because I'm busy."

"Precisely why I don't knock."

The curls *boinged* again as Erin leaned over the top of his computer. "Did you have some purpose in coming here today, or is this playground-bully routine your way of telling me our resident anesthesiologist needs more work assigned to him?"

Oh yes, this was precisely what Owen had come for. Narrowing his eyes, he gave Erin a thin, menacing smile. "I have a bone to pick with you about this ridiculous auction."

Flinching, Erin lowered his eyes to his computer screen. "I don't have any authority over that. I'm only on the committee."

Owen hesitated, thrown off his game. Okay, what in the hell was that about? This was decidedly not in the script. Thinking he must have stepped in something without realizing it, Owen softened. "I get the concert, the overpriced dinner, the usual crap. Where in God's name did this auction come from, though, and why is every single male roped into it whether they want to be part of it or not? I'm the last person you want up there. I'm either going to be laughed into the wings or bought up by a cabal of nurses with a grudge."

This was Erin's cue to tell Owen to stay out of committee business unless he wanted to sign up and do the work, to remind him everyone in the hospital had to volunteer, to point out he could do this duty since he hadn't signed up to do anything else. Any of those responses would have been fine and given Owen an excuse to snarl in response again. He was *ready* for them.

Instead Erin… paled. When he spoke, he didn't sound irritated half as much as he sounded nervous. "I don't have time to entertain your pointless questions right now, Dr. Gagnon. If you don't mind, I want to finish preparing for the meeting. I'm certain you have somewhere else to be."

Owen was so stunned he had no idea how to respond, could only gape at Erin, who in turn stared at his laptop screen, face flushed.

No acrid rejoinder. No demands Owen leave his office with a heat that said, in fact, he wanted him to stay and keep shouting until they nearly burned down the hospital. Nothing at all.

This was… weird.

There was no denying Erin had been off his game for some time, a little more frazzled around the edges, slightly more inward than normal. It was easy to pinpoint ground zero for his transformation: *he'd* been the person who'd stood up in front of the hospital board, after all. Except he hadn't stood. He'd sat defiantly in the middle of the hospital cafeteria, waiting for his father—the hospital board president—to gut him after Erin sent a particularly nuclear staff memo.

This reaction was different, though. Was it about the committee? Owen frowned at Erin, disquiet settling in his gut. Everyone in the hospital rejoiced at the freedom Erin's reversal of the policy had granted them. How much of the cost had come on Erin's shoulders?

Had everyone ignored that and left him to face dragons alone? Had Owen done that too?

Well, now he felt like an ass.

Erin glanced up from the computer, saw Owen regarding him with concern, and immediately swapped his hollow expression with an icy glare. "Why are you looking at me like that?"

The disdain was such a relief Owen had to suppress a fist pump. He wanted to ask Erin what was wrong, but he was smart enough not to make a direct line of questioning. "What's your meeting about?"

Internally he winced—well, that wasn't a direct question, but it was a ridiculous angle to take. The delivery was too bald, almost politely inquisitive. Now Erin regarded him warily, as if he were a snake about to strike. "My office is not a social lounge. If you don't have business with me, please leave."

Nice save. Owen leaned forward so his elbows rested on his knees. *Think of another topic. Another topic, anything, anything....* "This Valentine's Day auction is a mess. There's got to be time to kill it."

What the fuck was with him? Totally the wrong tone, completely the wrong approach, and the *dead worst* thing to bring up.

Maybe it would be okay. Maybe he'd pissed Erin off with this out-and-out begging. Maybe he'd fix Owen with an icy smile and tell him off as he'd never been told off. Then everything would be normal again.

Erin shrank into his chair, color draining from his face as he lowered his gaze, his voice going quiet. "The auction is nonnegotiable."

An ill wind blew over Owen's neck, and he forgot all about fighting, all about delicately dancing around the topic. "Erin, what is going on with you?"

Erin iced over and aimed a long, slender finger at the door. "Leave."

"Why are you closing up like this every time I bring up the auction? Why are you barely fighting with me?"

Why do you look so... lost?

Erin said nothing, and Owen angsted in a conflicted private storm, at a loss over what to do. He'd sparred with Erin since he'd come to St. Ann's, and they'd never been anything close to friends, but it wasn't as if he didn't care about the man as a human being. Particularly since that stunt with the memo, Owen had begun to rethink his stance on Erin Andreas entirely, because clearly this man whom he'd thought of as aligned with the old guard on the board had been an ally all along. For some time now, Owen had wanted to know what other secrets this man was hiding, but it was difficult when their entire relationship was built on arguments.

Looking at Erin now, feeling the fractures in him, Owen had never been more motivated to craft a bridge toward a new understanding between them. What could be the problem? Maybe if he nudged him in the right direction, Erin would loosen up and tell him what was going on.

It wasn't hard to guess what the problem likely was, the more he thought about it.

"Your father." Owen hesitated, trying to figure out what to add, then decided that was enough to get started.

Erin didn't loosen up. "At whatever point you'd like to leave, please do so."

Owen was so frustrated. "I just want to help. Let me help. You don't want help?"

He didn't know if it was an improvement or not, but Erin wasn't frozen or hollow-looking anymore. He was coldly furious. "Why would I want *your* help?"

Yikes. Also, ouch. Owen rubbed his cheek. "Harsh."

Erin gathered a pile of papers and shuffled them, banging the bottoms with excessive force against the desk. "I'm perfectly fine."

"That is the biggest line of bull I've ever heard. You're completely wooden, you can barely maintain eye contact with me, and you get weird every time I bring up the auction. Usually you can argue with me until we're both blue in the face, but you can't keep up more than a few lines of banter today. Something is wrong." He pursed his lips. "It's got to be your father."

For a moment Owen had him. Erin had softened—and looked at him—when Owen pointed out he couldn't maintain eye contact, and just before the end, he seemed almost ready to, if not confess the problem, at least admit there was one.

The second Owen said *your father*, though, he lost him. His cool, dead mask sliding back into place, Erin averted his gaze again. "Leave, or I'll tell the entertainment committee you've volunteered for a violin solo."

Owen drew back as if he'd been slapped.

Rising, he pushed Erin's desk light into the most obscene angle possible and exited the office without a word. If he was going to play that kind of dirty pool, he could damn well save himself.

HEIDI CULLINAN has always enjoyed a good love story, provided it has a happy ending. Proud to be from the first Midwestern state with full marriage equality, Heidi writes positive-outcome romances for LGBT characters struggling against insurmountable odds because she believes there's no such thing as too much happily ever after. Heidi is a two-time RITA® finalist, and her books have been recommended by *Library Journal, USA Today, RT Magazine*, and *Publisher's Weekly*. When Heidi isn't writing, she enjoys cooking, reading romance and manga, playing with her cats, and watching too much anime.

Visit Heidi's website at www.heidicullinan.com.

You can contact her at heidi@heidicullinan.com.